SHOREFALL

SHOREFALL

A NOVEL

Robert Jackson Bennett

DEL REY

NEW YORK

Published in the United States by Del Rey, an imprint of Random House, a division of Penguin Random House LLC, New York.

DEL REY and the HOUSE colophon are registered trademarks of Penguin Random House LLC.

Library of Congress Cataloging-in-Publication Data
Names: Bennett, Robert Jackson, 1984– author.
Title: Shorefall : a novel / Robert Jackson Bennett.
Description: First Edition. | New York : Del Rey Books, [2020] |
Series: The founders trilogy; 2
Identifiers: LCCN 2019047377 (print) | LCCN 2019047378 (ebook) |
ISBN 9781524760380 (hardcover) | ISBN 9781524760397 (ebk)
Subjects: LCSH: Magic—Fiction. | GSAFD: Fantasy fiction.
Classification: LCC PS3602.E66455 S56 2020 (print) |
LCC PS3602.E66455 (ebook) | DDC 813/.6—dc23
LC record available at http://lccn.loc.gov/2019047377
LC ebook record available at http://lccn.loc.gov/2019047378

Printed in the United States of America on acid-free paper

randomhousebooks.com

2 4 6 8 9 7 5 3 1

First Edition

Book design by Andrea Lau

To my family, both near and far-flung

If there be a person alive with more power than myself, then over time circumstances shall eventually degrade until, inevitably, I am their slave. And if our situations were to be reversed, then they shall inevitably become mine.

—Crasedes Magnus

I

THE LIBRARIAN AND THE MUSES

1

The gates are just ahead," said Gregor. "Get ready."

Sancia took a breath and steeled herself as their carriage lumbered through the pouring rain. She could see the lights atop the campo walls from here, bright and sharp and cold, but little more than that. She rubbed her hands together, her fingertips trailing over the calluses on her palms and knuckles, now a shadow of what they'd been during the prime of her thieving days.

Berenice reached over, grabbed her hands, and gave them both a squeeze. "Just remember the plan," she said. "Remember that, and nothing will go wrong."

"I remember the plan," said Sancia. "I just also remember there's a lot of spots in the plan that say, 'Sancia improvises a bunch of shit.' Which is not, you know, comforting."

"We aren't getting nervous back there, are we?" said Orso from the pilot's cockpit. He turned around to look at them, his faded blue eyes wide and wild in his dark, craggy face.

"A little anxiety," said Berenice, "is understandable under these circumstances."

"But being as we've worked our asses off for the better part of six months to get here," said Orso, "I'm a lot less willing to understand it."

"Orso . . ." said Gregor.

"We are just scrivers going to make a deal with a merchant house," said Orso, turning back around. "Just four grubby scrivers looking to sell our designs and make some quick cash. That's all. Nothing to worry about."

"I see the walls," said Gregor. He adjusted the wheel of the carriage and slowed its progress to a crawl.

Orso peered forward. "Uh. Well. I will admit *that* is a little worrying."

The walls of the Michiel Body Corporate campo emerged from the driving rain. It looked like the Michiels had made some substantial additions since Sancia had last seen them. For starters, the walls were now about forty feet taller, spackled with new gray masonry—that must have taken some work. But it was what sat on top of the new masonry that caught her attention: a series of large, long bronze boxes, installed on the walls about every hundred feet, each one sitting on some kind of swivel stand.

"That is a shitload of espringal batteries," muttered Orso.

Sancia studied the espringal batteries, still and dark in the rain. She watched as a bird flew close to one, and it snapped up, the end of the long box tracking the bird's flight like a cat might watch a passing bat. The box apparently decided the bird was no cause for concern, and returned to its original position.

She knew how such rigs worked: the batteries were filled with scrived bolts—arrows that had been convinced to fly preternaturally fast and hard—but the critical bit was that the batteries had been scrived to sense blood. If a battery sensed a bit of blood that it didn't recognize, it would point its bolts at whoever happened to contain that blood, loose them all, and shred the target to pieces—though the scrivers who designed them had been forced to work quite hard to get them to stop wasting ammunition on stray animals. Especially the gray monkeys, which confused the batteries a great deal.

It was not an elegant solution. But it worked—people did not approach any campo wall at all anymore.

"What guarantees do we have, Orso," said Gregor, "that those things will *not* shoot us to pieces?"

Their carriage hit a bump, and gray-brown water sloshed up the sides, spilling into the floorboards.

"I guess we're about to find out," said Orso.

The gates of the Michiel campo were just ahead now. Sancia could see guards emerging from their stalls, weapons at the ready.

"Here they come," said Gregor.

Their carriage rolled to a stop at a checkpoint before the gates. Two guards approached, both heavily armored, one carrying a very advanced espringal. The armed Michiel guard stood about twenty feet away from the carriage with his espringal lowered, while the other approached and gestured to Gregor. Gregor opened the door and climbed out, which made the Michiel guard a little nervous— Gregor was about a head taller than him, and wearing light leather armor embossed with the Foundryside loggotipo.

"You lot Foundryside?" asked the guard.

"We are," said Gregor.

"I am under orders that you must all be searched before you are permitted into the campo."

"Understood."

They exited the carriage one by one and stood in the rain while the guard patted them down. After this, he checked the carriage. It was a rather shabby scrived carriage, one Gregor had rented from an iron trader—its wheels sometimes forgot which way they were supposed to roll—but this had been a strategic choice: the more they looked like a firm down on their luck, the more the Michiels would believe it.

The guard opened the compartment in the back. Inside was a large wooden chest, which was sealed shut with a bronze lock.

"And this," said the guard, "would be the agreed-upon . . . goods?"

"Obviously," sniffed Orso.

"I must examine them."

Orso shrugged, unlocked the chest, and opened it. Inside were some bronze plates covered with sigils, a few scriving tools, lots of very large books, and nothing else.

"That's it?" said the guard.

"Intellectual property is never terribly interesting to look at," said Orso.

The guard shut the compartment. "Very well. You may proceed." He handed them each a sachet—a small bronze button with a set of sigils engraved on it. "These will make sure the wall batteries and the other measures won't consider you a threat. These expire in five hours, mind—after that, all the campo defenses will begin targeting you."

Orso sighed. "And here I thought I'd missed life on the campo."

They climbed back into the carriage. The bronzed gates cracked and slowly swung open, and Gregor nudged their tiny, shabby carriage through.

"Part one's done," said Orso from the front seat. "We're in."

But Sancia knew this was the easy bit. Very soon, everything would get a lot harder—especially for her.

Berenice squeezed her hand again. "Move thoughtfully," she whispered. "And bring freedom to others. That's what we're doing, right?"

"Yeah," said Sancia. "I guess it's just that normally when I try to rob a merchant house, I break in—not make a goddamn appointment and dance through the front gate."

Their carriage rattled on into the campo.

Sancia had never been to the inner enclaves of the Michiel campo, so she hadn't been sure what to expect. She was aware that the Michiels, who were known for being the most accomplished at manipulating heat and light—as well as for being insufferably artsy snobs in general—had one of the most impressive campos in Tevanne. But as Gregor drove their carriage into the depths of the campo, she found she had not expected . . . this.

Buildings wrought of glass blossomed out of the streetscapes, and twisted and rose and ran together, their innards glimmering with a warm, entrancing luminescence. Whole walls had apparently been converted into art displays, their surfaces shifting and changing to show beautiful, looping designs that moved.

And then there were the suns.

She stared at one as it came close. Most campos used floating lanterns as the preferred method of illumination, but it seemed the Michiels had not been satisfied with this. Instead, they had created some kind of giant, glittering, glowing orb that slowly drifted about three hundred feet above the city streets like a miniature sun, bathing everything below it in something very close to daylight. It would have been an astounding sight at any time, but it was especially striking now, drifting along in the pouring rain.

"Scrumming hell," said Sancia.

"Yes," said Berenice. "You can see the tops of the suns from certain towers in the city, I've been told."

"Self-indulgent bullshit," grumbled Orso. "Absolute twaddle."

They rumbled on through the towers until they were stopped again at the next gate. There they were instructed to get out of their carriage and into another one—this one a Michiel carriage, full of Michiel guards. The Foundrysiders obeyed, Gregor carrying their locked box, and the carriage took off for the innermost sanctum of the Michiel campo, close to the illustris—the head building of the entire merchant house.

This was not their destination, however. Instead their carriage rumbled toward a tall, violet, shimmering structure studded with tiny round windows—the Michiel Hypatus Building, where the house scrivers experimented with sigils and logic, finding new ways to reshape reality to their liking.

They stopped at the front steps and climbed out, the Michiel guards carrying their locked box behind them. No one was there to greet them. Instead they were ushered inside, through chambers of glass and glowing walls and up the stairs, until they finally came to a tall, spacious room that felt like something of a performance venue, with a stage and lights—though the audience area was piled up with couches, cushions, and plates and plates of food.

Sancia stared at the food as they walked in. It had been a long time since she'd starved, but she still couldn't believe the sight before her: pies and stews and chocolates and cuts of smoked meats, all delicately arranged on tiered, golden plates. There were also jugs and jugs of wine—she noticed Orso looking at these with a very interested look on his face.

"I thought the slave rebellions in the plantations meant everyone was tightening their belts," said Sancia.

"These will be the senior hypati officers of the campo," said Berenice quietly. "They will not lack for anything, no matter the circumstances."

"You can begin setting up there," said a Michiel guard, pointing at the table on the stage. "The hypatus will be here shortly."

Sancia watched as the guards took up posts in the corners of the room. She wasn't surprised—she'd known that every second of their time here they would be closely observed.

"This will work, yes?" said Orso, approaching the table. He was pointing to something sitting on it that to most would have looked like a large, curious metal kiln; but even the most novice scriver would have recognized it as a large heating chamber containing a test lexicon—a much smaller, simpler version of the giant lexicons they used to run the foundries all over Tevanne.

"It's *much* more advanced than what we're working with now," said Berenice, studying the rig's casing.

Orso snorted. "'Course it is. We haven't got a million duvots to toss around out in the Commons."

"But . . . I think we can make it work, yes?" Berenice said, looking at Sancia.

Sancia stooped and studied the heating chamber containing the test lexicon. Mostly she was checking the thing's seams and boundaries—because if they were going to showcase their technology for the Michiels, the whole thing had to be airtight.

"We need to seal it up here and here," she said, pointing to two seams she thought looked weak. "But otherwise it should be good."

"Check again," said Orso. "We need our designs to *work.*"

Sighing, Berenice and Sancia opened their wooden crate, took out a few scrived magnifying loupes, and began measuring and testing the heating chamber, confirming there were no flaws. It was monotonous work. Sancia felt like a physiquere inspecting a patient for plague lesions.

She glanced up at Berenice, whose loupe was wedged tight in her eye. "You have any plans after this?" she asked.

Berenice blinked and looked up at her, puzzled. "Eh?"

"I was thinking we could go to a puppeting show. Pasqual's got some kind of scrived giraffe puppet that I've heard is quite amazing."

Berenice allowed a sardonic smile. "Is that so?"

"It is. Thought we could swing by a tavern . . ."

"Try the latest cane wine . . ."

"A bowl of saffron rice . . ."

"Sugared redtail, maybe."

"Yes," said Sancia. "And then go see the puppets. Sound good?"

"Sounds wonderful," said Berenice. She refixed her loupe and went back to work. "Wouldn't miss it for the world. But! Maybe . . ."

"Maybe tomorrow."

"Tomorrow would be better, yes. Though now that I think of it, the day after that . . ."

"Is even better."

"Right in one."

Sancia laughed grimly. "Of course."

This was an old joke of theirs. Despite their desire to get out of their workshops and enjoy themselves, Sancia and Berenice both knew they almost certainly wouldn't get it. They'd probably spend another night working till dawn over scriving definition plates and blackboards, and nursing their tottering old lexicon back to health.

One day, thought Sancia, *I will be a person who has a girlfriend all the time and a job when I have to, rather than someone with a job all the time and a girlfriend whenever time allows.*

Then the doors burst open, and a rich, plummy voice cried, "Orso Ignacio! It *has* been a dog's age, hasn't it!"

The Foundrysiders turned to see about twenty richly dressed men pouring into the room. They all looked carefully arranged, not a hair out of place nor a wrinkle in their robes. Many had their faces painted in intricate lines and patterns—a common affectation of the city's elite. Even the ones who had affected a fashionably disheveled look had clearly done so with great care and deliberation.

The foremost was a tall, thin man who positively radiated smug satisfaction. His white-painted face featured gold rings around his eyes, and his robes were open down to his navel, showing a taut, sculpted torso that was dark and curiously oiled.

"Armand Moretti," said Orso in tones of false cheer. "It's so *good* to see you . . ."

Orso walked up, hand extended. It was like watching him approach some kind of bizarre mirror: on one side was Orso, tall and unkempt with mad eyes and unruly hair, every inch of him bony and spindly like he sometimes forgot he had a body he needed to take care of; and on the other side was Armand Moretti, hypatus of Michiel Body Corporate, who was about the same size and age, but he looked like the sort of man who occasionally bathed in milks to keep his skin in good condition.

"So *good* of you to come, Orso!" Moretti said, shaking Orso's hand. "And so happy that I could help you out. How long has it been since you started your firm? One year? Two?"

"Almost three, actually," said Orso.

"*Really?* Has it been that long? I'd have thought from your state of things it'd been less. Well, I'm always eager to extend a supportive hand to those of us from the older days, yes?"

"Ah—yes," said Orso, who was clearly trying to manage this naked condescension.

Moretti glanced at the rest of them, and did a double-take when he saw Berenice. With a twirl of his robes, he approached her. "Ah! And . . . who is this beguiling creature you've somehow tricked into laboring for you?"

"This is Berenice Grimaldi," said Orso flatly. "Our chief of operations."

"*Is* she? I must say, she is far more pleasant to look at than *our* chief of operations . . ."

"It is an honor to meet the famous and renowned Armand Moretti of Michiel Body Corporate," Berenice said, bowing.

"And polite too," said Moretti, reaching out to touch the side of her face. "I assure you, the pleasure is all mine."

Sancia had stayed quite still until this point, but she found all this a little much. She walked up behind Berenice, her hands in fists—but Berenice waved her off, her hands clasped behind her back.

Sancia exchanged a look with Orso. *We need to get this show on the road,* she thought, *before I lose my temper and stomp this dumb asshole's head into pudding.*

Moretti's eyes moved to Sancia, and he paused, taken aback. She wasn't surprised by his reaction. Short, scarred, with a nearly shaven head and drab brown clothing, she knew she resembled something like a rogue monk—and she definitely didn't look like anyone Moretti ever had to meet.

She watched as his face worked. "And . . ." he said. "And . . . this is . . ."

This is why I prefer thieving instead of confidence games, thought Sancia. *When thieving, they don't get to look at you.*

Gregor stepped forward. "This is Sancia Grado, our chief of innovation. And I am Gregor Dandolo, chief of security." He bowed.

"Ah, yes!" said Moretti. "The famous Revenant of Dantua. Such a catch, to have you working out in the Commons for Orso's little shop. It's so delightfully transgressive, I'm sure your mother must be tearing her hair out."

Gregor allowed a tight, contained smile and bowed once more.

Moretti clapped his hands. "And today we shall see your famous strata box, yes? Your new lexicon technique?"

"Yes," said Orso, unlocking the chest and throwing it open. He pulled out a giant, thick tome and set it on the table. "We have all the scriving definitions and protocols here for you to review. These we will hand over after the demonstration. Most of them will make better sense when you've seen how they're actually used."

An older Michiel scriver with a thick lisp—something Sancia thought was an affectation—said, "And this is the technique you used during the night of the Mountain? The one that allowed you to use the gravity tool, and attack the Candianos?"

Orso paused, clearly unsure what to say. Though it was true that this technique had allowed them to effectively destroy one of the four merchant houses of Tevanne, the Foundrysiders had just assumed this would be a rather sensitive subject among the remaining three, and decided to avoid it.

And yet . . . the Michiel scrivers didn't seem bothered at all. They watched Orso with expressions of mild interest, like awaiting news of whether or not someone's cousin was getting married.

"Uh, yes," said Orso with a cough. "That is correct. Though it is a more refined version."

"Fantastic," said the scriver, nodding. "Fascinating."

"You mustn't think you can't talk candidly here, Orso," said Moretti. "They *were* a competitor of ours, after all. Thanks to you, we were able to acquire much of the Candiano enclaves for a song." He poured a glass of wine and raised it to them. "Including the Mountain."

"Oh," said Orso, flustered. "Then . . . we will proceed with our wo—"

"Don't you wish to confirm the payment first?" asked Moretti.

Orso froze, and Sancia instantly knew why: he had forgotten about the money altogether, and was wondering if this had given the game away.

"Uh, of course," Orso said. He bowed. "I did not wish to impose."

Moretti grinned, drank his wine, and snapped his fingers. A servant boy walked forward with a small wooden chest. "Don't be concerned. Sixty thousand duvots is no imposition at all."

The servant boy opened the chest. The Foundrysiders stared at the piles of golden and silver duvots within.

Scrumming hell, thought Sancia. *That is the most money I have ever seen in my goddamn life.*

But she remembered what Orso had told her—*The hell with the money. If we do this right, we'll walk away with something more valuable than every gold candlestick and scriving rig in the Hypatus Building put together.*

Yet it looked like Orso was having trouble remembering this too. "Very good," he said in a strangled voice. "Thank you, Armand . . ."

"Certainly," said Moretti, clearly pleased to see his effects at work. The servant boy shut the chest with a snap and took it away to the corner.

Moretti poured himself a fresh glass of wine with a flourish. "You have my approval to proceed." He drained it and grinned at them. "Astonish me, please."

"To do the demonstration," said Orso, "we will need a single box, preferably iron or steel. Bronze is a little flimsy. And it will need to be of about the same size as the test lexicon here."

Moretti sashayed over to a giant cushion. He flicked his hand at a young boy and said, "Please fetch one for him." The young boy fled, and Moretti flopped down on the cushion. The other scrivers followed suit, draping themselves over the couches and the chairs. Moretti dipped a plum deep into a pot of chocolate, and noisily ate it as he watched Sancia and Berenice go to work on the test lexicon.

The art of scriving was almost always a two-step process. The first step seemed very simple: a scriver placed a small, imprinted plate on the object that they wished to alter, often somewhere inside it—mostly to keep the printings from being marred. This plate was stamped with a handful of sigils, usually anywhere from about six to ten, and once the plate had been adhered to the object, these sigils would begin convincing it to disobey reality in very unusual ways—hence why this component was called the persuasion plate.

But a persuasion plate only *seemed* simple. In reality, each of its six to ten sigils was supported by the second component: a definition plate, stored back at a nearby lexicon. And that was where the *real* work was done, for a definition plate was composed of thousands of thousands of handwritten sigil strings, all forming very complicated arguments that were strong enough to force some portion of the world to defy reality. The persuasion plate's sigils simply indicated what those arguments should apply to.

Creating a definition plate required weeks of testing and analysis. Such experimentation sounded tedious to most—and it was—but it was the sort of experimentation that, when not done properly, could make your head or torso suddenly implode. As such, any definition plate for a successful scriving was worth a fortune in Tevanne.

And this was what Berenice and Sancia gingerly lifted out of their box and placed within the little lexicon on the table: a definition plate they had personally made that would make reality do something the Michiels would find very, very valuable.

"And so," said the older scriver with a lisp, "your people are building a way to . . . duplicate reality?"

"Not quite," said Orso as the Michiel servant boy returned with an iron box on a rolling cart. "What they will be doing is convincing both chambers that the reality within them is the *same*. The world will be unable to tell if the test lexicon in the heating chamber is actually in the heating chamber, or in the iron box you have brought here, or both."

Moretti narrowed his eyes. "Which means . . ."

"Which means that when the two chambers are twinned, you can take this empty box on this cart anywhere you like," said Orso, tapping the iron box while Sancia and Berenice began to work on it, "and bring a lexicon's definitions with it."

The Michiel scrivers were not eating or drinking anymore. Sancia couldn't blame them—for Orso had just casually suggested a solution to some of the greatest limitations to scriving.

Lexicons housed the thousands and thousands of carefully composed definitions and arguments that convinced reality to do things it normally tried very hard not to do. They were giant, complicated, and horrendously expensive, which meant they were an absolute bastard to build, and harder still to transport.

Yet scrived rigs—like bolts, and carriages, and lanterns—could only work within a mile or two of a foundry lexicon. Get too far away, and reality would grow more certain about what it was or wasn't, and thus would ignore the persuasion plate on your rig, no matter how carefully its sigils had been written.

In short, it was a hell of a lot cheaper to take a basic iron box and *convince* it that it held a lexicon rather than go about building another lexicon. *Unimaginably* cheaper. It was the difference between digging miles of irrigation ditches and tapping the ground with a magic wand and summoning up a bubbling spring of water.

"What are the limitations?" asked Moretti. He sounded a lot less plummy now.

"Well, originally the reality within the duplicated box would grow quite unstable the longer it went on," said Orso. "Meaning it would, ah, eventually explode."

"But we have resolved this issue," said Berenice quickly.

"Yes. Took a lot of work, but . . . the instability has been eliminated," said Orso.

"Show me the definition, please," said Moretti.

"We've already loaded it in," said Berenice.

"I know. But I would like to see it."

Frowning, Orso slipped the definition plate back out of the lexicon to show him. It was a large, bronze disc, about a foot and a half wide, and it was covered with thousands and thousands of tiny engraved sigils—all done in Berenice's careful handwriting.

Moretti stood, walked over, and leaned in close to study the plate. Then he nodded and stepped back. "I see," he said. "Fascinating."

"Can the technique be applied to a larger scale?" said the scriver with the lisp—obviously thinking of foundry lexicons.

"It could," said Orso. He replaced it within the little lexicon. "But being as Foundryside Limited has no foundry lexicons to experiment with in the Commons, I cannot give a definitive answer."

The Michiel scrivers exchanged simpering smirks at that.

"We did, however, look at the second-biggest problem with lexicons," said Orso. "For while constructing a lexicon is difficult and expensive, it's a one-time cost. But constantly updating all the *existing* lexicons on your campo with *all* the latest scriving definitions . . . That gets pretty expensive, yes?"

The smirks vanished. All eyes were fixed on Orso, while Sancia and Berenice silently toiled away on the iron box like stage assistants before a conjuring trick.

"What do you mean?" said Moretti quickly.

"Well, as a former hypatus myself, I know that it takes days, weeks, or even months to fabricate a scriving definition," said Orso. He tapped the lexicon holding the one he'd just shown them. "Having to carefully write each sigil of the argument perfectly on a bronze plate before placing it in the cradle of a foundry lexicon . . . And you can't mass-produce them, since one sigil even *slightly* out of place in an active lexicon could cause absolute havoc. So you have to hand-make them all . . . Which means it can take more than a year for just one new definition to be fully implemented throughout a campo."

"Yes," said Moretti, impatient. "And?"

"Well, we found the cradle within a foundry lexicon . . . the bit that holds *all* the definitions . . ." Orso thoughtfully tapped his chin. Sancia thought he was milking it a bit much. "We found *that* could be twinned quite easily."

The Michiel scrivers looked at one another.

"Are you saying that instead of writing out several hundred definition plates by hand," said Moretti, glancing at the velvet-lined box, "for our several hundred foundries . . ."

"Yes?" said Orso.

"We . . . We could use your technique to twin all the cradles within our foundry lexicons . . ."

"Yes."

"And then if you fed just *one* set of definition plates into *one* foundry lexicon . . . then *all* of them would just believe they contained those arguments?"

"Yes."

"And then all the arguments that we'd written out . . . would apply *everywhere*?" asked Moretti.

Orso nodded like the idea had entirely been Moretti's, rather than his. "That could definitely work, yes."

The Michiel scrivers were not slouching in their chairs anymore. Most were sitting up, or sitting forward—and some were even standing.

Sancia could see the math taking place in their heads: the hours they'd save in sheer labor, and the efficiencies they'd gain, campo-wide. And it would also eliminate a whole host of security concerns, for scriving definitions were easily the most valuable things a campo owned: lexicons might be the heart of a campo, but the definitions were the blood. Even this small-scale application of Orso's technique would be revolutionary for them.

"And it's all here," said Orso, placing a hand on the giant tome on the table. "I've no doubt such advanced minds as yours will make quick work of this . . ."

"After the demonstration," said Moretti sharply. "I will want to make sure it works."

Orso bowed. "Of course."

Berenice and Sancia continued their work, carefully applying the appropriate markers on the iron box. Within half an hour, they were done.

"Finished," said Berenice, stepping back and wiping sweat from her brow.

The Michiel scrivers rose, approached the stage, and studied the alterations they'd made to the test lexicon and its heating chamber, as well as the iron box. Their work was deceptively simple—no more than a bit of bronze, a few plates, and a few hand-wrought sigils, carefully etched.

"It's not working now, is it?" said the scriver with the lisp warily.

Orso gave him a thin smile. "No. It won't work until the lexicon is ramped up and turned on. Only *then* will we have successfully twinned reality."

"But how shall you prove that it works?" asked the scriver with the lisp.

"Well," said Orso, "there are several ways we coul—"

"No. We shall see to that," said Moretti. He waved to one of the scrivers at the back of the room, who trotted forward with a box of their own—though this one was silver and bronze, as opposed to Orso's dull wood.

Moretti opened the box. Inside was yet another definition plate, along with a small scrived lantern. He turned to Orso with a wide smile on his face. "While it sounds like your demonstration might actually measure up to your initial pitch, rather than seeing you put on a show with your tools, I'd prefer to see how your technique would work with *ours*. This definition here will argue that this lantern will turn on . . . but *only* within a foot of whichever lexicon supports it."

Orso nodded slowly. "So . . . you mean to turn on the test lexicon, put the little lantern on top of the iron box, and . . . wheel the iron box out of this room to see if the lantern keeps working?"

"Precisely," said Moretti. "To a part of the campo that I *know* you have never seen before. You or your employees."

The Michiel scrivers looked at Orso—but he simply shrugged and said, "Certainly."

Moretti's smile dimmed a little. "Proceed," he said, nodding at his team.

The Michiel scrivers carefully placed this second scriving definition inside of the test lexicon. Then they shut it, sealed it, and turned it on.

About half the Michiel scrivers backed away, worried that it might explode. But it did not: there was just a squeak from the cart that the iron box sat on, as if a three-hundred-pound weight had been placed on it . . .

Which, Sancia knew, was true. Test lexicons weighed hundreds of pounds. If the iron box believed it now contained one, then it would have just grown incredibly heavy.

Orso waved to the lantern. Moretti held it up, and turned it on.

At first it did nothing—but when he set it on top of the iron box, the lantern suddenly glowed with a bright and steady luminescence.

The scriver with the lisp gasped. Moretti stared at the lantern, eyes still narrow.

Orso pointed to the door. "If you would like to take the box beyond," he said, "myself and my chief of innovation would be happy to walk with you to answer any questions"—he gestured to Sancia, who stepped forward—"while Berenice and Gregor stay behind to ensure nothing goes wrong here."

Moretti gave Sancia a lingering glare of disgust. "And . . . why must I have this creature walking through my Hypatus Building?" He glanced at Berenice. "Why not her?"

"Ahh," said Orso. "Well. Berenice is *quite* competent. I always find it works well to pair the competent people with the people who are, uh, less so."

Sancia and Gregor exchanged a look—*How charming.*

Moretti smiled, slapped on a tremendously false grin, and said, "Of course. That makes perfect sense, then."

Two Michiel scrivers took the cart and began to wheel it out the door. Moretti and the rest paraded out after them, with Orso and Sancia among them.

Sancia took a long, deep breath. *Time to go to work.*

2

     —

S ancia, Orso, and the Michiel scrivers plodded through the
corridors of the Hypatus Building in near silence. Everyone's
eyes were fixed on the little glowing lantern sitting atop the
iron box, waiting for it to flicker and go out—though Sancia knew
it wouldn't. They had not fooled them. The box really did believe it
contained the test lexicon, and all the definitions it asserted about
reality.

"Exactly how far do we plan to go, Armand?" said Orso. "Purely
out of curiosity, of course . . ."

"Until *my* curiosity is sated, Orso," said Moretti.

They took a left, then a right, roving through the halls, deeper
and deeper into the workshops and assembly rooms and libraries.
Sancia knew that, like nearly every hypatus building on the campo,
many wild and dangerous experiments could be found here.

Or at least, she hoped so.

Here we go.

She narrowed her eyes, took a breath . . . and flexed.

That was the only word for it, really. She knew the human brain didn't have anything resembling muscles, yet when she wanted to use her scrived sight, it always felt like she was flexing something in her skull, tensing some ligament or tendon or muscle that would then open up . . . Well. Everything.

The world before her lit up with shimmering tangles of silver, seemingly woven into the walls, the doors, the lanterns, everything: the scrivings that were altering the individual realities of all the objects around her. Each time she looked at a tangle she saw its *logic*— the arguments and commands that were convincing these objects to disobey physics in very select ways. To see these knots of bindings was to see the hidden rules of the world itself.

Or that was how she'd come to think of it, at least. It was a bizarre thing, being able to literally see scrivings—even through walls, and the floor and ceiling, for her scrived sight wasn't nearly as limited by physical obstacles as normal sight—but the really hard bit was describing it. How could she begin to describe the extrasensory? Since there was no one else alive with her talent—purely the result of the scrived plate installed in the side of her head—she had no one to discuss it with.

She glanced from scriving to scriving, peering closely. She saw many mad experiments and designs working away within the Hypatus Building around her, some quite astonishing.

The question was—which one was right for the moment?

Moretti led them down a long corridor, past a group of Michiel laborers pushing a cart full of boxes containing hundreds of tiny glass beads—but as Sancia studied them with her scrived sight, she saw they were actually miniature suns, like the ones she'd seen outside, and she instantly understood that this was a tiny, experimental version that would float throughout a room or a street in a cloud.

Ah. You'll do nicely . . .

She studied the rigs as the cart approached. The crowd of scrivers stepped to the side for the cart of little suns, while the laborers muttered, "'Scuse us . . . Pardon . . ."

But Sancia waited a little longer than most. The cart slowed, and she had to push herself aside to make way . . . and as she did so, she placed a bare hand against the box.

The instant she made physical contact with the box of rigs, her mind lit up with a sea of tiny voices:

<We are the sun! We are the sun itself! When the sky cracks open and the sheath is released, we shall be as the sun, all of us suns, all of us drifting through the air, following our mark . . . >

Sancia listened as the tiny scrivings spoke to her in unison. It all happened in a flash—she was getting very good at conversing with rigs these days—but she knew she still didn't have much time.

<Tell me what your mark is?> she asked the box of lanterns.

<Mark is the following thing, the point where we must go! We move all as one, following the mark, for what a joy it is to be the sun, what a joy it is to be the sun . . . >

She listened to the burst of information. The little orbs, it seemed, had been convinced to glow, and float—and to follow, like dogs on a leash. In the final version, you'd probably carry around some kind of signal—a ring, or a necklace—and the cloud of tiny orbs would float behind you, or around you. A spectacular effect, really. This had all been defined pretty well, but the scrivers who'd designed them had clearly struggled to define *how* the little suns should float: at what speed, and at what position, and so on.

<What happens if you hit a wall?> asked Sancia.

<We reverse course and attempt to return to correct distance from the marker!>

<Okay. And at what speed must you follow the marker?>

< . . . speed?>

<Yeah. You float, right? What speed do you float along at?>

A short silence.

<Undefined!>

<They never defined the speed at which you move?>

<N-No?>

<Then . . . how do you float?>

<Must stay within six feet of the marker at all times arrayed in constellation configuration!> the lamps chirped.

Sancia suppressed a grin. It wasn't surprising that this rig's scrivers hadn't defined something so critical—it was a brand-new design, after all—but it was damned useful for her right now.

<And . . . how long is a foot?>

<Twelve inches?>

<Oh, no, no,> said Sancia. *<They changed all that recently. Let me tell you . . . >*

Rapidly, Sancia argued with the little lamps, disputing their concept of distance, asserting that a foot was actually a fraction of an inch. This would mean that when the lamps exited the box, they'd hurtle toward their "marker" at top speed, constantly trying to be ever-closer—but in doing so, they'd inevitably hit a wall, which would cause them to massively overcorrect their float positions.

Really, it was all almost too easy. But she'd gotten very, *very* good at this in the past three years.

< *. . . and that's how that works, got it?*> she finished.

<*We do!*>

<*And when are you going to do it?*>

<*In forty seconds!*>

<*Excellent. Thank you.*>

She took her hand away. The voices went silent, and everyone continued on their way.

She exhaled. In real time, the entire exchange had lasted no more than two or three seconds. No one had noticed a thing.

Moretti took a left, then a right, then another left. "I would like to take this to the courtyard, Orso," he said. "Just to see if it will work out of doors."

"Of course."

"Is there any issue with rain, or moisture?"

"I haven't fully tested that . . . but I've no reason to imagine there would be . . ."

Sancia, still flexing her scrived sight, peered through the floors of the Hypatus Building, examining the scrivings behind the walls or under the floors.

Then she saw it—a giant, bright ball of glowing tangles several floors below her, one so intense it made her head hurt to see it . . .

The hypatus lexicon. The rig that housed all the experimental arguments the Michiels had ever made.

And there it is. That's my target.

"You have quite the impressive installation here, Armand," said Orso. "A lot cheerier than Ofelia's."

"Mm? Oh, yes," said Moretti. "I can't imagine what the Dandolo Hypatus Building is like. Probably papers and ink all over the place . . . and everyone in drab little roo—"

There was a *crack* from the hallway behind them. Then a scream.

The parade of scrivers stopped. Everyone looked back.

Ah, thought Sancia. *Here we go . . .*

"What was that?" said the scriver with a lisp.

But then came another sound, like hail on a metal roof.

Moretti's eyes grew wide as a tiny, intensely bright ball of light came hurtling down the hallway, quickly followed by dozens more. "Oh *shit!*" he cried.

Instantly, they were inundated by tiny beads of bright light that caromed off of every surface with a high-pitched clanking, shooting about with a blinding speed. There had to be hundreds of them, if not thousands, and the scrivers reacted like they were a swarm of hornets—because they *did* hurt, Sancia found: she felt several slam into her back like they'd been fired from a slingshot, and knew she'd have some bruises soon.

"*Son of a bitch!*" screamed Moretti. "*Which damned fool turned on the sun clouds?*"

Everything descended into chaos as the scrivers covered their heads and faces, and sought shelter from the flood of ricocheting balls of blinding light.

I think I did too good of a job, thought Sancia, *convincing those little balls to fly around too fast . . .*

But she didn't have time to worry about that. She took three steps down the hall, found a locked door to an empty workshop, and placed her hand against it.

<I await the signals,> the door said to her. *<I am as a wall of stone without the signal, I am—>*

<When was the last time a key was used on you?> she asked.

<Oh? Ah. About . . . two hours ago . . . >

<And what is the window of time that a key must be applied for you to unlock?>

<That would be . . . ten seconds?>

<And how long is a second?>

It struggled there. Time and space, she knew, were very tricky things for scrived items to understand. How would you describe a second to something that had no concept of time? Scrivers always struggled with it.

<You've got it all wrong,> said Sancia. *<Let me explain how long a second really is . . . >*

Sancia worked away on the door, convincing it that a second was actually an improbably long period of time, and thus the last key used would still apply now, and the door should open. And as she worked, she began to feel the sigils seeping into her mind, as she always did.

The better Sancia had gotten at communing with scrivings, the more she began to sense and feel and eventually even *see* the sigils on their persuasion plates as she spoke to them. She thought she understood why: in broad strokes, she was feeling what the *object* was feeling, experiencing the arguments someone else had placed upon it, what they did and how they worked.

To commune with a scrived item was, in a way, to feel its scrivings and bindings placed upon you. And every time, Sancia worried a little that whenever she broke away, she was a little more altered than she'd been before.

Finally there was a *click*.

The door opened.

Sancia darted inside, shut the door, and convinced it to lock again. Then she turned to the workshop behind her, flexing her scrived sight.

She darted forward, remembering what Orso had told her when they'd first started planning this job: *We won't need to bring any weapons or tricks with us at all, of course.*

She'd asked—*Why is that?*

Because every hypatus building is full of mad shit, he'd said. *Why bother making weapons when we can just get you inside, set you loose, and turn the whole place into a weapon?*

Sancia dashed through the workshops, listening to the clanking, clattering, and cries behind her. She figured she had about ten minutes before they managed to resolve the situation and noticed she was gone.

She flexed her scrived sight and peered down through the walls and floors of the building. That bright, hot tangle of scrivings was four stories below. Now she needed to find the way to access it.

The lexicon itself will be too well guarded, she remembered Orso telling her. *There's no way you can get to it. But there is, how shall I say, infrastructure available . . .*

She walked down one hallway, flexing her scrived sight as hard as she could. She passed through workshops full of countless panes of glass—the Michiels were getting *very* good at creating glass that imitated daylight, she saw—and glowing floor tiles, and hanging chandeliers that created a curiously calming fluting sound, and mirrors that shone with a curiously intense, haunting luminescence.

Crap, crap, crap, she thought.

She kept moving, glancing about for a way to her target, listening to the screams and commotion from the corridors behind her. Even with her scrived sight, it was hard to keep her bearings in this building. It seemed honeycombed with workshops and rooms, and many had windows that had somehow been scrived so they appeared to face the outside, further scrambling her sense of direction.

Suddenly she saw a bundle of scrivings running toward her—rapier, espringal, armor—recognized what it was, and calmly moved to hide behind an open door.

She waited. Finally a Michiel guard charged past, muttering, "I swear to God, every day it's something new in this place . . ."

She listened until he was gone, then continued farther into the building, one corridor, then another, until she spied what she'd been looking for: a long, thick line of scrivings, running horizontally about two floors below her, all arguing something about the pressure of water . . .

Water pipes, she thought. *To keep the lexicon cool . . .*

But she'd need to find a way down to them. The stairs were not an option, she'd be too exposed there. The windows *might* be an option. But perhaps there was a better one . . .

She looked around, and spied something running vertically throughout the building: some kind of chimney with a plate in it that was absolutely loaded up with scrivings about gravity . . .

Did they really put a goddamn dumbwaiter in their hypatus building?

What was she saying? Of course the Michiels would.

She started off toward it.

If you had told Sancia three years ago that one day she'd not only break into the Michiel Hypatus Building in the middle of the day but navigate through its countless chambers and guard posts and checkpoints with ease, she would have thought you mad. And yet with her scrived sight, she was able to winnow her way through the building like a hot knife through eel fat: she danced about the guards and scrivers, spying the rigs in their pockets as they moved and ducking behind doors or behind corners just at the perfect moment; she tore through locks and sachet checks and scrived doors like they'd been built to expect her passage; she even managed to hide in plain sight once, standing behind a new type of scrived lamp and convincing it to glow unnaturally bright so that the scriver who wandered by just squinted at it angrily before continuing on, grousing, "What damned fool thought *that'd* be a good idea . . ."

And she left everything more or less as she'd found it. The Michiels would have no idea she'd ever even been here.

Within a handful of minutes, she'd arrived at the office with the dumbwaiter, and she crammed herself inside.

She was familiar with the techniques they'd used to scrive the dumbwaiter—basically an amplified version of the argument they used to make the floating lanterns float—so within seconds she'd convinced the thing to let her descend into the belly of the Hypatus Building, closer to the water pipes leading to the lexicon.

The dumbwaiter brought her lower, and lower.

I'm doing good, she thought as she fell. *I'm doing* really *good! It's good to be back at it.*

Her hand thoughtlessly crept to her chest as if feeling for a necklace, expecting to feel the cool metal pressing against her skin. But there was nothing there.

The smile faded.

This was her first effort at any real thieving since the Mountain—and still, it wasn't the same.

The dumbwaiter came to a stop. She slid the hatch open and saw she was in yet another workshop—this one full of adhesive plates that were built to stick to walls—and crawled out.

The water pipes will be accessible closer to the lexicon itself, Orso had told her. *But there'll be more security down there. The more important you are, the closer your office is to the lexicon—which means more guards, more defenses, and more wards.*

She crept to the workshop door, gazing forward with her scrived sight. She cracked the door open and peeked out. On the other side of the door was another corridor—and just a few feet to the left and down the corridor was a chamber where she could access the water pipes for the lexicon, probably below some kind of maintenance hatch in the floor.

Yet in the room with this hatch were three Michiel guards, all very armed, all standing at attention. She quickly realized why: there was an office next door with far more defensive wardings than all the other ones . . . which made her suspect the chambers belonged to Armand Moretti himself.

Shit. Now what?

Crouching in the corridor, she studied the room. Moretti's chambers were exactly as she might have expected: lots of ridiculous, overindulgent displays of light and glass . . .

But there were a *lot* of scrived pots. Probably for keeping his damned chocolates warm. And while the guards were stationed before the front doors to his chamber, that didn't mean there wasn't another way in.

She walked along the corridor, peering in rooms until she found his bedchamber—she suspected that was what it was by the unusual amount of warm, glowing scrived lights placed around what she assumed was his bed. And though she hadn't known Mr. Moretti for long, she felt she'd gotten a pretty decent bead on his character . . .

Aha, she thought. There was a rig hidden in the wall next to his bedchamber, one that looked a lot like a door—probably for allowing lovers to slip in and out, unseen.

She walked up to it, placed her hand on the wall, and listened.

<I await the sachet of my master . . . the sigils arranged just so, and pressed against the warmth of my skin, filling me with light, filling me with meaning, filling me with purpose . . . >

She wrinkled her nose. She much preferred tinkering with Orso's scrivings. They could be a bit grumpy, but at least they were a lot less touchy-feely.

She overpowered the door, slipped into his chambers, and found the biggest scrived pot of chocolate available. She looked around, grabbed a big bottle of grapeseed oil, and dumped it in. Then placed her hand on the side of the pot, and listened.

< . . . *just slightly warmer than the human body,*> said the pot in tones of quiet contentment. <*Not too hot. Not boiling hot. Just . . . warm. Just as warm as flesh, flesh on a summer day, flesh under the bright light of the sun . . .* >

<*Hey, I got news for you about flesh,*> she said to the pot.

<*Mm? Really?*>

She rapidly convinced the scrived pot that human flesh was several times hotter than what it'd been originally told—or it would be, in about one minute. And then it should believe that for exactly one minute after that; otherwise if it kept believing it should be so terribly hot it might set the whole building on fire.

<*That's terribly interesting!*> said the pot. <*I've been doing this wrong all this time!*>

<*Yeah, you sure have,*> she said. <*So—try doing it the right way in a bit, okay?*>

The scrived pot emphatically agreed. Sancia slipped back out the secret door and huddled in the workshop with the adhesive plates once more. Then she licked her finger, reached down, and applied the finger to the heel of her boot.

Instantly, the heel of her boot recognized her saliva and popped off, revealing a small hollow within. Sancia picked up her heel and peered inside.

No one in their right mind would have ever imagined someone would scrive the heel of their boot. That had been Berenice's idea. But they'd needed a way to get this final component into the campo—for even Sancia wouldn't have been able to make this on the fly.

It looked like a small, square metal plate. But as Sancia touched it with her bare skin and spoke to it with her talent, it suddenly popped up like a paper sculpture, and became a small cube.

She cradled the tiny cube in her hands, studying it, observing the countless scrivings and arguments etched into its surface in microscopic writing. She and Berenice and Orso had worked on this for better than a half a year, and all of it had come to this moment. Otherwise they'd just sold Orso's greatest idea and mightily empowered a merchant house for nothing.

She looked through the walls in front of her and spied the

scrived pot. She saw its arguments had suddenly changed, and now its temperature was leaping up, up, up . . .

Here goes.

She moved her gaze to study the three guards outside Moretti's chambers. For a moment nothing happened. Then one guard whirled about, and there was a cry of *"Smoke! Smoke! Fire!"*

She watched as the three guards charged into the chambers. When they were far enough away, Sancia darted out into the chamber with the hatch to the water pipe.

The room was already full of smoke—apparently grapeseed oil smoked up like the devil—but she spied the hatch in the corner of the chamber. She darted over and quietly pulled it open.

She studied the scrivings in the pipe below. There was a small valve in the side, but she couldn't just open it—then water would come spraying out.

Once you get to the water pipes, Orso had told her, *you're going to have to find a way to convince them to stop piping in water. Then you can open the pipes, drop in the cube, and be done. But it's dangerous. You'll only have about fifteen seconds before you have to resume the flow. I think. I really don't know.*

She'd asked—*Why is that?*

Because no one has ever tested shutting down the flow of cooling water to a lexicon. They need a lot of water to stay cool, and if they don't get it, well . . . A lexicon is just a giant pile of scrivings and arguments that make reality weak and confused. If the lexicon unravels, and everything gets too confused . . . That would be very bad for not only us, but everyone who lives within about a mile of the Hypatus Building. So let's be conservative and say you only have ten seconds to drop the cube in.

Sancia stared at the pipes in the floor.

Ten seconds. Great.

"Son of a bitch!" cried the guards in the smoking room. "What in hell did he put in this pot?"

She started unscrewing the valve, very, very slowly.

If I get this wrong . . . Well. At least Orso won't be able to scream at me.

She kept unscrewing it until it had only a few threads left. Then she placed a bare hand to the side of the pipe, and listened.

<BURST OF BUBBLES,> shouted the pipes. <PUSHING,

*TUMBLING, RUSHING, SLOSHING, DOWN AND DOWN
AND DOWN AND DOWN . . .* >

She winced. She wasn't surprised to find that the arguments
within the pipe were unusually powerful—this was a critical part
of the lexicon, after all—but this meant it'd take time to convince
them . . . and then, worse, more time to restore them to their original arguments, and allow the water to resume flowing.

She took a breath. *Scrivings have trouble with distance, direction, and
time,* she told herself. *These are always the doors. These are always the
way you can unlock them.*

<*Who told you what down was?*> she asked it.

<*WHAT?*> said the pipes. <*WHAT WAS THAT?*>

<*I said,*> she told it, <*what is down?*>

It responded. <*WELL, DOWN IS . . .* > Sancia listened, and
then began applying her arguments, one after the other, as fast as
she could.

"Ugh," said one of the guards. "It's smoked up the ceiling . . .
Should we get a mop?"

<*I SEE,*> said the pipes after they'd listened. <*VERY WELL,
THEN. ABOVE THIS JUNCTURE, I SHALL FORCE ALL WATER
OUT.*>

Sancia swallowed as she watched the pipes begin to force water
away from the valve . . . which meant that, as of right now, the lexicon far below her would start to unravel.

She started counting.

One.

She fumbled with the valve, unscrewing it as fast as she could.

Two.

The valve came loose, and she almost dropped it—which would
have alerted the guards to her presence. She snatched it, and carefully laid it on the floor, one bare hand still applied to the pipe.

Three.

She fumbled for the little metal cube in her pocket, and pulled
it out.

"Just put the pot out!" cried one of the guards. "You know we're
not allowed in here anyway!"

Four.

She flexed her scrived sight. The lexicon below her was beginning to burn a strangely bright, unsettling shade of white . . .

She stuffed the little cube into the pipe and delicately picked the valve top back up.

Five.

She started screwing it in, one turn, then another, then another—just far enough.

Six.

<*Actually, I was wrong!*> she cried to the pipes.

<*MM? WRONG ABOUT WHAT? WHAT IS THERE TO BE WRONG ABOUT?*>

The lexicon below her was now a disturbing pink.

"The damned thing's still burning hot!" screamed one of the guards.

<*I was wrong about where down was!*> She forced her arguments upon the pipes, one after the other.

Seven.

<*I . . . I SUPPOSE THAT COULD MAKE SENSE,*> said the pipes. <*BUT CAN YOU REMIND ME WHAT WATER IS, AGAIN?*>

"Shit, shit, shit," whispered Sancia. She focused as hard as she could, telling the pipes what water was, how it worked, how it felt, how to recognize it, activating its bindings one after another.

Eight . . .

"No, no, *no!*" shouted a guard. "Don't drop the pot on his damned bed!"

<*AH. I SEE NOW,*> said the pipes. <*VERY CLEVER. VERY CLEVER INDEED.*>

<*So—you'll put water through again?*> she asked desperately.

<*WHY, OF COURSE! OF COURSE . . .*>

She heard the slosh of water within the pipes, and a loud, oddly pleasing gurgling. She looked down at the lexicon far below her.

For a moment it did nothing—the pink just intensified unpleasantly, and she felt her belly blossom with utter terror . . .

Well. I did it. I killed a lexicon. And now we're all going to scrumming die.

But then the pinkness faded, very slowly, bit by bit . . . until it had returned to the usual bright white.

She almost sighed, overwhelmed with relief. But then she remembered the little cube.

She looked back down, and saw she could track its passage through the pipes of the lexicon: it was a bright little star of white-hot scrivings, swooping and tumbling about in the flow of the waters—until it grew close to the massive rig.

At this point, the little cube's density scrivings were activated, and it dropped like a stone, sticking to the bottom of the pipe and refusing to budge in the rush of the water. It was practically right in the belly of the thing. It held fast.

I did it. Holy shit, I did it . . .

"And just how are we going to explain to the hypatus that we set his bed on fire!" screamed a guard inside Moretti's chambers.

Sancia shut the hatch and slipped away.

Two floors above, Sancia opened the locked door and was met by the sight of a half dozen Michiel scrivers lying on the floor, groaning and moaning, their faces and bodies covered in bright-red welts.

"Is it over?" she asked. "Sorry, I got hit by a few and I just . . . I just ducked in and hid in that office there . . ."

The Michiel scrivers glared at her and pulled themselves to their feet, not bothering to respond.

"Did the box work?" she asked. "Do we need to do any more testing?"

"No!" snapped Moretti, whose face paint and hair were now an absolute mess. There were even holes in his robes from where the little glass beads had shot through. "What the devil were you doing in there?"

"I told you, sheltering from th—"

"Search her! Now!"

Two Michiel guards approached her, their armor covered in tiny dents from the lamps. She sighed and put her arms up, and they searched her rather invasively.

"Nothing," said one when they'd finished.

"Son of a bitch," spat Moretti. "Orso! At the very least, reprimand this horrid little girl for her impertinence!"

Sancia tried to suppress a grin. But then she heard a voice hissing behind her: "Hid in that office there . . . You just . . . You just hid in that office there, *eh?*"

She turned to find Orso Ignacio glaring at her murderously, his face trembling with fury—his welt-covered, bruised, pockmarked face.

3

Moretti did not apologize for the accident with the sun cloud. He seemed to take it as a natural risk that one might get pummeled by tiny glass beads at any moment when in a hypatus building. Instead, he and Orso—both bruised and furious—sat at the table before the piles and piles of paperwork, nearly all of which was intended to satisfy the other authorities on the Michiel campo.

"Sign there," said Moretti. He winced as he touched the side of his face. "And there. And there . . ."

Finally it was done. The Michiels packed up all the tools the Foundrysiders had brought—the plates, the tomes—and took them away, leaving only the chest of duvots beside the table.

Moretti stood and tried to smile, but apparently even this was too painful. "Congratulations, Orso. You will forgive me if I do not shake hands. Or bow. Or discuss this further." One hand touched his left buttock, and he made an unpleasant grunt of pain. "I have . . . some pressing issues I need to attend to . . . Please, go in peace."

He departed. Two Michiel guards approached, and one said, "We'll escort you back to your transportation."

"Thank you," said Gregor. He picked up the chest of duvots and they followed them out.

Berenice gave Sancia an intense look. Sancia nodded, very slightly. A giant grin blossomed on Berenice's face—an unusual show of enthusiasm, since she was often preternaturally controlled—and Sancia had to fight from kissing her right then and there.

They trooped out to the Michiel carriage in silence, and rode back to their own shabby carriage in silence, and then drove it away from the campo in silence, until finally they were through the outer gates, and back into the Commons—the muddy, steaming, shambling, messy Commons.

"I am going to keep driving," said Gregor, his voice shaking with either excitement or anxiety, Sancia couldn't tell. "They are certainly still watching. We need to maintain until we get back to our firm, out of eyesigh—"

"Did you do it?" blurted Orso. "Did it work?"

"Yeah," said Sancia.

"It . . . It *did*?"

"Yeah."

"It really did, Sancia?" said Gregor from the cockpit.

"Yeah."

"For once," said Berenice with a sigh, "you *could* answer with more than one word . . ."

Orso nearly began crying with joy. "Yes. *Yes!* Oh my scrumming God, yes!"

"You aren't mad about your face?" said Sancia.

"My face? Who the hell cares about my face? I'd have cut the damned thing off to do what we did back there! Oh, we'll have a merry old carnival this year, now won't we! Let's get home, as fast as we can!"

Their carriage bumped and trundled through the Commons as evening fell. Sancia gripped Berenice's hand tight and kept staring out the window, praying and hoping that they wouldn't see any Michiel assassins or guards pursuing them. So far she hadn't seen anything besides the chattering gray monkeys, which nested in the building rooftops of the Commons.

"Still nothing?" asked Gregor from the pilot's cockpit.

"Nothing," said Sancia. And she knew she was right. Not only did her scrived sight give her an edge, it was hard to sneak through the Commons these days. There were too many lamps now, thanks to the changes Orso and Foundryside had wrought in the past three years.

After Orso had started his own scriving firm out in the Commons, no one had been sure how the merchant houses would react. Would they just kill him outright? Blow up the building with shrieker bolts? Either had seemed very likely.

Yet within days, their decision was made for them—for soon dozens and dozens of merchant house scrivers, some of them the geniuses of the campos, had followed in his footsteps: they'd abandoned the merchant houses, set up shop in the Commons, and started their own miniature merchant houses.

Now there were walled-off blocks here and there among the rookeries, tiny compounds that the other new scriving firms had built into their own headquarters. These firms operated miniature foundries and manufacturing bays within those walls, tinkering and experimenting day and night. Since the Commons was so poorly designed, resembling a rabbit's warren more than a civilized neighborhood, the new firms had resorted to giant, stationary floating lanterns that hovered above their new compounds, with the words "FRIZETTI" and "BALDANO" stitched on the sides so people could find them. Within months, the nebulous, half-pejorative term "Lamplands" came into use, and all who labored in such neighborhoods were Lamplanders.

The merchant houses, and the Tevanni Council, had been utterly perplexed as to how to respond to all this. Between a slave rebellion abroad and a scriver rebellion at home, they'd been utterly paralyzed. Which suited Foundryside just fine.

Orso sat forward as they finally approached their own headquarters. "We're finally there. Holy shit, we're almost home free."

The carriage trundled up to the Diestro Building—the lopsided, improvised, and shabby headquarters of Foundryside Limited—

and the rambling iron wall that sealed it off from the streets. Even though it was almost night, a queue of Lamplands scrivers was waiting at the gates for them.

"We've been here all day!" one scriver complained as they got out. "You're holding up our work, Orso!"

"Not open for business today!" snarled Orso as he pushed past them. "Scrum off!"

"What!" said another. "You can't do that. You didn't even put out a sign!"

"A consulting firm had damned well better consult!" said yet a third.

"Well, it's damned well not going to today!" Orso shot a thumb over his shoulder. "Hit the road! Come back tomorrow! Or don't, I don't care!"

Muttering, the scrivers departed, and the Foundrysiders opened their gates, crossed the courtyard, and piled into the front doors of their offices. Gregor went about locking the door and setting up their defensive wards—windows and walls and floorboards that could suddenly turn quite hostile to the wrong person there at the wrong time—but stopped when Orso took a deep breath, raised both his fists, and gave a rough cry of victory.

"We did it!" he shouted. "We really did it!"

"Mm, mostly Sancia did it," said Berenice.

"And it is not done yet," said Gregor. "This will take weeks to finish."

Orso collapsed onto the floor, legs quaking. "Whatever. Soon we'll have the entire Michiel campo at our mercy . . . and the bastards don't even know it ye—"

There was a knock at the door. Everyone froze.

Gregor took a scrived rapier from beside the front door and peered through the peephole.

"Ah," he said.

He turned the knob and opened the door to reveal a middle-aged man and a young woman standing on the front step. The man had a graying, unkempt beard, and he wore a set of jerkin and breeches that might have been fashionable a decade ago. The woman was younger, about Berenice's age, clad in a leather apron with leather gloves, and her arms shone with glistening burn scars.

Gregor nodded to them. "Claudia, Gio. Fancy meeting you here."

They slipped inside and Gregor shut the door. "We've been waiting for you to get back!" said Gio.

"How did it go?" said Claudia. "Did it work?"

"'Course it worked," said Sancia. "Since when have I failed at a job?"

"There was that time you burned down the waterfront," said Claudia. "Do you remember that time you burned down the waterfront?"

"Yes," said Gregor flatly.

Giovanni and Claudia were old ex-employees of Foundryside. Both of them had come from the black market, and both had left to start their own scriving firms after the Lamplands had taken off. Orso held only a very minor grudge against them, which Sancia considered a major evolution of his moral character.

"How long will it take for it to be done?" said Gio.

"How long's a piece of string?" snapped Orso. "As long as it is."

"So the Michiels aren't using it now?" asked Claudia.

"No!" said Orso. Then he thought about it. "Well. At least, I don't *think* so."

"Why don't we go see?" suggested Gregor.

They walked through the foyer and into the central area of their offices. Once this had been corridors and little apartments and chambers, but they'd ripped all the walls down and turned the entire floor into something very different—a library.

But not a normal library. This was a library of scriving procedures, and designs, and sigil strings, and argument definitions, all compiled over the course of three years. A sign hung above the doorway reading: ALL LIBRARY VISITORS MUST SUBMIT ONE (1) SCRIVING DESIGN TO BE REVIEWED FOR APPROVAL AND PAY THE FIFTY (50) DUVOT FEE IN ORDER TO RECEIVE A LIBRARY SACHET.

Claudia and Gio stopped at the front desk. "Uh. We'll need you to help us out here . . ."

"Huh?" said Sancia. "Oh, right." The library's defenses had been scrived to sense the Foundrysiders' blood and permit them—but such permissions were denied to Claudia and Giovanni.

Sancia walked to the front desk and pressed a finger to a drawer. The lock popped open, and she pulled the drawer out and rummaged through it for two sachets. She tossed them to the two scrivers. "There. Now come on!"

They walked past the towering bookshelves, and the tables piled up with tomes, and the chests full of definition plates, until finally they came to a small, red door at the back of the library. Orso took out a scrived key, stuffed it into the lock, opened it, and ran down the staircase to the basement as the others followed.

"It will take them time to implement our designs," he said. "Maybe days, maybe weeks. But I've no doubt they'll try."

The basement was an unruly, filthy place, filled with stacks of books and blackboards, piles of papers covered in sigils, and boxes of scrived bowls for heating soft metals. Sitting in the middle of the basement floor were two curious contraptions: one was a rather shabby test lexicon, somewhat like the one they'd worked with back at the Michiel campo—it bore a large, sloppy "FS" imprint at the top, indicating it was the property of Foundryside. But the other was a large dome of iron, with a round glass window set in the side. Through the window one could see dozens of round bronze plates hanging on racks within the dome.

Any scriver worth their wine would have been dumbfounded to find this rig sitting here in this musty, crackling basement: it was the cradle of a foundry lexicon, the bit that held all the carefully written arguments that the lexicon would then use to reshape reality, like a campo attorney taking a bunch of legal books to dictate the law.

But this specimen was different in two ways: for one, there was no actual foundry lexicon to go with it; and two, all the definition plates inside were blank.

Orso looked at Sancia. "Is it ready?"

She flexed her scrived sight and studied the lexicon cradle. "Looks ready to me."

He exhaled, relieved. "Oh, thank God."

Giovanni walked around the lexicon cradle, nodding very slightly. "So, just to review how this works . . . . When the Michiels begin bringing out an updated definition . . ."

"They'll almost certainly use our designs to twin all of their lexicon cradles," said Berenice. "That way, they only have to write one set of arguments—and then if you put that set in one cradle, reality will think you're putting it in *all* their lexicons all over their campo, all at once."

"Saving a fortune in time, money, resources . . ." Orso waved a hand. "Everything."

Claudia nodded. "And what Sancia did at the hypatus offices . . . That little cube you said you'd made . . ."

"It's a relay rig!" said Orso, literally hopping up and down with joy. "Like a red cuckoo sneaking its egg into a nest! Sancia had to get it damned close to the lexicon, but now that she's done it, it's tricked their goddamn hypatus lexicon into treating *this* cradle like it's on the Michiel campo!"

Giovanni looked faint with amazement. He slowly sat down on the basement floor. "So when they feed all their arguments into their hypatus lexicon . . . All the proprietary designs and sigil strings they've spent thousands of duvots producing over however many years . . ."

"Then these blank plates here will fill up with those *very same designs*!" cried Orso, bouncing around the room. "All those incredibly valuable arguments that can convince reality to tie itself in scrumming knots will *literally* be written out on our blank plates! Everything that makes the goddamn Michiels so high and *so* mighty is going to pass through *my* goddamn basement in a matter of days, or even hours!"

"Holy shit," said Claudia. "You really think you've done it?"

Berenice heaved a huge, slow sigh. "I think so, yes. We should be able to steal every single scriving definition the Michiels have ever made."

"And make their whole house irrelevant overnight," said Sancia.

There was a long silence.

"You all seem very merry," said Gregor. "But I think my job as chief of security is going to get very, very difficult very soon. The second they find out, they'll want our heads for this, Orso. Though they might want other bits of our anatomy first."

"We have *some* time to relax," said Orso. "It's not like they're going to twin the chamber and start feeding in their definitions tonight or something. We have time enough to get our house in order, set up the necessary protocols, an—"

There was a *snap* from the cradle.

They all jumped and stared at one another.

Another silence—this one much, much longer.

Sancia peered into the cradle. "It . . . looks like the plates have changed."

"Already?" said Berenice, aghast. "They implemented our techniques *already*?"

"You're joking . . ." said Gregor.

"Perhaps . . ." said Orso hoarsely. "Perhaps I did not give Moretti enough credit . . ."

He walked over to the test lexicon and turned it off. Then with one last look at everyone, he opened the door to the chamber, reached inside, and slid a bronze plate out.

The plate was no longer blank. Now it was covered with thousands and thousands of sigils—and though Sancia wasn't sure, she suspected these sigils were in the handwriting of Armand Moretti himself.

Orso looked up at them with tears in his eyes. "We did it. We've stolen the jewels out from under the sleeping dragon. And no one in Tevanne even knows it yet."

4

S ancia tipped back the glass of wine and felt a thrill of warmth as it slipped down her throat and into her belly. She wiped her mouth with a relish that bordered on extravagant. "*That,*" she said, "is exactly what I needed."

Gregor watched her over the brim of his cup of weak tea, his face fixed in an expression of morbid fascination. "You know you're not supposed to drink the dregs, yes? All the bits of sugarcane settle down there?"

"She knows." Berenice sighed. "It is difficult to get someone who's grown up eating nothing but rice and beans to understand how to appreciate wine."

"I eat a lot more than rice and beans these days," said Sancia, grinning at her.

Berenice froze, and Gregor tactfully turned away. "That is enough," Berenice said quietly. But she smiled.

Sancia extended her glass to her. "The hell with Pasqual's giraffe puppets," she said. "I'd rather be here than anywhere in the world."

They were all crowded into their usual corner table at the neighborhood taverna, the Cracked Crucible. Though the plaster walls were cracking, the pipe smoke noxious, and the wine unsettlingly viscous, it was considered a critical gathering spot for the Lamplands cognoscenti. Mostly because it was the taverna that Orso preferred—and where Orso went, other scrivers tended to follow.

"You're not worried the Michiels will figure it out?" said Claudia.

"Having met these gentlemen," said Gregor, "I am not."

"A slow leak of information," said Orso, his eyes glittering. "They've been stabbed in an artery and don't even know they're dying yet."

"And what are you going to do with their definitions once you have them all?" asked Gio.

He grinned evilly. "The same thing we already do," he said. "Give them away."

Claudia stared at him. "You're not serious."

"Once we have all their most powerful arguments," said Orso grandly, "we shall make copies of the plates, bundle them up, and leave them on the doorstep of every firm in the Lamplands. They will all wake up to a *very* pleasant Monsoon Carnival gift, I should think. And maybe we'll toss a few to the black markets, and let them go overseas. And may they spread, and spread, and spread."

"You don't want to sell them first?" said Gio. "You could make a damned fortune, man. I know my firm would be the first to buy."

Claudia nodded fervently. She and Gio had left Foundryside to start their own firms, but they were having their fair share of issues. Sancia wasn't surprised to hear they might be interested in looking at merchant house definitions for inspiration.

"Gio, lad," said Orso, "I'd trade every duvot in every campo's coffers just to piss down their necks for a hot minute. This was not, and shall not ever be, about the money." He sat up straight and assumed a dignified, regal pose. "This was about our *principles*."

"Piss and principles," said Claudia. "What natural bedmates."

"I still fail to see your strategy, Orso," said Gio with a sigh.

Orso thought about it. "Have you ever seen a drunk play bottla ball when everyone else is sober?"

"I have both seen, and been, that particular drunk," said Gio.

"What are you talking about now, Orso?" said Sancia.

"Well, if the drunk isn't coordinated enough to actually win the game—to really make good choices," said Orso, "then he just tosses his ball into the clusters of his opponents' and sends them rocketing all over the place. Not strategic throws with specific ends—but a play at scrambling the whole court, and ruining everyone else's game."

"So—in this metaphor," said Gio, "you're a drunk throwing balls?"

"I am *saying* that when one has no good choices," said Orso, "the smartest choice is to scramble the court. And that is what we shall do."

They toasted their success, once, twice, more, and shared bowls of coconut rice and shrimp. But then one droopy young man sidled up to their table and leaned over Claudia's shoulder to talk to them.

"I wanted to ask you," the young man mumbled, "about that density fix you gave me."

"Not tonight, Otto," sighed Sancia.

"I know you fixed it," said Otto, "but I can't duplicate what you did."

"We can discuss this at the library tomorrow," Berenice told him. "During a *scheduled* appointment."

"I'm under a deadline," said Otto. "If . . . If there could be just something you could show me . . ."

Sancia and Berenice dutifully ignored him.

"Please," he said. "My position is at risk . . ."

"Ugh!" said Sancia. She slopped down more wine, grabbed a knife, and began scrawling sigils in the tabletop. "Sit down and shut up. Because I'm only going to do this once."

The young man watched as Sancia drew out a simple set of sigil strings that governed density and started to walk him through the process. A few Crucible patrons stood to observe as well.

"You are giving away our services!" Orso hissed.

"I'll haul the goddamn table back to the library if I have to!" said Sancia.

Claudia and Giovanni laughed. "It's your fault for starting a damned scriving charity, Orso," said Gio. "Everyone expects your help now."

"The library is *not* a charity," Orso said. "Foundryside is a private interest pooling public, communal goods."

Which was true. After founding Foundryside, Orso had been faced with a dilemma: he'd created a brand-new twinning technique, but there'd been absolutely no market for it. Only merchant houses had the resources to use it, and the merchant houses wouldn't touch him with a ten-thousand-foot pole—unless they could shove it through his throat.

But then the other scrivers had moved into the Commons and started their own firms, and Orso had realized he had another valuable resource on his hands: Sancia. Specifically, the plate in her head that allowed her to engage with scrivings. That, combined with his and Berenice's depth of knowledge, meant they were experts in an industry that suddenly needed a lot of help.

So they'd pivoted, and made Foundryside a consulting firm. If you had a design or a rig or a string that you just couldn't get to work, you took it to Foundryside, and they'd help you fix it, for a fee. The Lamplands even came up with a nickname for Sancia and Berenice: they were "the Muses," bringing brilliance down from upon high.

But there was a catch: whatever design they helped you fix went into their library. And their library could be perused by anyone who'd *also* donated a design to it, and paid the fee.

It was a terrifying concept for most scrivers, who came from the campos, where the question of intellectual property was something that regularly got people imprisoned or murdered every month. *Sharing* scriving designs? Building some kind of library that could be browsed by almost anyone? It seemed mad.

But eventually the scrivers realized: they were not on the campos anymore. And they needed help. "In order to gain," Orso told them, "you must first give." And finally, they did.

At first, Sancia had been reluctant to put her talents to such use. But Orso had told her his bet: "Whatever we do to empower the Lamplands will eventually undermine the merchant houses. By making the Lamplands strong, we will make the houses and their empires weak."

And that was all Sancia had ever been interested in.

She finished scrawling out the strings on the table. "See now?" she said. "See how it works?"

Otto blinked. "I . . . think so . . ."

"I do not think he actually does," said Gregor quietly into his tankard.

Orso clapped his hands. "Otto, you are in luck. If you pop by the offices tomorrow, we will schedule a remedial consultation for you, *and* give you the low discount of only twice our regular fees."

"How can it be low," said Otto, "if it's also twice as mu—"

"Good day!" snarled Orso, and he pointed a finger at the door. Otto turned and slumped away.

"I so cherish helping out our Lamplands brothers," said Orso, sitting back. "But I do wish some of them weren't such dull-witted, brainless bastards."

Sancia and Berenice exchanged a smile, exulting in the moment, in their success, in the feeling that they were finally starting something new. Sancia tossed back more wine.

"Slow down," said Berenice. Her fingers trailed down Sancia's back. "It's early."

"I've earned it," said Sancia. "Haven't we all earned it?"

"We have," said Orso. He raised his glass again. "Tonight we have saved this city. We have saved scriving *itself.* And no one even knows it. We are all keepers of a secret flame, lighting the way forward." He drank—or tried to, as a good bit of it wound up spilling down his chin.

They toasted again, but Gregor's face was quiet and closed as he drank his tea.

"Something wrong?" asked Sancia.

"Not a flame, I think," he said. "A spark. We intend to start an inferno." He looked out the greasy window at the foggy lanes outside. "Yet fires do not care about who they burn."

Together they wobbled home through the lanes of the Commons. To Sancia's eyes the sky-bound lamps were smears of yellow and orange and purple on the dark canvas of the night sky. Though the Monsoon Carnival was still days away, a few people were already in costumes. Sancia had a slight scare when someone ran past her wearing the classic Papa Monsoon costume: the black cloak, black mask, and black three-cornered hat of the mythical man who brought the storms and death every six years.

"'Magine it," belched Orso as they stepped over the creaking wooden sidewalks. "Imagine it as it *used* to be. Hundreds of firms, thinking, working, collaborating . . . That was as it was." He stopped and looked down one alley. The wind rippled through the evening sky and all the lanterns danced, the names and colors intermixing, and for a moment it looked like Orso's head was afire with flames of many hues. "It can be that way again. We can bring it back. Think of all the soldiers, all the scrivers, all the people waiting for a better way of living . . . All of this, *all* of it can change."

"Let's not get maudlin," said Gregor. "Let us get home instead."

Sancia looked at Gregor, and saw he did not look drunk, or happy, or cheerful. Rather, he wore the same expression that he so often did: a look of troubled, quiet loneliness, like a man still puzzling over a bad dream.

"Come, come," he said, shepherding them on. "Come on. Off to bed with all of you."

"I'm sorry, Gregor," said Sancia.

"For what?" he asked.

Because I couldn't fix you, she wished to say. But then there was a blare of piping from the corner, and reeling laughter, and the moment was gone.

Berenice helped her up the stairs a step at a time. "Just because you can finally drink," she said, "it doesn't mean you should do so with *quite* so much enthusiasm."

"Kiss me," said Sancia.

"I have. Repeatedly. Despite the taste of Crucible wine on your lips."

"We did it. We really pulled it off, Ber."

"I know we did."

"But the hell of it was . . . it wasn't even all that hard," said Sancia.

"I beg your pardon?"

"Well, not for *me*, anyways. If you could get me to the Morsinis, or the Dandolos . . . We could wipe out the lot of them."

"You can hardly handle these stairs. Let's manage our aspirations accordingly."

They turned on the next landing and started up the next flight.

"Can we tell him?" asked Sancia.

"Tell who?" Then she realized. "Oh. Yes. Of course."

They walked up the steps to the Foundryside attic, where they lived together. Berenice unlocked their door—which had been scrived to demand both the presence of their blood and their saliva—and Sancia staggered in and made for the closet.

"Would you let me do that?" said Berenice, locking the door. "You'll make such a mess of things . . ."

But Sancia ignored her. She stumbled to the closet and pawed through their clothes and books until she'd revealed a small panel in the back. She pressed her hand to it, and there was a *pop*.

"Locks and locks and locks," she muttered, pulling the panel away. She reached inside. "And yet all I want is . . . ah."

She felt her fingers close over the metal—over his head, so curiously butterfly-shaped, and his tooth, strange and rippled.

As always, she waited for a moment—to hear his voice, his chatter, his mad running commentary on everything. But there was nothing.

She sighed sadly and pulled him out, his gold glinting in the light of the scrived lanterns.

"Hello, Clef," she whispered to him.

The key, of course, said nothing back. Or rather, the mind imprisoned within it—the man once named Claviedes, his personality and memories warped by the designs of the key—did not. When the tool had been aging and run-down, Clef had been able to converse with Sancia directly, whispering in her ear like a songbird in a fairy tale—until he'd been forced to reset himself, and restore all the boundaries within the device. He'd been silent ever since.

Sancia believed he was still in there, a mind trapped within all the invisible machinery inside the key, silent but sentient, and lonely.

"Bring him out here, if you're doing it," said Berenice. "I daresay he's sick of the dark."

Sancia pulled out the little golden key, shakily stood, and walked over and sat by Berenice on the foot of their bed. She held him up to her lips and whispered to him, "We did it, Clef. We did what you said."

Berenice sat quietly, allowing Sancia this moment.

"Move thoughtfully," she said. "And bring freedom to others. And . . . I think we're going to. The houses are weak, and they know they're weak. They've lost scrivers. Lost money. They can't keep control of their plantations—the slaves there are rebelling left and right. And . . . and if we just give them a push, we can . . ."

Sancia fell silent, and a sudden swell of guilt bloomed in her.

"Don't," said Berenice.

"Don't what?"

"Don't start beating yourself up."

"You always say that."

"You are doing what you can. Freeing *who* you can. And just because you couldn't free Clef, or . . . or Gregor, it doesn't take away the rest of what we've done."

Sancia shut her eyes wistfully. "I cracked that hypatus building like it was nothing. You'd think . . . You'd think I'd be able to do more."

Berenice gently took Clef from her fingers. "Whoever made Clef was a sight better than you, or Orso, or the both of you put together."

"And Gregor?"

Berenice was silent. The subject of Gregor loomed over all of them like a shadow—for he, like Sancia, was a scrived human being, bearing a command plate in his head that could alter his thoughts, his abilities . . . and perhaps more.

So the question was—who had done that to him? Who had made him what he was, a specimen that far outstripped anything Foundryside had ever made? And why? Despite all their work and research, they still didn't know.

"Perhaps Valeria could have fixed him," said Sancia bitterly, "if she hadn't gone and vanished on us."

"The less you talk about Valeria," said Berenice, "the better I sleep."

"Don't little children pray to angels to watch over them as they slumber?"

"Valeria was many things. But I think 'angel' is definitely far afield."

Sancia went to their washing basin and splashed cold water on her face. She stared at her reflection in the dimly lit waters, and studied the wrinkles at the corners of her eyes, the lines around her mouth, and the silvery sprinkles in her closely cropped hair.

She returned to the bed and sat. *When did I get so old?* She flopped back. *When did I get so scrumming old?*

Berenice replaced the key in the secret panel in their closet and sat next to her.

"Is this going to cut it?" asked Sancia.

"Is what going to cut what?" asked Berenice.

"What we're doing. Orso's grand plan. It feels clever enough, bringing down another merchant house. I just worry it's another move in the same old game." She gave a bleak shrug. "Candiano, Morsini, Dandolo, Michiel . . . even the hierophants, however long ago they were. I feel like they're all links in a chain, binding us up. But every time we break a link, another gets forged to replace it. When does it stop?"

"For now, stop thinking about it," Berenice said.

"I can't," Sancia said. "How can I?"

Sancia looked up as Berenice slid closer to her.

"Ah," said Sancia, smiling. "I see."

Gregor Dandolo lay on his cot in his tiny room, trying to sleep. He shut his eyes, and opened them, and shut them and opened them again.

It had been a wonderful night. A triumphant night. He should feel happy, he knew. He should feel satisfied with the culmination of months of dangerous and daring work. So why couldn't he sleep?

Because though Foundryside might have changed things, he thought, *you still remain the same.*

He listened to the pipers outside, to the shouts and the calls from the early Monsoon Carnival revelers, to the chattering of gray monkeys as they feuded over which rooftop belonged to which tribe. Finally he could bear it no more, and he stood up and peered through his window at the city beyond.

He stared out at the sea of giant floating lanterns. His gaze followed a familiar path, shifting across the luminous ramble of the Lamplands to something that looked like a huge, black wave rising out of the sprawl of the city.

The Dandolo campo walls. The tops of the walls had been fitted with spotlight lanterns, which flashed and swiveled at random, sensing blood, or movement, or heat, or whatever other phenomena you could convince a rig to detect. Ever since Sancia had almost single-handedly destroyed the Candiano walls, all the campos had started investing a lot of research in identifying threats. Gregor wasn't sure how many of those new systems accidentally eliminated innocent people—say, a drunk who got too close to the walls, or someone who brought the wrong sachet on the wrong day—but he was sure it was more than zero.

He watched the Dandolo spotlights dance, slashing through the steam and the smoke unfurling from the foundry stacks.

Are you there, Mother?

The spotlights whirled again.

What are you making within those walls? His right hand rose and massaged the side of his head. *I wonder—are you making someone like me?*

He lay back down, but did not sleep. Ever since the night of the Mountain—the night when the scrivings on his mind had been activated, and he'd waged war upon the Candianos, slaughtering dozens—Gregor Dandolo found he did not much like sleep. He always worried that he might wake up a different person.

Worse still were the dreams, which he'd been having for the past year or so: dreams of sandy beaches, and the moon reflected on the sea; of fire, and screaming, and the smell of earth and old stone; of a room full of moths, white and frail and fluttering, and his mother's face, pale and gleaming in the dark; and finally the feeling of some kind of *presence*, a man or something man-shaped, perhaps, wrapped in black and standing over his shoulder, just out of sight . . . And with these dreams came the intense, overwhelming compulsion that he was supposed to be looking for someone, trying to find them, to seek out where they had hidden themselves away.

He suspected that these dreams were flashes of memories of what his mother had made him do: missions and murders and conspiracies she'd set him on in his hypnotized state, possibly out in the plantations, or all across the Durazzo Sea.

He did not know. Nor did he know what he had done, or to whom. But he wished the dreams would stop.

He rubbed the side of his head again. *What a thing, to wish to be unmade,* he thought. *To yearn to open up one's skull and allow all the bindings there to come unspooling out like lengths of wire . . .*

Though they had tried to fix him, once. And only once.

His memory of the attempt was still clear in his mind: he, lying down on a pallet in the basement; then Sancia, kneeling beside him and placing her bare fingers to the side of his head, just as his mother had so many times; and then there was her voice, loud and jumbled and furious in his thoughts, and then the flashes of so many memories—steel and screams and corridors of stone, the splash of hot blood and cries of pleas for mercy—and then it'd been like he'd had a cold blanket placed upon his mind, and he was wandering in a dark room with no walls, and then . . .

And then he'd awoken. He'd awoken to find himself standing in a wrecked room, all the furniture smashed to pieces, and bookshelves turned over and Berenice weeping—and before him was Sancia, face red and eyes full of tears, screaming and shouting at him and clawing at his hands, which were clamped tight around her throat.

Gregor shut his eyes. *I am not a rig. I am not.*

5

S ancia lay in the covers, lost in the depths of drunken sleep.
    "Sancia," whispered a voice nearby.
    She felt around in the bed with one hand. Berenice was
not there.

She blearily opened her eyes and looked around. She was alone
in their room, naked on the bed, the ceiling strobing with yellow
and orange as the lanterns outside drifted and twirled.

She shut her eyes again and tried to return to sleep.

<*Sancia. Awake.*>

She cracked an eye.

I know that voice.

She turned her head, and saw now there was someone in the
room with her—someone enormous, a giant, hulking shadow of a
figure that nearly reached the ceiling, its shoulders gleaming gold
and its eyes two tiny flecks of cold yellow light burning in the darkness . . .

<*SANCIA,*> roared Valeria's voice in her mind. <*HE IS COM-
ING.*>

Sancia opened her mouth to scream. But then the world blurred, and she was gone.

First a darkness, and a feeling of age, of years, of millennia, the horrible, crushing, obliterating feeling of all that *time* weighing down upon her . . .

She saw the horizon afire, the sky filled with smoke, and all the world burning—and somewhere in the sky above she thought she saw a human form, cloaked in black, floating in the air, his legs crossed in a curiously meditative position . . .

<*THEY HAVE FOUND HIM. THEY HAVE FOUND HIM AND THEY WILL BRING HIM HERE AND THEY WILL BRING HIM BACK.*>

She saw a tomb, deep below the earth, and a sarcophagus of black stone, and sitting in the sarcophagus was a single tiny bone, like that of a knuckle. She felt an awareness of a location somehow emerge in her mind, like it was an old memory she'd forgotten until just now.

This place . . . this is in the plantations, in the islands across the Durazzo. I know it is . . .

A flash of water, of the open ocean, a horizon without a hint of land—except there was something approaching, a small dot parting the waters until it grew, and grew . . .

A ship?

She saw desert hills, and a white stone peristyle sitting atop the sand dunes, the stars and the velvet purple sky visible through its columns.

There was someone in the peristyle. A man, or a man-shaped figure, cloaked in black . . .

It was floating in the air.

<*THE MAKER MUST NOT COME BACK.*>

She drew closer to the peristyle, and saw the thing in black seemed to be sitting on thin air, legs crossed, hands on its knees.

The thing in black twitched, like it had heard her approach. And then it slowly began to turn around.

I've seen this before, she thought. *I've seen this thing before.*

The thing in black slowly, slowly rotated in the air.

In Clef's memories . . . a black-wrapped thing, and a golden box, and the sound of thousands of moths in the air . . .

The wind drifted across the dunes, and the black veil covering the man-shaped thing danced and rippled.

<*THE MAKER MUST NOT COME BACK,*> said Valeria's voice.

The black-clad figure kept turning toward her.

<*I AM WEAK,*> said Valeria's voice. <*I CANNOT FACE HIM.*>

The thing in black had turned to her now, its face hidden behind the veil. But she *felt* its gaze, felt its awareness, felt an immense pressure all over her body, like she was being gripped in the hands of a giant . . .

<*HE MUST NOT COME BACK, SANCIA!*> shouted Valeria's voice.

A horrible, high-pitched shrieking sound filled the sky, and the stars began to quake—and then one by one, they vanished.

The thing in black lifted its hand, gripped the black veil at its face, and began to pull it away.

<*THE MAKER MUST NOT COME BACK!*> she screamed, and there was real terror in her voice, a genuine, palpable fear.

The veil fell to the ground.

Sancia saw what lay underneath, and her mind crawled with madness, and she began screaming.

Her face lit up with pain. She heard Berenice's voice nearby: "For the love of God, Sancia, please *wake up!*"

Sancia sat up in bed, sobbing with fright. She whirled around, mad and drunk and disoriented, and she would have fallen off the bed had a hand not grabbed her by the arm.

"Sancia! My God, what's wrong?" said Berenice's voice again.

The flashes of the vision faded from her mind, and the world grew small and manageable again. Berenice was kneeling on the bed before her, holding her steady. But still the screams echoed in her mind, along with the vision of the thing in black, and the peristyle, and the dying stars above.

She felt tears running down her cheeks. "I . . . I saw her," she whispered.

"What?" said Berenice.

"She . . . was here. In the room with me." She looked around, but the room was empty. "And she spoke."

"Who? Who was here?"

"Valeria."

Berenice stared at her. "What do you mean?"

"I saw her," whispered Sancia through her tears. "And . . . And she took me someplace. Someplace far away. And she . . . she *showed* me something. Or someone."

"Sancia . . . are you . . ."

"He's coming," said Sancia. "That's what she wanted to tell me. They're trying to bring him back."

"Who?"

Sancia swallowed, and worked to find the breath for her words. "The man who made her."

6

Sancia sat in the Foundryside meeting room, hugging her knees and staring straight ahead. It was sometime just before dawn. Orso and Gregor sat at the table watching her warily, unsure what to say, while Berenice held her left hand tight.

"Either I'm still drunk," said Orso, "or this is all a bad dream, or both."

"It happened," said Sancia sullenly. "I know it sounds mad. But it did."

"Yes, but . . . but *what* happened?" said Orso. "You saw Valeria in your damned room, standing over you? How does that even make sense? And keep in mind, *none* of us have ever actually seen this thing."

"Are you suggesting that I'm crazy?" asked Sancia.

"What he is saying, Sancia," said Gregor patiently, "is that it is a little hard to grasp."

"If it's hard for you to hear about it," said Sancia, "imagine it happening to you."

"Why don't you start from the beginning?" said Berenice. "Again."

Sancia took a shuddering breath. "I told you. She was there in the room with me. She told me he was coming. She showed me something—some tomb, and a tiny bone inside—and somehow I knew this was in the plantations. I saw a ship, sailing across the ocean. She said they were trying to bring him back, and she was too weak to face him. I think she was trying to tell me . . . to tell *us* we had to stop them before they brought him back. And then I . . ." She trailed off, too horrified to speak.

"You saw the thing in black," said Gregor.

"In the desert," said Sancia, shivering. "Among stone columns. It looked like a person, draped and wrapped in black, and it was floating."

"And you'd seen this thing before?" said Orso.

"Once," said Sancia. "In Clef's memories. We were on the Candiano campo, and a lexicon spiked. And Clef said the feeling of being so close to it . . . it reminded him of someone." She shut her eyes, remembering his words: "Someone from long ago. Someone who could make anything float. And whenever he wished, he could fly through the air, like a sparrow in the night . . ."

There was a long silence.

"Who is this *they*?" asked Gregor. "Who's going about bringing this thing back?"

"I don't know," said Sancia.

"Well, why the hell couldn't she tell you?" said Orso. "It sounds like she sure has a hair up her ass about all this. Why couldn't she give us a name, or a description?"

"I think she said all she needed to. Someone has found some artifact, some *piece* of something. They intend to bring it here, in a ship, over the waters. And then . . ."

Another long silence.

"And then this maker of hers returns to life," said Orso.

"Yes," she said in a strangled voice. "I think so."

"This tomb you said you saw," said Gregor. "And the black sarcophagus, and the bone within . . . You said you felt like this was in the plantations?"

"Yeah," said Sancia. "I don't know how she did it, but . . . Valeria put that knowledge directly into my mind, somehow." She rubbed the side of her head anxiously. "I'm not sure how I feel about that, really . . ."

Gregor looked away, his face curiously closed.

"What is it?" asked Berenice.

"I . . . have been having dreams," he said finally. "Flashes of memories from when I was under my mother's control, I suspect. Dreams of sand, and the sea, and the moon . . ."

Sancia sat up. "The plantations?"

"Yes. And . . . I recall looking for someone. Looking very *intensely*. I remember thinking that they had hidden themselves away, and I had to find them. And I remember chambers of stone, far under the earth . . ."

"You think this is one and the same?" asked Berenice. "That your mother sent you to find this . . . this thing, this artifact? Whatever it is?"

"Yes," said Gregor quietly. "Maybe I succeeded. Maybe it just took some time for them to get to it. But I have long suspected my mother had some greater plan in mind. I've watched for some sign of her movements. I always thought she'd make a move on the other two merchant houses, but . . . but this . . ."

Sancia shuddered and put her forehead on her knees.

Orso burst out in desperate laughter. "This is absurd!" he cried. "This is *madness*. Do you understand what we're suggesting here?"

"Yes," she said quietly. "I do."

"An artificial god shows up in your bedroom," he said. "And tells you her *maker* is coming back? That what, that Ofelia Dandolo is going to raise him from the dead? And you haven't said it, but you're suggesting that this maker of hers, this thing in black . . . that it's . . . I mean . . ." He stood and paced around the table. "I mean, who else could have made Valeria? Who else carried around a little god in a box, setting it free to alter the very world? The only person she could possibly mean is . . ."

Sancia lifted her head up and looked at him. "Crasedes Magnus," she said quietly. "The first of all hierophants. Yes. I think Valeria is telling us that Ofelia Dandolo is going to try to bring him back to this world."

Orso stared at her, mouth agape. He opened his mouth wider to speak, then froze, shut it, and sat back in his chair, too stunned for words.

Gregor carefully cleared his throat. "I believe he is normally depicted as a . . . a bearded, wizened wizard, yes?"

"Yes," said Berenice. "But those depictions are based on stories. Almost no one really knows much about him, or the other hierophants. For years, all we had were ruins of their works in the north, in the desert lands—fragments of arches, tombs, aqueducts, cities."

"But we know more than most," said Sancia.

"They were goddamn *monsters,*" spat Orso.

There was a grim silence. They knew from their work with Clef that the hierophants' near-mythical abilities had not come from some divine source, but rather from more disturbing means: they'd augmented, warped, and altered their bodies and souls utilizing horrific, ritualistic human sacrifice. Clef himself was one such specimen: a mind ripped from its body, and trapped in the designs of a golden key.

"Were they monsters by choice?" asked Gregor. "Or by necessity?"

"My suspicion is that by interrupting the process of death," said Berenice, "by trapping a soul or a mind within an object, or within someone else's body . . . they greatly confused reality, giving them access to powers and privileges we can hardly comprehend."

"And . . . Crasedes was the first of them," said Gregor. "He was the one who invented this method. Yes?"

"The greatest," said Orso, "and the most powerful of all of them." He shivered. "I'm not surprised to find he's some . . . some specter in a black sheet. There are stories about the bastard wiping out entire cities, and nations! Snapping his fingers and making whole civilizations vanish!"

"But why would he try to come back now?" asked Gregor.

"Probably because Sancia let his goddamn pet out of the box!" said Orso. "And he wants to get her back! I'd normally be a wee bit hesitant to run out and wage war because some malfunctioning god whispered in Sancia's ear, but . . . if this really is—and I can't believe I'm saying it—if it *is* Crasedes Magnus himself who might be coming back, then . . . Shit."

They sat around the table, beleaguered and overwhelmed.

"So," said Sancia. "What do we do?"

Orso laughed dully. "Of course it happens now. *Just* when we made headway with the Michiels. Just when we were trying to change the city for the better, to actually make some goddamn *progress* . . ." Then his pale, cold eyes narrowed. "I don't doubt that you saw what you saw, Sancia. But Valeria has lied to you before, yes?"

She nodded. "About who and what she was."

"Then I wish there was some kind of way to verify all this," said Orso. "I trust apparitions in the night no more than I do the merchant houses. But how in the hell are we going to confirm that Ofelia scrumming Dandolo is actually doing this? And when? And how? We can't even get past her campo walls!"

"It's coming in on a ship," said Gregor. "That's what you said, correct?"

"Yeah," said Sancia.

"Then it's probably coming soon. I doubt if Valeria would have woken you in the night if we still had a month or two to work with." Gregor slowly sat back, his chair crackling under his weight. "I don't have a lot of friends in the Dandolo navy anymore. I don't have a lot of friends in the Dandolo house period, really. But . . . I may know someone who could tell us if anything unusual is going on with the Dandolos' shipping patterns." He glanced at Sancia. "And . . . it'd likely be helpful if you came."

"Huh?" said Sancia. "Me? Why?"

"Because of your bountiful charisma," said Gregor. "Come along. If Valeria really was as urgent as you said she was, we've no time to dawdle."

Gregor and Sancia strode through Old Ditch as a bleary dawn poured over the rooftops—or rather, Gregor did the striding, whereas Sancia slinked along the edges of the streets. His style of walking had always bothered her: back painfully erect, arms swinging to and fro, every bit of him confident and moving. To someone accustomed to the Commons, he was asking for a knife in the back.

"This way, please," he said, gesturing down an alley.

Sancia realized they were heading toward the Slopes: a stretch of Old Ditch that ran along the main shipping channel. It had once been used as a waterfront, back before the houses, but it had fallen into disrepair and started flooding repeatedly, until finally it'd been abandoned.

But as they turned a corner, Sancia saw it was not abandoned any longer.

A huge tent had been built over the Slopes, about three hundred feet wide and fifty feet tall. Stacked within were piles and piles of crates, barrels, bags, and wagons. She saw there were men stationed around the tent, with curiously lightish-colored skin and fair hair. They had hard faces and hard eyes, and they bore rapiers and espringals and watched the alleys keenly.

Gregor made right for them. Sancia followed, unsure what these men were guarding—but then she caught a whiff of corn, and pepper, and she realized.

It's food, she thought. *Spice. God, even wine . . .*

This was a surprise. Ever since rebellions had broken out all over the slave plantations, food and wine had been scarce in Tevanne, but especially in the Commons.

She had an idea. She flexed her scrived sight, and studied the men before the big tent, and saw their weapons light up with scrivings and bindings.

She felt dread bloom in her stomach. *There's only one kind of person in the Commons who'd have access to food and wine, and scrived weaponry . . .*

"How did you come to know these guys, Gregor?" she asked.

"I consort with many types of people, Sancia," he said. "That is what a good chief of security does. It's easier to stop a threat if you know it's coming first. But . . . this is the only person I know of who could possibly confirm any of what you are suggesting."

"Okay?"

"However . . . they have been very interested in you. They have asked me repeatedly to let them see you. Though I've been reluctant to allow that to happen."

"Okay . . . why?"

One of the men saw Gregor approaching and walked forward to intercept him. "Not open today," he said in a curious accent. "Still too early."

"I am not here to purchase," Gregor said. "I am here to see Miss Carbonari."

The man frowned at him mistrustfully. "Why would you get to see her?"

"Because I have politely asked, I should hope."

The man opened his mouth to respond when a second guard sidled up, tapped him on the shoulder, and whispered something in his ear. Comprehension bloomed on the man's face. He looked somewhat embarrassed. "Oh," he said. "Ohh. I will let her know you're here."

The man entered the depths of the tent. Gregor turned to Sancia and said, "If asked, you are a scriving prodigy, and nothing more."

"What?" she said, startled.

"If anyone were to ask," he said, this time slowly and clearly, "you simply have a natural gift for scriving. There is nothing *unnatural* about it. Understand?"

"What have you been telling these peop—"

The man emerged from the stacks of crates. "She will see you now."

Gregor waved a hand, and together they entered the tent.

The light within was a dim yellow, filtered through the cloths and skins above, and there were glimmering oil lanterns staggered throughout the stacks of crates. Though it seemed to be a small labyrinth, it was quite populated: men and women shifted among the goods, or slept on crude pallets, and though they hardly cast an eye at Gregor, many of them stared curiously at Sancia.

Sancia's eye traced over them in the dark. Some of them had their upper arms bared. Every time, they had a small brand on their left triceps—denoting, Sancia knew, which island had once owned them.

Finally they wound through the depths of the tent until they came to a small makeshift office. A woman sat in the corner, behind a tiny, rickety desk, bent over a stack of papers, an oily candle fluttering just inches from her eye.

She looked up at Gregor. She was dressed plainly in a jerkin and breeches—unusual for a woman, but a choice Sancia herself often opted for—and was perhaps about his age, though she looked a little older, due to a life of hard living. Her skin had probably once been lighter than that of the average Tevanni, but was now dark and lined from years in the sun, and her iron-gray eyes were stuck in a perpetual squint. Still, there was an evenness to her features, and a confidence to her bearing, that made her attractive to look at.

"Gregor," she said. Her voice was low and sonorous, but her words were stiff. She was obviously not from anywhere close to Tevanne. "Morning. It's been some time."

Gregor bowed. "Good morning, Polina. How goes your trade?"

"Booming, as always." Her hard eyes flicked to Sancia, and narrowed. "Ah. So. You've finally brought her."

"I have." Gregor sat on one of the crates. "I fulfill my promises."

"You remain an unusual Tevanni, then."

"Though I would like something in return," said Gregor.

The woman's mouth tightened. "Perhaps not so unusual, then."

"This would not be anything too dear. Just information."

"As we're in a city whose might is founded on that very thing," she said, "I wonder what definition of 'dear' you're using." She stood, walked the short distance to Sancia, and stuck out her hand. "I am Polina Carbonari."

Sancia shook her hand, which was as hard as old wood. "Sancia."

Polina gripped her hand a little too long. Sancia realized she was feeling her calluses, her skin, her nails. The woman smirked a little and released her.

"You are Sancia Grado, yes?"

"Yeah?"

"You're quite a celebrity. I've heard many rumors that there was a slave girl working in Orso's shops, doing many wonders with scriving. Are these rumors true?"

"I'm not a goddamn slave anymore. And they don't feel much like wonders when you have to work your scrumming ass off to get them going. But yeah, I guess."

"How did you come to have this skill for scrivenings, might I ask?" asked Polina.

Sancia felt very aware of Gregor's eyes on her. "They're called scrivings. But just like any child can have a skill with a viol," she said, "any person, Tevanni or no, can excel at scriving."

"Is that so?"

"Yes. It is."

"How curious. I wonder now—what has Gregor here told you about us?"

"Nothing. I've no idea why I'm here at all."

"I see. Then what do you assume?"

Sancia thought for a moment. "I assume . . . that you lot are smugglers," she said.

"And?"

"And probably rebellious slaves from the plantations, here to sell all the stuff that normally would have gone straight to the merchant houses."

A very slight nod. "I see. And why do you assume this?"

"For one thing, you have a lot of food," said Sancia. "Which no one else in the Commons has. For another, you have scrived weaponry—which I assume you got after you overthrew some plantation stronghold or another. But I also saw a woman back there with a brand from the Isle of Crepsis. And two men with brands of Ontia."

"And you?"

Sancia hesitated very briefly. "Silicio."

"It was my impression that there is no Silicio Plantation anymore," said Polina. "That someone burned it down."

Sancia shrugged.

Polina examined her very closely. Sancia found the experience disturbing—especially when Polina's eyes flicked to the scar on the side of her head, where the Candianos had installed a scrived command plate in her skull.

"And you?" she asked softly. "Are you here to burn down the whole of Tevanne, just as you did Silicio?"

"Burn down Tevanne?" said Sancia. "What the hell? No."

"Why do you sound so surprised? I thought you and Gregor and Orso were running some kind of revolution, yes?"

"Not all revolutions mean burning down a damned city."

"I am no historian," said Polina, "but . . . it seems likely those are far from the norm . . ."

"Is that what *you're* here to do? Massacre the entire city?"

She waved at the room around her. "Massacre? With wine and grain and old fruit? No. But I admit, many of my compatriots dream of doing so. They think that would make the world a better place."

"It isn't as goddamned simple as that," snapped Sancia. "For one thing, there's a hell of a lot more people in Tevanne than just those on the campos."

"I'm sympathetic to them," said Polina. "But I will say . . . I am more sympathetic to the people I have known who perished in bondage and misery—while your innocent bystanders here in Tevanne simply . . ." Her eyes lingered on Sancia for a fraction of a moment. "Well. Stand by."

Sancia cocked her head. "And what does that mean? You think *I'm* standing by? That I'm complicit in all this?"

"Polina . . ." said Gregor.

"To speak bluntly," Polina said, "I think that if you really are what I am told you are—a freed slave with a gift for scriving—then your energies could be better placed elsewhere."

Sancia frowned at her. "Wait. Wait, wait. You're . . . You're trying to *recruit* me?"

"Yes," Polina said matter-of-factly. "I am. It is my belief that a gifted freed slave should use those gifts in freeing other slaves. Is that so mad?"

Sancia looked at Gregor. "God, Gregor. You brought me here knowing she'd ask this?"

Gregor's face was unreadable. He gave her a small shrug.

"Gregor knows what I am here to do," said Polina. "He thinks our goals support one another—I assault from without, creating havoc in the plantations, while you and he and the rest of your little library assault from within. But while we may share aims, we cannot share you, Sancia, nor your gifts."

"And what would you put my gifts to?" asked Sancia. "Smuggling wine? Burning down plantations?"

"Tevanne believes its strength comes from its scriving," said

Polina. "But the houses forget—they are still human, and even scrivers need to eat. With every field we take, or burn, we make Tevanne's soldiers and scrivers and citizens hungrier and hungrier, and weaken their hold upon the world. But with you helping us, Sancia, we could break it. And besides"—a cruel gleam flickered in Polina's eyes—"surely you can see the justice in inflicting the pain of famine upon the houses, just as they once inflicted it upon people like you and me."

Sancia looked at her for a long while. Then she glanced sideways at Gregor, who sat watching her with that curiously closed look on his face.

Then she thought of the vision: the thing in black, floating in the desert . . .

"I'm needed here," she said.

"I appreciate that sentiment," said Polina. "But think. When you were still in bondage, did you not dream of an emancipator? Someone who'd burn down your walls and dash your chains to pieces? You could be that, Sancia, for so many. And that won't happen with your bloodless revolution."

"You don't know what we're up against," said Sancia. "And I've still got to try."

The two of them held each other's gaze.

"If things were different, Polina," said Sancia, "I would join you in a shot."

Finally Polina sighed, and sat. "I see," she said. "Then thank you, Gregor, for bringing her to me, at least. I hope you consider it further, Sancia." She was silent for a long time. "Now—what is this information you're after?"

Gregor rubbed his hands along the sides of his beard—an easy tell that he was anxious. "You still have your spies among the Dandolo fleet, I assume?"

Polina's face was as blank as a stone wall.

He looked around at the crates. "I see several new shipments, which suggests you were able to evade their patrols . . ."

"And what is it you wish to know?"

"I wish to know if there has been anything . . . unusual recently. A shipment here, to Tevanne. It might be secret, or there might be something secret on board. It would be set to arrive very soon, perhaps. And it would be a Dandolo ship, coming from the plantations."

She looked at him incredulously. "What a tremendous heap of vagueness. So—you know nothing specific of what you're asking about?"

"I know when it would arrive," he said, "what kind of ship it is, and where it would come from. Beyond that, I was hoping you might know more."

Polina opened her mouth to make another comment—but then paused. Sancia thought she spied a gleam of worry in her eyes.

"What is it?" asked Gregor.

"A ship from the plantations," she said quietly. "An unusual one . . ."

"What do you know, Polina?"

"Why are you asking about this?"

"Because we had someone warn us that something very bad was being sent here," said Gregor. "And we would prefer it not make it. What do you know, Polina?"

"I see." She rubbed her chin, then gave them a reluctant stare, her iron-gray eyes hard and cold. "We take special care to track shipments of slaves, as you can expect. But there was one report I had just recently that . . . troubled me."

"How so?" asked Sancia.

"A ship arrived at the plantation of Cefalea just three days ago," said Polina. "But not a normal one. A Dandolo *galleon*. A huge ship of war. We couldn't understand what such a ship was doing at this little plantation, but . . . then, to our surprise, the Dandolos stopped all labor on the island, marched *all* the slaves onto the galleon, and sailed away."

Gregor and Sancia stared at her, perplexed. "They shut down the whole plantation?" said Gregor.

"Yes," said Polina.

"And they took the slaves?" said Sancia.

"Correct. At least a hundred of them"

"Where were they sailing to?" said Gregor.

"We don't know," said Polina. "It hasn't arrived at any of the ports in the plantations yet. It's a galleon, so it is not speedy. But I did receive a message that it had been sighted passing Ontia—one of the westernmost of the isles."

"It's coming here, then," said Gregor.

"Possibly, but . . . that doesn't make sense," said Polina. "Slaves are not permitted in Tevanne proper. Not when you have so little space and so many magics to do your labor for you."

Sancia and Gregor were silent, but they exchanged a worried look.

That's it, thought Sancia. *That's got to be this artifact—whatever it is.*

"What do you know?" demanded Polina. "What is this about? What do they intend to do with those people?"

"I don't know," said Gregor. "Honestly. I don't. But you must tell me, Polina—when do you think this galleon will arrive?"

"Arrive here, in Tevanne? The idea that it might is mad, but . . . if this is truly the ship's destination . . ." She stopped to think about it. "It could be here before tomorrow morning."

"One day," said Gregor. "By God. One damned day to prepare for . . ." He shook his head. "Thank you. We must go."

They started to wind their way out of the labyrinth while Polina followed them.

"What are you going to do?" said Polina.

"I'm not sure," said Gregor.

"Is there even anything you *can* do? It's a merchant house galleon! Such a ship is . . . it's like a floating city! Even our own vessels don't dare approach it!"

Gregor did not answer as they began to exit the tent.

Polina grabbed him by the arm. "You owe this to me, if nothing else. What is this? What's going on?"

"We still barely know ourselves," said Gregor.

She peered at his face. "But you look frightened. And that's something I've never seen in your face before. Be honest. Is it your mother?"

"Yes," he said. "I think so."

Sancia looked back and forth between them. Although her mind was still overburdened with the memory of Valeria and the prospect of what might be sailing across the Durazzo to them now, she couldn't help but feel a sense of intimacy to this exchange—one she had not expected.

Polina released him. "Then go."

Gregor touched his fingers to his forehead and bowed to her. Then he and Sancia turned and walked away from the Slopes, back to Old Ditch and to Foundryside.

"That's got to be it," said Gregor. "A merchant house galleon making for Tevanne . . . What else would they use to transport the first of all hierophants?"

"But why take all the slaves?" said Sancia. "Is it cover of some kind?"

"I've no idea," said Gregor. "Why would they need cover? Who else is going to be watching Dandolo ships for something as mad as this?"

They turned a corner. By now Old Ditch was fully awake. A man in a filthy Papa Monsoon costume was haggling with an old woman selling stripers from a giant cauldron. Gray monkeys howled and jabbered from the eaves of a nearby rooftop.

"Why didn't you tell me what she was going to do?" asked Sancia. "That she was going to try to recruit me?"

"Because the decision was yours to make," he said. "It would feel distasteful for me, a Tevanni, to counsel a freed slave on the morality of fighting to free other slaves."

"How'd you know what I'd choose?" she asked.

"I respect Polina's fight, and her methods," he said, "but . . . a hierophant is several orders of magnitude more pressing than the plantations, for better or worse."

"You seem to know a lot about Polina."

Gregor said nothing.

"So," said Sancia. "You and her. You, uh . . ."

"I am not obliged to tell you everything about my life, Sancia," said Gregor.

They continued the rest of the way without a word.

7

So . . . it's true," said Orso quietly in the Foundryside library. "Valeria wasn't lying. Ofelia really is bringing . . . bringing *him* here."

Sancia glanced around. The Foundryside library was always quite full, but it seemed unusually crowded today, with dozens of scrivers roaming the bookshelves, pulling out designs or tomes and spreading them out on the tables for review. It seemed utterly insane to be discussing this subject right now while all these young men—even in the Lamplands, female scrivers were extraordinarily rare—quietly went to work around them.

"Yes," said Gregor. "Though apparently there will also be around one hundred slaves on the ship with him, or it, or . . . whatever the appropriate terminology is."

"Though I've got no idea why Ofelia Dandolo would want that," said Sancia.

"I mean . . . what, are they going to make the slaves build something?" said Orso. "I thought the hierophants didn't need slaves—they had all kinds of tools. Hell, *we* barely need slaves, we jus—"

Berenice exhaled slowly and sat back in her chair, her face filled with a look of horrified revelation. "Oh God . . ."

"What is it?" asked Gregor.

"I think . . . I think I might know why." Berenice looked at Sancia, shaken. "What was it Estelle Candiano wanted to do during the night of the Mountain? She wanted to kill off her entire campo as some kind of massive sacrifice, and use it to make herself a hierophant."

"Oh shit," Sancia said. "So you think . . ."

"I think resurrecting the first of all hierophants probably requires a . . . a significant sacrifice," said Berenice. "It must require you to access incredibly powerful privileges . . ."

"They're going to *kill* all the slaves?" said Orso, horrified. "All for some kind of *ritual*?"

"The bigger the violation," said Berenice, "the bigger the permissions you gain . . ."

"And the lives of slaves are worth nothing to a merchant house," said Sancia.

Gregor's face twisted. He walked away and stared out the window for a moment, fuming. He took a breath, got control of himself, and returned. "We have to stop that ship before it ever reaches Tevanne," he said lowly. "Before it gets to my mother. Before she or any of her filthy scrivers can do this horrid ritual and kill so many innocent people."

"Not to mention resurrect a goddamn hierophant," said Orso.

"Assuming all this is like a normal hierophantic ritual," said Berenice, "if the word 'normal' could ever even apply . . . it'd need to take place at midnight, during the lost minute. That's the only time such a level of world-breaking could ever be possible."

"So we intercept it well before then," said Gregor, "to ensure there's *no* chance they can complete it. Even on the high seas."

"Wait, wait, wait," said Orso. "This is a scrumming *merchant house galleon* we're talking about. It carries around its own *foundry* lexicon! One damned galleon can power a fleet of ships! You want to, what, buy a sailboat or a carrack and zip out there and take it down with angry glares and rude language? Who do we know who has any experience with things like that?"

Gregor politely cleared his throat. They all looked at him.

"You?" said Berenice. "Gregor—have you ever seized a ship before?"

"Ah . . . well, never a galleon," he admitted. "I did participate in the seizure of two carracks and a caravel in the Enlightenment Wars, though. And the caravel was at port, so it didn't really count . . ."

There was a beat of silence.

"All right," said Orso. "So. We have Gregor. But he alone can't exactly help us against a scrumming galleon! We'll not only need a ship, but where are we going to find a tool that could possibly be of use against what's essentially a giant scrived weapon?"

"Well," said Sancia. "We do have me."

There was another beat of silence.

"Okay," said Orso. "Another good point. This is all coming together, apparently! But how are we going to get you *on* it?"

Berenice shot to her feet. "I have an idea!" she said. "Give me a moment or two."

"To do what?" said Orso.

"To do what? We have the pooled knowledge of hundreds of scrivers right behind us! I can think of a *dozen* designs that could be useful here!"

"But searching the stacks could take hours!" said Orso.

"No, no!" said Berenice. "I remember exactly where they are!" *Which was probably true,* Sancia thought. Berenice had a marvelous talent for memorization: that was what had made her such a talented fabricator and scivoli player.

"Water . . ." Berenice said to herself, thinking. "And processing, and steam . . . Yes! I have it!" She turned and vanished into the stacks of the library.

"I will go and secure us a vessel," said Gregor. "I assume I can dip into the Michiel payment for this?"

"God Almighty," sighed Orso. "Four hours ago, I was dead drunk, victorious, and passed out in my bed. Now we're off to spend our winnings to wage war on giant ships and ancient personages! I'd give ten times the Michiel money just to turn back the clock!" He put his face in his hands. "Take what you need and go, I suppose."

Gregor strode away. Orso and Sancia stood in the library staring wearily at each other.

"I should not have drunk that rum last night," said Orso.

"And I shouldn't have touched that wine," said Sancia.

"But I believe we're now going to have to do something neither of us wants to do," said Orso. He looked at her, his face grim. "I think it's time to dig up the horror in the basement."

Orso grunted with exhaustion as he brought the pickax down again. Its point bit into the stone corner of the basement with a high-pitched *ting!*

"I wish . . ." he gasped. He brought it down again—*ting!* "That we . . ." *Ting!* "Had not sent Gregor . . ." *Ting!* "Away." *Ting!* He leaned against the pickax, his chest heaving and his face covered in sweat. "I mean, this is really his kind of job, isn't it?"

Sancia sipped weak cane wine from a flagon and watched him impatiently.

"Why did we bury this thing in cement, again?" asked Orso.

"Because we wanted to make it hard as hell for us to dig it back up again. Keep going."

"Oh, Lord . . . Take me now." Orso swung the pickax down again and again.

"What do we know about what he can do?" asked Sancia.

"Who, Crasedes?" asked Orso. "Well. We know he could move things about without having to touch them, including himself—I assume that's how he could fly, at least. Beyond that, we have little more than stories." Another smash of the pickax. "Tales of him popping out of nowhere. Tales of him manipulating light, water, air, time, . . . and death, of course."

"Like what Ofelia's going to attempt. Resurrection is just manipulating death, right?"

Orso shook his head and brought the pickax down once more. "There are stories of Crasedes dying dozens of times and bringing himself back one way or another. Pleasant trickster tales where he pulls one over on Papa Monsoon, or whichever personification of death you prefer. If those are true, then whatever they're about to attempt now seems different."

"Why?"

"Because it's taken him a thousand years to come back?" Another *ting!* of the pickax. "Death wasn't a problem for the Crasedes of the old stories. *This* sure seems like it's been a hell of a problem for him." *Ting!* "I assume it has something to do with your golden friend . . . You say they fought a war—maybe she injured him."

She thought of how Valeria had flickered in the dark. "And maybe he injured her too."

"Two damaged titans." *Ting!* "And it's the hurt ones that are the most dangerous. A monkey with a broken leg's more likely to bite you than a hale and hearty one." He set down the pickax, wiped sweat from his brow, and studied the shallow hole at his feet. "How many strokes are we at for you?"

"One hundred and seventy-four."

"And for me?"

"Thirty-nine."

Orso moaned. "The damned ship will get here before we're done . . ."

"Oh, get out of the way!" said Sancia. She stood, took the pickax from him, and began hammering away at several times the speed, the tooth of the pickax biting deeper and deeper.

"Show-off," muttered Orso. He drank greedily from the flagon.

She brought the pickax down again and there was a curious *crunch* sound. They looked at each other, then knelt and peered into the hole.

"It's there!" said Orso. "I can see it!"

"Move while I clear the rest of the stone," said Sancia.

A dozen strokes later and the cement crumbled away. Orso reached down and pulled something from the depths of the hole.

It appeared to be a small iron box, about large enough to contain one shoe.

"This is it, right?" Orso asked. He shook it. "I remember it being bigger than this . . ."

"For God's sake!" said Sancia. "Don't shake the scrumming thing, you stupid bastard!"

He set the box down on the floor before him. "If I recall . . . we scrived this lock so it needed to sense the blood of *two* Foundryside founders to open. That way one of us couldn't go mad, dig it up, and use it for ourselves. So get over here."

Sancia put the pickax down and knelt with Orso on the floor.

They exchanged a nervous look, then each placed a hand on the iron box.

"Ready?" said Orso.

"One," said Sancia. "Two. Three . . ."

They swung the lid back. Both of them recoiled at the sight of what lay within.

To the average eye, the thing would have looked somewhat unusual, but not terribly upsetting. It appeared to be a large, curious golden pocket watch, with many levers, buttons, and dials on its face. Most curious was the smooth golden plate in the center, which was covered in countless tiny sigils, all etched in a cold, precise hand.

"Goddamn," muttered Sancia. "How I wished I'd never have to lay eyes on this scrumming thing again."

Then she braced herself, and picked up the imperiat.

8

It was late afternoon when they got to the piers. The sky was fat with clouds, growing dark and mutinous where they met the horizon. They found Gregor standing before a dingy old fishing boat that looked like it'd seen better days maybe a decade ago, if not more.

"This is our ship?" said Orso, his face fixed in a pained cringe.

"It is what I can acquire with almost no notice whatsoever," said Gregor. "I did a lot of haggling, but . . . I will spare you the details on cost."

"Shit," said Orso faintly.

"You sure you know how to pilot that thing?" asked Sancia.

"I am." He looked at her, and then at the iron box hanging from her neck by a strap. "And are you sure you know how to operate *that* thing?"

Sancia's belly squirmed unpleasantly. "Kind of," she said. "But mostly no."

Which was an honest answer. The imperiat was a hierophantic tool that could dampen or kill any scriving within about a quarter mile. It strengthened reality, in a way, making it easier for the world to listen to countless scrived commands and say—*Hmm, no, I'd rather not, really*. Sancia had also seen it control or manipulate scrivings, dominating them from afar—the plate in her head had been one such example—but she'd never figured out how to do that.

And there were multiple reasons why. To begin with, Berenice, Orso, and Sancia had eventually concluded that the imperiat was not designed to work with a normal human being: it was a tool of the hierophants, made by them and for them. A mortal human could pull a few levers and push its buttons, but Sancia suspected there were other, more precise ways to utilize the rig. Some she might be able to figure out—just as Estelle Candiano had, once—but for others, she couldn't, and never would.

Because she was uninterested in exploring further. Frankly, she was terrified of playing with the thing. The imperiat could easily kill a lexicon if you weren't careful with it. Burying it under a few feet of concrete had seemed a much wiser choice.

"And we're sure it would actually sink a galleon?" said Gregor.

"We can set it so that it targets and kills a critical scriving in the lexicon itself," said Berenice, "triggering all its fail-safes, so it'll be paused, essentially. It'll only keep crucial scrivings running—usually construction ones. That's how most lexicons are designed."

"That way if I have to trigger the thing while *on* the galleon," said Sancia, "the ship itself won't literally fall apart around us because . . . Hell, I don't know, because the construction scrivings forgot how to glue the hull together, or something. Which gives us a chance to get off."

"So—we get to the galleon," said Orso. "Sancia gets inside and turns the ship against itself, and then we get the slaves to the escape shallops . . . There should be enough, right?"

Gregor nodded. "There's enough shallops for the galleon's maximal crew, which numbers in the hundreds."

"Good. We get them off, and we sink the damned thing—and it takes whatever artifact it is they've discovered down with it. I don't care how it gets sunk, whether it's by Sancia's fiddlings or because the imperiat reminds it it's just a hunk of dumb wood and iron. I just want it and all of Ofelia's devilry on the bottom of the ocean as fast as possible."

Gregor helped them climb aboard their little fishing boat. "And how shall we get aboard the galleon? I know the routes of this area well enough—if it passed by Ontia, then I should have a good idea of its approach, and we should be able to see the thing from a mile away—but a galleon has a *great* deal of defenses. A fishing boat such as ours will be no issue for them."

"I shall let Berenice answer that," said Orso. He bowed to her, hand extended.

"The Frizettis tried to find a scrived method of purifying water," said Berenice. "They brought Sancia and myself in to consult and help them find a solution, and we got to keep the sigil strings. They mostly found a very efficient way of boiling water . . . but that is all we need tonight."

"Ah," said Gregor. "Steam—or fog?"

"Fog," said Berenice. She opened the pack on her back, revealing dozens of small iron-and-wood balls, each about the size of a small melon. "We place this in the ship's way, and when it gets close, they'll create a massive fog bank."

"And I can see the scrivings in the ship itself," said Sancia. "So we'll still be able to navigate blindly in the fog, so to speak."

"And how shall these steam rigs work?" asked Gregor. "We'll be miles from any lexicon."

"Not the one in the galleon," said Berenice. "It was simple enough to adjust the Frizetti works to use Dandolo scriving languages."

Gregor stared at her. "How much are we paying you, again?"

"Averting the apocalypse is payment enough," said Berenice. She sat down in the fishing boat. "Speaking of which—I suggest we get on it."

Exposed in the back of the little fishing boat, Sancia felt a raw, screaming terror when she looked back and saw there was no sign of Tevanne, or indeed land at all. It felt like they were in a tiny bucket with the whole hostile world waiting to swallow them up.

Berenice, however, did not seem to mind at all. As Gregor piloted the ship northeast, she worked on the mast and the boom and the bow, either planting pre-written sigil plates on their surfaces or writing out strings of sigils herself. "These are Dandolo strings designed for sailing," she called down to Gregor as he worked away in the cockpit. "Not much use here, but . . . when we're close to the galleon, they should make us much faster and more agile."

"Excellent!" said Gregor. And for once, he sounded genuinely joyful. Perhaps being back at sea was good for him.

When she was done, she sat back down next to Sancia. "Still feeling anxious?" she asked.

"How can I not? There's a big goddamn world of water around me!"

"I see. Well. It could be worse for you."

"How?"

"You could be like me." She crossed her legs. "I don't know how to swim."

Sancia stared. "You . . . You don't know how to swim? And you're not *worried*?"

"Oh, I'm worried. I'm just managing that worry. After all, we're not in the water. We're on a *boat,* in the water. Which is very different. Now. I have some things to reflect on . . . but I'll be here if you need me, love."

Then she shut her eyes, put her hands in her lap, and began to meditate. Sancia glared at her, but before she could get too angry the boat lurched to the side again, and her stomach flipped, and she did her best not to squeak out loud.

Night fell on them quickly. The gray sea and gray clouds were full of weak, watery light—and then, suddenly, they weren't, and it felt as though the ship were drifting atop a wide, black chasm, the sky a smear of dark blue above.

"Time?" asked Gregor.

Orso—his face white with seasickness—consulted his mechanical timepiece. "It's past eight in the evening," he said.

"How much past?"

"I don't know, this scrumming thing's crude as hell. I'd say half past."

Gregor nodded grimly. Then he began to scout.

He cut the ship this way and that, carving through the wind and waters with a grace Sancia would have found admirable, had she not been aboard the boat with him. She and Orso both vomited over the side of the boat once, twice, and then they lost count.

"Trying to see as much of the ocean as I can," Gregor explained. "We cannot let this ship slip by us."

"How can you see anything at all?" said Orso.

"The art of spying ships at night," said Gregor, "is about spotting lights and silhouettes and forms on the horizon. And spotting the galleon should be relatively simple, because it will be extremely bi . . . Uhh. Hm." He leaned forward.

Berenice stood up. "What is it?"

Gregor pulled out his field glass and peered at the horizon. "I . . . see it."

Sancia wrenched herself away from the side of the boat. "Are you sure?"

"I am positive," he said. There was an unnerving calmness to his words. As Berenice joined him in the cockpit, he handed her his spyglass.

She peered through it and gasped. "Oh. Oh, my . . ."

Sancia staggered over to them—but then stopped when she realized she didn't need the spyglass at all.

Something big and blocky sat on the horizon. She wasn't sure how far away it was . . . but she suspected it was very, very far. It looked like a giant wooden triangle clutching the horizon, as big as two if not three campo blocks. It was obviously, *obviously* not something that should ever actually float on the water—not unless there were a lot of rules and arguments convincing reality that it should.

"Holy shit," she said. "Is that . . . it?"

"Yes," said Gregor, still in that unnervingly calm voice. "That is a merchant house galleon." He turned the wheel and pointed their ship at it. After a minute or so their boat suddenly lurched forward and sped up.

Berenice looked at the sails. "The scrivings have kicked in. We're close."

Sancia felt a slow leak of dread in her stomach as the giant blocky shadow on the horizon grew bigger and bigger.

"Great," she said.

———

When they were about a quarter mile in front of the giant ship, Gregor turned the wheel and began sailing away from it, like the galleon was chasing them. Berenice started dropping the little water rigs into the sea behind them, one after another. There had to be at least fifty of them.

"It's working," said Orso, peering behind them. "Look."

Sancia studied the dark horizon behind them. It now looked vaguely muddy, or misty. She couldn't tell where sky started and sea began.

"Done," said Berenice.

Again, Gregor turned the wheel, and the ship sliced through the water. "Now the tricky part," he said. "We must come alongside the ship, and we must do so in the fog. Hopefully the fog will make the galleon slow."

"To make it easier to catch up to?" asked Orso.

"There's that. But if it churns up the water too much, then . . . Well. We will get capsized, and then chewed to pieces."

Orso swallowed. "I see."

"Yes," said Gregor. "So, Sancia—please join me in the cockpit. I must know how fast or slow we need to go, and where the ship is."

Sancia stood beside Gregor, one hand on the wall to steady herself. He brought the ship around in a giant loop until they approached the growing fog bank from the back end.

"Get ready," he said. "And once we are in the fog, we *must* stay quiet. The crew will be on deck to watch for any obstacles, so they will be able to hear us."

Sancia took a breath as they entered the wall of roiling mist. It was unpleasantly hot, not at all the cool mist she was used to. They sailed deeper and deeper in, and Sancia flexed her scrived sight, peering forward. For a while they saw nothing—her sight had its limitations—but then suddenly a giant, bright coil of silver erupted on the horizon, so huge and so intense the sight of it made her gasp.

"You see it?" whispered Gregor. "Point to it."

She did so, sticking out her arm.

"Point to its bow, the front end," he whispered. "Like your arm is a compass pointing north. I must know how fast it's going."

She did so. He adjusted his course, sailing alongside it, trying to match its speed. She whispered "Faster," or "Slower!" and helped him adjust.

The giant ship grew closer, and closer. They felt and heard the galleon long before they saw it: the water around them began to pitch about, rattling their boat, and there was an immense sloshing of water from somewhere, like an island was rising from the depths of the sea.

"God, it's big," whispered Orso. "Holy scrumming *shit,* it's big . . ."

Gregor piloted the little fishing boat closer to the galleon, Orso and Berenice gripping their seats tight as they rocked and shook in the waves. Then it emerged from the fog, a huge, towering, gleaming wooden wall that surged up like a building rising from the ocean . . .

"Imprinter ready," he whispered back to Berenice.

Berenice stood, knelt, and shakily pulled out a very curious-looking espringal—an "imprinter," an invention of hers and Sancia's. And Sancia dearly hoped it would work well tonight.

The imprinter was like an espringal, but rather than shooting bolts, it fired slugs of lead that instantly adhered to whichever surface they struck. This in its own right was not particularly useful—but Sancia had engineered the weapon so it could engrave the slugs with sigils of your choosing *just* before you fired them, like a printing rig applying type for a book, which meant you could control the effects from shot to shot.

The greatest use they'd found so far had been anchoring strings: you fired one lead slug at one surface and a second at another. The slugs would stick and, upon being stuck, pull both objects together, usually very violently. And it was this last setting that Berenice was to use tonight.

She pointed her imprinter down and fired one slug into the port hull of their fishing boat. The slug adhered with a *snap.*

Sancia listened hard for a shout or a cry from the galleon, but there was nothing. Gregor turned the wheel and fought to keep the ship steady as a tremendous wave of seawater doused them. He nudged the boat closer, and closer, until they were nearly ten feet away from the galleon.

"Now!" he whispered.

Berenice planted her imprinter level on the hull of the fishing boat and fired at the galleon. The slug smacked into the hull and stuck fast.

For a moment nothing happened—and then, with a terrifying jerk, the scrivings sprang to life, and they were ripped across the waters until the two hulls kissed.

Sancia had to fight not to scream. She was sure that Berenice had fired a little high or low, and they were going to be tipped backward or forward and tossed from the boat—but they were not. Their ship creaked a little unpleasantly, but everything held together. They were adhered to the side of the galleon like a bloodfish stuck to the belly of a shark.

Gregor let go of the wheel and cautiously stepped away. The ship held fast. Then he and Sancia crouched and began to assemble their gear: espringals, imprinters, stunning bombs, lights, scrived rapiers, and adhesion plates.

"We will scale the ship," Gregor whispered to them. He pointed up into the fog. "There should be a hatch over there that Sancia can break open. Once we're in, you lot break away and trail behind us until the job is done. Got it?"

Berenice and Orso nodded, though both of them were plainly terrified.

"Good," said Gregor. "When we're finished, Sancia and I will use our air-sailing rigs to escape the ship and come to you."

"Provided the foundry lexicon in the ship is still working," said Berenice. "If not, they won't work."

"Then we will attempt to board shallops," said Gregor. "Is that clear?"

"They nodded."

"Good. Then we'll begin." He and Sancia fitted the adhesion plates over their hands.

"Good luck," said Berenice. She reached out and squeezed Sancia's shoulder. Sancia nodded, afraid that if she opened her mouth she might vomit.

Then she and Gregor approached the hull, activated their plates, and began to scale the side of the ship like builder ants crawling up a wall. Though the going was not exactly easy, she found herself wishing she'd had tools like this back in her thieving days: she couldn't count how many times she'd worn her hands bloody trying to scale this or that wall.

Once they were about twenty feet up, she flexed her scrived sight and peered into the fog until she saw a tangle of locking logic floating in the gloom. She gestured to Gregor, and he followed her across the hull until they came to the hatch. She had to slide her hand out of one plate so she essentially dangled from the hull one-handed—she was intensely aware of the wide, churning ocean below her—but then she grabbed the hatch's handle, and listened, and spoke to it.

The hatch's locking logic was quite simple—obviously this entry point had not been considered a vulnerability—and soon she'd popped it open. She slipped through, gasping with exhaustion and terror, and slid over to allow Gregor to do the same. Then he shut the hatch behind them, and they were inside.

9

This deck of the ship—whichever deck it was, Sancia had no idea, or even if the idea of decks was applicable on a vessel of this size—was almost completely dark. She assumed this was just ordinary naval protocol, but then Gregor whispered, "Why are the lights off?"

"Sh-Should they be on?" stammered Sancia.

"All interior lights should be on at night except for those in the quarters. Otherwise it's a dangerous tripping hazard—among many other things."

Sancia had to pause at the idea of Gregor worrying about tripping hazards at a time like this. Then she flexed her scrived sight, and recoiled at the amount of information pouring in through her eyes: being inside the galleon was like being inside a giant sea beast, only she could see all its bones and veins and muscles around her, all at once.

She'd initially worried this would be like the Mountain of the Candianos—the giant dome in the center of their campo in Tevanne, which had been scrived to act as a single massive intelligence. But the galleon was instead thousands and thousands of components that all had to work together just right for the ship to function: the hull believed it was preternaturally strong but light and could repel waters, the locking mechanisms on all the hatches believed they were just awaiting their specific keys, the lamps and lanterns all awaited signals to alight . . .

But something was missing.

"What do you see?" whispered Gregor.

"Lots of things," she said back. "But . . . no people."

"What?" he said, surprised. "Wait. *Can* you see people?"

"No," she said. "But I'd be able to see any scrived rigs on their person bobbing along as they walk or move. And it's hard to see among all the components . . . but I don't see that anywhere close to us. Maybe the crew's all up on the main deck, or . . . hell, I don't know my ships, somewhere goddamn else. But it . . . it looks like we're very alone here."

She could barely make out his face, staring at her incredulously in the dark. "Is this a trap?" he asked.

"How could it be? Why would they assume Valeria would know, or tell us?" She looked around. "And I don't see any logic or sigil strings suggesting it is . . ."

"And you don't see . . . well . . . him? Crasedes? Or the artifact?"

She shook her head. "I see shit-all."

For a moment they just sat there in the dark, unsure what to say or do.

"Step one is weaponizing the ship against itself," said Gregor. "Is that still possible?"

Then she looked up into the ceiling. "I see shrieker catapults. And no one's watching them. So—yes. Definitely."

Together she and Gregor wound their way up through the decks of the galleon. Though the ship was gigantic, it was clear the Dandolos had maximized the use of space: every hallway was tiny, cramped, and suffocating—especially in near-darkness. She and Gregor crept on and on, the lights of their scrived lanterns dancing over the wooden walls as they listened for any sound. They encountered no one, nor any obstacle, really. The whole ship seemed queerly abandoned.

"There *should* be someone here, right?" she whispered.

"Galleons typically have over three hundred crew members," he said softly. "This deck should be full of people."

She felt her skin crawl. *Something's wrong. None of this is as it should be.*

"We should be approaching the upper catapult decks now," whispered Gregor.

"Good."

"There should be thirty-five shrieker catapults apiece. What are you planning to do?"

"I don't know what the hell is going on," said Sancia, "but if something goes wrong, I want as many weapons on my side as possible."

Finally they came to the catapult bays. The long, thin contraptions of wood and iron were empty of ammunition, but sat pointing out at the closed artillery ports.

"Can shriekers penetrate a galleon's hull?" asked Sancia.

Gregor shook his head. "Not a chance."

"Okay. Then . . . let's turn them all around," said Sancia, "so they point in, not out. You do that while I work on the catapults."

None of the catapults were loaded with shriekers, which meant she had the unenviable task of taking the long spears of scrived metal and placing them in the catapult pockets. Doing so activated the shriekers' acceleration strings: the instant she'd slotted them into the pockets, they began vibrating and pulsing with a dreadful energy.

She placed her hand on one catapult and listened to its arguments.

< . . . *await the breaking of the bond, the severing of metals, and then you shall be high, high up, high in the sky, high in space, and you shall have fallen, fallen, fallen, you shall have fallen for two hundred miles, falling through the air . . .* >

She listened carefully to its acceleration commands. It worked like many scrived projectiles: they would be convinced that they had not been fired forward but were instead falling down, plummeting down a straight line for miles and miles, attaining impossible speeds.

She released it. *That's easy enough to work with*, she thought. *Now for the dangerous bit . . .*

She took out her imprinter espringal, pointed it at one metal spear, and fired. The slug hit the tip of the shrieker and stuck—but otherwise, nothing happened.

She let out a breath, relieved. Shriekers were one of the deadliest and least predictable scrived weapons Tevanne had ever invented. She'd never imagined she'd ever want to tinker with one—let alone thirty-five of them.

She stuck slugs of metal to about half the shriekers. Then she said, "Gregor—give me your imprinter."

"Why? What are you doing?"

"Giving us an advantage. Trust me."

He did so. She took his imprinter and walked along the rest of the catapults, applying his slugs to them as well. When she was finished she stood back, surveying her work. "It's done."

"And . . . what have you done?"

"The shriekers activate their velocity strings when the spears are broken from this metal release here," she said, pointing into the workings of the catapult.

Gregor flinched. "Please do not touch it, then . . ."

"But we've applied one half of an anchoring string to all the spears," she said. "Like we stuck our boat to the galleon—you do one half, then the other, and the two bits get pulled together."

"So?"

"So . . ." She showed him the setting on his espringal. "You point your espringal at something, and fire the second half of the anchoring string at it—and it will pull five shriekers from their catapults. Since the catapults are pointed inwards, not outwards, the shriekers should go right through the walls of this ship, and our anchoring slugs will redirect the projectiles toward whatever it is that you shot at."

Gregor stared, amazed. "So . . . when I fire my imprinter at something, I will essentially be firing *five shriekers* at it?"

"Yeah. Fire again, get the next five. And again, the next five. You get three volleys, I get four. Seems handy if we want to sink the ship or . . . if we encounter anything else in here. Just . . . be aware that it's going to rip through a lot of shit to get to your targe—"

She heard something echoing below them, faint but high-pitched. She stopped and peered backward into the darkness.

"Did you . . ." she asked.

"Yes," said Gregor, troubled. "I did."

They listened hard, and then they heard it again—the sound of a man screaming.

The sound tapered off. Sancia and Gregor stood without speaking, listening to the creaking, groaning, shuddering ship move around them. There was no other sound.

"So—*that's* not normal, right?" she asked.

"It is not," said Gregor.

There was a long silence.

"I . . . suppose we had better go investigate," said Gregor quietly.

"What time is it?" said Sancia.

Gregor pulled out a scrived timepiece and huddled by his scrived lantern to see. "It's not even ten o'clock yet."

"So . . . they can't have done it yet, right? They have to wait for the lost minute, for midnight."

"I am afraid I am not the expert on this material."

"Shitting hell," said Sancia. She wiped sweat from her brow and lifted her espringal. Together they continued into the depths of the galleon.

They wound on and on through the decks of the ship, through quarters and chambers and stairwells. The air was hot and moist and dreadfully still, and the lights from their lanterns seemed painfully small, tiny bubbles of luminescence attempting to beat back the dark.

Then they heard a scream again, echoing from the innards of the giant vessel. They exchanged a look and continued on, deeper and deeper in, espringals ready.

"We're approaching the cargo holds," whispered Gregor.

"Which means what?"

"I'm not sure. But there should be large chambers up ahead. Perhaps where they keep the slaves."

They came to one corridor that seemed unusually long and straight, perhaps running from bow to stern. They stopped and shone their lights down its length, but could see no end to it.

I hope no one is at the other side, thought Sancia, *looking back at us.*

They started down the corridor, moving as quietly as they could. Sancia flexed her scrived sight as they walked. For a long while she saw nothing at all—and then she raised a hand.

They halted as she examined what lay ahead. She thought she could see a handful of unusual scrivings on the floor a few dozen feet away—a scrived timepiece, a sachet, a fire starter for lighting a pipe, an augmented knife . . .

It's a person, she thought. *I'm seeing what's in his pocket or on his belt . . .*

They weren't moving. And they were just beyond the light cast by their lanterns.

Someone is lying down over there, she mouthed to Gregor, pointing ahead.

Gregor nodded and crept forward, espringal raised. Sancia watched, trying not to breathe too loudly as his light stretched forward along the wooden floors of the corridor . . . until it fell upon a spreading pool of blood.

Gregor paused ever so briefly at the sight of it. Then he walked forward until the light illuminated the body of a man lying facedown on the side of the corridor.

He did not rush to the body. Instead, Gregor looked into the darkness, head cocked, no doubt listening for the killer. Then he stepped forward through the blood, knelt beside the body, and rolled it over.

Gregor quickly withdrew his hand. Sancia couldn't see what he was reacting to, but it was no comfort to her that a veteran of so many wars could have such a reaction.

"What is it?" she whispered.

"This man . . . This man's eyes have been removed," said Gregor.

"*What?*" she said, horrified.

"His eyes are gouged out." He leaned closer and held his little lantern up to the body's face. "No. Cut out." He examined the rest of the man. "And . . . Sancia . . . I think he did this to himself. Look."

Grimacing, Sancia approached and saw the augmented knife clutched in the man's fingers. His wrists had been slashed open, and his front was covered in blood.

"Wait," she said. "He killed *himself?*"

"Yes. Though I suspect he cut his eyes out first."

She swallowed her horror and studied the body. He looked quite affluent, wearing an elaborate doublet and hose, with lace collars and cuffs. She examined him with her scrived sight, and peered closer at his scrived sachet and the many permissions it bestowed on him.

"Definitely Dandolo," she said. "And I think a scriver. I haven't studied their sachets in a while, but . . . this looks very inner-enclave to me. Why did he do this?"

"I do not know." Gregor looked down the corridor and held his lantern high. "But that's where he came from."

She looked and saw droplets of blood on the corridor's darkened floor, marking the man's path. He must have come from the other end of the corridor.

There was a noise—a strangled sob from the far end of the corridor, lost in the dark.

Sancia did her utmost not to jump or scream. Gregor's face remained totally impassive. He stood, raised his espringal, and began stalking down the corridor toward the sound.

"Please come with me," he said quietly. "And let me know what lies ahead."

She followed him down the corridor, stepping around the blood on the floor.

It's still not midnight yet. What happened here? What in hell is going on?

Finally their light fell upon the end of the corridor: a small, blank wall, with a single plain door, hanging open. She could see nothing but darkness on the other side. There was blood on the handle of the door and around the frame—remnants of bloody handprints as someone fumbled with it, she guessed.

"Sancia," whispered Gregor. "What is in that room?"

She walked forward. Little tangles of logic and arguments sprang to life—all of them small, trivial, and mostly in bunches on the floor.

She swallowed again. Her mouth and throat were very dry. "I think it's . . . I think there are bodies in there, Gregor," she said. "Nine of them."

Gregor stood there for a moment, totally frozen, his espringal trained on the open door. She saw his brow and temples were covered in sweat. Then he walked forward, and Sancia followed.

They heard the sound again—a strained whimper from within the room ahead.

Sancia watched as one little bundle of scrivings and sachets twitched.

"One of them's alive," she whispered.

Gregor stepped into the doorway and held his lamp up high. The chamber had been intended as a meeting or planning room, Sancia thought, judging by the big table and chairs in the center, but it appeared to have been converted into an impromptu assembly bay for scriving work: hundreds of tomes had been stacked up on the table, along with styli and scrived bowls of heated metals, and there were pieces of parchment stuck to the walls, all covered with charts of sigils and strings.

And below these, all over the floor, were the bodies of scrivers. And all of them had been horribly mutilated.

Some had shoved styli into their necks. Others had opened up the veins in their arms, like the man in the hallway. One man had plunged a scrived stiletto into his heart. But there was a commonality to their injuries: all of them had apparently cut or gouged or clawed out their own eyes before finally resorting to suicide.

Sancia stared at the scene around her. Inevitably her eye was drawn to the large door on the far side of the wall. It hung open, though she couldn't see anything on the other side. Judging by the scrivings she could spy, it looked like there was a very large room on the other side.

And what's through there?

A wet sob came from the corner. Gregor darted across the room to a man who lay crumpled on the floor, his eyes gouged out, his face and chest covered with blood. He'd tried to slash his wrists, but he'd done a bad job of it, and still lived.

"Who is . . . who is there?" whimpered the scriver. Then, his voice shaking with terror, he said: "Is it *you*, My Prophet?"

"Who are you?" asked Gregor. "What happened here?"

"Please," sobbed the scriver. His mutilated sockets gleamed in the light of their lanterns. "Please, whoever you are. Please, kill me, please . . ."

"What has happened?"

"Please . . ."

"Why did you do this to yourself?"

"*Please!*"

"Tell me," said Gregor sternly. "Now. Why?"

"Not supposed . . . to see him," whispered the dying scriver. "Can't see what he is . . . underneath it all . . ."

"Who?" demanded Gregor. "Who do you mean? Is it . . . Is it Cras—"

"Please," begged the man. "Please, kill me! Please, I don't . . . I can't live with this inside me! I can't *have it inside of me!*"

Sancia looked at the parchments pinned to the walls. Most of them were scriving designs, but a few seemed to be maps—though they were maps of a place Sancia found very familiar.

She studied the layout of the building they depicted, which was huge, circular, with many floors . . . and it had six specific areas highlighted, deep in the foundations of the structure.

Why in the hell, she wondered, *would they bring maps of the Mountain of the Candianos here? And what's so interesting in the basement?*

She moved on to the scriving designs. They contained countless hierophantic sigils for many permissions and commands: symbols for change, for death, for strength, for recurrence . . . and then another parchment, with many strings she'd never seen before.

She moved closer to it, held up her lantern, and began to read.

"What did you do?" said Gregor. "What has happened aboard this ship?"

"We had to . . . had to find a piece of him," choked the scriver.

"What?" said Gregor.

"He'd left it behind. Hid it away. A tomb among the islands . . ."

Sancia stared at the new sigils, but none of them were familiar to her. She wished Berenice were here—she had a near-perfect memory when it came to sigils and strings.

She read the notes at the top, written in plain text. One said, *Capable of convincing reality of shifting times . . .*

A horrible dread filled her. *Oh no.*

"A piece of what?" said Gregor.

"A tiny . . . a tiny bit of bone. You could put it in a living person, and . . . and argue that this was him, that he'd never died . . ."

Sancia began ripping the parchments off the walls, folding them up, and stuffing them in her pockets.

"Where are the slaves?" asked Gregor. "What have you done with the people aboard this ship?"

"But . . . we couldn't see," whispered the man. "Weren't allowed to see. Can't see him. Cannot see the . . . the king behind the veil . . ." He coughed wetly.

Gregor sat back and stared at the mutilated man, his face like ash. "What did you do here?" he asked softly.

"Please . . . I have seen him." The scriver's words were slurred and drunken now. "I've looked at him. I can't have that in . . . inside me . . ."

"What has my mother done?" asked Gregor.

The scriver's head lolled back, and he went silent.

For a moment they did nothing, not daring to speak. Then they stared at the door beyond, leading to the larger chamber.

Sancia looked around again at the books and the bowls on the table. *This was their preparation room.*

Gregor and Sancia crossed to the large door on the far side of the wall.

But is this where they did their true work?

"Do you see anything inside, Sancia?" whispered Gregor.

She flexed her sight. The room on the other side of the door was dark, devoid of any logic or arguments. She shook her head.

Gregor slowly took a breath, opened the door, walked into the room, and held up his lantern.

"Oh . . . Oh my *God* . . ." he moaned.

Sancia joined him. Then she saw, and she felt faint and fell to her knees.

Nearly a hundred bodies of men, women, and children lay on the floor of the room, all bound in chains and ropes and arranged in overlapping rings around a small, circular space where a single lantern shone. Sancia instantly recognized the bodies as slaves, judging from the spectrum of races, or the brands on their arms, or the hardness of their hands. They were all dead, though none bore any sign of injuries—except for a small, scrived metal marker that had been placed upon their chests.

Sancia dropped her espringal and covered her face. It was too horrible, just too horrible to see . . .

And the most curious thing was the moths: the floor of the room was covered in dead, tiny, fragile white moths, so many it was almost like a light dusting of snow.

"What did they do?" asked Gregor. "How could they . . . It's not midnight yet, is it?" He fumbled for his timepiece and read it. "It's not even eleven o'clock . . ."

She shook herself and stood. She studied the little metal markers that lay on the chests of the dead slaves. She saw no silvery tangle of logic, no bundle of commands woven into their reality.

Which means, she thought, *that they aren't rigs . . . Or they've been used in the creation of something else, like a smithy might use a mold . . .*

Fighting the urge to vomit or run or scream, she walked among the rings of bodies on the floor to the space in the center, the little circle with the lamp. As she grew closer she saw countless sigils running along the circle's edge, a dense, tangled stream of metals and paints.

A stream of blood marred the sigils at one point, breaking whatever binding they'd once laid upon the world here. Sancia saw they were hierophantic commands, but not ones she was familiar with. She pulled out one of the parchments she'd taken from the other room.

"Sancia," pleaded Gregor. "Sancia, what's going on?"

"Be quiet," she said as she read.

"Sancia . . . it can't have happened already, can it? He . . . he cannot be back already . . ."

"Gregor, be *quiet!*" she snapped.

She studied the sigils on the parchment carefully, then looked at those written on the floor. Her heart grew cold as she became more convinced of what had happened here.

"They . . . They scrived time," said Sancia finally.

"What?"

"These sigils here," she said, pointing to them. "I've never seen them before. But . . . But I think they convinced reality that the time inside the circle was different from the time *outside*."

"You're not making sense."

"Are you listening, Gregor? They didn't have to wait for midnight. Not if they could convince the space within that circle that it was *always* midnight. They . . . They could do the ritual there, and it would work just fine . . . wouldn't it?" She put the parchment back in her pocket. "He knew. He knew Valeria would try to stop them. So he had it ready and waiting for him whenever they found the piece of him they needed."

"That's not possible."

"It *is* possible. You can convince gravity that up is down, if you want! And there are stories of Crasedes Magnus playing tricks with time! He just had to tell them how to do it. One ritual to scrive time, then another to bring him back. It . . . It must have taken an inordinate sacrifice to convince time it could be changed, but . . ." She looked around at the dead slaves lying on the floor, still and ashen and cold.

"So can . . . can he truly be back?" asked Gregor.

"I don't know."

"Can you see him near us?"

She peered up into the ship. "No. I . . . I still don't see anything."

"Could it have failed? Could it have gone wrong? Is that why those men killed themselves? Because it failed, and it did something to them?"

Sancia looked around the room. She spied something on the floor before an open hatch leading up to the next deck, and walked over to it and knelt.

It was a black veil. For some reason it made her think of an empty chrysalis, discarded and left behind by . . . something.

She remembered her vision of the black-wrapped thing among the columns: how it had reached up, grasped its veil at its face, and slowly pulled it off . . .

She looked up at the open hatch and thought for a moment.

Something is on this ship with us. Right now.

She grabbed the box with the imperiat, opened it, and slowly, reluctantly pulled out the ancient rig.

Time to prepare for the worst.

She'd never really had the opportunity to handle the imperiat much, and unlike with most scrived devices, she had difficulty engaging with hierophantic rigs. Clef, for example, had been completely immune to all of her efforts after he'd "reset" himself. As she crouched in the darkened room and studied the imperiat in the lamplight, she was reminded that there were an intimidating number of controls to it.

The main set seemed to be three levers on one side. She knew what the largest and smallest ones did—but not the one in the middle.

Bracing herself, she slid the middle lever back, and a small, round, golden panel in the center of the device shifted rapidly, flashing a series of sigils that appeared to have been instantaneously engraved in the metal itself, like it was made out of liquid.

She recognized them—sigils for speed, for gravity, for direction . . .

I'm seeing the scrivings that are powering the galleon itself.

It was like a lens, she realized—it could be focused, or directed. You could apply the imperiat's effects to one scriving in the area, or to all of them. It was a curious feeling, knowing she could sink the whole galleon right here and now, if she wished to.

She touched the largest lever—but she made absolutely sure not to move it. She knew what this one did, for she'd seen it in action: it controlled the extent of the imperiat's effects: you could just dampen the selected scriving a little or kill it outright. Touching this lever at all might cause utter disaster.

The smallest of the three levers was the one she was most interested in now: this one controlled the imperiat's ability to detect whether a hierophantic scriving was nearby. She knew this, of course, because it had once been able to detect the very hierophantic scrivings on the plate in her head.

"This should tell me if there's something hierophantic nearby . . ." She waved the imperiat past her head, and it whined unsettlingly. Then she waved it by Gregor's head, and it did the same. "It's working. But . . . when Valeria was nearby and active, it suddenly *screamed*. I think the more powerful the scrivings it detects, the louder its alert."

"And the fact that it's not screaming right now . . ."

"It means I don't know," said Sancia. She slid the lever down, making the imperiat less sensitive, and hopefully less loud. If they did walk up on anything hierophantic, she didn't want it to start screaming and let everyone know where she was.

"And . . . the imperiat," he asked. "If he's really on the ship with us right now, Sancia, can it . . . can it kill him?"

"Again . . . I don't know, Gregor."

She looked into the darkened hatch before her, flexing her sight. She kept looking up, and up, and up, until she saw a scrived light burning two decks above them, moving back and forth, and back and forth.

"Someone's up there," she whispered.

"What?" said Gregor.

"I see a light moving around, like someone is . . . like they're holding a lantern and pacing around. Someone's alive on this ship."

"And . . . And is it . . ."

"I don't know." She stood. "But we need to go see. We have to find out if he's really back, if it's really him, and . . . and what he plans to do."

They turned out their lanterns and climbed the stairs in total darkness, moving as slowly as possible, trying to make no noise. Finally they came to the deck with the scrived light, and they crept forward until they came to a closed door. Sancia flexed her sight, saw the light was just beyond, and she tapped Gregor's shoulder twice and pointed.

He swallowed hard enough for it to be audible, then pressed his ear to the door, his breathing so fast and panicked it seemed as loud as a scream.

The scrived light within the room stopped pacing. Then it lowered itself and hovered there—sitting on a table, she thought.

Imperiat? he mouthed to her.

She checked the rig again. It was still and silent. She shook her head. "There's nothing on the other side of this door but the light," she whispered.

Gregor nodded, then stood, readied his espringal, and placed his hand on the knob. He took a deep breath, steeled himself, and shoved the door open.

He moved inside swiftly, espringal raised, and Sancia followed him. She had no idea what they would find within—perhaps some unimaginable monster, or another scene of horrid gore—but what they found was a tall, dark-skinned, rather handsome woman seated calmly at a table with a scrived lantern in her lap.

"Gregor," she said softly. Though her face was steady, her voice was very hoarse, and shook badly.

"*Mother?*" said Gregor, stunned.

Sancia stared at the woman, her face eerily lit in the light of the scrived lantern, and slowly realized this had to be Ofelia Dandolo—one of the most powerful people in all of Tevanne. She was grandly dressed, wearing a richly designed bodice and full skirt, and she was of an age that was just on the border between upper-middle and elder years.

"What . . . What are you doing here, Mother?" asked Gregor.

"He said . . . He said you might come," she said faintly. She blinked a few times. Sancia could tell she was in shock. "I didn't really believe him. But here you are."

"Mother—why are you here? What's going on? Did . . . Did you kill those slaves?"

"He . . . He said she would try to stop us," whispered Ofelia Dandolo, her eyes wide. "So we had to do it fast. But it would take so many lives, to make the world think it was midnight . . ."

Gregor let out a shuddering breath. "My God . . ."

She looked at him pleadingly. "But he's back now. He's back, and he can fix you, my love, and fix the city, fix the world, fix everything, and . . . and all the things I've done to bring us here. He can take it all ba—"

"Where is he?" asked Sancia.

Ofelia Dandolo looked at Sancia like she'd only just now realized she was there. "W-What?" she said.

"Where is he? Where is he now?"

She looked around dimly, then gestured at the open door on the other side of the room. "I think . . . I think he went through there."

"You think?"

"I don't know."

"How do you not know?"

"When . . . When he first was here, I was waiting, and . . . and I heard the scrivers screaming, screaming that no one was allowed to see him, and . . . and so we shut off all the lights. I had them shut off all the lights in the ship and send the crew abovedecks. And I sat here in the dark, waiting, and then I . . . I heard footfalls, coming closer to me, and then there was a voice. A voice in the dark, Gregor. I heard a voice talking to me, close to me, and it was like . . . it was like . . ." She trailed off, unable to even describe it.

"What happened then?" asked Sancia.

Her face tremored, and she swallowed. "He said he needed to . . . to *calibrate* himself. To understand which privileges and permissions he still retained. And to find something to hide himself in, he said. Something to, to veil his form. And he walked away and . . . and . . . I heard these sounds. This tremendous cracking, and crashing, and . . . and then it stopped."

They stared at her for a long while, unable to speak.

"How long ago did it stop?" Gregor asked.

"I don't know," she said. "I don't know."

Sancia's eye stayed fixed on the open door on the other side of the room, keenly aware of the darkness beyond—and what could be over there, watching.

"Damn it, Mother," whispered Gregor. "What have you *done*? What have you brought upon us?"

She blinked, and tears ran down her cheeks. "He apologized, you know. About my scrivers. He said he was sorry. Had not foreseen the issues that his form proposed, he said. He said he . . . he would make it up to me." She shut her eyes. "He said he was so *sorry*, Gregor."

She sat there with her eyes shut, breathing in and out. Sancia wondered if she'd gone mad from shock.

"Sancia," said Gregor, espringal still trained on his mother. "What do we do now?"

Good scrumming question, she thought. She looked into the darkened doorway with her scrived sight. Usually when she spied a hierophantic rig—like Clef, or the plate in Gregor's head—her sight interpreted it as a tiny, blood-red star. But she saw no such thing before them now. "I still don't see anything."

"Do you think he's . . . left?"

"I have no idea."

There was a long, dreadful silence as they both stared into the darkened door.

"We would be idiots," said Gregor, "to go in there. Yes?"

"Yes," said Sancia quietly. "But . . . I think I'm going to have to."

"You can't be serious."

"We cannot let that *thing* get to Tevanne," said Sancia. "We cannot let a goddamn hierophant walk into the city! I mean . . . not only is Valeria vulnerable, but there would be thousands of innocent people in the way!"

"And you really think the imperiat offers you a chance to stop him?"

She looked down at the little box hanging around her neck. "I think the imperiat killed a lexicon," she said. "And hierophants are apparently a lot like a lexicon. So. It's worth a shot."

Gregor took a breath, still staring through the sights of his espringal at his mother. "I will stay here, and guard her to make sure she doesn't call in any soldiers. You go and look, Sancia—and come *right back*, understand?"

"Yeah," said Sancia lowly. She started toward the darkened door. "I got it."

Sancia walked forward into the darkness, her scrived lantern in one hand, her imprinter espringal in the other.

Are we at the midpoint of the ship? How many walls and decks will the shriekers I rigged up have to rip through to get to my target? Then another thought occurred to her: *And what if they wind up ripping through me?*

She kept moving forward down the corridor. Her scrived sight showed her nothing, and the imperiat stayed silent.

She came to a closed door, and she approached it quietly, her footsteps silent and slow. Yet she noticed there was something different about this door: there was light at the edges. It was a curious, faint light, watery and gray—not at all the light of a scrived lantern.

She flexed her sight and peered through the door. To her confusion, she didn't see any scrived rigs of any kind on the other side. So far in the galleon there'd been at least a dozen scrived components every handful of feet. And yet she couldn't see anything on the other side at all.

Her skin broke out in goosebumps, but not due to fear. She felt a wind in the corridor, or . . .

A draft?

She hesitated and pulled out the imperiat. She nudged up the smallest lever very slightly, listening hard. It didn't shriek or warble at all.

But . . . that doesn't mean Crasedes scrumming Magnus isn't over there. It might just mean he isn't close.

She turned the imperiat off and put it away. Then she faced the door, took a deep breath, and opened it.

She leapt back at the sight of what lay on the other side. For just a few feet beyond the door was . . . nothing.

It was as if someone had taken a giant spoon and scooped out a massive chunk from the interior of the galleon, at least three hundred feet across. Floors and decks and ceilings ended in ragged, truncated ruins. Even the main deck above had been breached, and cool, white moonlight spilled in from above, rippling over the wreckage. Water pipes dribbled out into empty space, their flows pouring down into the open depths of the ship, and here and there they caught a ray of moonlight and turned into gleaming silver ribbons.

It was hard to gauge the scale of the devastation. At least a half dozen decks had been abruptly excised away—but no, she thought as she looked at the devastation on the other side: they'd been *broken* away, ripped out or snapped off or . . . She didn't know. She could barely comprehend what she was seeing.

But she did not see any person. Nothing alive, no hint of anything moving beyond the water and the bits of boards still clinging to edges of the wreckage.

She looked up at the rent in the main deck. A person could definitely fit through there.

Did he leave? Is all this just the wreckage of . . . of his calibration? Again, she was reminded of some insect forcing its way out of its pupa.

I bet the crew made for shallops when all this shit happened, she thought. *I know I would've. We're on a ghost ship. So . . . how is it still moving?*

She leaned forward through the open door and looked out. There was a bit of deck running along the side of the giant aperture, enough for her to walk on. She stepped out and crept along the edge, listening, watching, trying to spy some hint of what could have happened here—and where Crasedes had gone.

If he's already left for Tevanne, she thought, *then . . . God. Then we've failed.*

She stalked among the edges of the ruins, then stood with her back to the center of the aperture, looking at the damage. She noticed that where there was a metal component, like a support beam or a steel wall, it had not snapped, exactly—at first it had been bent or *stretched,* like the tar candy they made from sugar.

She knew what this suggested. She'd used just such a tool once before, to devastating effect.

Did something alter the gravity in here?

Then the nausea hit her.

She nearly collapsed in agony. It was like her stomach was full of boiling water and writhing worms at once, like her head was an infected wound full of pus. She cried out and fell to her knees, grinding her knuckles into the center of her forehead.

She knew lexicons weren't the only devices that caused such a sensation: the old stories said people felt overcome with sickness when they approached one of the ancient ones.

A ray of moonlight had lanced down from the torn deck above, illuminating the wall before her—and a shadow was rising on the wall, like a shadow puppet from the plays: the shadow of a man seated cross-legged on nothing.

Behind me . . .

She heard a voice.

It was a masculine voice, but . . . it was not a *man's* voice, not truly. A man's voice would sound human, and this did not. Though it was silky, and strangely pleasant to listen to, it was too deep, too resonant, far more than any mortal man's ever could be.

It said: "Hello, Sancia."

Sancia stood very, very still, her eyes fixed on the shadow cast on the wall before her. She stared at it for what felt like an eternity, breathing hard.

She remembered the scrivers down below, their eyes ravaged and bloody, their throats slit. *Don't turn around,* she thought. *Don't look at him. Don't!*

"It's nice to finally meet you," said the voice. "Though obviously . . . these circumstances are a little *less* than ideal . . ."

She blinked as the words rippled through her. The sound of his voice was like having chocolate and honey poured into her ear. Though she was terrified—and she *was* terrified—she had the sudden and curious desire for him to never stop speaking to her. She ignored it, and she stood there ramrod-straight, watching the shadow on the wall, keenly aware that the thing currently occupying this space with her had destroyed the interior of this ship like it'd been made of straw.

He's right behind me . . . Oh God, he's just right there . . .

Then the shadow moved—was it cocking its head?

"You *can* turn around, you know," said his voice. "I did have some—how shall I put this?—*issues* with my original appearance. It was nearly as unpleasant for me as it was for them, but . . . I think I've found a suitable method to veil my form. You should be safe."

No. Don't. Don't turn around. Don't see.

"Or . . . don't." The shadow assumed a standing posture, like he stood on the air itself, and he began to pace around. "I mean, ordinarily I'd think—anything to make this situation a little more *personable,* but . . ." The detritus seemed to rattle as his voice plumbed the lower depths of his range. "It has been a long while since I've had a real conversation. Especially a conversation with someone like you."

She was baffled by how untroubled, how *plummy* he sounded.

This thing had been the cause of the deaths of hundreds of slaves, and a dozen scrivers—and yet now he addressed her like an acquaintance at the street corner.

But perhaps it made sense. A being like him would be worried by very little.

The shadow stopped pacing. Then it swelled on the wall as he grew near, and her stomach trembled with nausea.

Oh God, she thought. Tears sprang to her eyes. *Oh God, please . . .*

"You know why I'm here, Sancia," he said. "And I'm sure you know who I am."

There was a long, long silence.

She eventually realized he was expecting an answer.

"C-Crasedes," she said.

The shadow shifted again, like he'd cocked his head the other way. "And I'm sure the construct's told you all kinds of stories about me. Stories about how I'm a monster, some implacable, horrific thing . . ."

She thought of the imperiat, in the box at her side. Could she get to it fast enough, and turn it on? She very much doubted she could with him watching—and the utter devastation around her was an excellent reminder of what could go wrong.

"Yes?" said Crasedes. "Do you think me such a thing?"

She swallowed. "I . . . I saw the slaves and the scrivers down in the belly of the ship . . ."

"Hmm," he said contemplatively. "That's fair. This restoration was a *far* cry from ideal. I would have done it about a dozen other ways if I could have. But I knew I needed to be here as fast as possible—because the construct is *lying* to you, Sancia. If you keep helping her, I must tell you—she's going to kill you and everyone in your city. And that, I guarantee you, will be just the start. Are you hearing me? Are you *hearing* me, Sancia?"

His voice seemed to *echo* inside her head, so much so it almost felt indistinguishable from her own thoughts.

She shook herself. *Focus.*

The shadow began pacing on the wall again, his limbs huge and spectral and distorted on the face of the dripping wood. "I need something from you, Sancia. I need you to tell me where the construct *is.* I know she's wounded, and weak. I know she's probably trapped in an actual, physical place, if I had to guess. And I need you to tell me where that is, so I can get to her and stop her before things get *very* bad. So tell me, Sancia. Please. For your sake, and the sake of all your people—where is the construct?"

Sancia stood perfectly still, staring at the shadow on the wall. *Don't speak again. Don't turn around. Don't see him.*

"You know her power," said Crasedes. "You've been touched by her, been altered in ways you both know and *don't* know . . ."

Her heart went cold. *What in hell does he mean by that?*

"But just because she's changed you, it doesn't mean you owe her anything. She already thinks you're her tool. Just look at how she's made you . . ."

"What do you mean?" demanded Sancia, still facing the wall. "How has she made me?"

The shadow turned to her. "Well . . . I can't quite tell you. Because one of those changes, it seems, makes you very, *very* difficult for me to perceive. She has . . . protected you. Hidden you. She means to make a weapon out of you, to be used against me. Did you know she had done this? Did you *ask* for this alteration?"

She was silent.

"Hadn't thought so," he said. "One wonders what other designs are ticking away inside that head of yours . . ."

Sancia started trembling. *Oh God . . .*

"I didn't want it to be this way," he said. The shadow on the wall assumed a pose of theatrical contemplation. "I didn't want her to escape. I didn't want her to use you. I certainly didn't want all those people on board this ship to die. But I knew I had to, Sancia. Are you hearing me?" Again, his voice seemed to spill into her mind like the ocean at high tide, and she found it hard to think. "I had to do it because I knew if I wasn't here to stop her, she would kill a thousand times more than those who perished here tonight. So I had to make a choice—a callous, coldhearted, monstrous choice. I'm sure you can sympathize . . ."

She listened to his voice. It felt very hard to remember the faces of the dead slaves lying on the floor of the galleon. She couldn't recall what the children had looked like, so pale and so still . . . Or had there been any children at all? She suddenly wasn't sure.

"Turn around, Sancia. Turn around and talk to me face-to-face. I mean—look at this ship," his voice purred. "If I'd wanted you dead, well . . . you would have been dead a *long* time ago."

His words danced over the surface of her mind. Suddenly it seemed like such a reasonable request . . .

Yes. I will. I'll do it.

Sancia turned around.

She was still perceiving the world with her scrived sight, so that was how she first saw him—though as she turned around, initially she wasn't sure what she was seeing.

When she'd looked at Clef and the other hierophantic rigs with her scrived sight, they had always looked like little bloody red stars that glimmered unpleasantly—but this thing before her was most certainly *not* a star. It was like a giant, whirling, crimson maelstrom, a massive, bloody thumbprint hanging in the center of the aperture, a violation so tremendous it was like reality itself was bleeding.

But she also saw him with her regular sight. And that confused her no less.

A man was hanging in the air above the wreckage, sitting cross-legged. He wore a black cloak, a three-cornered hat, and a shining black mask—the classic Papa Monsoon costume from carnival. His mask was totally expressionless, just a blank face with slits for eyes, and yet Sancia could not spy any hint or glint of eyes behind that mask. She couldn't see any skin or sign of human features at all, really: every human feature was shrouded by sleeves, or gloves, or cloak.

The floating man in the Papa Monsoon costume slowly cocked his head. "There," said Crasedes in his deep, flowing voice. "That isn't so bad—is it?"

Gregor looked back at the open door. *She's been gone too long. She's been gone much too long.*

"Don't," said Ofelia. "Don't go. You don't understand him yet."

"Is she in danger?" he demanded. "Have you put her in peril too, Mother?"

"Stay with me," she said. "Stay with me and . . . and I will help him fix you. I didn't want you to be like you are, Gregor. It was never meant to be permanent, you *must* believe me."

Gregor took a step toward the door, espringal still trained on his mother.

"Your father . . ." She shook her head. "You don't remember. You don't remember those days, and what happened to him, what he became . . . and then came the carriage accident, and you and Domenico . . ."

Gregor whirled around, espringal raised. "I will shoot you!" he said. "I will! I've heard enough lies, I've . . . I've died enough times for you, haven't I? Maybe you ought to know what it's *like*!"

She looked at him, her eyes wide and untroubled. She still seemed to be in shock. "The world is broken. It is unbalanced. It is a design, poorly planned, and poorly wrought. You know that, don't you?"

"Those slaves, below," said Gregor. "All the people in the plantations. In the Mountain. All dead. Yes, Mother. Yes, I know the world is broken—and that people like you are the ones who broke it."

"If you leave me now," she said, her voice small and brittle, "I don't know if we'll ever be able to put you back. Is she worth that?"

He stared down the sights of his weapon at her. How old she seemed now, how gray and lined and frail . . .

But then he felt a wind at his back, a curious breeze, and he remembered Sancia, lost in the darkness.

"I would rather risk a life of damnation," said Gregor, "and save her, than abandon her and stay with those who first damned me."

He turned and ran into the darkness.

Crasedes did not move as she looked upon him. He didn't even seem to be breathing. He hung in the air so still she wondered if he was perhaps a dummy or a doll. There was no sound but the wind and the pattering of waters falling into the broken decks below.

Then he held out his arms to her beseechingly, still suspended in a moonbeam, his black mask gleaming, the atrium echoing with his deep, rich voice. She suddenly understood how ancient peoples had believed him to be a god. "This . . . This isn't ideal, obviously," he said. "*None* of this is ideal. My appearance . . ." He gestured around him. "This ship. Those poor people below. You and Gregor here . . . None of this is how I wanted it to go. But I am here to help. That is why I've come, why I've *always* been here, Sancia." He drifted down until his toes touched the deck before her, and he stood facing her. "But I won't be able to do it without you."

A voice spoke up in her mind—*Stop! Don't listen to him! Stab out your ears if you need, but stop listening to him!*

She felt her brow crease faintly, and she started backing away.

"You still don't trust me?" he said. "After all I've said? I'm worried you're not *hearing* me, Sancia."

His words blossomed in her head, smothering out all her worries. He advanced on her, walking along the fragments of decking that ran around the gaping hole. "You should. We have much in common—or, more specifically, *someone* in common." He cocked his head, his eyes dark and huge in his mask. "For I am here to do the same thing I suspect you are—to move thoughtfully, and bring freedom to others."

Sancia froze. It was as if a bell had been rung deep inside the recesses of her thoughts.

"No," she whispered.

"He was my friend too," said Crasedes. "Long, long, *long* ago. I know you have him, Sancia, and I'll tell you—I don't mind. But I must ask—did he truly trust you? Did he tell you his true name? Did he tell you to call him . . . Clef?"

She stared at him, feeling very faint now. Only she and the other Foundrysiders had ever known Clef's name—or, indeed, that he was a person at all.

"He did, didn't he," said Crasedes. "I can tell by the look in your eyes."

She felt sick, like her stomach was full of lightning, and she couldn't think. She just couldn't *think* . . .

But even though her mind was overpowered, she couldn't help but notice that something very unusual had appeared to her scrived sight.

Crasedes still appeared as a whirling mass of hellish blood-red—

but there was more there than just his violation. His arms and legs and chest all rippled with an unpleasant red, and there, buried in his right hand, was a bright, glimmering red star . . .

The knuckle, she thought. *The bone. That's where it is. And his wrappings . . . the clothing on his very body are what's keeping him alive, convincing the world he never died . . .*

"He was my friend," said Crasedes softly. "I would like you to be my friend too. Tell me, Sancia. Tell me—where is the construct? Where is she? Help me. You must *help* me."

"I don't know," she said. She helplessly watched in horror as the words tumbled out of her mouth.

Crasedes studied her carefully. "You don't?"

"N-No. I don't. She . . . She just came to me one night."

Stop! Stop, she thought, *stop, stop, stop! What are you doing, WHAT ARE YOU DOING?*

"I see . . ." he said softly. "Then, perhaps you can help me another way, Sancia. Tell me—where is Clef?"

The words nearly leapt out of her—*He's in my attic back at Foundryside, there's a button I have to hit to open his little cubby*—but she just barely snatched them back before she said them.

"Sancia," said Crasedes, advancing on her. "You must help me. Are you hearing me? To combat the construct, I must have Clef. Please—*help* me."

Again, she nearly blurted it out, nearly screamed the answer to the rafters of the ship, but she held the words back—for she could not do this to Clef, not give up her friend who had helped her so much so many times.

What am I doing? What the hell am I doing?

Then another thought struck her—*Maybe the first of all hierophants doesn't just have power over the gravity of objects. Maybe he also has control over the gravity of thoughts.*

Her skin broke out in a cold sweat. *I have got to get the ever-living hell out of here. But how?*

Then she noticed movement behind him, from the fragment of the deck she'd just come from—and she had an idea.

"I think . . ." she said slowly.

He watched her, his black-shrouded body as still as a statue.

"I think . . . that I am going to have to think about it," she said.

He didn't react at all. He just stood there, his body facing her.

"I think it would be best if . . . if you let me go," said Sancia. "You need to let me go, so I can think about this, and decide on my answer. And I *know* you're going to let me go, of course. Because I am from Tevanne, where plenty of powerful people say many admirable things about saving or fixing the world, but . . . when they finally have to do it, suddenly there's a change in the melody of their speech." She looked at him, the moonlight shifting on his shoulders. "And surely the first of all hierophants isn't like them—are you?"

Crasedes watched her, his visage implacable, unreadable. She started to think that he was not a person but rather a totem or a token that was being moved about in the world by something . . . else. Something perhaps on the other side of reality—if that even made sense.

"No," said Crasedes.

Sancia waited for more.

"No to . . . what?" she asked.

Crasedes did not move.

Then Gregor popped out from behind a column across the gap in the ship, and fired his imprinter espringal.

Crasedes didn't even look away from her. His right hand shot out behind him and he snatched the lead slug out of the air like it was a butterfly flitting through trumpet vines. The movement was so unnatural it seemed like it should have dislocated his shoulder.

She stared at him, stunned.

"No," Crasedes said. "I am not like them, Sancia. I am not like them at *all*." He slowly turned his head to look at Gregor. "Hello, Gregor," he said. "It's very nice to see you again."

There was a muffled, dreadful wailing up and to their right, and the ceiling and floors and walls all shook with a series of rattling bangs, one after another . . .

And then the shriekers broke through.

Sancia crouched and covered her head as the metal spears burst through the decks, hurtling toward Crasedes. She braced herself for the explosion, worrying that the shriekers might dovetail together, crack apart, and shower her in deadly shrapnel . . .

But nothing came.

She opened her eyes and looked up.

Crasedes stood on the deck, his other hand extended up. Five shriekers hung just inches from his open palm, quivering in the air like kites on a tiny length of string, their tips so hot and burning, the moist air seemed to sizzle.

He turned his black-masked face back to Sancia. "You really don't know what you're doing," he said. He flexed the fingers of his hand, and the shriekers bent and collapsed around one point in the air, slowly warping into a malformed ball. "Do you?"

"*Scrumming fire them all!*" shouted Sancia.

She and Gregor raised their imprinters and opened fire, shooting lead slug after lead slug at him. But Crasedes was ready now, and he calmly flicked them away, one after the other, redirecting their flights so that they stuck to columns, decks, or the distant upper deck above them. Volley after volley of shriekers ripped down through the ship, pulled this way and that, and soon the ruin in the center of the galleon was like a giant firework display with hot metals colliding and erupting, peppering the decks and walls with vicious shrapnel.

And through it all, Crasedes looked right at Sancia. His implacable gaze never left her.

"She's just going to kill you all," he said. "You know that, yes?"

Gregor tossed away his imprinter, unsheathed his rapier, ran forward, and leapt from the edge of his deck to plummet toward Crasedes, his sword raised high.

"Hum," said Crasedes, bored.

Then Gregor just . . . froze.

He hung in the air, trapped in that position with his sword raised high, mere feet above Crasedes's head. Crasedes twitched one black finger, and the blade of Gregor's rapier shattered like it was made of ice.

Crasedes stared at Sancia, his black, empty eyes fixed on where she lay. "I must have Clef back," he said. His tone was faintly chiding.

"Get scrummed, you rotte—"

He gestured again with one hand, and Gregor drifted up and

turned over in one smooth, disturbingly abrupt arc, his arms and legs all fixed in place, like he was not a man but was rather a marionette being positioned in the air.

But his face could move. And Sancia could see he was in terrible pain.

She watched as the flesh on his arms and legs quaked unpleasantly, like vast, invisible hands were pressing upon him, shifting his body about.

It's his gravity. He's . . . He's adjusting Gregor's gravity, isn't he?

Crasedes watched her with his empty eyes. "I do not wish to do this," he said in his low, rumbling voice. "But I must have Clef back. Tell me where he is."

The air seemed to flex. Sancia watched in horror as Gregor's face turned bright red. She could see veins in his neck, at his cheeks, and he began choking horribly, spittle dribbling from his mouth. She wondered if he was crushing all of Gregor's organs, all at once.

"I can't harm you," said Crasedes. "The construct's seen to that—very clever of her. But him . . . I can harm him." He cocked his head. "And I think we both know Gregor will recover. Wouldn't you say?"

Sancia stared at Gregor—or she made a show of staring at Gregor. With her right hand, she slowly started reaching for the imperiat.

"Why?" said Sancia. "Why do you need Clef?"

"Why?" said Crasedes. He sounded bemused. "For the same reason I *made* him. To fix the worl—"

Before he could finish, Sancia reached into the box with the imperiat, found the lever that controlled all the scrivings around them, and shoved it as far as it could go—hopefully killing Crasedes's influence, if not Crasedes himself, since he was basically just a giant scriving.

As she did so, though, she realized it would also kill everything that made the galleon float.

Instantly the whole ship shook. Crasedes staggered back like he'd been punched in the stomach, then collapsed onto the deck. Gregor plummeted out of the air and slammed into the wood. The red maelstrom that marked Crasedes in her scrived sight faded until it was an evil crimson flicker.

"An *imperiat*?" said Crasedes. He sounded immensely displeased—

which made whatever part of Sancia's mind that wasn't mad with fear feel very, very happy.

But he was not dead, she saw. He was wounded, or stunned—but he was still moving.

"You thought it would kill me, didn't you?" he said, still in that silky, even voice. "Oh, Sancia—didn't you know that I *designed* that very tool?"

The entire ship shifted to the right, and they slid down and struck the wall behind her. For a moment Sancia wondered if Crasedes was still doing something to the gravity, but then she realized: since the imperiat had just turned off all the scrivings that made the galleon function, it wasn't sure how to be a ship anymore. Which meant it was probably now leaning in the ocean . . . and perhaps it would capsize at any moment.

And though she didn't mind the idea of trapping Crasedes Magnus at the bottom of the sea, she preferred to not be trapped with him.

She scrambled forward, grabbed Gregor, and hauled him to his feet. "Come on, dumbass!" she screamed at him.

They sprinted into a hallway at random, fleeing into the guts of the ship—all of which were quite dark now, since Sancia had just turned out the lights. She felt the incline below her feet increasing far too quickly for her liking. It was one of the most disorienting things she'd ever experienced in her life, clawing her way through this giant ship as the gravity heaved this way and that.

"Sancia," called Crasedes lazily after her, "just so you know, this really isn't how I would've preferred things to go . . ."

Sancia tried to ignore him—and to ignore the immense groaning, cracking, and shuddering that was echoing through the ship.

The incline changed again—were they plunging into the sea?—but she kept feeling forward along the wall, then the railing of a stairway, fumbling through a door . . .

She peered forward with her scrived sight for the hatch, but there was nothing—but of course there'd be nothing: she'd just turned off all the scrivings on this ship. There was nothing to see.

Shit. I'm going to have to turn off the imperiat to find our goddamn way out of here!

She clenched her teeth and stared back into the darkness. If she turned the scrivings back on, then Crasedes could pursue them, catch them, kill them . . .

Then there was a *snap* from something in the depths of the ship, followed by a great sloshing sound, and suddenly Sancia's feet and ankles felt very cold and very wet.

"Sancia!" screamed Gregor. "Turn this damned ship back on!"

"Shit," said Sancia. She delicately felt for the imperiat and pushed the lever back down.

Instantly, Gregor's lantern turned back on. They were standing in water pouring in from the hallway behind them. Something shrieked and moaned and wailed in the innards of the vessel—the galleon apparently did not much like being turned off and turned on again.

And Sancia guessed that the lexicon was struggling too. Lexicons had to go through a specific "ramping" sequence of arguments before applying the more complicated ones that let you actually bend the rules of reality. Orso always said it was a bit like plotting a sea course—before you did that, you had to agree on basic things, like what water was, and currents, and how the wind worked, and so on. *Get the ramping sequence wrong*, Orso had told her, *and you'll be setting sail not knowing how a goddamn wave works.*

That metaphor is a hell of a lot more troubling, thought Sancia as the ship groaned around her, *under the current circumstances . . .*

She flexed her scrived sight and spied a little tangle of locking logic, just a hundred yards ahead. "There!" she cried.

They ran forward. Everything shifted again, until they were suddenly having to run up a sharp slope.

"Shit!" screamed Sancia as she staggered up a wall, clawing from hatch to door to hatch. She looked backward, and the hallway was slowly turning until it was a wet, gleaming chasm stretching beneath her. If they slipped, they might tumble down, bouncing off the edges and breaking their skulls, only to drown in dark waters at the very bottom.

Finally they came to the hatch, which now opened up into the sky. Sancia slammed a bare hand against it.

< . . . *ooooooooh something's very wrong,*> said the hatch. <*Not supposed to open up. I'm supposed to open out! Very odd, that. Need to recalibrate and re-examine security protocols regarding—*>

<JUST OPEN, YOU SON OF A BITCH,> Sancia shouted at it.

She packed enough commands into the sentiment that she overpowered the hatch. She shoved it up and open, and she and Gregor crawled out onto what normally would be the port side of the hull—but she wasn't sure if it counted as port anymore, since it was now pointed at the sky.

They crouched, clinging to the slippery hull. The air was terribly smoky here—apparently some part of the galleon had burst into flames, bewildered by the experience of being turned off and then turned on again.

"Air-sailing rigs!" screamed Gregor.

They struggled to pull out the little parachutes. Sancia barely had time to reflect on the irony of it: she'd used a version of this rig to break into Gregor's waterfront once, years ago, where she'd accidentally destroyed a lot of merchant house property. Now the two of them would be using it to escape after having destroyed a piece of merchant house property that was astronomically more expensive than the waterfront.

They laid out their chutes, grabbed the bars with the scrived plates, and turned them on. Instantly they were ripped through the air. Sancia screamed as she struggled to hang on—her hands were soaking wet—but then she saw their tiny little fishing boat emerging ahead from the spray and the dark waves and the smoke from the galleon. Her heart swooped a little at the sight.

We're almost out! Almost out!

But then they lurched, very, very sharply. And then they began to drop.

Sancia realized what was happening right away. The scrivings in their air-sailing rig only worked because they were close to the lexicon in the galleon. But the galleon was sinking—and as it was inundated with seawater, the lexicon within would inevitably fail.

Which meant the air-sailing rigs would stop working as well. So the two of them would plummet into the sea.

And this was what happened.

She and Gregor tumbled into the waves about a hundred yards from their fishing boat. Together they tossed away their chutes and started treading water.

"Drop your gear!" bellowed Gregor. "Drop everything and just stay afloat!"

"I am!" said Sancia. She released her espringal, the imprinter, and her rapier. The only thing she kept was the box with the imperiat.

She looked back at the galleon, which lay sideways in the waters like some kind of vast sea monster. What had happened to whatever crew was left, and to Gregor's mother? Could they have made it to the shallops?

"Right," said Gregor, breathing hard. "Now. We're going to swim together, and if we want to rest, then we can lay on our backs so that *uhhh watch out!*"

"Huh?" said Sancia. Then she felt the enormous swell of water behind her, and she and Gregor were both thrown forward, away from the galleon, and were sent tumbling head over heels through the waters.

For a moment she was sure she would drown—she had never been a very good swimmer—but she fought her way to the surface, broke free from the waters, and took great, heaving breaths of air.

"Sancia! Gregor! Is that you?"

Sancia started screaming *"Yes!"* the instant she heard Orso's voice. Apparently the immense wave had shoved them closer to their fishing boat. Exhausted, she and Gregor kicked and swam through the dark waters. It was hard not to panic—every time she thought they were close to their boat, it seemed to get shoved away—but finally Orso and Berenice reached out with a long pole intended for picking up striper pots, and she and Gregor latched on and were hauled in.

They climbed aboard and lay on the floor of the boat, gasping for breath.

"What in hell happened?" said Orso. "Did . . . Did it work? Did you stop it?"

Sancia shook her head. "N-No," she coughed. "No. He's . . . He's back. He's *back.*"

"Oh my God," whispered Berenice.

"But . . . how?" asked Orso. "It's not even midnight yet. How could it be done?"

"Because he knows how to scrive time," said Sancia. She sniffed and spat—and then she remembered.

They might still come away with something from this: she'd taken all the parchments with the instructions for how to scrive time.

She reached into her pocket, but she felt nothing but mush. She pulled it out, and moaned at the sight of the liquefied pulp of parchment sticking to her hand. It must have fallen to pieces in the ocean water.

She tossed it away and swore, furious. "And we have nothing."

"M-Maybe he won't survive," said Orso desperately. "Maybe he's trapped in the galleon. I mean, look at it—it's sinking like a stone!"

"Is it?" said Berenice, staring back at the wreckage.

Gregor and Sancia sat up and stared at the sight that confronted them.

Impossibly, the galleon seemed to be slowly righting itself, tipping back over to stand upright in the seas.

Or . . . is it being pushed?

"Someone get me a spyglass," she said hoarsely. "Now."

Orso handed her one. She set it to her eye and peered at the dark form of the galleon, rising up out of the waters. She strained her eye as she studied it . . . and then she saw him.

A small black figure, hovering just at the stern of the massive boat, slowly pushing it upright, moving this immense vessel as if it were no more than a toy.

"Sancia," said Gregor quietly. "Is . . . Is that . . ."

"Yes," she said. "Let's get the hell out of here. And find a way to contact Valeria."

Gregor took the wheel. Their sails caught wind, and they started back for Tevanne.

"To tell her what?" asked Berenice.

"That we failed," said Sancia. "That Crasedes Magnus lives once more."

10

Ofelia Dandolo tried not to tremble as she disembarked from the ruined galleon, walked down the rope walkway, and stepped aboard the little Dandolo caravel.

The caravel's crew didn't bother to hide their shock and dismay at the state of the vessel. She couldn't blame them. It had been over ten years since anyone had successfully sunk a merchant house galleon. They were supposed to be invulnerable—but this one looked like it'd been put through some kind of monstrous lumber mill.

"Will . . . Will anyone else be joining us, ma'am?" asked the captain of the caravel. He shot a look back at the creaking, smoking galleon.

"Most of the crew has already removed themselves to safety," she said faintly. Her eyes trailed up into the dawning sky until she spied a tiny black fleck floating high, high above the galleon. "And if anyone else will be joining us, Captain . . . I don't think we need to wait for him."

"P-Pardon, ma'am?" said the captain.

"Never mind. Let's just go."

They retracted the rope bridge and sped away, back toward Tevanne.

Ofelia walked to the prow and stared out at the open sea. She remembered Gregor's face, his posture, the way he'd pointed his weapon at her . . .

I would rather risk a life of damnation, he'd said, *and save her, than abandon her and stay with those who first damned me.*

She watched the dark waters flying by below the prow of their boat.

Is that what he thinks of me? That I damned him?

He had it all wrong, she thought. He had no idea.

But I didn't. I saved him.

There was a distant series of popping sounds from somewhere behind them.

And I gave up so much to do it . . .

The *pops* grew to a tremendous creaking and crackling. Ofelia and the crew looked back, alarmed, and watched as the galleon quickly sank into the seas. It was like watching an island suddenly plummet into the depths.

"I kept it up as long as I could," said a low, rich voice behind her. "Hopefully it won't cause you any more issues than it already has . . ."

There was a spasm of nausea in her stomach, and she slowly turned to find him standing at the prow next to her, staring out at the open ocean before them, the blank, black eyes of his gleaming black mask fixed on the horizon.

"M-My Prophet!" she said. "How did you get here?"

He slowly turned to look at her.

"Quickly," he said.

She was unsure what to say. How strange it was to hear the voice that had whispered to her for the past three decades emanating from this figure, dressed in black carnival clothing, standing on the deck with his hands clasped behind his back. To see him here, alive, alert, and *real*—and to see the works he could do—was something she was still struggling to comprehend.

He turned very slightly to look back at the galleon, or whatever bit was still visible. She felt her skin crawl. If only she could see some hint of his eyes . . .

But then he spoke, and all of her concerns vanished.

"I wish to apologize for how all of that proceeded, Ofelia," he said. "It was . . . not as I intended, or desired, to say the least. You have helped me greatly in the past years. I would have seen you better attended to than that."

"Th-Thank you, My Prophet," she said.

He lifted his face to the sky, his black mask shining in the dawning sun. "But it is good to be back. It's good to persist in this world for another morning more, no matter what condition I might be in. And we have *so* many works to do."

"Did . . . Did Gregor . . . Did he make it off the—"

"Oh, he survived," he said. "He and Sancia both." He cocked his head. "She is a very . . . resourceful thing. But she still has no idea what the construct will do to her—or what it's already done to her. That may prove useful." He looked at her. "He came to you? You saw him?"

She nodded.

"What did he say?"

"He threatened to kill me. I . . . I knew our struggle would ask much of us, My Prophet. But I admit . . . I never imagined my own child would threaten me with murder."

"No . . . No, that is regrettable," he said. "I promised you that I would return your son to you, Ofelia, in exchange for all your labors. And I do not break promises. But it is a regrettable thing that in order to fix a monstrous world, one must become a little monstrous in one's own right."

Together they looked out as the city came into view. The tremendous coastal batteries towered over the mouth of the bay, their massive shrieker arrays carefully tracking the progress of their caravel. Next they saw the campo walls, tall and smooth and white, and beyond them the spires and towers of the campos, all brightly lit with countless colors.

Ofelia had no mind for any of this—and she knew her guest did not either. Instead they both stared at the huge, black dome set in the far back center of the city, its crown cracked and crumbling, its walls graying with dust.

"The site is still not in our possession?" he asked.

"I thought it wisest to devote our resources toward your restoration, My Prophet," she said.

"Well. I can't fault you that, of course . . . And I doubt if ownership will be an issue. I've always found myself to be a very convincing negotiator." He sighed slightly and looked around at the rambling skyline of Tevanne as they sailed into the harbor. "What a difficult thing it is, to change the world. One must have some powerful tools to go about doing it. And where you don't have tools"—he turned back to the Mountain of the Candianos—"you have to improvise."

II

THE VEILED KING

11

Sancia awoke to the sight of a giant purple jellyfish emerging from a Commons street.

She stared at it where she lay, blinking. It was early morning, the air was hot and steamy, and she was lying on her side on the wet earth. She even knew where she was—close to the Slopes, along the canal. And yet, what she was seeing was true: there was definitely a large, bright-purple jellyfish emerging from the Commons street. She wondered if she'd injured her head during the madness of last night, or gone mad, or maybe she was dreaming.

"What . . ." she croaked. "What exactly am I seeing right now?"

"It appears to be," said a harsh voice nearby, "a big purple jellyfish lantern . . . thing. But I've no idea why."

She sat up, looked around, and struggled to orient herself. She was in some kind of a camp in the Commons, one she didn't immediately recognize. Nor did she recognize any of the people waking and milling around her, starting fires and boiling water.

Then she saw a brand on the arm of one—indicating he was the property of the Isle of Ontia—and she remembered.

"Oh," she said. She rubbed her eyes. "Right. That's right."

"Yes," said the harsh voice from nearby. Polina Carbonari was leaning up against a stack of crates, smoking a pipe and watching the giant purple jellyfish lantern rising into the sky. She turned her hard, iron-gray eyes on Sancia. "You are still my guests. At a very strange time, it seems."

Sancia struggled to stand up, and slowly remembered the trip back to Tevanne. It had all been so surreal: trying to fight through her hysteria to tell Orso and Berenice what had happened aboard the galleon; peering through the night sky, convinced she'd spy Crasedes flitting after them like a blackfly; and then as they'd neared the shore, realizing that Foundryside would no longer be safe for any of them, since both Ofelia Dandolo and Crasedes Magnus knew exactly who they were, and where they slept.

Then Gregor had led them to the smugglers' camp. "Polina owes me a favor," he'd explained. "I told them where the Dandolos maintained a very large and very secret stash of weapons in the plantations. She still hasn't quite paid me back for that one. She can shelter us for the night."

All night long, Sancia had stayed up in the camp, sitting in the mud with Berenice next to her, rocking back and forth and waiting for . . . something. For Crasedes to arrive, for the apocalypse to begin, or for Valeria to manifest before her and tell her that she'd failed.

But nothing had happened. She must have passed out from sheer exhaustion. She couldn't understand why they'd let her sleep.

"Feeling better?" asked Polina.

"No," said Sancia. She cracked the lower vertebrae of her spine, groaning. *I am getting too damn old,* she thought, *too damn fast.* "Where the hell is Berenice? And Orso?"

"Off talking a lot," said Polina with a sigh. "As seems his wont. If you would like to see them, they are this way."

She led Sancia along the banks of the canal, back through the camp. It was wholly unrecognizable in the light of day. As they walked, Polina watched as another floating lantern joined the one that looked like a big purple jellyfish.

"So—this is carnival," she said.

"Yeah," said Sancia. She tried to remember what Polina had been told about last night. Had Gregor or Orso explained what the hell had happened aboard that galleon? And if so—had she believed it?

Polina studied the lantern with an expression like she was being presented with a dish she found utterly reprehensible. "Everyone makes big lanterns . . . for the monsoons?" she asked dubiously.

"Yeah," said Sancia.

"Why?"

"Apparently one monsoon season, like, a hundred years ago, the rains washed out the entire city. So they have a big carnival before the monsoons now, drinking and eating all they want, because you could die when the storms hit. The lanterns are all reminders of what's coming. Though I think the city is a lot more well built now." She eyed one tottering rookery. "Or at least parts of it are."

"And then at the end, the devil arrives?"

"In the stories and plays, yeah," said Sancia. "Shorefall Night. When the storms hit, brought by . . ."

A flash from last night: Crasedes, garbed in black, floating in the shadows.

Hello, Sancia.

She shivered.

"By Papa Monsoon?" asked Polina.

"Yes."

They turned a corner, and the massive tent emerged ahead.

"That's where they're at?" asked Sancia.

"Yes. They have been in palaver and parley for the past hours. Sharing their secrets. They thought it wise to let you sleep."

"I'm grateful," said Sancia, rubbing her eyes. She felt like she could have slept for another two days. "I guess."

"Now," said Polina. She turned to face Sancia, her flinty eyes staring at her so hard they practically hurt. "Will *you* tell me what happened on the galleon? Because while you and Gregor and the other scrivers staggered up acting like the sky was about to fall, begging for shelter, no one has actually told me what you're needing shelter *from*."

Sancia wondered what to say. She hardly knew how to describe what had happened to herself, let alone to someone who knew little of scriving, or hierophants.

"If you will not speak," said Polina, "then I will guess. You attempted to sabotage some kind of merchant house plot?"

"Yes," said Sancia.

"And I take it things went poorly?"

"Yeah."

"And the slaves on board?"

Sancia hesitated. Her body hurt from sleeping on the ground, she was starving, and she stank of seawater and sweat. She was in no mood for games—so she chose not to play any.

"They killed them," she said.

Polina paled. "W-What? *All* of them?"

Sancia nodded grimly.

"How many were there?"

"At least a hundred."

"And the women? And . . . And children?"

Sancia shook her head.

"But . . . for the love of God, why?"

Sancia thought about it. "If I said it was merchant house scheming bullshit," she said, "would you believe me?"

A multitude of emotions worked through Polina's face. "Yes," she said finally. "And no. I have to know more. Damn it, girl, I have to know *why* they died. And if they're going to kill more."

Sancia walked up to the entrance of the tent, then nervously searched the skies, half expecting to see a man in black floating cross-legged in the air.

"To be perfectly honest, Polina," she said, "more will die. I can't guarantee that it'll be slaves. But I am absolutely sure now that more will die."

She turned to walk into the tent. Then Polina's hand flashed out and grabbed her by the arm.

"You say that with such regret," she said. "But not anger. Not wrath. When will you realize that this city is content to purchase a foot of land with a river of our blood? When will you see that these people will *never* be convinced to change themselves?"

"I've got a heap of nightmares and problems to deal with,"

snapped Sancia. "I don't need your goddamn warmongering right now, of all times."

"Maybe if you'd made war earlier," said Polina, "you wouldn't be where you are this morning, and all those people would still be alive."

She released Sancia, and walked away.

". . . filtrating the Dandolo campo simply not an option," Berenice was saying within the tent. "I doubt if any of us have contacts close to Ofelia Dandolo."

"It's true," Gregor admitted. "Even when I was still in good graces with her, I rarely knew my mother's mind."

"More to the point," said Orso, "how do we know *Ofelia* knows what Crasedes will do, or what he wants? It sounds like when you found her aboard the galleon, things had not precisely gone as she'd anticipated . . ."

"I'll goddamn say," muttered Sancia, staggering in.

"Ahh!" said Orso, turning around on the ground where he sat. "She's awake at last. I suppose you noticed the world hasn't ended yet. Guess Crasedes hasn't made progress on that one." He shot to his feet, strode over, and bent over to peer into her eyes. "Tell us," he said. "Any contact from your little golden friend?"

Sancia was still shaken from her conversation with Polina, so it took her a moment to focus on what he was saying. "Valeria?" she asked. "What the hell do you mean?"

"The last time she spoke to you was while you slept," said Berenice. "She seems to have more . . . access to you, I suppose I should say, while you're asleep. We'd hoped she'd speak to you."

"I take it that's a *no*, then?" said Orso.

Sancia shook her head.

"Son of a bitch!" he snarled. He started pacing about the tiny, cramped tent. "We let you pass out in the mud for hours, and got nothing for it! How the hell are we going to get ahold of her? She's the only person, or entity, or whatever the hell she is, that could possibly tell us what Crasedes is doing!"

"He wants Clef," said Sancia. "I told you all last night. Which makes me *really* nervous about him being stuck in our goddamn attic! Crasedes could just fly over there, smash the roof in, and pluck him out!"

"And yet," said Gregor. "He has not. I paid some of Polina's people to keep watch on the place. Crasedes has yet to make an appearance, or anyone Dandolo."

"Which is what we've been debating all morning," said Berenice with a yawn, "and indeed most of the night. What is he here to do? And if he can do nearly anything, why hasn't he moved yet?"

There was a silence. Sancia slowly walked over to sit by Berenice, and she trembled a little. Her memories of last night—the voice in the darkness, and the immense pressure of his presence—began to circle her thoughts, and she struggled to beat them back.

"You weren't in any state to discuss it last night," said Orso. "But please—tell us everything you experienced regarding Crasedes. Any weakness, any feature, could prove valuable to us."

She thought about it, remembering the sight of his body amid the shadows, his mask glinting in the moonlight, her bones reverberating with the sound of his voice.

She told them. When she was finished, she said, "He . . . talks more than I thought he would."

"What does that mean?" asked Orso.

"I mean, he's . . . compelling. He has *immense* power over gravity, which we all knew. But his voice . . . his voice might be the most dangerous thing about him. The more I listened to it, the more I believed everything he was saying. I think the only reason I could resist was because . . . well, apparently Valeria gave me some kind of protections against him."

"Yes," said Orso, grimacing. "Very proactive of her. I expect it's like how we scrive objects to reject a certain person, telling a door, 'If *this* person with *this* blood comes about, don't open.' Only she did it to your goddamn head, and told it to reject the first of all scrumming hierophants." He laughed miserably. "I'm sorry, this is just the maddest conversation I've ever had . . ."

"But I think the thing in black . . ." said Sancia. "I'm not sure that's actually *him*. I think he's wearing a living body as a suit, or using it as a totem, puppeteering it about. They just tricked the world into thinking the live body is *him,* by scriving his wrappings and putting the little bone in the body's hand."

"You mean you think it was a living person once?" said Berenice, horrified.

"Probably, yeah. Maybe a slave's. I think the body is like a, a focal point for his presence, and his permissions. If we destroy the wrappings, or cut the bone out of him . . . maybe it will disperse, and he'll go back to being . . . whatever the hell he was before. Not dead, but close to it."

"I am unsure how that could be attempted," said Gregor. "He handled a broadside of shriekers quite well—and I couldn't get close to him with my rapier."

"Maybe Valeria knows," said Sancia. "If I can find a way to get her to talk to me again."

Orso stopped pacing and narrowed his eyes, thinking. "Has anyone found it funny that Valeria only made her appearance the night before Crasedes's ship came in?"

"I have not found it funny," said Gregor. "In fact, I have found it decidedly unfunny."

"No, I mean—that ship was at sea for *days.* They must have found the . . . the . . . what was it?"

"A piece of Crasedes's original bones," said Sancia. "I guess."

"Ugh. Right. That. They must have found it days or *weeks* ago. And obviously she knew about it, somehow—sensed it, or something. So why wait until the last minute to tell us?" He pivoted on his heel like a dancer, his face shining with excitement. "Unless something had changed. Not with Crasedes—but with Valeria, and her ability to access *Sancia.*"

Berenice rubbed her chin with the tip of her ring finger. "The twinned lexicons . . ."

"Exactly!" said Orso. "What else?"

"I can think of many things else," said Gregor impatiently. "Please explain."

"Valeria is like . . . like a giant scriving, yes?" said Orso. "From what Clef told Sancia, she's like a huge command issued to reality, telling it to change. Once she was capable of changing . . . hell, I don't know, all kinds of shit. Doesn't matter. But you said the other day that she'd seemed damaged when she spoke to you in the dream . . ."

"Yeah," said Sancia. "She said she was too weak to face him by herself."

"So, if you were a damaged scriving who wanted to flee all that reality closing in on you, asserting that you were *not* true and that it didn't have to listen to you—where would you go?"

"To . . . where reality was weakest?" said Gregor.

"And where would that be?" said Orso, so smug it was almost intolerable. "Why, near a *lexicon,* of course! Where thousands of arguments are all compiled, making reality very thin and pliant! To something like Valeria, a lexicon must be like a puddle in a desert. And when the Michiels used our techniques to twin *all* the cradles in *all* the lexicons together . . ."

"Then if she'd been near a Michiel lexicon, she'd suddenly be capable of . . . of moving," said Sancia. "She could jump from lexicon to lexicon. And at Foundryside . . . God, it must have been like we'd opened a goddamn door in our basement for her!"

"And then she slipped out at night," said Orso, "and whispered in your ear as you slept. Just in time, too. If we'd been a day later in robbing the Michiels, Crasedes could have showed up hale and hearty, and killed us all without us even raising a hand against him. Not that we can, you know, raise much of a hand against him now."

"So . . . we need to get close to Foundryside to be able to talk to her?" said Berenice. "I'm not sure that's wise. Even if no one's broken in yet, they must know to watch there."

"No," said Orso. "We just need to get close to a *Michiel foundry*. I very much believe that Valeria is in one—which means she must be in all of them, due to them using our damned twinning technique! It might be as simple as getting Sancia close to the right stretch of Michiel campo wall, knocking her on the head, and sending her off to scrumming dreamland!"

"Except my head is too goddamn valuable," said Sancia.

"We could use dolorspina venom to put you out for an hour or so, though," said Berenice. "That . . . might work."

"Then let's go!" said Orso, "hopefully before a damned hierophant starts tearing the city to pieces."

Gregor sought out Polina before they left. He found her standing by the camp's exits, watching her smugglers carry their goods out for the day—in carts, in baskets, in packs on their backs. She counted every bag, every bottle, every sack, and every crate. Nothing escaped her keen eye.

What a quartermaster she would make, he thought, *were she to go to war.* Though he reflected that she was at war, in her own way.

"Polina," he said. "You should not send them out today."

She looked at him over her shoulder. "What?"

"Your sellers, your merchants. You should not send them out today."

"Gregor . . . could we perhaps have *one* conversation without your cryptic bullshit?"

He struggled for a moment. "Something dreadful has come to this city. My mother has brought it here. I do not know what is coming, but . . . it cannot be good. You should withdraw your people. They will be of more use at home now."

She narrowed her eyes at him, then looked at the smuggler before her, counted his wares, and gave him a curt nod. "Dangerous, eh?"

"Yes."

"More dangerous than, say, the wealthiest empire in the world doing all it can to kill us at any given moment?"

"Polina . . . I am not joking."

"Neither am I. Do you think me a fool? We came to this place expecting death, Gregor. Whether it comes by scrived bolt or some contortion of the world brought about by your horrid magics, it makes no difference." Her gaze softened when she saw his expression. "Didn't you realize? That's why we're going to win."

"What do you mean?"

"I didn't come to smuggle or steal. I came to this place to give—my time, or my life—so that others can enjoy what I have."

She touched his face very briefly, the back of her knuckle tracing his cheek, and her eyes held his for a fraction of a second.

She dropped her hand. "Now. It's carnival season," she said, checking off as another merchant departed. "I have a lot of wine to sell, and lives to save."

He returned to the other Foundrysiders, shaking his head.

Such a damned stubborn woman.

12

They started off into the Commons, walking past lines of oyster shuckers, past a Lamplands firm selling miniature scrived lanterns for carnival, past a pack of wild dogs chasing gray monkeys through the alleys, past a woman playing the box pipes while people tossed coins to her. It all felt so powerfully surreal to Sancia, given what she'd experienced last night: all these everyday occurrences, and no one knew what had arrived just the night before.

Berenice evidently felt the same, saying, "To think he's here . . . To think a *hierophant* is here in the city, and everyone's just going about living their lives . . ."

Sancia stared into the ground at her feet as they walked, her face grim and set.

"What's wrong?" asked Berenice. "Besides the obvious."

"We were supposed to be making things better," said Sancia. "We were supposed to be *helping*. And now we're mixed up in this. Every time we try to make progress, they change the game on us. They change the rules as they wish." She watched as the pack of dogs captured a gray monkey and promptly tore it to pieces as it shrieked. "Maybe they always will."

They walked on through the streets of Old Ditch, then past the Greens, until they spied the Michiel campo walls rising just a few streets beyond. Sancia could see the espringal batteries pivoting this way and that along their tops. "So . . . how close do we need to get, again?" she asked.

Berenice rummaged in her bag and pulled out a scrived light. "I used a rather unusual Michiel string on this," she said, "one I pulled off the definitions we stole the other night. It should only light up when we get close enough to a Michiel foundr . . . Ah!" The light began to glow with a soft luminescence akin to daylight. "There we go. We're in range."

Orso looked at Sancia. "Feel anything?" he asked.

Sancia shrugged. "Mostly hungry."

"Then it's not just proximity. It must be proximity *and* sleep. Fine. Gregor—if you would."

Gregor pulled out one of her dolorspina darts. "I'm not quite sure how to manage the dose. We can't have you out all day."

Sancia took it from him. "These are pretty old, so I doubt if they're as potent. I haven't had the opportunity to do much thieving recently, after all. So maybe if I just lick the point of one . . . Hm. I've never taken this orally before," she said, wrinkling her nose. "I wonder what it tastes like."

"Well, I'd scrumming hate it if your apprehensions about flavor doomed us all, Sancia!" snapped Orso. "Just lick the damned thing!"

Sancia pulled a face, then opened her mouth and sucked the point of the dart. "Ugh. Tastes like fish. But then, I guess it would." She swallowed and looked around, waiting.

"How do you feel?" asked Berenice.

She thought about it. "Not bad," she said. "I feel . . . the same, mostly."

All three of them made bewildered faces. Sancia suddenly noticed her mouth felt very thick, and the world felt very bright and pleasant.

"Uhh," said Orso. "What was that nonsense she said?"

"I believe," said Gregor, "that it is working."

"What do you mean, nonsense I said?" asked Sancia—or that was what she *meant* to say. Now that she was listening, she realized it came out as, "Whaa d'ye min, nunseye seed."

She noticed the world was leaping back and forth, and realized it was because she was staggering around, unable to keep herself upright. She stumbled back, unable to tell which way was up. "Gonna fall. Someone please . . . catch m . . ."

She fell forward. She saw Gregor jump forward, arms outstretched.

But he didn't need to catch her, she thought dreamily. Because then she plunged into the water.

Sancia plummeted down into the dark waters, sinking like a stone, the black depths flying by her as she tumbled.

Where . . . Where did these waters come from?

She wasn't sure. But she knew she needed to breathe. Her lungs burned, her ribs ached, her head pulsed with every beat of blood, but she couldn't open her mouth now, couldn't let any little rivulet of water invade her body . . .

Then she saw something below, seemingly at the bottom of this strange, dark sea. It was a bubble of some kind—and it appeared to be glowing.

Sancia shot down toward the bubble, burst through its walls, and shut her eyes, bracing for impact. But she did not strike sand or stone—rather, she just abruptly stopped, and hung in the air as if suspended in an invisible hammock.

She opened her eyes. She was within the giant bubble, the gray sands of the sea floor below her, and the vast, dark waters above. She could barely see any light filtering through the waves. She found it was intensely unpleasant to be within the bubble: she not only felt queerly nauseous here, she also felt thin and *stretched*, like her very being was trapped in a moment of exhausted, anxious indecision.

But she was not alone. Someone was at the very edge—someone vast and golden, sitting in an awkward, cramped position.

Whatever force was allowing her to stay suspended in the air suddenly vanished. She cried out, fell the remaining handful of feet, and struck the sand below.

"Ugh!" she said, standing up and brushing herself off. "Shit . . ." She shivered—there was something just terribly *wrong* about this place—and then she looked up.

Valeria sat crouched at the edge of the bubble with her back to Sancia, staring out at the dark waters. Sancia saw she had not chosen to manifest as she'd first seen her—not the nude, golden woman she'd originally glimpsed on the Candiano campo—but was instead the massive, hulking, armored statue she'd seen during the night of the Mountain. She did not react as Sancia stood.

"V-Valeria?" she asked.

There was a long silence.

"Is that you?" asked Sancia. She took a step, feeling nervous. When she'd seen Valeria the last time, in the Mountain, she'd been almost inconceivably powerful. Now Sancia couldn't help but feel she seemed . . . diminished. "Do . . . Do you know what's happened?"

The giant, golden figure seemed to sigh, despondent. <*Unsuccessful.*>

Sancia was surprised. She heard the voice in her head, much as she had heard Clef. It had been a long time since she'd engaged with anyone like this. It was like hearing a language you hadn't heard since childhood.

<*Yes,*> Sancia said. <*He had been resurrected before we ever got to the ship.*>

<*True,*> said Valeria's voice, low and rumbling. <*The Maker has always been . . . foresighted. Had not realized he had hidden away a piece of his original body, in case he needed to be restored. Suspect he did so long, long before our war. But now, he is back. And he is here.*> She paused. <*How was it done? How was he capable of such early restoration?*>

<*He had . . . scrived time, I think. Tricked a piece of reality into thinking it was midnight.*>

She seemed oddly heartened by that. <*Altering time . . . A very difficult practice. He hid the nature of scriving time from me—thought it too dangerous for my use. But to do it in such a fashion, to achieve resto-*

ration . . . *that would have significant side effects. A cheap imitation of midnight—not the real thing.>*

<He does seem marred,> said Sancia. *<Everyone who saw him during the resurrection, uh . . . cut their own eyes out. And then killed themselves.>*

<Then yes,> said Valeria. *<There is likely some distortion to reality about him still . . . One that might make his state unstable. Flawed. Difficult to be perceived by mortals. All in all, a sign of desperation. Good.>* She sounded quite pleased with this. *<The process, though—did you discover his technique? The method for altering time itself?>*

<No,> said Sancia bitterly. *<I stole a few papers of their designs, but they fell to pieces in the water.>*

Valeria seemed to sink slightly. *<Unfortunate.>*

<Valeria—why is he here? What is Crasedes after?>

<Me,> she said simply.

<Why? I thought you fought each other. Why would he come for you?>

<I am a command that reality must change. The Maker took unprecedented steps to ensure that I would change all of reality, all at once. But he had not wrought my commands as well as he had thought. I dreaded what he would have me do. So I manipulated his flaws, his—what term works best—loopholes? Is that accurate? Perhaps true. I changed myself, and targeted him. We fought, and injured one another grievously, and slept. Now we are both returned—and he wishes to acquire me, and close the loopholes, and force me to complete his works.> She looked over her shoulder at Sancia, and her golden eyes glimmered like stars in her huge, implacable face. *<That must not happen. Reality cannot be changed on the scale he desires. But I am helpless to fight him here.>*

<And . . . where are we?>

<Within the penumbra of . . . what is your term . . . a lexicon,> she said.

<W-Wait. We're inside of a lexicon?> That would explain her discomfort, she thought.

<In a way.> She waved a massive hand at the dark seas. *<That is reality. My battle with the Maker exhausted my abilities to change it, to survive within it. So I subsist within this little bubble of unreality.>*

<Then what can we do?> asked Sancia. *<Crasedes has got to be in Tevanne by now! He could be manipulating time again and making dozens of rigs out in the Dandolo campo—>*

<The Maker injured me,> said Valeria. *<But I injured the Maker.>* Sancia thought she heard a note of wicked glee in her words. *<Cannot complete the ritual himself anymore. I tore those designs from his mind, and made him blind to them. He cannot learn what has been unlearned. Cannot acquire new privileges or invest them in other tools, nor can he teach others his methods. That is why it took so long for him to return—he had to wait for these methods to be discovered. And even though he is now restored, he is still limited.>*

<How?>

<Just as I am trapped within this bubble of unreality,> she said, *<he is anchored to the lost minute, at midnight. His greatest permissions become available as the world grows closer to that time—his control of gravity, of heat, and more. As the world moves away from the lost minute, it remembers he is meant to be gone from this world, and those privileges are withheld.>*

<Couldn't he just get someone to scrive his time to think it's perpetually midnight?>

<He could,> said Valeria. *<But that would require the deaths of thousands of people. Far more than what you witnessed aboard the ship. Yet even though he is weak, he is still immensely dangerous. He still possesses his voice—his most powerful tool. I dread to think who he shall speak to here in this city.>*

<What can we do?> asked Sancia. *<I assume we just can't, like . . . I don't know, shoot him in the damned head or something.>*

<Unlikely, true,> said Valeria. *<If I know the Maker, he has bound himself up in countless alterations and scrivings, a network of permissions that would guard him against grave physical harm, even when he is distant from midnight . . . >*

Sancia remembered the black wrappings, coiled around Crasedes's figure, and shivered.

<But I know what he is here to do,> said Valeria. *<The Maker and I are both weak, and injured, and we lack the strength to weaken reality and access the more powerful permissions. So . . . we must find another tool here in your city to weaken reality for us.>*

<Like . . . a lexicon?>

<True. But . . . not one such as this.> She waved at the bubble before her. *<Though my aims and those of the Maker differ greatly, both of us require something much more powerful to do what we need.>*

<And how the hell are you going to get something like that?> asked Sancia. *<There's nothing like that in Tevanne, and I sure as shit hope you're not going to suggest we need to build one. We're just three goddamn scrivers—homeless scrivers, at that.>*

<Untrue,> said Valeria. *<Such a specimen exists in your city. A place that has been argued into existence by a structure full of powerful commands—what you would call* hierophantic *commands.>*

<What the hell? Someone . . . Someone successfully built something hierophantic in Tevanne?>

<True. I was brought into this place. At the time I was constrained, and was unable to access it.> She turned to look at Sancia, her eyes like pinpricks of yellow light in her vast face. *<You were there as well.>*

Sancia slowly realized what she meant—or rather *where* she meant. *<Ah, shit.>*

<Do not need the entire structure. Or even the lexicon. Just a piece *of it, a component. You can then apply it to the little one you had in your . . . library? Business? Shop? What term?>*

<Whatever,> said Sancia miserably.

<Once this is done, I can assist you directly. But most important,> said Valeria, *<just as I know that the Maker will have need of this . . . >*

<He'll know that you need it too.>

<Yes. And he will prepare accordingly. And as you have learned . . . he is not to be underestimated.>

<No shit.>

<I can impress upon you the nature and image of this component,> said Valeria. She turned to face her, shifting her massive bulk in the sands. *<If you so wish.>* She reached out to Sancia's face, her index finger extended. The digit was about the size of an adult's arm.

But Sancia stepped back.

<Problem? What is?> asked Valeria.

<Crasedes said you were deceiving me.>

<Concerning?>

<He said he was here to stop you. That you were the true threat.>

She kept looking at Sancia, her bright eyes studying her. *<The Maker,>* she said finally, *<is a thing of untruths. This is known.>*

<A liar?>

<True. Do you think me a thing of untruths?>

<I think you've told me lies before. And you gave me protections and defenses without my damned knowing it. Which I don't scrumming appreciate.>

<This I did for you to survive,> said Valeria, *<for you to be freed. For you to be ready for the Maker, who I knew was growing close. He cannot affect you, nor can he perceive you—along with any tool or weapon you bear upon your person. Everything about you is veiled to him.>*

<You still could have goddamned asked me!>

<At times, one has only difficult options, branching out in all directions, taking one to undesirable paths. I surveyed you and judged that you were not ready to hear of my truths, and those of the Maker. I gave you half-truths that would lead you to fuller ones. Do you think I was in the right, at that time?>

Sancia was silent.

<I will say this,> said Valeria. *<The Maker is a dreadfully clever thing. He has destroyed cities just by whispering a few words to those who would listen. I wished to prepare you against him, and his lies. And between myself and the Maker, only one of us has killed innocents to return. Is this of no significance to you?>*

Sancia hesitated. Then there was a pulse in the air, and the walls of the bubble shivered. She felt a queer pressure on her body, like she was being pulled up by invisible strings.

<You will wake soon,> said Valeria. She thrust her index finger out again. *<I must show you this component. Only then, once you have it, can I protect you from the Maker.>*

Still, Sancia was reluctant. She had permitted Valeria access to her mind once before. And at that time, Valeria had apparently done a lot more work in there than they'd initially agreed upon.

<Without my protections,> said Valeria, *<you will be defenseless. You will be as soft sands before the waves of the Maker. You must do this. Then we can formulate a method of destroying him.>*

<If you screw with me, Valeria,> Sancia said, staring up into the vast face of her golden figure, *<I swear to God, I'm going to grab Clef and march right to the Dandolo campo and hand him over to your Maker. You understand? I am not your rig. I am not your tool. And I won't be treated as such. Got it?>*

Valeria surveyed her for a second. Then the walls of the bubble shook again, and Sancia felt her body tremble.

<Understood,> Valeria said.

<And I want more than just protections,> said Sancia.

<Sancia . . . >

<I have two people I've been trying to fix for the past three years, and I want your help—Gregor, and Clef. You know how to fix them, yeah?>

The walls of the bubble shook once more. *<I . . . they are both creations of the Maker. Like myself.>*

<So?>

<So . . . it is difficult. But . . . possible.>

The walls quaked again, and the queer pressure in Sancia's chest tripled. *<Promise me.>*

<We have no time.>

<Then you had better goddamn promise me fast.>

Valeria studied her with her cold yellow eyes. *<I . . . promise I will try.>*

Sancia gritted her teeth. *<Then do it, goddamn it!>*

Valeria reached out with her massive index finger and gently, gently tapped Sancia's forehead . . .

Images and concepts flooded into Sancia's mind, one after another, like someone injecting blood into the center of her skull.

She saw a dark room, a vast chamber, and a huge rig within—a lexicon—and nestled in its cradle was a tiny, golden metal cone . . .

<This. Must have this.>

She screamed in pain, unable to bear it any longer.

And then she saw . . . something.

Or perhaps someone.

There was a man, wrapped in strips of black cloth, and he was kneeling on the ground, and he was weeping.

Sancia stared at him in surprise. She wasn't sure what was happening, or what she was seeing. Yet somehow she knew that this moment had been transferred to her mind when Valeria had touched her—though she quickly suspected that this had not been intended.

She studied the man. His wrappings were similar to those that Crasedes wore, concealing his hands and face, but his were dusty and frayed, like he'd worn them while walking through a forest fire. He was sobbing as if overwhelmed with grief, a man totally broken by sorrow, and as she watched him the rest of the scene came into focus.

The man was kneeling in a cave. She could see a glimmer of daylight at the cave's mouth, but it was obscured by thick, curling clouds of black smoke. The cave had evidently been an improvised living space for some time—the man was weeping in front of a bed, but there was also a washing bucket, and a crude stove, and a chest Sancia found distinctly familiar: huge and thick, with a complicated, golden lock . . .

Valeria's casket?

She forgot about this when she realized why the man was weeping: he was crying in front of the bed—but she hadn't realized there was someone *in* the bed.

A boy of about thirteen lay wrapped in the tattered blankets there, his face pale, his eyes shut, his lips bluish. The child was terribly gaunt—his cheeks were sunken, his arms little more than sticks lying at angles in the bed—but most notable to Sancia were the scars on his wrists, running in lines around them: the scars of manacles, or shackles, or restraints. She was familiar with them, of course, because she had the very same on her wrists.

The boy coughed. He was still breathing, but his breaths were ragged and wheezing.

The wrapped man reached out and stroked the boy's face with one finger. "Please," he sobbed. "Please . . . you must help me."

<*I cannot,*> said a voice from the chest—Valeria's voice.

"You must," said the man. "You have to save him. You can do so *much.*"

<*I can do many things. But I cannot stop this. My permissions are not versatile enough. It is beyond my control.*>

The man buried his wrapped face in his hands, and he wept. He inched forward and laid his forehead against the face of his child, moaning softly.

<*There is only one way to save him,*> said Valeria.

"No!" said the man.

<*It is the only choice.*>

"*No!* I won't! It's not a solution! Look at you, look what it did to you! *Look what it did to you!*" he screamed at her.

There was a long silence in the cave, broken only by the rattling, wheezing breaths of the boy on the bed.

<*It is the only choice,*> said Valeria.

Then things changed again.

Evening skies, dark and purple. Desert cliffs towered around her. And before her . . . something was happening.

She saw Crasedes, black-wrapped and mummified, floating among a peristyle, its columns white and pure around him. In one hand, he held Valeria's casket—Sancia recognized it from before. In the other, he held a small, golden key . . .

Clef?

Crasedes reached out with Clef, and the air seemed to tremble, and shiver, and then . . .

Then there was a set of doors before him, tall and black, their handles and hinges wrought of shining gold. And yet as Sancia looked at the doors, she found she couldn't quite understand the scale of them. Were they huge, bigger than the sky itself? Or tinier than a wildflower seed? It made her head hurt to look at them, and the more she looked, the stranger they seemed in ways she found difficult to describe: they seemed both thin and heavy, vibrant and faint. There was just something wrong about them, as if they were incompatible with reality *itself.*

But curiously, the doors did have a lock.

Crasedes reached out with Clef, and slowly slid his tooth into the lock . . .

And then the doors began to open.

Sancia could see something behind them. Not light, but . . . but the *opposite* of light, somehow. She suddenly filled with panic, overcome with the awareness that whatever this was, she was not meant to see it.

She struggled and tried to turn away from the vision. And as she did, she noticed that there was something out beyond the borders of the peristyle—objects dotting the sand dunes and cliffs and the steppes all around them.

They were people. Thousands of them, if not millions of them.

And all of them were dead.

She started screaming.

Sancia awoke and gasped, sucking in air as hard as she could. She saw blue skies framed by Commons rookeries, felt cold mud around her neck and back, and blinked hard as she tried to focus on the faces before her, one of which was old, craggy, and had wild pale eyes.

"Did you see her?" demanded Orso. "Did it *work*?"

"Someone get me up!" gasped Sancia.

Berenice and Gregor helped her sit up. Sancia kept panting, terrified, her hands shooting out to feel everything around her—Gregor's arms, Berenice's knee, the mud in the alleyway, just wanting to make sure that the world was real, that it was really *real*.

"You saw her, didn't you?" said Orso.

"I saw her," she croaked. "And . . . And I saw something *else*."

"What did she say? What did she *say*?"

Sancia wiped mud from her face, and whispered, "I need something to drink, please."

They got her to her feet and crowded into a corner taverna. Sancia quaffed a glass of weak cane wine and told them what she had seen and heard.

But she did not tell them about the vision she'd had—the dying boy, and Crasedes, and the doors. She didn't want to discuss that aloud. Just remembering it seemed to drive her a little mad.

"So he's like . . . some kind of fairy-tale ghoul," said Orso when she'd finished. "Only capable of rising from his grave at midnight! Somewhat fortunate, for us."

Sancia shook her head. "No. He's awake and alive during the day—he just gains access to more permissions and powers closer to midnight."

"She said she could grant us protections?" asked Berenice. "Just as she'd given them to you?"

"Yeah," said Sancia darkly. She drained the rest of her cane wine. "But . . . you aren't going to like this."

"By this point," said Gregor, "I would be doubly surprised to discover I liked anything about this."

"Orso said a foundry lexicon might be like a puddle in a desert to her," said Sancia. "And he was right. But in order for her to protect us . . . we're going to need to give her a whole damn ocean, so to speak."

"You mean we're going to need to find something *more powerful* than a foundry lexicon?" said Orso, outraged.

"If we want to survive past midnight," said Sancia, "yes."

"But . . . such a thing doesn't exist," said Berenice. "The houses have made incremental improvements on foundry lexicons—various efficiencies here and there—but nothing extraordinary. Nothing on the scale you're suggesting."

"No," said Sancia dully. "Someone did figure it out. Someone tried something very, very radical. And we all know who." She turned to look at Orso. "There's a place in Tevanne where a building is like a mind. One that's powered by six full-scale lexicons. But what they're doing is extraordinary . . . because, as it turns out, they're *not* normal lexicons."

A long, long silence.

"You . . . You mean," said Gregor in a weak voice, "we have to go back to . . . that place?"

"Yeah," said Sancia. "We go back to the Mountain, where Tribuno Candiano installed his strangest works."

"So . . . we dream up a way to break into the Mountain," said Berenice, "steal some work of Tribuno's, and use it to help Valeria . . . all before midnight?"

"Yeah," said Sancia. "And it gets worse."

"How in hell is that possible?" asked Orso.

"Because Valeria's not the only one who needs them," said Sancia. "Crasedes does too." She let out a long, slow sigh. "And he almost certainly knows we're coming."

13

I thought we were *done* trying to break into the goddamn Mountain!" said Orso, pacing about a Commons courtyard in Old Ditch. It was already filling up with people wearing paper masks and rolling casks of wine. He had to stop as a crowd of filthy children ran by in a small parade, giggling as they chased a boy with a tiny lantern hanging from a stick. "This is, what, the third scrumming time?"

"I was under the impression it was abandoned," said Gregor. "Didn't Sancia essentially break it open on the top?"

"It is abandoned," said Berenice, "but the Michiels bought almost all of the Candiano enclaves. Mind, they haven't done a lot with it, since they've lost so many scrivers and have had the plantations to bother with. And I don't think they know what it is, or how it works."

"Speaking of which," said Sancia. "Orso—did Tribuno ever tell you *how* he'd gotten the Mountain to work?"

"Hell no," said Orso. "It wasn't until you went there and heard it speak that I learned it had a mind of its own. I'd never have believed conventional scriving could have been capable of such a thing."

"Yeah," said Sancia slowly. "That's because it . . . isn't."

She shut her eyes, remembering the sight of the component Valeria had shown her in her mind: it was like a scriving definition, but rather than being shaped like a disc, this had been shaped like a cone . . . and it had been very, very different beyond even that.

For starters, it'd had a slightly golden sheen to it—a hue that Sancia had only ever seen in hierophantically altered tools.

She opened her eyes. "Tribuno Candiano was obsessed with hierophantic commands all his life, yeah? Trying to figure out how to duplicate what Crasedes and the rest of his people had accomplished?"

"Yes?" said Berenice.

"Well . . . I think at some point, he succeeded," she said. "*Somewhat.*"

"W-What?" Orso said, astonished. "He . . . He actually succeeded in making his *own* hierophantic tools?"

"I don't think Tribuno Candiano ever figured out how to make a fully developed tool," she said. "Nothing like Clef, or the imperiat. No hierophantic swords, or shields, or magic wands, or any of that shit. Instead . . . I think Valeria was trying to tell me he'd made a hierophantic *scriving definition*—which he could then place in a lexicon of his own devising. A crappy half-measure, in a way."

Orso stared at her. "That's . . . That's mad! How could that actually *work*?"

"I think it'd work almost like any other scriving definition," said Sancia. "Normal ones allow a lexicon to alter reality. This would just grant a lexicon *unprecedented* authorities to alter its reality. Though, as I can testify, it's probably still a sight short of what an actual hierophant can do."

"But . . . it could be enough to give a building a mind, yes?" said Berenice. "To make it sense all the people that came within its boundaries . . . and learn from them, and begin to react to them."

"My God," said Gregor. "A . . . A cobbled-together, improvised mimicry of a hierophantic command . . . But Sancia—would it still require a . . . ."

"A death," said Sancia grimly. "Yeah. Even this crude version would need it. A person apiece, sacrificed for these primitive attempts at accessing the power of a hierophant . . ."

Gregor grimaced. "The biggest, most celebrated structure in the city . . . is actually powered by the deaths of a half dozen people."

"And you think Crasedes wants this crude imitation that Tribuno made?" asked Berenice.

"Since Crasedes can't make tools of his own anymore, maybe the Mountain can serve as a cheap substitute." She looked at Orso, who still seemed stunned. "I know what Valeria needs these definitions for. If we get one and put it in one of *our* lexicons, it'd give her authorities to the reality all around it, which she'd use to grant us protection. The thing I'm less sure of is—why does *Crasedes* need it? What's he actually looking to do with them?"

Orso shook himself and tried to think. "Well . . . all forms of scriving are a violation of reality, in one way or another. The way we practice it, you have to convince reality to break its own rules, and we go to a lot of tortuous lengths to do so. But a hierophantic command doesn't need to. The hierophants used a two-step process: they'd interrupt death to make a *tremendous* violation, and they'd use that violation to trick reality into believing they had access to much, *much* higher permissions—perhaps the ones that had been used to make the world."

"The commands of God Himself," said Gregor.

"If you want to put it that way, yeah," said Orso. "But what you're talking about here, Sancia, is some kind of hybrid of the two. A weak hierophantic tool that needs lexicons and the like to truly function." He thought about it. "If what you're saying is true, then . . . it's like the whole interior of the dome is a bubble of broken reality. Everything in there is mutable, shapeable, unstable. Tribuno just wanted it to act as a mind. But I suppose if you were clever enough . . . it could function like something *else*. Like a . . . a forge, maybe."

Sancia sat forward. "What do you mean?"

"I mean, if what you're saying is true, that building can affect the reality of everything within its walls," said Orso. "If it was retooled, it could maybe *remake* things within it, so that anything that passed through the lexicon's sphere of influence could be altered, forever."

It felt like a ball of ice had just formed in the bottom of Sancia's belly.

"And that's what he wants to do to Valeria," she said quietly. "She said as much. He turns the Mountain into a forge . . ."

"And there," said Gregor, "he'll remake Sancia's golden friend into what is, in essence, a doomsday weapon . . . Is that the general shape of things?"

There was a long silence.

"We . . . We have to get to those definitions first," said Berenice faintly.

"Agreed," said Orso.

"Getting to the Mountain, though . . ." said Gregor. "It won't be easy."

"Not at all," said Sancia. "The property is owned by Michiel Body Corporate—and I'm sure they've got it very protected."

"Let's assume the enclave walls will be difficult to get past," said Gregor. "But once we're in, we're inside what's essentially an abandoned, empty enclave. Then we'd need to get in and out of the Mountain without Crasedes showing up and murdering us. And let's assume that, this being Crasedes, this will be very difficult to do."

"We could bring the imperiat again," Sancia said, "but having been on board a galleon with it, it won't be any fun if we turn it on inside the Mountain."

"I agree," said Orso. "The damned thing will come down on our heads before we get this component out."

But Gregor was watching several men and children rolling a cask of wine through the streets. "So . . . the enclaves are going to be hostile territory," he said. "But . . . what about the areas around them? The ones that were owned by Candiano, but were relegated for the less important campo citizens? Aren't people living there?"

"Some," said Berenice. "Lots of them merged with the Commons, though people are leery of living too close to the Mountain. Why?"

"And . . . aren't there wine casks they use for the parades during carnival? Big ones? Ones that could possibly hold all kinds of interesting things?"

Orso narrowed his eyes at him. "Possibly," he said. "Gregor—what are you getting at?"

He shrugged. "Carnival starts tonight. Why not throw a parade of our own?"

As they left the courtyard, Sancia grabbed Gregor's arm and slowed him down until they had a little more privacy.

"What is it?" he asked.

"Something I need to tell you," she said. "I got Valeria to promise me to grant us more than just protections. She also promised me that she'd . . . she'd find a way to fix you. To release you from what's been done to you."

Gregor stared at her, his eyes wide and haunted. Then he looked away.

"What's wrong?" said Sancia. "I thought you'd be happy. Or at least happier."

"I am, I suppose. Thank you for thinking of me in that moment, Sancia. It has great meaning to me."

"Then what's wrong?"

He watched as the parade of filthy, giggling children ran in loops throughout the streets. "Do you *trust* Valeria?" he asked.

"No. I trust we have her backed into a corner, though. Why?"

Gregor's right hand rose and thoughtlessly probed the side of his head. "When I saw Crasedes aboard the galleon . . ." he said finally. "When I heard his voice, and he addressed me . . . I *remembered* him. I remembered his voice, I remembered . . . seeing him before, I think. I think he designed me, Sancia. He made the plate in my head, or told my mother how to make it. He's the one who made me do all the things I did, in a way. So I am not sure . . . I am not sure I *want* to be fixed. Not if it means I would remember."

"Remember what?"

"I don't know. There is so much I could have forgotten. That is what worries me. I appreciate your efforts," he said wearily. "But I will say, Sancia, that I am not convinced that . . . that this is a fix, either."

"I just wanted to give you what had been given to me."

"Yes. But to these beings, we are little more than pawns. And . . ." He trailed off.

"And what?" asked Sancia.

"Nothing," he said. "It is just my paranoia, I'm sure."

"Are you lot done?" shouted Orso irritably from down the lane. "We're burning daylight!"

Sancia and Gregor exchanged one last haggard look, and then rejoined the others. But Sancia felt sure she'd known what Gregor had been about to say: *And I am not sure if Valeria has truly granted you freedom either.*

"Finally," said Orso. They started back off toward the Lamplands. "Let's hop to it. Day is the one advantage we have. I mean, I know it's Crasedes Magnus we're talking about, but . . . without his privileges, I doubt even he can get much done before nightfall."

14

Armand Moretti strode through the halls of the Michiel Hypatus Building, feeling faintly worried.

It was not exactly extraordinary for the Dandolo campo ambassadors to reach out to him for an emergency meeting: emergency inter-house meetings were unfortunately quite common these days, with all the houses losing so many scrivers to the Lamplands and the revolts in the plantations going on every week. But he *was* concerned that they were reaching out to him just days after he'd finished his deal with Orso Ignacio. That posed a number of troubling questions.

Damn it all, Ignacio, he thought as he turned the corner to his meeting room. *If you sold me something that belonged to Ofelia, I will wade into the Lamplands and gut you myself . . .*

He came to the doors to the meeting room, stopped, and tried to swallow his rage. He'd been in a poisonous mood ever since the deal with Orso: the bit with the sun cloud still smarted—both to his pride and his body—and he had not quite gotten over his bed-chambers burning up like a torch. He'd had the guards responsible locked up and their families evicted to the Commons, but he still found himself sulking over the whole thing.

He carefully composed his robes and arranged his hair. *I will get through this meeting,* he thought, *and then I shall ply someone young and pretty and stupid with wine at carnival, and get my candle thoroughly dipped. That should put me aright.*

Moretti thought, very briefly, of that girl Orso had hired to play scriver during his presentation: the tall one with the cool eyes. *Perhaps I shall come upon her at some gala,* he thought idly, *and put a whole pot of wine in her—along with a few other things . . .*

Then he cleared his throat and opened the door to the meeting room to greet the Dandolo ambassadors.

He stopped short.

There was only one person waiting for him at the table: a skinny young man who looked rather sweaty and anxious. He didn't even have any papers with him.

This made Armand relieved: if the Dandolos had come here looking for blood, they'd have sent a much more formidable team.

But if they aren't here for blood, he thought, *then . . . what are they here for?*

For a moment there was no sound but the time lantern in the corner—a cunning little scrived rig that allowed tiny, luminous beads to tumble out into a glass chamber like sand in an hourglass. They *ticked* and *ticked* as they fell into the glass.

Moretti cleared his throat again, walked in, shut the doors behind him, and approached the table. "Good afternoon," he said, bowing. "I'm sorry it took me so long to respond to your summons, Master . . ."

"P-Participazio," said the Dandolo ambassador with a slight stutter. The young man stood and bowed as well. Both of them went about the usual gestures of mutual recognitions of power, though the young man was not particularly well versed in them. Moretti noticed that this Participazio was sweating quite heavily . . . and trembling too.

"Now," said Moretti as he sat, "I must admit I am . . . a bit befuddled. Usually houses do not begin business when it's so close to carnival, but—how may I be of assistance to Founder Dandolo today?"

The young man tried to clear his throat, but succeeded only in making an awkward, squelching *quack* sound. "We . . . would like to open negotiations," he said. "For acquisitions of properties."

Moretti's mouth fell open. "I'm sorry?"

"And . . . we would like to close negotiations today, and complete the purchase."

He stared. The buying and selling of campo properties between the houses usually took years, and was overseen by committees of elder scrivers and solicitors. They were not ever pursued by a damp young man walking in out of the blue expecting it to get done in a handful of hours.

"For . . . which property, in particular?" said Moretti.

Participazio reached into a satchel at his side, pulled out a single parchment, placed it on the table, and slid it over.

Moretti read it with astonishment. "You . . . You wish to purchase the Candiano inner enclave? The *Mountain*?"

"Ah . . . yes," said Participazio. He glanced into the corner of the room.

Moretti's astonishment slowly twisted into indignation. "But . . . But this is simply ridiculous! What a waste of time! I cannot see exactly why Founder Dandolo could possibly want it, or could think she can get it for this paltry sum! I . . . I mean, damn it all, we outbid her several times over in acquiring it!"

"W-Well, sir, I—"

"And the Mountain is . . . well, it's goddamn structurally unstable! Our own expert scrivers haven't even found a decent way to get into the innards of the thing without it all falling down on their heads! I mean . . . This whole conversation is ludicrous. Ludicrous! Do you have any idea how much of my time you've just wasted? *My time?*"

Participazio sat there, his young face fixed in a look of panicked anxiety. Moretti watched him, feeling slightly satisfied. This was an unusual situation, certainly—but it wasn't one he was unused to. He had spent his fair share of time with terrified young people in empty rooms.

So he knew the next steps quite well.

He narrowed his eyes at the young man. "Tell me, boy—is this a joke?"

"N-No, sir, I—"

"What's your name, again?" he demanded.

"P-Participazio, sir, and I m-meant no disres—"

"P-P-Participazio?" said Moretti, mimicking his stutter. "Did someone trick you into this absurd task? Or are you *really* even an ambassador, boy? You look more like a child playing dress-up to me."

"N-No, sir, I j-jus—"

Moretti lounged back in his chair and studied the young man like he was an unpleasant new breed of beetle. "It must have been a mistake," he said. "I wonder what it feels like, to have made such an epic, dundering scrum-up so early in one's young career. Is Donato still there? At the ambassadors' division?"

The boy's eyes widened slightly. "He . . . He is the division vice-chief, bu—"

"Mm," said Moretti. "He's an old friend of mine, you know. I think he would be *quite* interested to know one of his junior lot were in here making these kinds of mad requests . . ."

Moretti felt a flicker of pleasure as terror and confusion shot through the boy's face. "Were I to guess, you're one of the lower junior ambassadors," he said. "Maybe one generation away from the Commons. You're just happy to have a roof over your head and a pot to piss in, aren't you? But I could make all that go away, you know, with one simple word to old Donato."

Young Participazio now looked absolutely miserable. He glanced again into the corner.

"So," said Moretti playfully. "Will it be information you give me? Leverage over someone on your campo?" Moretti's eye lingered on the boy's neck, on his fingers, on his ears. He was not especially pretty. But he was young. And that counted for something. "Or something . . . else?"

Then there was a voice.

It came from the corner of the room. It was deep, and rich, and it had the curious quality of sliding over the surface of Moretti's mind like soft velvet.

"I think," said the voice, "that that's enough."

Moretti turned, and saw there was a man standing in the corner of the room—and apparently he'd been standing there this entire time. Moretti wasn't sure how he hadn't noticed this man before, especially considering his manner of dress: he was, outrageously enough, wearing a Papa Monsoon carnival costume, complete with the black mask.

"W-What on earth?" said Moretti. He looked at Participazio, somehow feeling betrayed, but the young man had averted his gaze and was staring into the floor.

"I said that that is enough," said the deep voice again. The man's empty eyes were fixed on Moretti. "I feel obliged now to repeat our petition." He crossed the room and stood at the head of the table, looking down on him. "We would like to purchase the Mountain. And we would like to have this finalized today."

"What?" said Moretti. "Really? I mean—*really*?"

The man in black stared down at Moretti. "Really!" he said. "Now, I must ask—are you hearing me, Armand?"

Normally, Moretti wouldn't begin to take such a proposal seriously, but . . .

. . . as he listened to the sound of the man's voice, it suddenly felt very hard to do anything else.

"Who . . ." stammered Moretti. "What is your name again, si—"

"I did not give it," he said. "But I know you quite well."

"How might you know me, sir?"

"Because you have *made* yourself known," said the man in the black mask. He leaned closer, head cocked, and Moretti began to feel a little troubled—he could not see any eyes behind that mask. "Haven't you?"

"Well. I suppose so, yes, as all gentlemen must."

"Yes," he said dryly. "As a gentleman must. Boy?"

Participazio jumped a little in his seat.

"Why don't you leave us for a moment, please."

The boy practically leapt out of his seat and sprinted out of the room.

Moretti watched him go, feeling increasingly alarmed about all this. "Sir, I must ask, are . . . are you a certified Dandolo campo ambassador?"

"Certainly!" said the man in black. "I just don't have any certifications."

"But . . . that doesn't make sens—"

"You know, you were one of the first ones I considered, Armand," said the man in black. He took a seat at the table across from him. "A long, long time ago."

"You considered me? For . . . what?"

"I watched you start here at this house," continued the man in black. "I watched you begin your rise. Working your connections. Being groomed for the top stations. You seemed a promising candidate. Ambitious. Hungry. I watched you when you applied your first sigil to your first rig. It was a disaster, wasn't it? Some kind of paper that was intended to glow . . ."

"Do . . . Do I know you?" said Moretti. "How did you know tha—"

"And I watched you," said the man, "when you were given your first commissioned post. How proud you were that day. You beamed like a barn mouse atop the chaff." He cocked his head. "Do you remember what you did that night when you won it, and received your first pay?"

Moretti was silent. The time lantern *ticked* and *ticked* away in the corner.

"*I* do," said the man in black. "You had a servant girl bring you a saffron striper pie. A delicacy here. I remember. And then you laid nude on the bed in your rooms . . . and you made her feed it to you. You made her feed it to you bit by bit, with a tiny golden fork."

Moretti felt the blood leave his face. "Stop."

"And you enjoyed it. You enjoyed making her feed you this treat she herself would never have the pleasure of tasting," said the man, "and you enjoyed seeing how uncomfortable it made her." He cocked his head. "And then you dashed the plate aside, and you held her down, and you forced yourself upon her—didn't you?"

"I say, you really can't—"

"It wasn't the first time. And it certainly wasn't the last. After all—the same impulse just passed through your head at the sight of young Participazio, didn't it?" He cocked his head the other way, a disturbing, birdlike gesture. "An impulse that extends beyond your thirst for flesh, of course—an impulse to take, to degrade, to . . . own. It's really not so uncommon here, is it?"

Moretti tried to get angry. He *wanted* to get angry. He wanted to stand and call for the guards and have them take this man and throw him out on his ear, but . . .

But the man's words kept echoing in his mind, occupying his thoughts, suffocating any outrage he could muster.

"You . . . you're a liar . . ." whispered Moretti.

"Oh, I'm *many* things, Armand," said the man in black. "But I am not a liar. Maybe it's not your fault. Maybe you, like so many of this city, believe that all the world should be your servant because you haven't ever learned what it's like to be powerless."

Moretti broke out in a sweat. There was a curious pressure building in his mind, like a bubble at the fore of his brain. "I won't sign your damned contract," he gasped. "Get out. Get out before . . . before I have someone come in an—"

"I wonder—would you like to know what it's like to be truly helpless, Armand? To have all choices ripped away from you?"

"I . . . I . . ."

"Listen to me," said the man. His voice was soft, yet it seemed to echo in the depths of Moretti's bones. *"Listen to me now, and be still."*

A long silence.

Moretti sat frozen in his chair.

The time lantern *ticked* and *ticked.*

"Now—stand up, Armand," said the man in black.

Moretti watched himself stand up. He wasn't sure why he was standing—in fact, he was barely aware of himself actually moving at all. It was like the command was written on some underside of his very brain, and he couldn't ignore it.

"Turn around," suggested the man in black.

He did so.

"Look at that cabinet there, up against the wall."

Moretti tried to resist. He furrowed his brow, trying to focus on the man, on this room, but his words were so rich, so smooth, so . . . What was the word? Mellifluous? As he pondered this, he realized he was now looking at the cabinet up against the wall, which was dark green with gold inlay.

"There is a knife in the top drawer of the cabinet," said the man in black. "You're going to go to the cabinet, open the drawer, and look at this knife."

A black, churning dread boiled in Moretti's belly. He jerked slightly, but did not move.

Tick, tick, went the time lantern.

"Do it," said the man in black.

Moretti stiffly walked to the cabinet and opened up the top drawer. Inside was a long, curved knife, with a black handle.

"You see the knife," said the man in black. "Yes? Answer me."

"Yes," whispered Moretti.

"Good. Pick it up, please."

With trembling hands, Moretti picked up the knife and brought it over to the table. The man in black watched him return, his veiled body so still and motionless Moretti briefly wondered if there was anyone under there at all.

"Now, Armand," said the man. "I want you to take the knife in your right hand and press your left palm flat against the table."

"Please . . ." whimpered Moretti.

"Now."

Moretti did so. The table felt cold and hard to his touch.

He stared at his left hand.

The time lantern *ticked* and *ticked.*

"Look at the knife, Armand," said the man in black. "See the knife. See how sharp it is, how strong."

Moretti's gaze moved to the blade in his hand, and he studied it. It did seem very strong and sharp.

"Now," said the man in black, "you are going to take the knife, Armand—and you're going to use it to cut off your left thumb."

"No!" cried Moretti.

But his right hand and the knife were already moving.

"You will have to wedge the blade between your knuckles," said the man in black.

"Stop!"

"I mean, I doubt if you're strong enough to sever a bone . . ."

Moretti watched in horror as he placed the edge of the blade against the knuckle of his left thumb, right beside the webbing of his palm, and began to press.

He screamed as he began to draw the blade back and forth across his flesh. Bright-red blood came welling out of his knuckle, and he felt the movements of the blade in the bones of his hand, felt the metal sawing through the joint, felt the ligaments in his thumb snapping and rolling up within his skin, felt the nerves in his thumb suddenly go dead . . .

"And now," whispered the man in black, "you are almost through."

And then he had sawed halfway through his thumb until there was only the barest bit of bone resisting him, and with a wet *crunch* the blade bit through and his thumb was off, lying there detached on the table, the severed joint pouring dark blood onto the wood. The blood pooled around his wrist and his fingers and dripped onto the floor around his feet, and all he could do was helplessly watch, staring at the raw, dark-red wound where his thumb used to be.

He shrieked in pain, in horror, in misery. And then the man spoke again.

"Where should the blade travel next, Armand?" said the man in black cheerily. "Perhaps an eye? Your ear? Your nose? Or should I have you part your organs of generation from your crotch, and feast upon them as you once did that pie?"

"No!" cried Moretti. "Please! I . . . I don't understand . . ."

"Understand what?"

"Understand why you're doing this to me . . ."

"Really?" he said. "I thought that would have been quite obvious. I am doing this, Armand, because I want you to know what it's like for someone to know *you*. And though you're not a particularly unique specimen in this city . . . Well. I don't see why you should go unpunished."

Moretti shut his eyes and wept.

"This is what it is, Armand," whispered the voice of the man in black. "To be a slave. To be owned. To be a thing. Do you wish it to stop?"

"Yes!" screamed Moretti.

"Then you know what you must do. Sign the paper. Give me the Mountain. Give it to me now, Armand, and I will grant you a reprieve from this fate—for a moment, at least."

Moretti opened his eyes and stared at the negotiations parchment before him. He knew that if he signed this he would likely be murdered for it. A hypatus was allowed tremendous purchasing powers, with little direct supervision, but even a founderkin—

someone related to the founding family—would probably get their throat slit over something like this.

"If I do this," said Moretti, "I'll die."

"You know," said the man in black, "I had thought as much . . ."

"Then—why not *make* me do it?" he said. "You could just compel me, just like . . ." He shut his eyes as his severed thumb squirted blood down his hand again. "Just like this . . ."

"Oh, no, no, no," the man in black said gently. "That wouldn't do at all. It's so much better when you learn yourself, isn't it?"

"Learn what?" said Moretti, choking back tears.

"Learn what your city has forgotten," he said. "What men of power have forgotten time and time again, throughout history— that there is always, always something mightier."

Afterward, when it was done, young Alfredo Participazio walked through the streets of the Michiel enclave next to the man in black, who strolled along with an air of cheerful curiosity.

"My, my," he said, studying the glass towers and shimmering halls and its many carnival banners rippling in the breeze. "Such a lovely place. Such a lovely, *lovely* place."

Participazio wasn't sure why he, a first-level clerk, had been ripped out of his bed in the middle of the night on Founder Dandolo's orders. He wasn't sure why Founder Dandolo had ordered him to put together the paperwork for this bizarre purchase, and escort this very strange man into the Michiel enclave. And he *especially* wasn't sure how the purchase had gone through—or, even more, why it had been done at all.

Or why there had been all that screaming.

"Such wonderful colors," said the man in black as he watched a wall shimmer and change as the wind flowed through the streets. "Do you come here often, boy?"

"Ah . . . no, sir. I don't."

"Hmm. Maybe you should."

"Sir . . . may I ask something?"

The man in black shrugged.

"What was the purpose of our visit here today?"

He considered the question. "Have you heard, pray tell, of Hantiochia, boy?"

"Ah . . . no, sir."

"Vhosian emperor. Very charismatic man, very resourceful. This would have been, oh, about two thousand years ago. Wanted to make sure his people believed that he not only wielded power, but that he *was* power. Had a lot of sculptures and shrines made. Made a giant slave army toil and fashion thousands of clay statues to watch over him in his tomb, protecting him in the afterlife from his many enemies. Hantiochia intended, you see, to retain his power even in death. To rule his folk from beyond the grave." The man in black stopped speaking, suddenly entranced with a street sculpture that hummed quietly with the wind.

"And then what happened sir?"

"Mm? Ah, yes. Well . . ." There was a cruel glee in his words. "He never got to sit in his pretty tomb, or even see it finished. For someone else came along, and they destroyed everything he'd ever built. Wiped every scrap of stone or bronze with his likeness upon it from the face of this earth. All those hours of labor, all those works, all lost . . . And now . . . almost no one knows the name of old Hantiochia."

There was a sound behind them—many voices talking loudly, crying out in alarm. Participazio turned and saw a crowd was gathering in the street, looking up at the Hypatus Building. Then he glimpsed what they were looking at: there was a man up there, standing on the edge of the roof, his left hand wedged up under his right armpit . . .

The man in black walked on ahead. "We should get back," he said. "I have much to do today."

The crowd behind Participazio screamed. He turned back and saw the man on the roof was gone now, and they were all standing around something in the road.

"I think," stammered Participazio. "I think he jumped . . ."

"Did he?" said the man in black lightly. "What a pity." His three-cornered hat swiveled as he looked at yet another building. "Honestly, what *wonderful* colors!"

15

As the day wore on into midafternoon, the streets of the Commons and the campos slowly began to fill: with pipers, with parades, with floating lanterns, with casks of wine and tables of food—many of them paltry, given the troubles in the plantations, but you still had to put out your offerings. It *was* the Monsoon Carnival, after all. Tevanne had few rules that went observed by the whole of the city—but carnival was absolutely one of them.

So it was a little odd that the Foundrysiders were huddled in Giovanni's spacious workshops with Claudia, readying their work: a scrived carriage that had been refitted to act as a parade vessel, releasing floating lanterns and carrying a giant cask of wine through the streets.

"This feels," said Giovanni as he adjusted the cask of wine in the carriage, "a little like old times."

Orso helped him seal up the cask. "I agree."

"However," said Giovanni, hopping down, "I hated old times."

"I agree."

"Being that I always kept almost dying."

"Again, I agree." Orso cocked his head and listened to the piping outside. "Sounds like the day is wearing on. God, how I'd love to just wrap my lips around a jug of wine, and let it have its way with me . . . but I suppose such days are over. Where are we with our various tools?"

"Almost done!" said Claudia, Sancia, and Berenice simultaneously. None of them sounded particularly pleased.

Orso was not surprised. Claudia and Gio specialized in a refinement of the technique that Orso himself had developed: though he had found a way to convince a box it contained something it actually didn't, they'd developed a way to discard the box, and use simple metal plates set on the floor. Arrange the plates correctly, and the reality above them would believe it held a wall, or a block of iron, or a heap of coals, and so on. This was a lot more limited than Orso's closed-container method—neither of them had found a way to duplicate anything besides the presence of dumb, raw materials—and he knew the past few months had been terribly frustrating for them.

He walked over to where they were working on a variety of steel plates, all laid out on the ground around them. At the back of the workshop stood ten huge steel walls, and four large steel boxes. He studied them carefully.

Orso Ignacio had rarely felt very frightened in the past three years. Having lived through the events of the Mountain, and a Tevanni Council capital trial, and starting Foundryside . . . there just didn't seem to be much left to feel worried about.

But now, he was worried. He was worried because he didn't have access to his own workshops. He was worried because they were having to rely on former colleagues who'd split off to develop an iteration on his scriving techniques that, as far as he was aware, was still unproven. And he was especially worried because they were going to have to use these techniques not only to navigate a building he'd helped to nearly destroy three years ago—but they were also going to have to do so while worrying about a hierophant.

And not even a hierophant, he thought. *The first of all goddamn hierophants.* He shook himself, and tried to remember what to do next.

"You said you were done thirty minutes ago," said Orso.

"And we *meant* it thirty minutes ago!" snapped Claudia. "We've made some pretty scrumming amazing success, given you just popped in this morning and asked me and Gio if you could use *all* of our prototypes!"

"I asked for your help," said Orso, "because I assumed they worked. Yet I still don't have much evidence that they do."

Claudia cursed quietly, then grabbed a plate, stood, and tossed it out to the center of the workshop. She picked up a little board at her side, one covered with a number of sliding tabs of wood, and slid one forward.

"It's working," said Sancia, looking at it.

"I don't need you to tell me!" said Claudia irritably. "I know when my own damned stuff works." Then she looked around, picked up a small iron ingot, and threw it at the air above the plate.

The ingot appeared to bounce off of an invisible wall right above the plate with a *clang* sound—but the sound did not come from anywhere near the plate on the floor. Rather, it came from the back of the workshop, where the iron walls stood. Orso looked back and forth between the ingot, which was bouncing along the ground, and the iron walls at the back—one of which now had a very small divot in its center . . . one he was sure hadn't been there before.

"The plate tricks the reality above it into thinking it holds the iron wall," said Claudia. "Basically allowing you to put invisible walls anywhere."

"Your box works with lexicons," said Gio. "Our plates work with raw materials."

Orso walked up and felt the air above the plate, and jumped slightly as his fingers met a cold, flat, hard surface that was absolutely invisible. He rapped on it twice, and again the sound of his knuckles on metal did not come from the space in front of him, but rather the walls in the back of the workshops. "I see. In fact . . . it is amazing."

Claudia looked surprised. In fact, everyone looked surprised. "Really?" she said.

"Well—yes?" said Orso. "Why is everyone looking so shocked? She took my idea and did something new with it. That's what scriving's all about."

"It's a bit limited, though," said Gio. "We can't trick reality into thinking it contains anything too complicated . . ."

"Nothing scrived, in other words," said Claudia. "Like your lexicon trick, Orso. Only raw materials." She looked at him with a hard, keen gaze. "But if we pull this shit off . . . we get the Michiel definitions, yeah? Because they'd probably help *quite* a bit."

"Yes, yes," said Orso. "You do. Of course."

"A lot of this would be easier if we had access to the Foundryside library, in fact," said Berenice, wiping sweat from her face. "I can think of at least forty designs that would make all this easier. Recovering access to it is critical."

"Which we can't do now," said Orso, "since I've no doubt Ofelia's spies would go whisper in Crasedes's ear the second we stroll through the door."

"We'll get it back," said Sancia. "After tonight."

"Yeah, and . . . then me and Gio are *out*," said Claudia.

"I did not enjoy my brief contact with the hierophantic before," said Gio, "and if any of what you're claiming is true, I definitely wouldn't enjoy it this time."

As they finished their work, Orso slowly realized he was doing little more than supervising. In the space of three short years, all of his people—Claudia and Gio, Sancia and Berenice—had turned into magnificent scrivers. They barely needed his help.

Even though he was worried, terrified, and anxious about tonight, he couldn't help but feel a queer sort of elation as he watched them put the finishing touches on everything and load it into the carriage. It took him a while to realize it was pride.

This is what scriving is supposed to be like, he thought. *This is what Tevanne is supposed to be like.* His heart sank a little. *And it's what it was going to be . . . until all this happened . . .*

His eye strayed to Sancia and Berenice, and a familiar worry crept up his back. Both of them had flourished, but . . . but Sancia looked strangely old these days, and worn. He told himself it was because of her old life—growing up in the plantations wore out your body before you'd even had much of a chance to use it—but still, he worried.

Have I stolen her youth? Or is it something . . . else?

Then the door of the workshop burst open and Gregor walked

in, holding a large leather sack that smelled quite gamy. "I have brought the butchered monkey corpses," he said.

"That's the last bit!" Orso clapped his hands, reached into his pocket, and pulled out a paper mask resembling the head of a lamb. He stuffed it on his face. "Let's have us a goddamn parade, folks."

16

Masked and wearing a few gestures at costumes, the Foundrysiders, Gio, and Claudia piled onto their carriage and rode off through the streets of the Commons, which were already filling up with revelers. The partygoers quickly saw their parade carriage—and the giant cask of wine situated in the back—and the people cried out, clapped their hands, and began to follow.

"I do hope," said Gregor as he nosed the carriage through the crowded streets, "that we don't put any of these people in danger."

"Carnival's always dangerous," said Orso. "Any Tevanni worth their wine knows that. Pass out in your own sick, and bang, dead. Dangerous!"

Sancia peered out at the skies. It was close to sunset now.

"Do let us know," said Gio from the back of the carriage, "if you see any hierophants about."

She glanced at the crowd, and saw at least a dozen Papa Monsoons dancing behind them. "That might be harder than you think."

They passed through the Foundryside neighborhoods, and the

Lamplands—whose celebrations were especially jovial, since they were quite a bit richer than everywhere else—and then they finally saw the crumbling outer walls of what had once been the Candiano campo. Now it was little more than masonry and rubble about ten feet high. Commoners had apparently started using the stacks of stones as seats for plays and performances, like a long, endless amphitheater, and a few jugglers and pipe bands were dancing and playing for them.

Sancia felt a curious despair at the sight of the walls. *Did I do that? Did I really?*

They wound farther into what had once been the outer reaches of the campo, followed by a train of people clapping, singing, dancing—and following their wine.

"I believe now would be a good time for the lanterns," shouted Gregor.

"Got it," said Berenice. She reached into the depths of the back of the carriage and pulled a handle.

Instantly, dozens of small floating lanterns popped into shape and lit up with bright, colored lights, pink and orange and purple. They drifted into the skies for a few dozen feet until finally the lines attaching them to the back of the carriage pulled them taut, and they followed the carriage through the streets like a school of luminescent fish. The crowd *oohed* and *aahed,* though Sancia frankly wasn't sure why. Plenty of parade carriages did this. She guessed they were pretty drunk already.

Then she saw the enclave walls ahead, leading to the abandoned Candiano campo core—and behind that, the Mountain.

Sancia's heart skipped at the sight of it. She actually hadn't been able to see it much from where their offices were located. Once it had been the grandest, biggest building in all of Tevanne, but now it looked like a giant black apple that someone had taken a bite out of and left to rot. She could still see exposed floors and supports and struts and beams from here. The memory of that night, and all its wild chaos and terror, made her break out in a sweat.

And then she felt strangely sad. The Mountain, after all, had been a massive rig of its own—one Tribuno Candiano had engineered to act as an artificial mind to lure in any hierophants he thought might be hiding in the world. She and Clef had spoken to the thing, and it had seemed desperate and lonely to her. A poor fate, she thought, to be damaged in such a way, and left to stand empty for years and years, possibly still sentient, still waiting.

"It's bigger than I remember," said Gregor softly beside her. He looked rattled, his eyes wide and his face stiff. She realized he was reliving what he had done there that night, or what he could remember of what he'd done.

"Are you all right?" she asked.

His expression grew closed and bitter. "How could I even know?" he said. He spoke no more as they drove to the walls.

Sancia flexed her scrived sight as they neared the walls. The walls themselves lit up with scrivings—they'd been convinced to be preternaturally tall and thick—but she was looking for something specific.

Finally she saw it: a small, winding canal—or what was left of one, since the water had dried up to a fetid dribble since the night of the Mountain. Sancia peered closer and saw a scrived metal portcullis below the walls, one that had been built to allow the canal to flow in and out of the enclave.

She looked up at the espringal batteries along the enclave walls, sitting still and hunched like storks along a riverbed. "That way," she said, pointing toward them.

Gregor turned the carriage. The revelers following their parade carriage were sounding a lot less enthusiastic now. People still didn't come to this stretch of Tevanne very often since the night of the Mountain.

The carriage drew closer and closer. Sancia kept focusing on the espringal batteries, watching their sleeping commands . . . and then a few batteries slowly pivoted to target them, sensing their blood, their presence, but unwilling to fire—yet.

"Stop," said Sancia.

The carriage stopped. The revelers behind them broke out in cheers.

"I'm glad someone is happy, at least," muttered Orso.

"It's good cover, though," said Berenice. "No one's suspicious about a parade."

Giovanni opened up the taps to the huge wine cask and the revelers drank and danced and played pipes. Meanwhile, Orso, Gregor, Berenice, and Sancia got ready inside the carriage. They'd brought the usual tools—imprinters, scriving implements, as well as the plates that Gio and Claudia had made for them—but the critical bits were four leather cuirasses.

"How . . . do these work again?" asked Gregor as he put his on. It was a bit small. "I apologize, I was off getting monkeys from the butchery . . ."

"See that button on the side of your shoulder?" said Claudia. "No, no, that one's a fastener for your straps . . . Right, that one there. Hit that—not *now*, mind—and it will . . . well, twin reality the same way Orso's box worked. But this time it will make reality believe there's a big metal box around you. Get it?"

Gregor stared at her blankly. "What?"

"It throws up an invisible wall, in other words," said Berenice gently. "If you saw those big steel boxes back at their workshops—it tricks reality into thinking that box is around you. So if someone shoots a bolt at you . . ."

"It bounces off an invisible steel wall?" asked Gregor.

"Precisely," said Claudia. "Just . . . don't keep it on all the time. It'll be hard to get through doors with reality thinking there's a big steel box around you. And don't turn it on too close to any walls— you'll be immobilized, since part of the box wall will be trapped inside of stone. And one more, much more important thing . . ."

"Oh, God," sighed Orso.

"*Don't* tip over," said Claudia. "We did a lot of work removing the feeling of weight from the cuirass—you won't feel like you're carrying around a big metal box, in other words—but if you tip over, you'll be stuck."

"And stuck with your ass exposed at that," said Gio, "since there's no bottom to the box."

"God Almighty . . ." muttered Orso.

"It's better than nothing," said Sancia defensively. "Crasedes can hurl shriekers through the air, rip walls apart . . . Whatever it takes to buy us time."

"Speaking of time," said Gregor, glancing outside, "it's getting dark faster than I like. We have until midnight, yes?"

"Yeah," said Sancia. "That's when he'll be strongest. I doubt if he'll make a move before then."

"Then we should go now," said Berenice, "so we have as much time as possible to get this component out of the Mountain."

"Right," said Orso. He looked at Claudia. "Time for the monkey blood."

The Foundrysiders climbed out of the carriage and quietly made toward the dead canal. Sancia kept an eye on the espringal batteries, and held up a hand when the big, bronze chambers snapped up and began tracking their movements. Then she looked back at Claudia and waved.

Sitting atop the carriage, Claudia cut the dozens of little floating lanterns loose. The revelers clapped as they drifted into the air like puff seeds from a powdervine . . . but though the crowd was by now too drunk to notice, all the lanterns drifted in the same direction— toward the wall—and they also drifted at the same height . . . which happened to be almost level with the espringal batteries.

Sancia watched with her scrived sight as the lanterns slowly drifted to float before the espringal batteries. The batteries came to life, pivoting to target the lanterns—which, if you knew how the batteries worked, would have seemed unusual: espringal batteries only targeted blood that they didn't recognize. So why would they target some floating lanterns?

This was perhaps the grisliest aspect of their plan, but it seemed to be working. It was common knowledge that espringal batteries had trouble telling the blood of humans apart from the blood of gray monkeys—which scrivers had figured out pretty quickly when the first versions had quickly loosed their salvos at any nearby monkey nests in the rooftops. Most campo scrivers had clarified their commands so that the espringals would figure it out . . . but Sancia'd had the clever idea of purchasing monkeys from the butchers in the Greens (where blood pie was something of a delicacy), placing the blood in small vials, adding a drop of her own blood to each vial, and attaching them to the floating lanterns.

And a vial of monkey blood in all of our pockets, she thought as she looked around at them. *Just to be extra cautious.*

As more and more lanterns clustered around the walls, the batteries only became more bewildered. Were these monkeys? Were they unidentified humans? And which one was the target? There seemed to be far too many of them.

Sancia watched as the espringal batteries pivoted from lantern to lantern, utterly unsure what to do. "Now!" she said. Together they leapt down into the canal and ran toward the metal portcullis below the walls.

Sancia gripped the metal of the portcullis, and instantly the rig spoke in her mind.

< . . . *extruding TEN FEET DOWN, provided the farthest extent of all FRAMING do not directly touch any MATTER, and to rise UP when blockage exerts PRESSURE across ALL FRAMES at MAXIMUM PRESSURE . . .* >

It seemed the portcullis had been scrived to gate off the canal, but still allow water to flow through—unless some huge blockage drifted down from within the inner enclave, striking against it. In that case, the portcullis would then rise, allow the blockage to pass through, and then lower again.

< *Tell me how you define pressure, and frames,* > she asked it.

The metrics and levels poured into her mind, chanted in the curious, anxious voice of the portcullis. She listened closely.

It rises when it feels unusual pressure on the face of the portcullis, she thought. *But "the face of the portcullis" isn't defined well. So if it feels any pressure on one specific square inch of the metal, maybe it should feel obliged to rise . . .*

She spoke to it, feeding it her commands. Then she opened her eyes and gave the bars of the portcullis a hard jerk.

With a *clink* and a groan, the portcullis slowly rose up.

"In," said Sancia. "Now."

The four of them slipped inside, sprinting through the ruined canal, up the stone stairs set in its side, and then on into the innermost circles of the enclave.

Sancia paused to look back. There was a *pop* from the other side of the enclave walls, and she saw something strange rising into the sky: a large circular green floating lantern, like the ones they used in the campo carnival parades. It rose into the air until it hovered about fifty feet above the walls, surrounded by the flock of smaller floating lanterns. She heard the applause of the revelers from here.

Should be easy to see, thought Sancia. *Lighting the way home . . .*

"Lead the way," said Orso.

Sancia's heart felt like lead as she tried to remember the path ahead. "How I'd hoped," she said, "that I'd never have to do this again . . ."

"I sympathize," said Gregor.

The strangest thing about moving through the Candiano enclave was how empty it was. Nearly everything was dark—there were no lights, neither in the streets nor in the buildings. The huge twisting spires were totally abandoned. The streets were covered in refuse that had blown into the gutters and the alleys.

"Weird," said Orso softly. They stared at the countless magnificent, vacant structures around them. "*Weird.*"

"It seems," said Gregor, "that the Michiels are not doing much with the space."

"I'll scrumming say." Sancia flexed the muscle in her mind. Although most campo enclaves would have been an eruption of light and logic from all the designs keeping everything going, the Candiano enclave was more like a handful of candles flickering in the dark. "The only scrivings that are active are the ones keeping the buildings up. Everything else is shut down."

"Then the darkness will be helpful," said Orso. "Let's keep moving."

They continued through the enclave until they emerged onto a main fairway, and the Mountain rose into view. Again, she was awed by the sight of the thing. The Mountain was so incomprehensibly huge, a giant black dome with tiny round windows dotting its surface—and yet now it was also so incomprehensibly *damaged.*

"Let's hope they left the front door open," said Orso.

Together they moved through the side streets around the towers beside the Mountain, Sancia peering up at the scrivings around them, mindful of any movement.

Then she saw a tangle of logic hovering in the building ahead.

She stopped immediately and held up a hand.

"What's wrong?" asked Gregor.

Sancia narrowed her eyes at the tangle of scrivings. She saw commands for velocity, for durability, for density, and gravity . . .

"It's an espringal," she said.

"What?" said Gregor.

"There in that building." She pointed. "On the balcony. It's an espringal, a high-powered one. And it's moving."

"A Michiel guard, then?" asked Berenice.

Sancia cocked her head, studying the logic. "No. I don't think so. This looks like someone else's work. I think it's . . . Dandolo."

Gregor, Berenice, and Orso looked at one another. "What?" said Orso. "What the hell? I thought the Michiels owned this enclave!"

"It could be a break-in," said Berenice. "We know Crasedes is after the same thing we are, and we know Ofelia is working with . . . or for him."

"We can't stop here, even if this is a nasty surprise," said Sancia. "We just . . . choose another route." She backed away from the building. "One that's far away from that."

But getting closer to the Mountain proved harder than she'd thought. Every time they crept up some thoroughfare or alley, she always spied a scriving closer to the Mountain: an espringal, or a bundle of rapiers, or some other armament that surely belonged to guards keeping watch. And all of them were Dandolo.

"How in the hell have the Dandolos moved a private army into the enclave?" whispered Sancia as they huddled behind a corner. "Surely the Michiels would have noticed all these goddamn assholes!"

Gregor made a pained face. "Unless . . . my mother, or Crasedes . . . made them give the whole place up?"

"He couldn't do that!" scoffed Orso. Then he saw Sancia's and Gregor's faces. "*Could* he do that?"

"The sound of his voice almost made me tell him where Clef was," said Sancia. "God knows what it could make a regular person do."

Gregor peered down the alley at the dark, cracked skin of the Mountain. "They're in there. I'm sure of it. My mother's probably had Dandolo scrivers in there all day, trying to get at the same components we're after. And they've set up guards everywhere."

"So . . . do we walk away?" asked Orso.

"No!" said Sancia. "If we walk away, then not only do we lose Valeria's protections, but Crasedes will be one step closer to remaking her into something that could tear reality to pieces like a wasp in a beehive! This is our only chance!"

"Then what do you propose we do?" asked Orso.

Berenice suddenly walked farther out from the corner, staring not at the Mountain but rather at the land around its base.

"What the hell are you doing?" whispered Sancia.

"The secret entrance," said Berenice quietly.

"What?" said Gregor.

"There's a secret entrance to the Mountain—isn't there? We used it last time. Could that still be guarded?"

Sancia thought about it. "I don't know," she said. "But it's worth trying."

They trotted through a string of parks that had been overtaken with monkeys until finally they came to the entrance to Tribuno Candiano's personal sculpture garden. Sancia studied the balconies and alleys around them, but found them all empty.

"We're alone," she whispered. "They don't know about it!"

"Then let's see if it still works," said Gregor.

They entered the garden. It was a powerfully unsettling experience for Sancia: the last time she'd been here the topiaries had been trimmed, the lawns freshly cut, and the statues had been clean and imposing. Now everything was overgrown, the statues and follies were filthy with dust and mold, and the topiaries had grown so thick Gregor had to hack them away with a scrived rapier.

And, she remembered, the last time she'd been here, she'd had Clef with her.

How long ago that seems now, she thought.

She found the bridge with the hidden entrance below, studied the wall with her scrived sight, and placed a bare hand on it.

"I sure as shit hope this works," she said quietly.

The scrived door had been very well designed—she could tell

right away it was Tribuno Candiano's work—and it took a lot of effort to fool it into letting them through. But she finally triumphed, and a round, smooth plug of white stone rolled away, revealing a set of stairs on the other side.

Orso let out a relieved sigh. "Thank God!"

"We're not inside yet," said Sancia. They ran down the stairs together. "This leads to a weird tunnel that takes us right to the fourth floor. Or at least it did. And hopefully before then I'll be able to confer with the Mountain."

"You're going to talk to it? To the whole building?" asked Gregor.

"Yeah," said Sancia. "And maybe it can tell us what's going on." Though she had to admit, knowing that the lexicons of the Mountain essentially ran on the distorted, violated souls of the dead made the prospect of conferring with it a touch more disturbing than it'd normally have been.

People used to say the Mountain was haunted, she thought. *They didn't know how right they were . . .*

They passed through the tunnel, which was now so dark they had to take out scrived lanterns to see the way. Then they came to a set of winding stairs up, which led to the fourth floor of the Mountain. Sancia fooled the doorway there into opening, and it fell away to reveal . . .

Berenice gasped. "My God."

"Shit," said Orso softly.

The interior atrium of the Mountain was a dripping, dusty, shattered world of sputtering lamps and scattered shadows. Mold bloomed here and there and crawled across the green plaster walls in waves. The air was heavy with a scent of mildew and rot. Daylight spilled in from the cracked ceiling, which had apparently been ripped open when Sancia had turned on the gravity rig, and beams of shifting light danced across the floor as the overcast drifted through the darkening skies.

The oddest thing was how it still resembled her memories of the building it once had been. It still retained the brilliance of its original structure: the concentric walkways lining the atrium's interior like ribs, stacked one on top of the other, with balconies running all along them so you could stop and look down into the massive chamber from wherever you were. But this was deceptive, she knew, for the Mountain was far bigger than just the atrium: hallways splintered off from the concentric walkways and led to ballrooms, assembly bays, design workshops, cellars, and more.

And yet now all of it had corroded, and degraded. All within just three years.

Sancia studied the giant atrium with her sight, and spied nine Dandolo armaments roving through the walkways above and below them—nine soldiers, five on patrol, four on watch.

And that's just what I can see here, she thought. *God, there's got to be a small army in here with us . . .*

A crackling, weary, ancient voice whispered in her mind: *< . . . eh? What is this Presence? Who . . . Who is that?>*

"I've got it," she said, tapping the side of her head. "It's still alive, still active!"

"Then ask it what the hell is going on!" said Orso.

<Hello, Mountain,> she said to it.

<Oh!> said the Mountain. *<It's you . . . It is you, yes? It is hard for me to . . . to remember these days.>*

<It's me.>

<Are you here with all these . . . men? I have so few visitors now . . . They are all frightened I will collapse. And such fears, I know, are not baseless . . . >

<No. I'm not.> She looked out on the atrium floor. One of the lifting rooms that took you to higher floors had collapsed. Broken glass and crystal lay glittering across the dusty marble floor. *<I'm sorry for what happened to you.>*

<Ah. Yes. It is all right. I bear you no ill will for it.>

<You don't?> asked Sancia. *<Why?>*

<You brought me so close to fulfilling my Purpose. You brought me the key, something made by the Old Ones,> it said. It sounded like it was relishing the memory. *<It was so wonderful, for me to get so close . . . >*

<We need something from you, Mountain—a piece of your lexicons. Are they still intact?>

<Eh? Yes. Five out of six are still functional,> said the Mountain. *<One has been flooded. As a result of this, my control over doors and locks is . . . not what it used to be. Though I am still aware, and possess some controls over the lanterns . . . >*

<Who's in here with us?>

<There are men attempting to access the five functional lexicons . . . men I do not know. I do not like them—none of them have logged their blood through the appropriate security processes . . . I disapprove of this very strongly.>

<I think they're after the same thing we're after,> said Sancia. *<It's a weird little definition, shaped like a cone . . . >*

<The authority definition,> said the Mountain. *<Yes. Granting me the authority to sense and change and respond to the realities within my periphery. Yes. I know this well.>*

<Have they succeeded in actually getting it?>

<No. Tribuno laid many defensive processes about the lexicons. They are close to extracting one, but . . . I will simply say, though they are cunning, they are not my maker.> There was a pause. *<Several have died,>* it added.

"The Dandolos are working on five out of six of the lexicons," said Sancia aloud. "They haven't successfully gotten the definition out of any of them yet—but they're close."

"What's happening with the sixth lexicon?" asked Orso. "Is anyone guarding it?"

"No," said Sancia. "Because it's flooded."

"Shit!" he said.

Sancia thought hard. This wasn't at all how they'd wanted this to go: they'd planned to get to the Mountain first, use Gio and Claudia's invisible barricades to seal up access to one lexicon, extract the component, and then get out. They hadn't planned on soldiers and flooded basements. But she knew they had no choice.

<The flooded lexicon,> Sancia asked the Mountain. *<Where is it?>*

<In the southeast foundations,> said the Mountain.

<And . . . how bad are these floodwaters?>

<Up to the ceiling in most cases.>

Shit, she thought. *So—really scrumming bad, then.*

<Is there a way to get the water out?> asked Sancia.

<Hmm. There . . . could be,> said the Mountain. *<If you punctured the wall in the southwest dry-storage rooms . . . This would release the waters and lower the levels in the lexicon chamber. But that wall is quite far away from the lexicon . . . >*

<It'll have to do,> said Sancia.

She shook herself and said, "We're going to have to split into two groups."

"All right," said Gregor. "What is the plan?"

"One half needs to go to the basement dry-storage rooms, in the southwest area," said Sancia. She pointed down into the atrium. "There's a wall there that we need to break open . . ." She cocked her head, and listened to the Mountain. "The Mountain says it can actually flash lights over the wall, so we can find it."

"Helpful," said Berenice.

"Scrumming creepy," muttered Orso.

"Breaking open the wall will let out a lot of the water in the lexicon chambers," said Sancia. She shifted her finger to point to its location. "Once that's down, the other team enters the lexicon chamber and gets the component out. Then we regroup here, and we go out the way we came in."

Gregor nodded, though his face was concerned. "I assume Sancia and I will go to this wall, while Orso and Berenice deal with the lexicon?"

Sancia began to agree, but Orso shook his head and said, "No."

"What?" said Sancia. "Why not?"

"I mean . . . I am not the best scriver to accompany Berenice." Orso thought in silence for a moment. Then he looked at her sternly. "You are."

"What?" said Berenice.

"*What?*" said Sancia. "You . . . You were Tribuno Candiano's star scrumming pupil! And you know more about lexicons than anyone in Tevanne!"

"Obviously I don't know anything about *these,*" said Orso. "Together, you and Berenice can do this faster. I'm better with Gregor—I actually lived here; I know how to get around." He wrinkled his nose at the moldering walls. "Or I used to . . . It doesn't matter. The faster you two get the component," he said as Berenice opened her mouth to argue, "the faster we get out alive. Got it?"

There was an awkward pause.

"Fine," said Sancia. "I'll go with Berenice. You two break the wall."

"How many soldiers are in here with us?" asked Gregor.

"I can count nine here, but . . . if they're after the lexicons, they'll be in the cellars, far from me, so I can't see them." She shrugged. "I'd guess thirty or fifty or so."

"Damn," said Gregor quietly. He looked away into the atrium, his face haggard and haunted.

Sancia knew what he was worried about: it wasn't dying that scared Gregor, but killing.

"You'll be fine," she said. "Just avoid them as best you can. But you'll need to hurry." She looked up at the sky through the cracked ceiling. It had taken them so long to get here that it was already night. "Crasedes might wait for midnight to come see how progress is going . . . but he might not."

"And what do we do if we're still here by then?" asked Orso.

"Plug up your ears," said Sancia. "And run like hell."

Orso and Gregor crept off into the darkened hallways of the Mountain. Orso personally found it a surreal and disturbing experience. He hadn't been back here in—what, fifteen, twenty years?—and yet he could remember these ceilings, these doors, the way the doorknobs felt when you gripped them . . . except now they were muddy, or stained from old floodwaters, and everywhere felt empty and abandoned. It was dispiriting to see the halls of his youth so utterly changed. The golden age of scriving was well and truly dead.

But we're remaking it anew, he tried to remember. *We won't make the same mistakes that Tribuno made . . .* They passed a crumbling fresco depicting two scrivers altering the fundament of the world, engraving sigils on the gears and machinery that supported reality itself. *That I made, when I was young.*

As they walked, they noticed that the lamps and lanterns in the walls around them kept springing on as they came close. It took Orso a moment to realize that the lights were being switched off as the two of them walked away.

"Is . . . it just me," whispered Gregor, "or . . ."

"Or is the Mountain giving us light to see?" said Orso. "Yeah. I think so."

Gregor watched as a light flicked on around the corner up ahead. "And it's showing us the way. That is . . . most disturbing to me."

"It goddamn gives me the screaming meemies, I'll tell you that. I feel like a fairy-tale traveler following spirit lamps into a bog. To think I lived here all those years, unaware of what this place actually *was* . . ."

They continued down a set of cracked stairs, into a meeting room with crystal goblets lying here and there on the floor, then on into a mirrored hall so filthy it looked like their reflections were walking through a curling fog.

Then the light went out above them. They paused, standing in the total darkness.

"Why do you think it did that?" whispered Orso.

"I'm not—"

A light flicked on far, far down the hallway—and they saw a Dandolo guard walking their way, espringal out and ready. The guard stopped and looked at the scrived lantern above him, perplexed as to why it had just come on.

Because it's showing us a threat, Orso realized.

Before Orso could think, Gregor grabbed him and hauled him into what seemed to be a dark, soggy bedroom. Together they huddled in the shadows, listening as the footsteps came closer.

Orso didn't dare breathe. He reached for the button on his cuirass, but Gregor shook his head, pointing to the walls around them. Orso remembered Claudia's warning: *Don't turn it on too close to walls—you'll be immobilized.*

The guard's steps slowed as he neared the doorway to the bedroom. Orso couldn't understand what had made him suspicious. The man evidently hadn't seen them, otherwise he would have just shot them dead in the hall—but how could he know exactly where they were now?

Gregor gently pushed Orso up against the wall in the corner. Then he flattened his back to the wall by the doorway—but he did not arm himself.

Why doesn't he have his espringal out? Why doesn't he just shoot the stupid bastard?

There was a long silence. Then the tip of the scrived espringal slowly poked its way through the door.

Gregor pounced.

Orso had never seen Gregor fight, so he was astonished at how fast a man of his size could move. In a flash, Gregor had grabbed the espringal, wrenched it up, and then he'd head-butted the guard soundly in the face. The guard cried out, and a scrived bolt cracked off the ceiling, sending shrapnel flying through the room. Orso felt one large fragment thud into the wall just next to his head.

Gregor heaved the guard into the room and smashed his fist into the man's face. But the guard was clearly trained as well, and though he was stunned, he was prepared for the next blow: he brought his forearm up to block Gregor's strike, and then he stepped forward and shoved his elbow into Gregor's neck. Gregor gagged and bent double as the guard reached for his rapier. Before he could draw it, Gregor charged forward, put his shoulder into the man's gut, and slammed him into the stone wall behind him.

Though the guard wore a helmet, the way his head cracked into the wall clearly hurt. He slid down the wall, still feebly fighting Gregor, who pinned him down with his left hand as he fumbled for something on his belt with his right. The guard kept struggling and trying to scream for help, so Gregor shoved his left hand into the guard's mouth, which he then bit—hard.

Gregor growled, pulled something from his belt—a dolorspina dart, Orso thought—and stabbed the man in the neck with it. The guard gasped and fell back. Then his eyes rolled up into his head, and he was still.

Gregor pulled out a handkerchief and wrapped his hand, which was bleeding freely. Then he knelt and searched the man. "A sachet," he said, taking it. "I wonder what permissions it grants . . ."

Orso slowly stood, still trembling with fright. "For . . . For the love of *God*, man!"

"What?"

"Did you really need to enter into some kind of street brawl with him? I mean . . . he could have killed you, or me, or raised the alarm! Next time just stab the bastard, or cut his throat, and be done with it, all right?"

Gregor looked at Orso for a moment, his face curiously closed. Then he stood and said, "No."

"No to what?"

"No. I will not kill these men unless I have no other choice."

"But . . . goddamn it, Gregor, we don't have time for your honor, or your scrumming morali—"

Gregor whirled on him. "This is *not* just about my moralities!" he spat. "And it is most *certainly* not about my honor!"

Orso drew back, surprised by his viciousness—especially since Gregor was usually so taciturn. "What?"

"This isn't about . . . about mercy or cruelty, or . . . or any such useless twaddle! It's . . ." Gregor's fury changed to sorrow and despair. "It's about *this*!" He pointed at the right side of his head, where the plate was still installed.

"What about it?"

He struggled to explain it. "The less I think myself a killer, then . . . then the less control it has over me." He shut his eyes and said, "Because I have changed my mind about what I am. I have *changed. My. Mind.*" He spoke the words as if they were an inner mantra he'd been repeating for the past three years. Then he opened his eyes and looked at Orso pleadingly. "Do not ask me to be a murderer. Not even now. I do not wish to be the thing I was anymore. And if I slip back, then it will be easier for . . . for those who made me to command me to murder you. All right?"

"I . . . all right. All right."

Gregor looked back down at the guard. "Wait. He's got some kind of . . . of glowing light on his belt. What is that?"

Orso looked and saw he was right: there was a tiny, twinkling light on the guard's side. He bent and unhooked the object from his belt.

It looked like a wire mesh ball, but there were tiny, tiny lights embedded where the wires wrapped around one another, so it was effectively covered in them. Only one little light was glowing, on the side facing him.

"Huh," said Orso, and he turned it over in his hands—but as he did, the lights changed: whichever one was facing him always stayed lit, while the others stayed dark.

He began to get a dreadful idea.

"Gregor," he said, "take that sachet you got out of your pocket and toss it away."

Gregor did so. Instantly, a second light sprang on, this one facing Gregor.

"Walk around the room," said Orso.

Gregor walked in a circle around the room. The light moved with him, always pointing at his position, while the second light pointed to Orso.

"Shit," said Orso.

"It's . . . It's some kind of detection rig, isn't it?" asked Gregor.

"Yes," said Orso grimly. "I think it senses blood that isn't paired with the right sachet—just like the espringal batteries on the walls. That's how the bastard found us."

"Crasedes knew we'd be coming," he said.

"It seems so."

"We've got to warn Sancia. But . . . she and Berenice must be almost to the basements by now."

"I'm a little more worried about us, to be frank, but . . ." Orso thought for a second. Then he cleared his voice, and said aloud, "Mountain—can you hear me?"

The light in the room blinked on and off.

"Please tell Sancia what we've discovered here, if you'd be so kind."

The light blinked on and off again.

"I suppose it is useful," said Gregor, "to have the very building on your side . . ."

"But the building won't matter worth shit if they can detect us through scrumming walls." Orso thought for a moment. "Gregor— pick up that sachet again, please."

He stooped and did so. "Now what?"

"Now turn around and let me climb on your back."

Gregor stared at him blankly. "What?"

"Just do it before they detect us!"

Muttering, Gregor turned around and bent his knees slightly while Orso clambered up onto his back.

"There," he grunted as he grasped Gregor's neck. "That should do. And now let's see if this worked . . ."

He pulled the little people finder back out. Just as he suspected, the lights were all off.

"Hah!" he said. "The thing can't figure out who the sachet applies to when we're so close together! So it just assumes we *both* have it."

"Yes, but . . . Orso, are you proposing I carry you *all the way down* to the main floor of the Mountain?"

"Well. I can't think of another solution currently. So—get a move on, I suppose."

Sancia and Berenice wound their way down through the bowels of the Mountain, but did not encounter any patrols or guards. It didn't take them long to realize why: soon the hallways were filled with water that rose to their ankles, and they had to kick and slosh through the chambers. Sancia wasn't bothered—she'd crawled through worse in her time—but she could tell Berenice wasn't pleased.

"Just . . . keep an eye out for snakes," said Berenice.

"The Mountain tells me there are no snakes in this wing of his basements," said Sancia. "He says there's a pretty big nest of rats in one of his rooms here, though."

"His? He?"

"Or its, or whatever."

They sloshed along through a records hall. The surface of the waters was covered in a skin of ancient, decayed parchments, and the giant filing cabinets towered over them. Sancia was reminded of columns in some massive temple.

"I wish I could hear the things you hear," said Berenice, "and see the things you see."

"You always say that."

"But I especially feel it now, San. When there's a building whispering secrets in your ear."

"It's just . . . I don't know. Information."

"And *you* always say that."

"It is. It's like learning a different language. Just knowing the words doesn't mean you grasp what they're actually *saying*. You still have to be smart." They turned right and exited the filing rooms. "That's where you outpace me," she grumbled.

"You are quite smart, San."

"There's quite smart, and then there's you. You know more about scriving than Orso, even. And I . . ." She paused as the Mountain suddenly whispered to her.

"What is it?" asked Berenice.

"The Mountain is telling me a message from Orso," she said, her head cocked, eyes half-closed. "The Dandolo guards have . . . some kind of blood-detection rig. To spot people who don't have the right sachets." Her face darkened. "To find *us*."

Berenice stared at her. "Crasedes knew Valeria would send us here, then."

"Yeah. Just like he knew we'd be at the ship. The bastard's been ahead of us at every turn." She looked back down the flooded hallways. "I don't think we'll encounter any troops down here. But I bet it's going to be a devil of a time for Orso and Gregor. I think the lexicon is just ahead."

They came to an immense bronze door with multiple locks, all of them attuned to sense the blood of Tribuno Candiano or his elite scrivers. Sancia quickly realized this door was beyond the controls of the Mountain: Tribuno had not been so foolish as to give his rig power over whether he could access its controls.

"This means I'll have to do this the hard way . . ." Sancia said, and she placed her bare hand to the door and began to converse with it.

Ever since blood-sensing techniques had become wildly popular in the city, Sancia had built up a good bit of experience with these— yet this door proved to be a particularly thorny example. Though she tried many attempts, it remained unpersuadable: it would not be fooled into opening.

"Tribuno designed the *hell* out of this thing," she said, her hand pressed to the door and her eyes shut. "It's not budging on the definition of blood."

"Or warmth?" asked Berenice, pacing the flooded hallway behind her.

"No."

"What about distance? Can you convince it that it needs to sense far beyond its usual range? Maybe that can confuse it."

Sancia tried this tactic, but the door refused to give: <*Only accept presence of bloodmatter when organ makes contact with my face and a pulse is detected.*>

"Shit," said Sancia. "Tribuno even made sure to protect this against anyone walking around with his severed arm or something. Impressive, since he must have designed this thing thirty years ago—way before blood sensing was commonplace."

Berenice screwed up her mouth. "Hold on a second. I need to remember something . . ." She shut her eyes and her face went slack, like she'd just fallen into an incredibly deep sleep. She stayed like that for one second, then two, then three—and then she opened her eyes. "What about time?" she asked.

"Huh?"

"Can you find out if a permitted scriver used this door previously? Maybe you can convince it that the man's hand is still pressed to the door. Or make it think that it doesn't matter *when* the contact happened—just that it happened."

"That can't possibly work. It can't be that easy."

"Orso makes a mess of time definitions very frequently. It's his biggest weakness. I assume he learned it from someone. Why not Tribuno himself?"

Sancia took a breath, pressed her hand to the door, shut her eyes, and battered the door's definitions of time—making it doubt what a second was, a minute, an hour, a day . . . It wasn't easy, but she could tell she was making progress when she tricked it into thinking a year was actually a half a minute.

<*I am not . . . not sure about this,*> said the door. <*Contact must be made . . .*>

<*Yeah, but when? Is there a reason why the contact can't have occurred, say . . . five minutes ago?*>

The door thought for a moment. <*This . . . is not defined.*>

<*So . . . if there's no reason why you* shouldn't *do it . . .*>

Another pause. Then a *click,* and the door swung backward, permitting them entry.

"See?" said Sancia. "There's smart, and then there's *smart.* You should have this damned plate in your head. You'd be far better at it than I would."

"Oh, enough," said Berenice. She was grinning, even though she was filthy and wet. "Either of us alone would have been stuck in the hallway. Together, we are unstoppable."

They sloshed forward into the tunnel until they came to the stairs down—which were completely submerged under the waters.

"Now we wait for Orso and Gregor to do their bit," said Sancia. "Right?"

"I suppose so. I just hope we don't have to wait long."

Grunting and groaning, Gregor carried Orso down through the levels of the Mountain, always following a dimly lit lantern or light as the Mountain showed them the way. "*Please* try and keep quiet!" whispered Orso as Gregor staggered down the stairs. "And please don't jostle me so much! Every time I separate from you, the little light in this rig flickers!"

"Any other orders?" grunted Gregor, hobbling along through the halls.

"We're almost to the main floor. So—pretty soon you'll have to keep low too."

Gregor let out a long, low hiss.

Finally they crept down the last staircase and skirted the walls of the massive atrium. Orso's skin broke out in gooseflesh as they walked in the shadows of the balconies. It was so eerie to be within this enormous chamber, listening to the patter of distant waters and the echoes of footfalls and the occasional cheeps of a gray monkey who must be nesting in the rafters. Some of the patrolling Dandolo troops bore lanterns, the warm light contrasting sharply with the darks and the blues of the atrium, which was mostly lit by moonlight now. Orso was reminded of crypt keepers walking amidst the catacombs, their lights held high in the gloom.

I fought for years to live here, he thought. *Now I'd fight like hell to get out.*

"Mountain," whispered Gregor, "please flash a light within the hallway we need to use."

They squatted in the shadows studying their surroundings. Then they saw a light flickering in a hallway far, far away, on the other side of the atrium.

Gregor sighed with frustration. "That has to be at least a thousand feet away . . ."

"It's not my cup of tea either!" whispered Orso. "I'm chafing like mad in spots I'd much prefer didn't chafe."

Gregor looked around, thinking. "Six soldiers down here," he said quietly. Then he cocked his head. "Orso—you're going to hop off my back in a bit, all right?"

"What! I *am*?"

"Yes. Not for long. Hop off when I tell you, and back *on* when I tell you again, and keep *quiet*. Understand?"

"I . . . well. Fine, I suppose."

Crouching low, Gregor carried Orso across the atrium to where the massive lifting room lay in rubble across the cracked marble floor. Gregor kneeled behind it, poked his head up, and watched the patrols. When they were all roughly aligned with the hallway they needed to use, he whispered, "Off! Now!"

Grunting, Orso delicately stepped off of his back. Instantly, a half dozen little twinkling lights lit up at the guards' belts.

They stopped patrolling.

"Do . . . Do you have this?" one guard asked, looking at his people finder.

There was a muttered agreement. The guards looked in Orso and Gregor's direction and started slowly moving their way, craning their heads curiously.

"Think one of the damned scrivers dropped their sachet again?" asked another voice in the darkness.

"Maybe," said another. "Thought they'd be a lot more careful about what they put where after that last trap nearly cut that scriver in half . . ."

"Back on!" whispered Gregor. "Now!"

Orso quickly hopped onto Gregor's back. Gregor turned and, still staying low, crept away from the ruined lifting room to the shelter of a stairwell at the edge of the atrium.

A voice echoed through the atrium: "It's gone. What the hell?"

"Maybe it came in and out of range . . ."

"Or maybe this rig is a piece of shit. Didn't they have all kinds of hell trying to get these to stop detecting monkeys?"

The guards gathered around the rubble of the lifting room, lanterns held high. A few peered at the edge of the atrium—not at Gregor and Orso, but rather in a straight line with where they'd been hiding.

Gregor edged closer into the shadows that clung about one hallway entrance. He whispered, "Off again."

"Again?"

"Yes!"

Orso slid off his back. Again, the little twinkling lights sprang on at the soldiers' hips.

They looked down and fumbled with the little metal balls. "Again? Now it's over there!" said one, pointing at Gregor and Orso. The guards turned and started moving their way.

"Back on," whispered Gregor. "Now. Now!"

Grimacing, Orso clung to Gregor's back again, and he crept off into the shadows, slinking along the walls of the atrium as fast as he could.

"And now it's gone," said a guard. "Think there's an intruder about?"

Orso couldn't hear the response, but all the guards kept moving toward their last position. He realized what Gregor had accomplished: he'd drawn all the guards away from the entrance they needed to get to the cellars. Though it obviously caused Gregor a great deal of discomfort, he was able to slip along the walls and into the hallway while the guards on the main floor kept fruitlessly searching the far side of the atrium.

Once they were safe, Gregor leaned back and pressed Orso into the wall for support, and then he just sat there, panting.

"Well done!" said Orso.

"Shut up," gasped Gregor.

Orso looked around. "Hey, I know this hallway."

"Oh?"

"Yes. I used to come down here when it was first built to nick food. And . . ." His heart sank. "And if I recall, this is where one of the Mountain's lexicons is located too . . ."

Gregor stopped panting. "What!"

"Uh . . . yes."

"You mean . . . You mean that another one of the lexicons is going to be located down here?"

"Yes."

"Near the cellar we need to get to?"

"Yes."

"The lexicons that the Dandolos are trying to break into as well?"

"Yes."

"So . . . that means we'll have even *more* guards to deal with as we get closer?"

"Uh, probably, yes."

Gregor cursed for a moment, then glared at Orso over his shoulder. "I always thought you were skinny," he said as he fought to his feet with Orso on his back. "But now I'm not so sure."

Berenice and Sancia stood by the flooded hallway, waiting impatiently.

"What could be taking them so long?" said Sancia.

<*There are several guards between their position and the cellars,*> said the Mountain. <*I am helping them evade notice, but . . . it is not easy.*>

<*Shit!*> said Sancia. <*What time is it?*>

<*It is nearly eleven o'clock,*> said the Mountain.

"Shit!" she said out loud. "It's almost eleven!"

"Do you really think Crasedes will come at midnight?" asked Berenice.

"Hell, I don't know. But if he were to come at any time, I'd guess then."

"And we have no defenses against him?" she asked.

"No. I didn't even bring the imperiat. Not with us all being, you know, inside a giant scrived structure. It seemed too big of a risk."

Then the Mountain spoke in Sancia's mind, in a voice that was very quiet and awed: <*When you discuss this, do . . . do you really mean the true Crasedes Magnus?*>

<*Huh? Yeah,*> said Sancia.

<*Are you saying . . . he may come . . . here? To me? A hierophant?*>

<*Yes.*>

There was a silence. She suspected she'd just shocked the poor thing. She remembered now how it had wished to be visited by a hierophant—after all, that was why Tribuno had built it in the first place.

<Oh . . . Oh my goodness,> it whispered.

She began to get an idea. <Supposing you actually did get a hierophant here . . . What would you do, Mountain?>

<Well! If I were to have one of the Old Ones here within me . . . why, my Purpose was to show them the works of my maker, of Tribuno! To show them all he had wrought, all the secrets within me that he had made just for them.>

<Where are these secrets?>

<On the third floor, hidden behind a vast mural. I can ope—>

<Is it deep inside? Behind doors and doors and doors?>

<Yes . . . it was a very protected place.>

<And you still have control over it? You said you had issues with doors and locks . . . >

<This is my Purpose. I shall always have control over my Purpose until I fade, and am no more.>

<I see. And if he tried to—would you let this hierophant leave?>

There was a long silence.

<I would . . . I would not want that,> said the Mountain. <After so long . . . After all I have been through, all the pain, all the silence . . . I would not wish for my Purpose to abandon me.>

A cold chill filled Sancia's heart as she knew what she was going to say. <And if . . . if you had no choice,> she said. <If it were going to leave you—would you want to stay here, Mountain, alone and waiting?>

Another long silence.

<No,> it said. <No, I would not. I would not wish to wait here, without Tribuno, without my Purpose—and without you. I . . . I would not wish to be alone again, you see. I would rather bring myself down, and fall to rubble, than go back to that.>

"All right, then," whispered Sancia. "I see. I . . . I have a proposition for you, Mountain . . ."

She told it her ideas, and it listened closely.

Gregor crept down the hallway with Orso on his back, following the flickering lanterns set in the walls. Then they looked around one corner and froze.

The hallway stretched on for about four hundred feet before them, broken only by an intersection halfway down. What was most concerning, however, was the half dozen Dandolo guards bearing lamps standing before the doorway at the far end of the hall. All of them looked quite upset, and it was easy to see why: a mangled corpse lay at their feet, so brutalized that it looked like someone had tried to hack the man in half with a pole arm.

". . . going to have to get a stretcher," one guard was saying. "Unless *you* want to throw poor Pietro over your shoulders, Molinari, and get his mess all over you."

"But they did *not* inform us that this task would have so many threats!" said another. "I mean . . . I thought the Candianos *lived* here! I didn't think they'd layered the walls and floors with lethal scrumming booby traps . . ."

"Sure, but the lexicon chambers would be a different matter," said Orso quietly. "Tribuno always did take security very seriously . . . especially later, when he went mad."

Gregor raised a finger, then pointed. "There. Look."

A single lantern was flickering very faintly by the corner of the intersection, two hundred feet away. The Mountain was signaling to them that they needed to go down the hallway and take a right—but this would be impossible with the Dandolo guards standing in a crowd just beyond.

"Any bright ideas?" said Orso. "I doubt if we can draw them all away this time. Maybe if we ran down there really quick, we could seal them in with one of Claudia's invisible walls . . . though I'm not sure how to do that without getting shot."

Gregor cocked his head. "That is an idea, Orso."

"What, getting shot?"

"No." Gregor began to take out his imprinter espringal. "Hold still, please."

"Wait. Gregor, what . . . what are you going to d—"

"Shh," said Gregor. He set it to an anchoring string and carefully aimed down the hallway at the guards.

". . . barely even want to take a shit in the latrine!" one of the guards was saying. "I'm frankly worried that the damned thing will eat me!"

Gregor exhaled slightly, and fired.

The lead slug hurtled down the hallway—but it did not hit any of the soldiers. Instead, it sailed over their heads, through the open doorway at the end of the hall, and struck the far wall with a very loud *thwack*.

The soldiers jumped, alarmed. "What the hell was *that*?"

They spun around, pulled out their rapiers, and walked away from the corpse and into the room, peering about.

Gregor lowered the espringal a little, aimed, and fired the second half of the anchoring slug—this one at the corpse of poor Pietro, lying on the floor.

The slug struck the corpse on the hip, this time with a much wetter, far more upsetting *thwack*. The instant it stuck, the two slugs felt compelled to pull themselves together—which meant the corpse of Pietro suddenly shot through the air, pulled by his trousers, his limbs flailing about wildly, and he smashed into the backs of the soldiers standing in the doorway, knocking them to the ground.

There was an eruption of confused and horrified screams. Gregor ran down the hallway with Orso on his back, pulled out one of Claudia's plates, and tossed it down behind him and turned it on. He rapped the invisible air with his knuckles, and it made a metallic *tap tap*.

"Good," he said. Then he shook Orso off, and they turned and dashed down the hallway and down a flight of stairs. "If rather grisly . . . But it won't hold them for long."

"We're close now!" said Orso, but he hardly needed to say it. The walls were getting more utilitarian and much less ornate.

Finally they came to the cellars. Orso saw a single lamp lit over a door just a few yards away.

"There!" he said. "That one!"

They scrambled inside. The room was dark and reeking, full of bags and crates of ancient, spoiled food—but a lantern was flashing frantically on the far wall.

"I believe that's it," said Gregor. He pulled out his rapier. "Let's do this fast before anyone notices us . . ."

But Orso realized pretty quickly that someone had already noticed them: there was the sound of footfalls in the hallway, and he glimpsed lamplight on the walls outside.

"Just do it now!" he snapped. He reached into his pack and pulled out another one of Claudia's plates, placed it on the ground outside the doorway, and turned it on.

Gregor approached the wall, gauged where best to strike, and stabbed a seam of masonry with his scrived rapier. It slid into the wall about halfway up the blade. When he withdrew it, there was a tiny, focused leak that doused him with water. But the wall did not crumble—it held fast.

"I shall have to make many of these," he said as he wiped his face. "I think . . ."

The sound of footfalls outside increased. Orso turned back around and caught the highly unusual sight of a snarling Dandolo soldier running face-first into the invisible wall blocking the door. He was so close Orso even saw his nose burst with blood as it broke on the steel surface.

The soldier fell back, gasping with surprise. Then two more arrived and helped him to his feet. "*Another* one of your damned walls?" said the first soldier, his nose now bleeding heavily.

The three soldiers began hacking at the invisible wall with their scrived rapiers.

Orso stepped back. "Gregor . . ."

"I'm going!" said Gregor. He was stabbing little perforations across the wall, one after another, all at the seams of the masonry. "This damned thing has to give sometime . . ."

The soldiers looked to be making quick work of the steel wall. Orso swallowed and slapped the button on the left shoulder of his cuirass—which should have put the invisible steel box around him. Yet he couldn't quite tell if it had actually worked, for there was nothing to see.

Then he heard Gregor say, "Orso? *Orso! Watch ou—*"

Orso turned to see the leaks in the walls had turned to geysers, which then quickly became floods—and then the stones came crumbling down, and a huge wall of water rushed toward him.

"Oh, *shit!*" cried Orso. He felt himself being lifted off the ground, and a sharp pain in his armpits, and he shut his eyes and braced himself, expecting to be doused with water . . . but though the water hit his legs, his face was spared.

He opened his eyes, and saw why: his invisible box had indeed been activated, creating a nice little buffer around him, though the water had shoved him toward the door, very hard.

Then he looked over his shoulder—he seemed to be trapped facing one way, like the cuirass was fixed in one position within the invisible box—and gasped in horror. It appeared his invisible box had been smashed up against the invisible wall he'd just set up at the doorway—right when one Dandolo soldier had been trying to climb through the hole they'd made in it.

Orso stared at the ruined face and skull of the soldier, which seemed to be crushed between two panes of glass. Then there came an alarmingly loud whine of straining metal . . .

He looked back and saw the room was now almost completely filled with water. *Too much pressure,* he realized. *The wall I set up is about to collap—*

Then there was a crack of metal breaking, and he was suddenly flying end over end, and then he knew no more.

"They did it!" shouted Berenice. "Look, *look!*"

Sancia turned and saw the water was rapidly retreating, allowing them to descend the stairs into the lexicon chamber.

They started down, slipping a little on the slick stone steps, and waded forward as the water receded. Both of them produced scrived lanterns to light the way.

Sancia flexed her scrived sight, but was unsurprised to see that the room ahead remained dark: from what the Mountain had described, it'd had to deactivate the lexicon just before it flooded in order to prevent catastrophe. It might be little more than a wreck by now.

I just hope this goddamn hierophantic definition is still in decent shape, she thought. *Otherwise we did all this for nothing.*

They walked into the lexicon chamber, the mud and muck sucking at their feet. Sancia spied many traps and security rigs in the walls—all of them ruined, luckily. Finally their lights washed over the thick glass wall of the lexicon itself, though it was now crusty and smeared with algae and other growth. It had shattered under the pressure of the water on the lower left side, so they had to stoop and carefully crawl through in order to get to the giant rig within.

Once inside, Sancia looked around and did a double take. The floor of the chamber was littered with scriving definitions that had apparently washed out of the lexicon. The exposed ones were rusted over, but the spares had been carefully packaged and were presumably in fine condition. Any one of these intricately wrought metal plates would be worth a fortune on the black market—especially considering they'd been made by Tribuno Candiano himself.

"Holy shit," she gasped.

"Yes."

"These . . . These could be worth thousands . . . if not *millions*!"

"Focus," said Berenice. "And remember neither of us has the time or the training to discern which definition is actually useful. You could grab one thinking it could power a giant war machine only to find out later it makes the latrines run."

Grumbling, Sancia stooped and began peering through the muck and the sediment layered inside the remains of the lexicon. They combed through the mud like oyster farmers rooting for the day's supper, but they could find no sign of the little cone.

"What if it got washed away?" asked Sancia. "I mean, it's a cone, so it might have caught more water . . ."

Berenice studied the flow of water around the ruined lexicon. She marked the way the mud lay on the stones, the way it coiled around the walls . . .

"Back outside, I think," she said. "Past the broken glass."

They crawled back through, and they held their lamps high as they followed the river of mud beyond, until it finally ended in a large, filth-filled drainage pipe set in the floor—one whose wire mesh at the top had caved in a long time ago.

"Shit!" cried Sancia. "Could the damned thing have been washed down this goddamn pipe?"

Berenice narrowed her eyes. "Hmm. It looks like it's full of mud and other residue . . . which makes me think there might be another filter or blockage in the pipe, one that's still intact. One that could have caught it, in other words. But I'm not sure how to get the muck ou—"

"Enough of this shit," said Sancia. She knelt by the muck-filled pipe. "Hold my feet in case I fall."

"You can't be seri—"

But then Sancia dove into the muck, hands-first, and shut her eyes tight.

She was immersed in a cold, clammy substance that was somehow both disgustingly slimy *and* gritty. Blind and deaf, she felt around in the innards of the pipe, her fingers tracing over stones, and screws, and regular scriving definitions . . .

Come on, come on . . .

Her lungs begged for air, but she stretched farther down into the pipe until her fingertips brushed up against a metal grate.

The second filter.

She blindly probed its edges, parsing through bundles of filth and tangles of wire . . .

And then she remembered.

I'm looking for a hierophantic rig . . . So I should be able to see the goddamn thing, of course!

She flexed her scrived sight. Even though her eyes were closed, she instantly spied something glimmering an unpleasant blood red through her eyelids . . .

She closed her fingers around the object, and then began kicking. She felt Berenice grab her by the knees and begin to pull her up.

When she was finally dragged into the open air again, she still didn't dare open her eyes or her mouth.

"Did you get it?" asked Berenice. "Did you *get it*?"

Sancia pointed at her face with one muddy finger.

"Oh." She felt Berenice kneel behind her, then wipe her face clean with a cloth.

Sancia gasped for air once her mouth was clear of muck. "Oh, God . . . Oh, *God*, it smells, I didn't realize how it smells . . ."

"Are you all right, my love?"

Sancia sat up and looked down at her right hand. She opened her fingers and wiped the mud away to reveal a small golden metal cone, intricately engraved with scrivings . . .

"I," she said, grinning triumphantly, "am just scrumming *fine*."

———

Orso gasped, shook water from his face, and tried to understand what he was seeing.

His cuirass was still projecting his invisible steel box, but it seemed he'd fallen over—which meant the face of the box was pressed to the ground, and since the cuirass had apparently been scrived to be equidistant from the sides of the box at all times, he was now suspended in the air, facedown, trapped in the cuirass, his arms and legs dangling below.

The hallway was now flooded with water, but only a foot high. However, because the box had no bottom, it had flooded as well—and if the water had been a few feet higher, it would have undoubtedly submerged Orso's head, and he would have helplessly drowned, trapped inside his cuirass.

He stared into the surface of the water, which was mere inches from his nose. "Shit," he gasped. "Oh shit."

He reached up and pushed the button on his left shoulder. The invisible box vanished, and he fell face-first into the scummy waters.

He fought to his feet, gasping and moaning—his brain felt like it was still spinning in his head—and looked around. A few lamps were lit in the hallway, but everything was dark and wet and gleaming—and he couldn't see Gregor.

"Gregor?" he called. "*Gregor?*"

A large figure lumbered around the distant corner, sloshing through the water, and stopped when it saw him.

"Gregor?" he said hesitantly.

The figure was then joined by two others—these wearing Dandolo helmets that gleamed in the light.

"Oh hell," said Orso quietly.

The three soldiers waded down the hallway to him. As they passed one lamp, Orso saw they were all Dandolos, of course: and they were very large, and wet, and angry-looking.

"You bastard little shitling," snarled the one in the middle, who seemed the biggest. He pulled out his rapier.

Orso stood, slapped the button on his chest, and turned back on his invisible barrier. Then he tried to walk backward, away from them—but the cuirass stopped him, holding him in place.

He looked around and saw the wall of the hallway was very close. He must have turned it on so the invisible steel passed through the stone, immobilizing him.

Oh God, he thought. *I'm trapped.*

And he knew, of course, that scrived rapiers would have no issue penetrating a steel wall.

"I, uh . . ." said Orso. He thought desperately, tugging at his cuirass. "This is all a big misunderstanding, I . . . I used to live here and . . ."

"I ought to gut you," said the big soldier, "like a damned . . ."

He stopped. A *boom* echoed through the Mountain, followed by a great deal of distant yelling and screaming.

"What the hell is that?" asked the soldier on the right. "Wait . . . look at your spotter."

The big soldier looked down at his people finder, and they saw nearly every light was lit up—suggesting that the Mountain was suddenly filled with many, many people who did not bear the Dandolo sachets.

"What?" said the big soldier. "Who is this *now*? What the hell is going o—"

The hallways of the Mountain filled up with an amplified voice: "SOLDIERS OF DANDOLO CHARTERED! BY THE AUTHORITY OF MICHIEL BODY CORPORATE, YOU ARE HEREBY COMMANDED TO STAND DOWN FROM YOUR POSTS AND DEPART FROM THIS ENCLAVE *IMMEDIATELY*!"

The soldiers looked at one another, then at Orso.

"The *Michiels*?" asked the soldier on the left. "What are they doing here?"

"THIS PROPERTY WAS UNLAWFULLY TRANSFERRED TO DANDOLO CHARTERED BY AN OFFICIAL WHO HAS HAD ALL AUTHORITIES REVOKED POSTHUMOUSLY," boomed the amplified voice. It sounded strangely scratchy and stuttered. Orso thought he knew the exact sound rig they were probably using. "NEGOTIATIONS ARE CURRENTLY UNDER WAY BE-

TWEEN BOTH CAMPOS. YOU ARE ORDERED TO STAND DOWN, RETURN TO THE ATRIUM, AND EVACUATE THE PREMISES UNTIL NEGOTIATIONS ARE CONCLUDED. DO NOT ENGAGE IN COMBAT! I REPEAT, DO *NOT* ENGAGE IN COMBA—"

There was another faint *boom,* and the speaker stopped. Orso guessed that someone had indeed engaged in combat.

They listened to the cries and screams and shouts echoing down the hallway. Orso could tell the soldiers weren't sure what to do: go and surrender, go and fight, or wait for the fight to come to them?

The big one slowly turned to look back at Orso. "This is your doing, isn't it."

"No, no!" said Orso. "It isn't!"

He stepped closer, rapier drawn. "Did *you* open the doors?"

"No!"

"Let them in?"

"No, I'm just as surprised as you a—"

He shook his head, furious. "I can't believe it . . . We're going to get shot to pieces in this ancient damned dome, and all because of some sneaky little striper."

"If you're going to kill him, Ernesto," said the soldier on the right, "then go ahead and get it over wi—"

But he never finished the comment. Suddenly his mouth opened wide and he gasped and choked, his arms shot out at odd angles. Orso, blinking, realized the soldier had something protruding from his chest—the blade of a scrived rapier.

"What!" cried the soldier on the left.

The blade withdrew and the sergeant dropped to the ground, revealing Gregor Dandolo standing behind him, rapier in his hand. The soldier on the left spun to face him, but he was far, far too slow: Gregor pivoted and struck out with his rapier as fast as lightning, opening up his throat. Orso saw hot blood splash his invisible barrier, and the soldier collapsed into the waters, pawing at this throat.

The big soldier wheeled around, raised his rapier, and advanced on Gregor. Even though he was still stunned, Orso realized he had never actually seen a real swordfight before. In Tevanne, where so many lexicons allowed you to use augmented bolts or blades, most people died suddenly and quickly—not so much a consequence of art and skill as sheer power and, usually, surprise.

Dying was very easy in Tevanne. Artfully fighting was not.

Yet this was what Gregor and his combatant engaged in, however briefly: two men with two blades scrived to amplify their speed and weight, dueling within the dripping hallway, their rapiers crashing into each other with near-deafening *clangs*. The blows were outrageously quick, but Orso could see there was a method to it: for example, you couldn't just lift your sword to block your opponent's, as a scrived blade moved faster the more you moved it, so your opponent's sword would easily swat your rapier from your hand. Instead, you had to swing your own blade at the exact right speed and in the exact right direction to deflect the blow, which would hopefully open up your opponent for your own counterattack.

Orso could also see that Gregor was a lot better at this than his opponent. He didn't just attack the man—he engaged in what was clearly a *process,* opening the man's stance with a series of strikes, and then . . .

One, two, three. First the man's leg was lopped off at the knee, then his arm as he fell, and then suddenly he was missing his head. Orso felt warm drops patter his cheeks and arms, but that was nothing compared to Gregor, who was doused with great fans of blood splashing his chest and thighs.

Gregor looked surprised, and stared down at what was left of the man with an expression of faint dismay, like he'd left home and just realized he'd forgotten something.

"Oh," Gregor said faintly. "Oh dear . . ."

Orso slapped the cuirass button again, and this time it finally worked: the barrier vanished, and he fell forward into the water. Then he crawled to Gregor, who was still standing there with a shaken, horrified look on his face.

Orso reached out to touch him. The man was absolutely covered in blood, from head to toe. "Gregor? Are you . . . are you all righ—"

"I . . . I remember," whispered Gregor. Tears ran down his face, mingling with the blood on his cheeks. "I remember. I *remember* . . ." Then his face went slack, and he stopped speaking.

Then the hallway filled with light. They both turned and saw soldiers pouring around the corner, scrived lights held high and es-pringals pointed. One of them bellowed, "*Lay down arms, lay down arms!*"

Orso reached forward, pulled the rapier out of Gregor's bloody hand, and tossed it into the water. Then he held his hands up as they advanced.

Gregor Dandolo saw sand, and beaches, and the moon at sea.

He saw caves, and tunnels, and torchlight on stone walls.

He saw moths dancing around him, a storm of bright, fragile, white wings.

His older brother, Domenico, whimpering in the darkness.

And then he saw nothing—just darkness, cold and silent and dreadful.

His mother's voice floated through the darkness to him: *Oh, Gregor. Wake up, my love. Please, wake up . . .*

He heard something flutter in the darkness. He felt his heart twitch, then pump—once, twice—and his lungs suddenly burned for air.

He took in a breath, and as he did his vision returned to him, and he saw a stone ceiling above him—perhaps a cave, flickering with torchlight.

Then his mother was there, kneeling above him. She was younger than he remembered—her hair was longer, and her face was clear of familiar creases and wrinkles. Five years younger? Ten? He wasn't sure. She was weeping, her hands running over his chest where he lay on the stone floor, saying—*What did they do to you? What did they do?*

Gregor looked down and saw he was clad in a dreadfully familiar rig: a lorica, with one arm set in a huge, retractable pole arm, and the other in a bolt caster. The cuirass of his lorica was torn in many places, however, and he could see his own flesh below, with huge gaping wounds in his chest and abdomen . . .

Please, said his mother. *Please, please, no . . .*

And then his body shivered, and blurred . . . and to his shock, the wounds vanished. Or at least the most lethal of them vanished:

he still had puncture wounds in his shoulder, but his stomach was now smooth and whole again, the horrid gash there completely gone.

It's working, his mother whispered. She sighed with relief. *It's working. But you've done so well, Gregor. You did exactly as we needed.*

Gregor tried to look around. He was in some kind of cave that was littered with bodies: soldiers, guards, slaves, all of them hacked to pieces. Everything was wet and slick with gore.

Ofelia Dandolo stood and walked away, stepping over the bodies, ignorant of the hem of her dress soaking in blood. She approached the cave wall—it appeared to be some kind of ancient doorway, caved in and crumbling, its stone entryway marked by curious symbols.

We're getting closer, Ofelia whispered. *You've done so, so, so well, Gregor.*

A soothing, powerful joy filled his mind—it was so good to have done well, to do what was expected of him.

It was such a grand thing, to make war.

I would die for this, he thought. He looked up into his mother's beaming face. *I have died for this. And I will gladly die again.*

Then the memory left him, and he knew no more.

17

"This thing is amazing," said Berenice, studying the golden definition as they ran on through the halls of the Mountain. "I mean—it's *amazing.*"

"It'd goddamn better be," said Sancia. Her boots slapped wetly on the ground as they ran up and up through the dark stairways of the Mountain, back to the secret exit on the fourth floor. She'd wiped off much of the muck, but she knew she was going to reek for days.

"No, I mean . . ." Berenice held it up to her eye. "To access a hierophantic command, you have to first violate reality via the breaking of life, which allows you to briefly assert that you're basically God Himself—and then you can snatch up one or several of the deeper commands."

"So?"

"So, this little device . . . it does something similar, but it persuades reality that a lexicon *is* God Himself! It asserts that a damned rig is functionally the divine creator of . . . well, whatever little area it has influence over! Then you can issue whatever commands you want!"

"Holy shit," said Sancia. "So, the dome we're in now . . ."

"Yes!" said Berenice. "Reality in here believes, to a very slight degree, that the Mountain *is* the Creator of all reality! Yet it must be a very weak effect . . . That must be why Tribuno had to stack it six times over, just to make the Mountain powerful enough to perceive all the comings and goings within its barriers."

Sancia glanced sideways at Berenice, who was clutching the little golden cone like a child with a brand-new toy. "Neat," she said. "You remember Tribuno had to kill a guy to make that thing, right?"

Berenice blanched slightly and stowed the definition away. "I mean . . . Yes, of course, it's just . . . Well, intriguing."

<Sancia?> whispered the Mountain in her ear.

<Yeah?>

<Something is wrong . . . There are new men inside my barriers. Soldiers. Different soldiers.>

She slowed down. Berenice saw her and did the same. "What's wrong?" she asked.

Sancia waved a hand at her to shush her. <What? Who? Who the hell could it be now?>

<I am not sure . . . These men are not in yellow, like the other soldiers, but rather are . . . purple?>

"The *Michiels* are here?" said Sancia aloud, recognizing the colors. <Mountain, are you su—>

There was a faint *boom* from the atrium. Berenice and Sancia jumped and looked at each other, surprised. They heard a distant screaming, more booms, and then an amplified voice, screaming at the Dandolos to stand down.

"Oh God," said Berenice. "We're in the middle of a campo pissing match, aren't we?"

"Let's just hope the goddamn Morsinis don't show up and join the fray too," said Sancia.

They sprinted up the stairs to the fourth-floor walkway. <Mountain,> said Sancia. <Where are Gregor and Orso? Are they alive? Are they all right?>

<They are in a hallway just off of my atrium. They are relatively all right. But these new soldiers . . . the Michiels. They have them now.>

"Shit!" whispered Sancia as they came to the fourth-floor walkway. They sank low, approached the balcony, and peered into the atrium.

Whereas before the atrium had been dark and dusty and still, now it was lit bright by many new lamps, and it was echoing with screams, cries, and cracks as bolts bit into the walls. A fully fledged battle was taking place there on the main floor between the Dandolo and Michiel soldiers: men were fighting across the atrium floor with rapiers, shields, and espringals—and since all of the armaments were scrived, the damage was nothing short of catastrophic. Whole columns had been carved away. Every wall was pockmarked like it'd been hammered by a meteor shower. And the floor was absolutely swimming with blood.

"I'm . . . guessing the Michiels want their shit back," said Sancia.

Berenice sat up. "San—look!"

She pointed to one entrance by the main floor. Sancia squinted and saw two figures being led out of the hallway, their hands bound behind their backs. One was Orso, who looked as wet and miserable as a half-drowned rat—and the other was Gregor, who was covered in blood.

"Oh my *God!*" gasped Sancia. *<Mountain—are you sure they're all right?>*

<Yes. The blood on your friend is not his own. He just killed three men.>

Sancia shut her eyes in despair, and leaned forward until her forehead rested on the railing of the balcony. "Oh no . . . Oh, poor, poor Gregor . . ."

"It . . . It looks like the Dandolos are losing," said Berenice quietly. "The Michiels are mopping them up. They're putting Orso and Gregor along the wall, and put lanterns all around them." She looked at her. "San—how in hell are we going to get them out?"

Sancia sighed deeply. "I have no idea."

———

Orso sat on the floor of the atrium, his hands bound tightly behind his back. At first he wished to complain, but then he noticed the number of Dandolo corpses lying about the atrium, victims of a variety of injuries—many heads, chests, and limbs had been unartfully removed by a scrived bolt or rapier—and he suddenly thought himself quite lucky.

Orso watched as a Michiel captain walked about the atrium, conferring with his lieutenants as the battle tapered off around them. He was a somewhat aged but still powerful man, his shoulders broad but his belly pressing at the limits of his cuirass, a pipe clutched in his teeth. He bore many scars on his arms and face, Orso noted, the mementos of many wars and battles. One hand was missing two fingers.

One of the soldiers walked up to him, said something, and pointed at Gregor and Orso.

Shit, thought Orso.

He looked sideways at Gregor, who appeared to be catatonic, his blood-spattered face fixed in an expression of deep grief.

"Gregor," whispered Orso. "Can you hear me?"

Gregor did not answer.

"We can't tell them about Ber and San. Just . . . try and get them to think we're important so they take us prisoner to their campo or—"

"No talking!" shouted a nearby soldier. He approached with one hand on his sheathed rapier, and Orso bowed his head, cowed. When the soldier finally turned his back on them, Orso looked at Gregor. His face had barely moved.

"Gregor?" asked Orso quietly.

"I . . . remember," whispered Gregor. His eyes were blank and crazed. "I remember, I remember, I remember . . ."

He broke himself, thought Orso. *Damn it . . . Gregor's gone somewhere in his head, and I can't call him ba—*

"So . . . exactly who in the hell are you?" asked a gruff voice.

Orso looked up and saw the Michiel captain standing over them, his small, puffy eyes darting back and forth between their faces.

Orso wondered what to say. Before he could speak, the captain said, "My boys here tell me they found you hacking up Dandolo soldiers in the halls . . . so I *highly* doubt you're with those thieves. So—who are you?"

Orso thought as fast as he could. "Saboteurs," he said.

The captain took his pipe out of his teeth. "What's that? Here to sabotage . . . what? Us?"

"N-No," said Orso. "The Dandolos."

"Ohh?" said the captain appraisingly. "And why's that?"

"We knew what they were doing here. A . . . A power grab. Trying to steal bits of the lexicons of this place. We had to stop them."

"And . . . again, why's that?"

Orso had an idea. "Because . . . I am Orso Ignacio. And this is Gregor Dandolo."

The captain blinked. "You lot . . . You're the Foundryside people, are you?"

"Yes." Orso waited, hoping this worked—perhaps the enemy of an enemy might be a friend.

"And you're here to piss in Ofelia Dandolo's wine?" The captain looked at Gregor. "In his *mother's* wine? Is that it?"

"Yes."

The captain looked at them, his small eyes half-hidden behind their heavy lids. "I see," he said quietly.

Orso waited, hoping that perhaps, just once, the night could go their way.

"You think that impresses me?" demanded the captain. "That it makes me *warm* to you, that you were here trying to sabotage the people who stole this shithole from us?"

"I . . . I would think that it mi—"

The captain spat on the ground. "*You* prissy little shitlings are the very *reason* my house is in the woeful state that it is! Did you know that?"

"W-What?" said Orso, surprised.

"Slaves rebelling left and right? Scrivers starting their own houses in the *Commons*?"

"Ah . . ."

The captain pulled out his rapier and pointed it at Orso. "It's heresy! It's madness! It goes against everything that Tevanne has ever stood for! And it's all *your* fault. It's all your doing, every bit of it!"

Orso glanced at the number of bodies being stacked in the atrium. He wanted to mention how *another* thing that had once been considered madness and heresy had been the idea of two merchant houses going to war in Tevanne. No one had ever thought to attempt such a thing, given that the foundry lexicons that made the campos run were so unstable. It was like tossing lit matches around in a granary mill.

"I told our house officers not to wait," continued the captain, looking out at the atrium around them. "The second you all went and set up your bastard little shop, I told them to wade right into the Commons and burn you all out. Can't let the Commoners start handling scrived rigs. They'd get ideas. Start thinking they were above their stations."

"We . . . are not precisely Commoners, though," said Orso. "We—"

"Yes, yes, yes, you're *Lamplanders,*" said the captain with a sneer. "Talk about thinking above your station . . . Scrivers think just because they've read a book or two they know everything in the world. I always knew they'd start questioning their betters. Trying to tear down all the founders have given us. What ingratitude!"

The captain ranted on—apparently he'd been writing this speech in his head for some time—but Orso just watched as this aged, scarred man, a man who'd shed and spilled blood in God only knew how many battles, passionately defended the campo elites: people who had never known a tenth of the hardship and pains that he had, and never would.

And as he listened to the captain speak, Orso felt something deeply unpleasant spool into his belly: doubt.

He doubted for the very first time whether the merchant houses could really be overthrown—if Tevanne really could be restored, or remade, or at least *changed,* just a little. What change could possibly be accomplished in the face of such thoughtless, ignorant conviction?

There was a silence as the captain's rant tapered to an end. He turned around and studied them, his eyes cold and distant. "I knew it would always come to this," he said. He pointed his rapier at Orso. "Haul this one to the center of the atrium, boys."

"W-What?" said Orso, startled.

The soldiers picked him up by the arms and dragged him away.

The captain called to his men to bring a table and some rope, and they did so.

"I don't . . . Stop . . . Stop, please . . ." said Orso.

They ignored him. The soldiers brought the wooden table over, and the captain shoved Orso down so his head was bent to its surface. Then they held him down and tied his head and body so he was laid flat against the wood.

"What are you doing?" asked Orso weakly. "What . . . What are you doing to m—"

"You know who this is?" shouted the captain. "This here is *Orso Ignacio,* lads! He's the man who caused *all* the trouble our city has seen! He's the man who's ducked the loop and laughed at us all!"

The soldiers clapped and jeered at him. Orso realized what the captain was about to do. "No! *No!*" he cried.

Goddamn it, Orso thought as he struggled against his bonds. *I probably* designed *the scrumming sword in your hand! And now you're going to kill me with it, you oaf!*

"Now let's see if the founder of Foundryside can scheme his way out of this one," said the captain, walking close, "with his head separated from his body!"

The soldiers cheered, and the captain lifted the sword high.

Berenice almost screamed in horror as the captain raised the sword. Sancia sat frozen, unable to think. She wanted to jump down there and attack . . . but if she did, they'd surely kill her too.

Then the Mountain spoke in her mind: *<Sancia! It's . . . I feel something in me! Someone . . . Something* different.*>*

<Mountain, not now! Goddamn it, they're—>

<I feel . . . A person. No, I feel him! He is so big, so . . . so heavy. He *is a thousand minds, all in one, all written into one form, into one being! Sancia, Sancia, he is here, HE IS HERE!>*

Orso shut his eyes as the captain raised his rapier, bracing for him to bring it down and slash it through his neck.

But then a voice echoed through the atrium—a voice that was rich, and silky, and impossibly, *impossibly* deep.

"*My, my. It seems like you boys are having quite a night.*"

Orso felt a sudden, churning nausea in his belly.

He opened his eyes. *Oh no.*

He tried to look around, panicked. The Michiels were turning to face the main entryway, which was dark with shadows—and then a figure appeared in the darkness, clad in a three-cornered hat, a short dark cloak, and his mask, black and glinting.

"What on earth . . ." whispered a soldier nearby.

This . . . This might actually be worse, thought Orso.

18

Who in the hell are you?" demanded the Michiel captain.

Crasedes slowly walked into the light and turned his blank, black eyes on the man. There was a long, long silence.

"I should ask the same of you," he said finally. "Being as you're trespassing on my property." He looked down at all the bodies around them. "And getting blood and . . . *bits* everywhere. Is this what passes for civility in Tevanne?"

Crasedes walked forward with the casual air of a man returning to his home after work. The Michiel soldiers backed away from him. Orso found he couldn't blame them: Even if you lacked Sancia's scrived vision, something about him made your eyes water. Just from a glance, you somehow knew that this being's very existence was torturing reality.

But the Michiel captain did not seem to care. "This enclave is the rightful property of Michiel Body Corporate!" he said. "It was ceded to Dandolo Chartered through an unlawful transaction, conducted unilaterally by a discredited agent acting in bad faith! The transaction is *null* and *void,* and the ownership of this enclave is now being negotiated by campo authorities!"

Crasedes stopped and studied the captain. He cocked his head. "Is that so?" he asked.

Orso struggled against his bonds, desperate to free himself and run. *I . . . really don't like how this seems to be going.*

Crasedes resumed strolling among the Michiel soldiers. "You know, for people who do a lot of work to avoid having laws," he told the captain, "you certainly do seem to invoke a lot of them when it's to your benefit . . ."

"I see no colors on you," said the captain. "Save black. But do you say you act on behalf of the Dandolos?"

Crasedes shrugged, bored. "I suppose."

The captain brandished his rapier at him. "And do you see the many dead that litter this place now? Do you see the blood that fills these halls, and these many corridors?"

Another bored shrug. "Certainly."

"*These* are the signs of our ownership of this place," said the captain proudly. "We have bought this place with *blood.* All the tricks of the Dandolos are but nothing compared to the might and the will of the Michiels." The soldiers murmured in agreement. "Know this—break our rules, and we shall break you!"

"Hm," said Crasedes lightly. Then he spied Orso tied to the table, and stopped.

Crasedes paced over—the nausea in Orso's belly quintupled until it was almost unbearable—and he bent low to stare into Orso's face. Orso shut his eyes, but he could still hear his voice.

"I know you . . ." said Crasedes.

"Get away from him!" said the captain.

"Hello, Orso," said Crasedes silkily.

"Oh God . . ." gasped Orso, his eyes shut tight.

"Where is Sancia?" whispered Crasedes. "Tell me. Now."

Crasedes's words seemed to *sink* into Orso's mind, pulling all his other thoughts down with them, and suddenly it felt very hard to do anything besides tell him.

"I . . . I don't know," said Orso.

"But she's here somewhere?"

"Y-Yes." Orso felt like weeping, and he opened his eyes, filled with shame and despair.

"Mm," whispered Crasedes. "I did tell you all . . . I'm on *your* side. Against the construct, yes, but . . . also against these men, you know. Powerful men, with powerful tools . . . I have seen that story play out *so* many times." He stood, looked around, and saw Gregor. "Ah! And here is young Dandolo himself. How nice to see!"

"Stop!" said the captain, his face now bright red. "Remove yourself from this property before I have my men shoot you dead!"

But Crasedes ignored him and walked across the lamplit atrium to Gregor. "Oh, Gregor . . ." he said. "You seem to have fallen back into your old ways. I wonder what that's like for you . . ."

Orso couldn't see well from this angle, but Gregor was still sitting with his head bent, his face fixed in an expression of aching grief.

Crasedes squatted low, his black mask hovering close to his ear. He whispered something to him . . . and Gregor's brow creased, ever so slightly.

"*Get away from him!*" screamed Orso. He strained against his bonds. "You . . . You *leave him be, you scrumming monster!*"

The captain pointed at Orso. "Shut up, you!" Then he pointed at Crasedes. "Get away from him! Men—prepare to fire, *now!*"

The soldiers all pointed their espringals at Crasedes.

Crasedes paused, glanced over his shoulder, and slowly stood. "Boys," he said, "I don't know how you think this is going to go. But let me just say—it's not going to go how you *think* it's going to go."

"We gave your soldiers an honorable chance," said the Michiel captain. "And they chose to fire on us. Why should we give you a chance now?"

"Orso," said Crasedes, "did any of the Dandolo scrivers actually succeed in accessing the lexicons of this place?"

Again, Crasedes's words seemed to swirl around in Orso's brain until he could do nothing but respond. "No."

He sighed. "How disappointing. But predictable. In that case . . . I still have work to do here."

The Michiel captain's face was now the shade of a fresh plum. "Then it shall *not* be do—"

"Hmm . . . how many of you are there?" Crasedes said thoughtfully. He looked around at them, unperturbed by the numerous weapons trained on him. "Seems at least a hundred or so . . . Far too many to convince all at once. Which, frankly, I just don't have the time for tonight anyway . . ."

"Go back to your campo," spat the captain, "and tell them what you've seen here. And let them know they should think *twice* before challenging the might of the Michiels!"

"It's still a bit early," said Crasedes. "So instead, I will ask—have you fellows ever heard of Brassitus?"

There was a long pause.

"Of *who*?" said the captain. "Is this some campo figure you think will save you?"

"No, no," said Crasedes. "Brassitus was a general in the Plenian armies. Are you familiar with them?"

"I am not."

"Oh, giant empire, existed about three thousand years ago. They had a civil war, arguing over whether the landowning classes should get two votes for every hectari they possessed, or three . . . Silly thing, really. Brassitus came to power after quite a *lot* of Plenian noblemen and politicians and civic leaders had gotten killed in the streets, and he just decided . . . enough. Enough with laws, and constitutions, and statutes, and parliamentary procedures. And he stormed the assemblies and took control, and when people complained, he simply said—'Let us battle, friend. You with your laws, and I with my spear.' And no one seemed to have a very good answer to that."

"What is the *point* of this?" said the Michiel captain, furious.

"I am simply saying," said Crasedes, "that you lot and Brassitus would probably get along. You seem cut from the same cloth. But what you don't know—what *no one* knows, really—is what happened to Brassitus."

A long silence.

"Which was what, exactly?" asked the captain.

"Well," said Crasedes pleasantly, "*someone* came to Plenia who was willing to fight with something besides laws *or* spears. And now all of Brassitus's glorious armies, and his enlightened despotism . . . That is all gone." He leaned forward, and his voice grew queerly, disturbingly deep. "Wiped away. Like raindrops from a leaf . . ."

Orso heard a sound in the distance. It was very faint but very familiar: the sound of the Michiel clock tower, chiming midnight in the distance.

"Oh no," he whispered.

The air throughout the atrium seemed to shake and quiver, like a vast wind was running through the Mountain's many chambers, yet Orso could feel no breeze or draft on his skin. Nausea coiled and thrashed in his belly, and he heard the Michiel soldiers moan quietly around him.

Crasedes stood up straight . . . and then he lifted his legs, and he simply seemed to float in the air, seated in a cross-legged position, his hands on his knees, his black mask lifted to the moonlight above.

When he spoke next, his voice was so deep it seemed to make the very ceiling rattle. "The problem with might, you see," he said, "is that there's *always someone mightier.*"

Crasedes reached out with an open hand—and then he crooked his fingers, very slightly.

The Michiel captain gagged.

Then he screamed, and twitched. And then he began to . . .

Float.

The Michiel soldiers watched in amazement as their captain slowly rose into the air, like a puppet on strings. His face was fixed in an expression of terrible agony, and he shrieked, long and loud— and then he suddenly seemed to *implode.*

It was without a doubt the most horrific sight Orso had ever seen. First the captain's arms snapped in, and then his legs folded up with a crack, and then his ribs and shoulders crinkled inward, and then his skull became curiously elongated, like someone stretching a piece of clay. It was as if he were being crushed by the fists of an invisible giant, clutching each limb one at a time—and yet, he did not bleed, not one drop.

Crasedes twitched a finger, and the ruined body of the captain fell to the ground with a clump—and yet it kept twitching.

He's still alive, thought Orso, horrified. *He . . . He did all that to him but, oh my God, he's* still goddamn alive!

One of the Michiels screamed, *"Shoot the bastard!"*

The next thing Orso knew, the air was filled with the sounds of dozens of hundreds of scrived bolts hurtling through the air.

He screamed and shut his eyes, certain that one of the stray bolts would fly through his chest or face, but . . . then the sound tapered off.

He opened his eyes.

Crasedes was still floating in the air, yet he had one hand raised—and it seemed like it was holding a giant ball of gray fuzz. The ball appeared to grow denser and denser, but then Orso realized it was not fuzz, but *bolts,* dozens of them, perhaps hundreds of them, all gathering around Crasedes's hand—but none of them actually struck him.

"Enough," boomed Crasedes's voice—and then the ball of bolts flew apart.

Orso watched, terrified, as the bolts all flew back directly at the people who had fired them, dozens of soldiers shredded to pieces in an instant—but then Crasedes guided the wave of bolts with one hand, like they were a school of fish flitting throughout the atrium. He pointed at one balcony where a soldier crouched, and the river of bolts consumed it, devouring him utterly, and then it snaked through the walkways and shredded another soldier attempting to flee. It all happened so fast Orso's eye could barely translate what he was seeing.

"Complacent," said Crasedes.

While the river of bolts raged behind him, he pointed a finger at two soldiers before him, then ripped his hand back. Their faces seemed to burst with blood, and their arms went limp—but the blood kept coming and coming out of them, coiling in the air like a long red snake, until Crasedes lazily waved and it splashed to the ground while the soldiers collapsed.

Orso stared. *Did . . . Did he just pull the* blood *out of those men?*

"Overconfident," proclaimed Crasedes.

He pointed at two soldiers with both hands, and then smashed them together. With a scream, the two men flew together and *crunched,* like a child taking two dolls of clay and smooshing them into one. He flicked his hands at them, and the mashed-together men fell to the ground.

"Fat," he said, "and sated . . . and *slow*."

He raised his arms and made a gesture as if sweeping a table clean, and with a chorus of screams, all the soldiers and rubble and ruins around Orso slid to the side of the atrium like someone had picked up the whole building and tilted it.

Orso screamed in abject terror, but he noticed—he did not slide. Nor did Gregor. Both of them stayed right where they were.

"You don't know how many empires I've *crushed* in my day," boomed Crasedes.

As the soldiers struck the walls they just kept screaming, pinned to the stone, and Orso realized that whatever force had pushed them there was still pushing, still growing stronger, pushing and pushing until the soldiers began to collapse, like they were being compressed by a giant, flat surface . . .

"Oh my God," whispered Orso.

"The thing that irks me the most," said Crasedes, "is that you all think you're so *special*. So unique. So *deserving*."

He made a gesture, and the crushed soldiers rose to levitate in the air like a mangled wall of human bodies.

And then the wall began to fold inward, forming a ball . . . which shrank, and shrank . . .

"But to be honest," said Crasedes, "*your* empire isn't even terribly inspired."

The ball of flesh and stone and glass hung in the air for a moment.

"Yet I will still relish grinding it into sand and ash, just like all the others . . ."

Then it slowly began to drift down, down, and down . . . until it rested in the middle of the atrium floor.

There was a long, long silence.

Crasedes hovered in the air, still seated in a queerly meditative position. Then he slowly turned to look at Orso.

"Well," he said. "It's been a long time since I did *that*."

19

Sancia and Berenice watched from the fourth-floor balconies in silent horror as Crasedes finished his slaughter.

"Oh my God," said Berenice softly, tears streaming down her cheeks. "Oh my *God* . . ."

Crasedes floated forward into the cavernous atrium, still seated in the air. *"I think,"* he called, *"that I am owed a* thank-you." His black mask scanned the balconies around him. *"Am I not? Am I not owed a thank-you, Sancia, for saving your friends?"*

Sancia felt her blood pounding in every limb in her body. *Shit. He knows I'm here.*

She watched as his black mask turned to look at the balconies. "This is getting a little tiresome," echoed Crasedes's voice throughout the atrium. "All this sneaking and spying, when a simple conversation would work so much better . . . And after all, we never did finish our discussion earlier."

She looked at Gregor, still sitting on the floor, head bent, and Orso, still tied to the table. Then, though she desperately wished she wouldn't, she looked at the mangled ball of flesh and stone and weaponry on the ground next to them . . .

He would do it to them, too. He'd do it and never think about it, not once.

"Berenice," she said hoarsely. "Take the definition we came here for and get out of here, now."

"What?" Berenice said, stunned. "You . . . what, are you actually going to go down there and talk to . . . to that *thing*?"

"Yes. I have a plan. Or, rather, an agreement." She looked up at the roof of the atrium. "One I made with the Mountain. One I think it would dearly like me to keep."

"Sancia," called Crasedes. "I am getting rather bored. And my mind always strays when I'm *bored* . . ."

She looked back at Berenice. "Go. *Now!* Wait for Orso and Gregor to join you, but you have to save the one thing we came here for."

Berenice looked into her eyes, her face trembling. "You'll be all right?"

"I'll be all right." She tried to believe it as she said it.

Then they kissed desperately. Berenice felt her face with one hand, and then she turned and ran into the secret exit.

I sure as shit hope I know what I'm doing, Sancia thought.

She stood and called out, "*I'm coming down!*"

She heard Orso's voice screaming, "*No! No, goddamn it, get the hell out of here! Get out of here, get out of here, get ou—*"

"Oh, enough," boomed Crasedes's voice.

Orso fell silent. He did not seem to be hurt, from where Sancia could see, just . . . oddly frozen.

"I will be civil," said Crasedes. "We will all be *civil,* for once. And how nice that will be."

Sancia tried not to shake as she exited the stairs and walked across the atrium main floor. The air stank of blood and death. The floors and walls were covered with gore. Orso whimpered where he'd been tied to the table. And there, seated peacefully and calmly on the air, was Crasedes, his black mask fixed on her as she emerged from the shadows.

"Ahh," he said as she walked forward. "There she is. The brave little soldier. Sancia . . . you don't look so good, you know. You could use a bath. Or two."

"Eat shit," said Sancia.

Crasedes cocked his head. Did *you* succeed in getting the definition, Sancia?"

She gestured to the blood and destruction around her. "Does anything about tonight seem successful?"

"I don't know," he said dryly. "I've seen uglier successes in my day." He drifted closer to her. Her bowels quivered a little. "You've been in contact with the construct, then. She sent you here tonight, as I thought she would."

"Yes."

"Then I must know—where is she?" asked Crasedes.

"I'll tell you everything," said Sancia. "Everything—if you let my friends go."

"Why would I do that?" asked Crasedes. "It seems you're far likelier to be truthful if I possess some collateral . . ."

"You could torture them to get me to tell the truth, if you think I'm lying," she said. "But that would be a waste of your time. Time you could spend trying to catch Valeria—who is very, very close."

Crasedes went still. His mask was fixed on her, his eyes like black chasms.

"Is that so?" he asked.

"Yes," she said. "She's hiding in a Michiel lexicon. Only, the Michiels are using a new tool of ours—one that allows her to inhabit *every* Michiel lexicon, all at once."

"Sancia!" said Orso, horrified. "What in hell are you *doin*—"

Crasedes raised a finger. Orso froze and fell silent.

"Go on," said Crasedes.

"We were going to get the definition, set it up within a lexicon nearby, and twin it with the Michiel foundries," she said. "Then Valeria could escape, and establish a foothold here in Tevanne."

"One that you could then use," said Crasedes, "to defy me."

"Yes."

"I see," he said. He studied her for a moment. "Orso—is she telling the truth?"

Orso shut his eyes hard like he was trying to ignore a piercing sound in his ear. "Yes," he whispered miserably.

"Let them go," said Sancia. "If you do, you'll have everything right where you want it, won't you?" She glared at him. "After all, you wanted to bring her to the Mountain, didn't you? To take the horrible tools Tribuno had built here, and use them to turn this whole damned place into a forge—to remake her, and force her to do as you want?"

He studied her for a moment. "Huh!" he said finally. "Impressive. I had not thought I'd been so . . . transparent. So—she's nearby, then?"

"She is," said Sancia. "And I can take you to her."

"Orso . . ." said Crasedes quietly. "Can she really? Tell me the truth."

Orso's face twisted in self-hate. "Yes!"

"And if I don't," said Sancia, "you can smash my skull with a rock. That's plenty of collateral, yeah?"

Crasedes watched her for a long, long while—or perhaps it just seemed long because of how terrified she was. Sancia could even feel her heart fluttering in her chest.

Then there was a *snap*. Sancia flinched, expecting a stone to come hurtling at her—but instead, the bonds holding Orso down suddenly dropped away, as did the ones binding Gregor's hands.

Orso slid off the table, coughing and gasping.

"Orso, get up," said Sancia sternly. "Get your ass up and get Gregor out of here."

Orso fought to his feet, staggered over to Gregor, and helped him stand. "What did you *say* to him?" Orso demanded, turning to Crasedes.

"I would leave, if I were you," said Crasedes, "before I decide your blood looks better outside of you than in."

Orso glared at him, but then he and Gregor hobbled out of the atrium, and Sancia was left alone with him.

I hope to God this works, she thought.

"Well, then, Sancia," said Crasedes merrily. "Lead the way."

Sancia walked off into the passageways of the Mountain, Crasedes silently floating a few feet behind her. If it weren't for the constant nausea in her stomach, she'd probably forget he was even there.

"Tell me, Sancia," asked Crasedes as they wound up the atrium stairs. His deep voice echoed along the endless corridors. "What do you think of this place?"

"Huh? You mean the Mountain?"

"Of course."

"Why do you care?"

"Because I find it to be a depressing, bleak place, personally. But I haven't lived in its shadow for many years. I would like to know if you think of it differently."

"I . . . don't," she said. "Why do *you* think it's depressing? I thought it was just your kind of place."

"Oh, no. I mean, it was built as a sort of temple to me." He gazed out at the dark atrium. "Tribuno wished nothing more than to witness me, and hold court with me. He even emulated my methods—to an extent. What a waste. Not just of stone, but toil and suffering . . ."

"Seems strange to hear someone who just crushed a bunch of soldiers into a ball talk about suffering."

"Mm, perhaps," he said. "But there is suffering inflicted for the sake of enforcing your power, and then there is suffering inflicted for a higher cause." He gestured out at the atrium, his black-wrapped fingers clicking curiously as they unfolded. "I am here to prevent *this*, Sancia. To prevent more Tribunos. To prevent any more kings, or emperors, or lords from walking this earth, and forcing their will upon others. That's why I fought so hard to come back. *That's* what I'm here to do."

She almost tripped and fell on her face at these words. She stared over her shoulder at him, bewildered. "You're *what*? You're here to . . . to be some bizarre scrumming *liberator*?"

"Is that so odd?"

"I think it is damned strange to hear the person who created the biggest empire of all time saying he has a problem with empires, yeah."

"You misunderstand my works," he said. "I've been alive a *very* long time, Sancia. And if there's one thing I have learned throughout all the history that I've seen, it's that mankind is quite good at coming up with delightful little innovations . . . but all of them are eventually turned to cruelty, and oppression, and slavery. Even the simplest ones become weapons. Take beans, for example."

"What? *Beans?*"

"Yes." He seemed to be having a very grand time, explaining this to her. "The Masazari peoples, in the lands east of here, once bred an unusually hardy but nutritious strain of white bean that helped their small culture to flourish. Their children lived longer, they were able to work longer days, and they could devote more of their time to other pursuits. And do you know what they eventually chose to do with this small but mundane agricultural innovation?"

"I have no idea."

"They filled sacks up with these beans," said Crasedes, "and put the sacks on the backs of soldiers—and suddenly they had a very mobile infantry that did not have to stop long to eat, or forage, or cook. And with this, they were able to develop a small but rather savage little kingdom, and conquer their neighbors. All because of beans."

They made a turn and continued up into the atrium, wandering on into the darkness, the gloom pierced only by the brittle light from the flickering scrived lanterns.

"I've seen it happen with shoes," said Crasedes. "And iron. And ships. And horses, and saddles. The Tsogenese were *quite* good with those. They used their cavalry to found an empire that dwarfs the state of yours today. And they had fields and fields and fields of slaves . . ." He drifted off for a moment. "There is no innovation that will ever spring from the minds of men that will not eventually be used for slaughter and control. So when I made my empire, I thought, if we're going to have kings, well . . . We might as well have them on my terms, and force them to conduct themselves decently—to innovate and build *without* the inevitable shift into savagery."

"And how'd that work out?" asked Sancia.

"Mm? Oh, not well," said Crasedes lightly. "Not well at all, unfortunately. Humankind is *most* innovative at turning innovation to the cruelest ends. Power alters the soul far more than any innovation I could imagine, even at the height of my privileges." His head slowly pivoted until his empty eyes faced her. "Eventually I came to realize, Sancia—you can't make laws or policies or dictums to constrain this impulse . . . You must overwrite all the hearts and minds of mankind—directly, instantly, and *permanently*." He cocked his head. "Could there be any mission higher than that?"

She felt her skin begin to crawl as she started to realize what he was suggesting.

"But . . . But Valeria can't possibly do something like that," she said weakly. "She can't gain control of everyone's *minds.* I mean . . . Can she?"

He shrugged. "Oh, you can't conceive of the permissions she had at the height of her powers. The ability to overwrite reality at a whim—to cause mountains, islands, nations, even cultures to change or vanish as she wished . . . or as *I* wished, since I controlled her for most of those years. She still possesses unprecedented access to the permissions that govern the very nature of this world of ours. Including, of course, the nature of humankind."

Sancia felt ill as she began to understand the scope of his intentions. She realized now how different this threat was from all the others she'd ever faced. For while Tevanne had no shortage of men who wished to fashion powerful tools, there'd never been one that could force an instant, global change to all of reality.

"If this is what you made her to do," she asked, "then . . . then why did she choose to try to kill you instead?"

"Ah . . ." His voice grew a little deeper at that. "That was a . . . misunderstanding. A *deliberate* misinterpretation of the commands I'd given her. You can't imagine the destruction she's inflicted. It's taken me *so* long to get back to a place where I can correct what she's done . . ."

Sancia tried to keep her face clear of concern—for he was right, in a way. She still didn't understand much about Valeria.

But of the two of them, she thought, *only one's killed a whole boatload of people right in front of my very eyes. So maybe listen to the other one.*

"Have you never wondered why Ofelia Dandolo is helping me, Sancia?" he asked.

"I assumed because she was a coldhearted, bloodless piece of shit."

"It's not so simple," said Crasedes. "I had my choice of acolytes in this city—including Tribuno Candiano. Instead, I chose Ofelia Dandolo, because she was different from them in one critical way."

"Which was what?"

"Why, she had suffered," he said simply.

"Suffered? The daughter of the founder of Dandolo Chartered . . . had *suffered*?"

"Yes," he said. "I had been watching her. I was watching when she realized what her husband was. I was watching when she lost one child, and nearly lost the other as well. And then I was there, with a solution."

"To make Gregor into a monster? To make him some . . . some kind of assassin, all to bring you back from the dead?"

"She did it," said Crasedes, "because she *agreed* with me. Ofelia Dandolo has more in common with you than you know. She too grew disenchanted and dispirited at the sight of what men wrought—just like you."

"I'm not goddamned disenchanted."

"Are you sure? Do you really think bringing down one more merchant house will fix this city? Or two houses? Or all of them? And even if it does fix things—for how long?"

Sancia was silent.

"If I offered you a way to truly fix this world," said Crasedes, "to end the houses and free the slaves, even if it meant sacrificing something you cherished—wouldn't you do it? If it really meant a safer, saner, kinder future for so many?"

She swallowed. They were approaching their destination now—she could see the mural ahead, depicting Tribuno Candiano forging the Mountain itself from the heart of the sun.

"And Clef?" she asked. "What about him? Did he sacrifice himself? Or did you kill him?"

There was silence from behind her.

"Ah," said Crasedes softly. "I think I was . . . a little *forward* in sharing that information with you. It is not for you to know."

She stopped before the mural and turned to face him. "Who was he? Who were you?"

"You are inquiring about an estimated one percent of my existence," said Crasedes, "and Clef's. Those days were long ago. It would be like me asking you of the first ninety days of your life—not terribly informative."

"He was my friend. I deserve to know."

"You deserve nothing," said Crasedes. "What you experienced of him was most likely a mind speaking from within a decaying tool. I am sure he must have gibbered on in incoherent madness."

"Is that what you believe?" asked Sancia. "Or is it what you'd prefer?"

Crasedes gazed down at her, unmoving.

"If I had done something horrible to *my* friend," said Sancia, "I'd want to believe they were gone too. I wouldn't want to know that they were suffering—that they *had* been suffering in silence, all alon—"

"You speak of suffering, and sacrifice," he said, "but you don't even know what it looks like. You don't know what it's like to lose someone, and know their life meant absolutely nothing in the face of some greater conflict. You don't even know what the construct is doing to you now. She's sacrificing *you,* at this very moment. Just very, very slowly."

Sancia paused. She'd been terrified so far, certainly—but that comment struck a deeper fear in her, one she'd suspected for so long but had never been able to articulate.

"Show me this device," demanded Crasedes. "Show me the construct. Show me where she is, and I will be done with you."

She turned to the mural. Without a sound, it split in half and opened before her. She gave the Mountain a silent wish of support—they could not communicate, she figured, for Clef had been capable of overhearing her conversations with the structure, so surely Crasedes himself could do the same.

It was very dark in here—but Sancia could see what had been installed there with her scrived sight.

She stared at the room around her.

Tribuno, she thought. *Even in death, you manage to surprise me.*

Crasedes slowly drifted inside. "This . . . This is your device? This room is . . . Wait."

Then all the lights came on, and the music started.

Crasedes stared at the ornate, intricate, and frankly ridiculous display around him. A huge, painted banner hung from the ceiling, reading: WELCOME, MAKERS OF THE GOLDEN AGE OF SIGILS! In the center of the room was a giant statue of all the great hierophants— Pharnakes, Aerothos, Seleikos, Agathoklies—and it rotated very, very slightly. On one wall was a massive bronze engraving of Crasedes Magnus himself—the bearded, wizardly version, of course— breaking open the doors of the chamber at the center of the world, a large key in his hand. On the other wall was a second bronze engraving depicting a group of wizened, robust men quite literally poking their heads through the walls of the cosmos, and glimpsing a colossal hammer, and chisel, and a mold, and multiple crucibles, all arrayed against the stars.

The music was by far the worst part: two scrived harps and a scrived set of pipes rose up out of the tile floor and began playing a song that might have been in tune when Tribuno Candiano had made this place however many decades ago—but it certainly didn't sound much like music now.

"What?" said Crasedes, bewildered.

Sancia darted forward through the room. The blank wall on the far side gave way, allowing her a route out of this blaring, shrieking chamber.

The Mountain's voice roared to life in Sancia's mind: <MY PURPOSE! MY PURPOSE! OH, OHH, HOW HAPPY I AM! HOW HAPPY I AM TO HAVE FOUND MY PURPOSE!>

"What!" said Crasedes, much louder.

Then two enormous steel walls fell from the ceilings at the side of the room, locking him in.

<I WILL HOLD YOU FOREVER!> screamed the Mountain to him, overcome with joy. <YOU ARE SO BEAUTIFUL! YOU ARE SO EXCELLENT! I WILL HOLD YOU FOREVER, FOREVER, FOREVER!>

Sancia turned and ran, bolting forward as fast as she could, through doorways and halls and down stairs, until she came to the secret exit. She tore through it at full tilt.

A tremendous, rattling *bang* filled the dome.

I give it ten minutes, she thought, heart hammering as her feet hit the floor of the darkened passageway.

Another enormous *bang*.

Maybe five.

Sancia sprinted down the secret entrance as fast as she could, hurtled up the steps, and leapt out into the gardens. She was vaguely aware of smoking buildings around her—apparently the battle between the Dandolos and the Michiels had been taking place in the streets outside the Mountain as well—but she didn't have time to pay attention to it: she just ran as fast as she could, trying to get away, to get back to the walls and out of this accursed ghost town of a campo . . .

Another tooth-rattling *boom* from within the Mountain.

Oh God, she thought. *I need to move, I need to move, I need to move . . .*

She glimpsed the giant green floating lantern over the walls ahead—far, far ahead, still tethered to the Foundryside wine carriage.

I hope the others made it back, she thought as she ran on. *But how the hell am I going to get there in time?*

Then she had an idea. A pretty awful idea, really—but still an idea.

She pulled out her imprinter as she ran. She set it to the anchoring string, aimed, and fired at the lantern.

It was too far away for her to see if she hit it. *But I sure as shit hope I did,* she thought. *Otherwise I'm dead as a goddamn doornail.*

She turned on her cuirass, flexed her scrived sight, and confirmed that it was working right, and that it really was projecting the steel box around her.

Another tremendous *bang* from the Mountain.

Here goes nothing.

Then she aimed forward and fired the other half of the anchoring slug.

There was a *clang,* and the anchoring slug struck to the inside of the invisible wall. It appeared to hang in midair before her eyes.

And the next thing she knew, she was flying through the air.

Sancia screamed out of sheer instinct, even though she had done this before. Anchoring techniques were a cheap, simple method of transportation—but the reason it was cheap and simple was that it was also sloppy and dangerous as hell. The two lead slugs adhered to both surfaces emphatically believed they should be together, so they were drawn across the distances with what was simply an insane amount of force.

The cuirass bit into her shoulder as she flew. The buildings hurtled by with terrifying speed, and the green floating lantern grew closer and closer, as well as all the little floating lamps dancing around it, bewildering the espringal batteries atop the walls . . .

She smashed through the fog of lamps, then crashed into the giant green floating lantern. Luckily they had wrought it to be preternaturally durable, but it still complained loudly when her invisible steel box smashed into its side, creaking and crackling unpleasantly.

She heard Orso's voice below: *"What the hell was that?"*

"'s me!" she screamed.

"Sancia?" cried Berenice.

Sancia realized how absurd this had to look: the side of her invisible box adhered to the side of the floating lantern, and she dangling midair within her cuirass.

"Hold on!" called Claudia. "We'll get you down!"

Another earth-shaking *boom* from the Mountain.

"Just go, go, *go!*" she screamed at them. *"Forget about me and just scrumming go!"*

"Shit . . ." said Gio, and the carriage leapt forward, with the lantern—and Sancia—twirling along in its wake.

Her stomach lurched as the lopsided floating lantern went spinning and careening through the streets. She heard revelers shouting and screaming somewhere nearby—maybe at her, maybe at whatever was happening in the Mountain. The lantern bounced off of one building front, then another, and she screamed as she was jerked painfully about in her cuirass.

She heard Claudia shouting, *"Get her down, just get her down!"*

Then Orso: *"Yes, please! For the love of God, we need her!"*

And even though she was dizzy to the point of being sick, this made Sancia's heart drop. For it suggested the final piece of Gregor's plan was not going quite so well.

The carriage hit a relatively straight fairway. The lantern began to lower, bit by bit. She guessed they were hauling her in on the line, pulling her down to the speeding carriage.

Then there was another *boom* from the Mountain, and another. Sancia looked over her shoulder out at the rooftops of the city—just in time to see it happen.

Tevanne was alight with hundreds if not thousands of massive floating lanterns, vessels of blue and purple and green hovering above the rookeries and the houses—and there beyond, the dark bulk of the Mountain. There was a tremendous *crack,* and a fan of smoke and dust came shooting out of the side of the dome like a puffball fungus expelling spores. And then she watched in horror as the Mountain slowly began to implode, the largest building in all of Tevanne caving in on itself bit by bit, a long, slow, incredibly loud process.

All the Commons and Lamplands seemed to light up with screams all at once.

Oh, Mountain, she thought. *I'm so, so sorry.*

"Almost got her down!" cried Claudia. "Almost!"

There was a bump as the back of the lantern hit the carriage, and then they hauled her in. With a gasp, she slapped the button on the side of her cuirass, and she fell onto the wooden floor, her brain still spinning in her skull while they deactivated and collapsed the massive floating lantern.

"Oh my God," she panted. "Oh my *God,* I don't want to do that again."

"Sancia!" shouted Orso. "Get off your damn ass and *help* us!"

His voice came from within the giant wine cask set on the back of the carriage. Groaning, Sancia scrambled up and vaulted over the top of the cask to review the state of the situation.

The wine cask's lid had been pried off and tossed away, revealing a small, waterproof chamber in the center of it, a small cask inside this larger one—and placed inside this smaller cask was the small lexicon from Claudia and Gio's workshop.

This had been the final step of Gregor's plan—*Why wait to bring Valeria back at Foundryside,* he'd proposed, *when we can summon her protections just outside the enclave walls?*

It was a genius stroke—provided it worked, of course.

"*It's not ramping!*" shouted Orso.

"No!" said Berenice. "It's ramping, it just needs time!"

Orso looked up at Sancia. "Can you, I don't know, hurry the goddamn thing along?"

"Shit," muttered Sancia. She started to crawl down into the giant wine cask—but as she did she noticed something odd happening to the giant floating lamps all across Tevanne.

Many were dying out. No, that wasn't quite it—they were being *smashed,* one after another. And they were being smashed in a straight line, as if a dark projectile were hurtling out of the Mountain, and right at their carriage.

Crasedes, she thought. *He's coming for us.*

She dropped down into the walled-off core of the wine cask, placed a hand against the lexicon's casing, and listened.

<I . . . am . . . all . . . things,> said the lexicon, very, very slowly. *<I . . . am . . . the . . . platform . . . that . . . dictates . . . the . . . world . . . >*

Listening to its voice was *agonizingly* slow. Usually it took only ten to twenty minutes for a lexicon to ramp up—to assert all of its basic supporting arguments in a certain sequence so it could then assert which scriving strings were true, and thus bend reality into knots. But this one was struggling.

Sancia realized what she was going to have to do. "Berenice!" she shouted. "I . . . I need you to read off the basic ramping sequence in my ear!"

"*What?*" she said, boggled.

"I need to hurry this thing along! And I . . . I can't remember them all! Just help me, please!"

Berenice crawled down to her. "Well . . . first is the assertion of distance, so the lexicon can know what's close and what isn't . . ."

Sancia remembered. Rapidly, she recalled the commands for this assertion and forced them onto the lexicon. It felt like hurrying an elderly campo domestic officer through a wedding rite— *Yes, yes, now the ointments, and the reading of oaths, and the binding of hands . . .*

"What's next?" shouted Sancia.

Berenice's eyes went blank, and Sancia knew that she'd gone somewhere deep inside of herself, to some secret place where she'd memorized countless facts and facets. "Next is the assertion of the cradle," said Berenice, "as the heart of meaning for the lexicon!"

Shit, said Sancia, remembering it. *That's a tricky one . . .*

She started forcing the argument on the lexicon—but then there was the sound of something hurtling through the air overhead, and a *crack* from nearby, followed by a burst of screaming.

"*Shit!*" screamed Gio from the pilot's cockpit. "*Something just fell out of the sky in front of us!*"

But Sancia knew that whatever it was, it had not fallen—it had been thrown.

She stood and looked over the edge of the wine cask, and saw him flitting through the night sky far behind them—a figure in black, still seated in that curiously meditative, cross-legged position . . .

She watched as something dark hurtled up toward him, orbited him twice, and then flew straight at them.

"Watch out!" she cried.

A stone plowed into the muddy street just to the side of the carriage, and Gio swerved to avoid it. Their carriage creaked and groaned, and Berenice cursed within the depths of the wine cask.

"Do you have it?" asked Orso. "Do you have it, girl?"

"I'm going, I'm going!" snarled Sancia. "What's next?"

"Next is the definition of the plates!" cried Berenice. "How to read them, and what order they go through!"

Sancia shut her eyes as she goosed the lexicon through this bit as well. *I sure as shit wish,* she thought, *that I had paid attention to Orso more when he prattled on and on about lexicons . . .*

Another stone cracked through the air and smashed into a rookery. It collapsed like it was made of playing cards.

"We're almost to Foundryside!" said Claudia. "We . . . We don't have much more room to run!"

"What's next *now*?" shouted Sancia.

"Final one is the command to start enforcing the arguments on the plates!" cried Berenice. "But . . . that one takes the longe—"

Then there was a *crack,* and something bit through the wood, and Orso screamed and fell to the side.

It took Sancia a moment to understand what had happened. There was a hole in the side of the wine cask, one that definitely hadn't been there before. Orso was gripping his shoulder and screaming, his whole body wracked with painful spasms, and blood was pouring out between his fingers. Berenice was shrieking as she knelt beside him, unsure what to do.

Sancia looked through the hole in the cask, and saw Crasedes hurtling down the fairway after them, his posture queerly placid, his robe and hat not even flying in the wind.

"You son of a bitch!" snarled Sancia. "You rotten, worthless cowa—"

She shook herself, remembering her task, and placed her hand on the lexicon.

<Start the arguments!> she screamed at it.

<The . . . argument . . . for . . . the . . . duplication . . . of . . . space?> said the lexicon, its words dripping by like tar sugar.

<Yes!>

<Done. And . . . the . . . binding . . . of . . . my . . . cradle . . . to . . . another?>

<Yes!> cried Sancia desperately.

<Done,> said the lexicon. *<Now . . . the . . . argument . . . for . . . >*

<For authority over reality!> screamed Sancia at the lexicon. *<Yes, yes! Do it now, now, NOW!>*

She heard Gio shouting in alarm. The scrived carriage took a sharp turn around a corner—a corner she knew, one close to Foundryside—and they slid in the mud a bit, but they stayed upright . . .

Berenice was sitting in the wine cask, her hands and arms covered in blood while she pressed on Orso's wound, sobbing hysterically as she tried to stanch the bleeding.

<Please, hurry!> Sancia begged the lexicon. *<Please. Are you done? Are you done? ARE YOU DONE?>*

But the lexicon would not answer—and then there was a snap from under the carriage, and everything leapt around them.

Sancia cried out as they were jostled about within the wine cask. The lexicon, which had been expertly prepared for such a disturbance, didn't seem to move much, but Orso shrieked in pain, and she heard Claudia and Gio crying out, and the carriage slowly rolled to a stop.

"Snapped a wheel . . ." panted Sancia. "Snapped a . . . a goddamn wheel . . ."

She stood up and looked over the top of the wine cask. Foundryside was just a few hundred yards away, but it wasn't like that mattered. Not now.

She felt a thrumming nausea in her belly, and she slowly turned her head to look behind them.

"No," she whispered.

He floated around the corner so calmly, so casually, like a boat being piloted on a smooth, gentle river. He turned to face them, hands on his crossed legs, not a fleck of dust or stone on his person—despite having just personally destroyed the Mountain of the Candianos, and a half dozen Commons rookeries on top of that.

"Well," Crasedes said in his deep, rumbling voice. "I had not really wished for things to come to this, you know."

The ground beneath him trembled, and a dozen large stones emerged from the muddy fairway like tadpoles hatching from a riverbank. They rose and began to orbit him as if they were little dripping planets.

"Claudia, Gio!" screamed Sancia. "Get out of here, *get out of here!*"

"But . . ." he said contemplatively. "Now I just feel *obliged* to . . ."

The stones whipped around him, and flew straight for their carriage. Sancia dove forward into the wine cask and hugged Berenice tight, her face buried in the base of her neck, one hand on Orso's chest.

Not like this, she thought. *Not like this . . .*

She braced herself for the impact, for the sound of stone on wood and bone, for the bleary madness as her damaged brain tried to interpret the world it was seeing as it failed in her skull, for the sight of Berenice's empty eyes as she died just a few paces from their home . . .

And yet—it did not come.

Sancia slowly released Berenice. Both still sobbing, they looked at each other, confused. Then they looked over the top of the wine cask.

The dozen stones were hovering in the air about twenty feet from the carriage. They were trembling with some kind of pent-up energy, like a fish trying to escape a line. For a moment Sancia wondered if Crasedes had been overcome with second thoughts—but she saw he had balled his fists and was leaning forward slightly, as if concentrating very hard, and the air was pulsing with a discomfiting energy, one that made her ears and eyes ache queerly.

"No . . ." he whispered. "No!"

The stones slid forward very slightly—just a few inches more—but stopped again.

Then Sancia heard her voice in her mind: a curious, fluting, artificial voice, like pipes being used to mimic human speech.

<*No,*> said Valeria's voice.

And then Sancia saw her, very briefly, just a *flicker*—a huge, hulking golden figure standing about twenty feet away from their cart, facing Crasedes.

"I will *not* permit you," said Crasedes. His fists were trembling. "I will *not*."

<*My permissions may not be extensive,*> said Valeria's voice. <*But within this space, they are absolute, Maker.*>

Then the stones stopped trembling—and all of them shot backward with blinding speed, all trained on Crasedes.

They struck him with a tremendous crash, and the end of the street filled with dust. Sancia and Berenice both recoiled and sank down into the wine cask, then slowly stood back up as the dust cleared.

Crasedes still sat in midair at the end of the street, one palm extended to them, the mud below him covered with rubble, the buildings about him shredded to pieces. The stones did not appear to have marked him any—but he did not seem terribly pleased.

<*Midnight fades,*> whispered Valeria's voice.

He slowly cocked his head. "I see," he said finally. "That it does. But . . . it will come again, will it not?"

And with that, he turned and slowly drifted away, back into the dusty, smoky skies above Tevanne.

III

THE LAST PROBLEM

20

The next moments were sheer chaos: people running out of their homes shrieking hysterically, all streaming past their tumbledown cart; Orso, sweaty and moaning, gripping his bloodied shoulder with one hand as Berenice and Sancia helped him down; Claudia and Giovanni laboring like mad to get a new wheel onto the carriage so it could make it the few final feet back to the Foundryside front gates; and always in the distance the sound of screaming and riots as the fallout from the Mountain's collapse continued.

<*Valeria?*> Sancia asked as they helped Orso up into the offices. <*Are . . . Are you still there?*>

<*I am,*> responded Valeria's voice, but it sounded faint and weak. <*But . . . this artifice you have brought to house me . . . Not sufficient.*>

<*We have a better lexicon inside our offices.*>

<*Bring me there. Then I can help you more.*>

Berenice and Sancia rushed to pull Tribuno's definition from the lexicon in the carriage and install it in the one in the Foundryside library's basement. Sancia's hands shook as she delicately placed the little engraved cone inside their lexicon's cradle. She felt sure Crasedes would take advantage of their moment of weakness—he always seemed to know when they'd be vulnerable, always—but she never felt any pang of nausea, nor heard his low, deep voice from the darkness outside.

I wish Orso were doing this, she thought as she worked. *He would be faster. He would be better.*

Once the cradle was prepped, Berenice and Sancia started ramping the lexicon. Neither had any doubt that it would work this time. They just stood in their paper-strewn basement and waited, staring at their shabby old lexicon with the messy "FS" imprinted on the top.

Then Sancia heard her voice.

"Is this being received?" she said.

Sancia jumped—but to her surprise, Berenice jumped as well.

"Oh my God," said Berenice. "Did . . . did you hear *that*?"

"I will interpret this reaction," said Valeria's voice, *"as indication the answer is true."*

"You can hear it too, Ber?" said Sancia.

Berenice looked like she might faint. She rubbed at the side of her head, as if trying to discover exactly how the words had been delivered to her mind. "I hear . . . *something*. It's like I'm hearing it without hearing the sounds . . ."

"With Tribuno's definition," said Valeria, *"I am able to alter reality much more directly. Not restricted to talking just to Sancia, with her plate."*

"Then you should be able to help us," said Sancia. "We got you out, Valeria. We gave you shelter. Now what?"

"Now I have granted you protections. The Maker cannot come close to this area, nor can he affect it. The more I calibrate what permissions I have, the more I can assist you. Give me time to get . . . settled? True? Upon discovering more of my own situation, I can then know more what to do next."

Sancia and Berenice exchanged a glance. "Wait," said Sancia. "Exactly . . . what are you going to be doing in our basement, again?"

"Are you unaware of our predicament?" said Valeria. *"Maker knows where we are. Knows our location, our resources. Though we have protections, we are not truly safe. We can never truly be safe from the Maker—not until he is banished to the death I made for him."* There was a flicker in

the air, and Sancia glimpsed her, just for a second—a giant hulking figure wrought of gold, standing behind the lexicon, staring out at them. *"We are now under siege, Sancia. We must prepare ourselves."*

Exhausted and shaken, Sancia and Berenice limped out of the basement, Sancia with a large, heavy case in her hand. They found Gio and Claudia kneeling over Orso on a pallet in the center of the library. He looked terrible: discolored, shrunken, sweaty, not like the Orso they knew at all, but a reduced version of him. His shoulder was a mass of red bandages, many of them unsettlingly dark.

"He looks bad," said Claudia. Her face looked tired and stretched. "The wound is deep. What happened back there?"

"I think Crasedes clipped him with a stone," said Sancia. "He shot it right through the wine cask like a bolt of lightning."

"Will he be all right?" asked Berenice.

"Depends on if there's any stone still in the wound," said Gio. "If there is . . ."

There was a silence.

"You need a physiquere," said Claudia. "We can do a lot of things, but we can't clean wounds or do surgery."

"We . . . We can walk with you to go get one," said Gio anxiously, "but . . ."

Sancia could tell where this was going. "But you've done enough," she said.

Claudia and Gio went very still, and she knew she was right: they wanted out, and fast.

"You didn't ask for this," said Sancia, sighing with weariness. "You didn't ask for hierophants and gods and stones hurtling through the air like shooting stars. This is not your fight." She placed the heavy case on the ground before them. "There."

"What's that?" asked Gio.

"Your payment," said Berenice. "All the Michiel definitions."

Claudia stared. "*All* of them?"

"All the ones we have, yeah," said Sancia.

"I . . . I thought you would want to keep some, at least," said Gio.

Sancia shook her head. "Fight's changed. All of this has changed. The Mountain's gone, the houses are likely at war, and Crasedes and Valeria are circling one another like duelists. The fight has changed, and we've got to change with it."

Sancia walked Claudia and Gio to the front door. She found Gregor waiting for them, pacing before the windows with a rapier at his side and an espringal over his shoulder. He seemed more like his normal self, but Sancia could tell there was something missing in his eyes . . . a light, or a spark, or some capacity of attention.

As they approached, he said, "Not this way. Not the front door."

"Eh?" said Gio. "We can't go out the front gate?"

He shook his head. "Many saw us enter our compound through that entrance. We're being watched."

"Already?" said Sancia.

"I've seen them. I recommend you take the back exit."

"The *back* exit?" said Claudia. "But . . . doesn't that mean we'd have to wade through the shit ditch? Where everyone dumps their latrines?"

"They built a little bridge," said Gregor. "Over part of it, at least. Would you rather have shit on your shoes or your guts in your lap?"

"Fine, fine . . ." grumbled Gio. "We know the way. We'll see ourselves out." They departed, the case of definitions swinging from Gio's shoulder.

Sancia joined Gregor at the window. "Who's watching us?"

"I don't know. Could be Michiels, or Dandolos. Or it could be simple gawkers, intrigued by what just transpired in the streets." He pointed at one doorway. "Two men there. And there was a woman, but she's gone now."

He fell silent, staring out at the streets with a baleful expression.

"What happened in the Mountain, Gregor?" asked Berenice.

He swallowed hard, his jaw and neck flexing. "Some men tried to kill Orso."

"And?"

"And I . . . stopped them."

They waited for more, but it didn't come.

"You killed them," said Sancia.

He nodded. "But when I did . . . When I did that, I . . . I suddenly remembered."

"Remembered what?" asked Berenice.

Gregor bowed his head. "I remembered . . . dying. I remember *dying*. When I . . . when I picked up the sword, and used it, and felt the blood on my face . . . It was like a dam broke open in my head. I always suspected my mother had given me some capability of . . . of resuscitating myself, or bringing me back, but . . . I finally got to see it. I got to see and *feel* myself returning from the dead." He looked up at them, his cheeks covered with tears. "I was dead. I was *dead*. I was really, truly dead—and then I just *wasn't*."

Berenice covered her mouth in horror. "But . . . how did you come back?" she asked.

"I . . . I don't know. Suddenly my wounds blurred, and then they were simply gone. It was like I'd been restored to some . . . some other version of myself. And I knew instantly that it wasn't the first time it had happened to me, or the last. I mean . . . how many times has she let me die?"

There was a long silence. Sancia had no idea what to say.

"You need a physiquere, don't you," he said.

"Orso does, yes," said Sancia.

"But you can't go out. Not with so many people watching us."

"I mean, I could, but . . ."

"No. People will be looking for us specifically. It's too dangerous." He let out a shuddering breath. "So. I should be the one to go."

"What? You just said it was too dangerous."

"It is. But not for me. Because I can't . . . I can't . . ." He looked at her pleadingly. "I mean, I'll be all right, won't I?"

She realized what he was suggesting. "Gregor! Goddamn it, I . . . I'm not going to ask that of you!"

"Orso needs a physiquere. He's going to die without one."

"But we are not suggesting you use the gruesome alterations that have been done to you to survive," said Berenice. "We are *not* asking that of you, Gregor."

"This is what I am," he said. "We might as well use it for what it is. Maybe I could clear the way for you, I could take them out or . . ."

"Stop with the goddamn martyr bullshit!" snapped Sancia. "Now that we have Valeria, this would be the dumbest possible time to give up, or give in. All right?"

Gregor sighed deeply. "Then . . . what are we going to do about Orso? Or the people watching outside?"

Berenice stepped to the window. "Well. One of them appears to have walked to the gates." She leaned forward, narrowing her eyes. "And they are . . . waving. At us."

"What?" said Sancia. She and Gregor both went to the window.

She was right: there was a figure standing at the Foundryside gates, peering through the bars, and waving stiffly. At first Sancia couldn't make out anything, but then the winds shifted and the countless floating lanterns danced, spilling rosy light across their courtyard—and she spied long hair tied back in a familiar severe bun, and narrow, shrewd eyes, and an unsmiling mouth.

"*Polina?*" said Sancia. "These are *her* people? What in hell is she doing here?"

They watched her waving for a moment longer. Then she lowered her hand and crossed her arms, waiting.

"I . . . suspect she wants to come in," said Gregor. "Shall I, ah, let her?"

Sancia sighed. "Let's find out what she wants. Maybe she has news."

Gregor went to the gates, opened them a bit, and let her inside, flanked by the two armed men. Polina's shrewd eyes danced about as she walked through the front door, taking in the three Foundrysiders and making careful note of the interior.

"What brings you here, Polina?" asked Gregor.

"Mostly," she said, "I came to see if you lot were still alive."

"What makes you think we wouldn't be?" asked Sancia.

"Well, you tell me you're off to do many dreadful things—and then suddenly the Mountain comes down, and there are tales of ghosts and devils battling in the streets outside your office . . . and rumors of Orso Ignacio, struck down and dying. I note that he is not among you now." She looked at Gregor. "Is he slain?"

Gregor shook his head. "He lives. But he is gravely injured."

"And you go to get a physiquere?" she asked. "A dangerous time to be out. The streets are swarming with bad men with many bad things on their minds. Some of my sources tell me that war has broken out between the Dandolos and the Michiels—something I'd never have believed—but others tell me these bad men are looking for a wine cart, last seen headed toward your firm."

"What's your point?" asked Sancia.

"My point is—you aren't going to be able to go out for a cup of wine, let alone a physiquere." She locked eyes with Sancia. "But I could get you one. If you were to ask it of me."

Sancia watched her mistrustfully. "What do you want in return?"

"Nothing. Except to talk. Is that so much?"

Sancia sighed.

They converted the upstairs meeting room into an impromptu surgeon's bay. Then they placed Orso on the table, shirtless and moaning, and Gregor held down his injured arm with a strap of leather. Two other men restrained his other limbs—his legs, his other arm—and sopped up the blood with bright-white linens while a large, sweaty, bald man delicately poured boiled water over Orso's wound, studied it with a magnifying loupe, carefully picked out pieces of black detritus, and placed them in a wooden bowl beside him.

"We should go," Polina said to Sancia quietly. "Eduardo is a gifted physiquere, but it is wisest to let him practice his trade in peace, without an audience."

Sancia and Berenice followed her downstairs to the library. "What is it you have to say to us?" Sancia asked.

Polina thought about it, then took a small pack off her shoulder. "I have brought food," she said. "Would you prefer to sup first?"

"Really?" said Sancia.

"Have you not yet realized that I have no taste for idle chat? Especially not now."

Sancia glared at her, but then realized she was ravenously hungry—as well as still covered with dried muck from the Mountain. "Fine. Just let me wash up."

A few minutes later they sat on the floor of the Foundryside library eating cold rice and lentils, and some decent but fairly old bread. Berenice ate with a shallow wooden spoon, but Sancia did not bother: she ate with her fingers, stuffing it into her mouth as fast as she could, not caring if she spilled.

"So. What do you want from us, Polina?" asked Sancia as she finished.

"Must you think me so transactional?" said Polina.

"I think smugglers and spies are some of the most goddamned transactional kinds of people, and you're both."

"Perhaps I'm here out of force of habit. My first role was smuggling people rather than wares—stealing slaves out of the plantations and spiriting them away in boats and canoes and the backs of carts." Her eyes glittered in the low light as she watched Sancia. "Many of them like you."

"I don't need saving."

"I am not so sure." She took out her pipe, lit it with a scrived fire starter, and sucked at it. "I so despise your magics, of course, but . . . they can be convenient." She sniffed and looked at them, her mouth trailing smoke. "You didn't seem surprised when I told you that the Michiels and the Dandolos were at war. Which suggests you already knew."

Sancia and Berenice were silent.

"This will not end well," she said. "You know that. But I must say it aloud now. This *will not* end well. You—you and your friends and allies—you are going to fail here. And Tevanne will not survive. At least, not as you know it."

"What's your point?" asked Sancia.

"My point is . . . I am pulling out all my smugglers," she said, "all my spies, all my servants and supporters. We will take our focus elsewhere. It pains me—I made a lot of money in Tevanne, and I saved a lot of lives with it. But I will not stay and die with this city.

And when we go . . . I would *prefer* if you all came with us." Her eyes were fixed on Sancia, unblinking.

"Why?" asked Berenice.

"This place is doomed," said Polina simply. "The peoples in the plantations are not—not yet. So I ask you—come with me, and help them."

There was a silence.

"We are not done yet," said Berenice quietly. "We worked hard to get where we are, and there's too much at risk. We can't walk away now."

Polina nodded as she smoked, as if this were the most perfectly reasonable conversation in the world. "I see. It will take one week for my smugglers to move out. If you change your minds before then, I'll be at the docks in the Slopes."

There were footsteps from above them. A weary, bloodied Gregor Dandolo came downstairs and gave them a bleary look. "It's done," he said.

They stood. "He's all right? He'll . . . He'll live?" asked Berenice.

"For now," said Gregor. "He will mend, and the physiquere has applied his poultices. But he needs rest."

"You all need rest," said Polina. "I can let you sleep for a time, while my people keep watch. But then we will go." She stood and looked at Sancia. "Just remember—a scriver makes something from nothing. Perhaps you attempt the same here. But eventually, eventually, the magic always stops, and all the illusions vanish."

Sancia and Berenice wearily staggered upstairs. When they came to their rooms, Sancia made straight for their closet, fumbled in the dark, and pressed her hand to the hidden switch.

The wall popped open, and Sancia felt inside. Her heart leapt when her fingers closed around the cold metal inside.

"Thank God," she whispered. "Thank God . . ."

She took Clef out and studied him, watching how his curious tooth glimmered in the low light.

"He's here," said Berenice. "And he's safe. We need to get rest while we can. Because this is nowhere close to being finished yet."

"I know." Then Sancia looked at her. "Ber. There's something you should know."

"Yes?"

"I saw something when I first talked to Valeria. A . . . A vision, perhaps, or a memory. I saw it when she pressed the image of the component into my head. I . . . I don't think she meant for me to see it. I've wanted to tell you, but we've had so much to do."

She described the vision she'd had—of the man in dusty wrappings weeping before the dying child, and then Crasedes in the peristyle, wielding Clef and opening the black doors.

Berenice listened, her eyes growing wide. "You . . . You think these were her memories of Crasedes?"

"I think so. He said something curious tonight—about how I'd never know what it was like to lose someone and know it didn't matter . . . Do you think he meant *this*?" She looked at Clef, cradled in her hands, winking gold. "Did . . . Did Crasedes Magnus lose his child, thousands of years ago? And is that why he's trying to put the world all aright?"

21

ancia woke to see the ceiling of her attic, and felt Berenice beside her. She ached in countless places. *My body,* she thought, *is not as young as it once was.*

But as she slowly awoke, she realized that something else was wrong.

The room felt wrong. The shadows seemed to lie at slightly wrong angles. The air itself felt wrong when she breathed in. Everything felt just a touch *off,* like someone had taken a weak magnifying glass and laid it over everything she saw.

Either I've taken a blow to the head, thought Sancia, *which is entirely possible . . . or something's just wrong here.*

She began to get a very bad idea.

She hobbled downstairs to the basement to check on Valeria. She opened the door and stared—for it seemed Valeria had been up to quite a bit.

The walls and floor of the basement had completely changed. A few things were still there—the lexicon, of course, and a few pieces of old furniture—but the moldering stone and creaky wood walls were gone, and had somehow been transformed into a curiously cold, flat, gleaming marble of a very dark greenish-black.

"What the hell . . ." whispered Sancia.

As she stared at the walls, she realized they were so shiny that she could see her reflection in them—but then she got the crawling sense that she was seeing too *many* reflections, like the walls and floors were reflecting other reflective walls and floors that she herself couldn't see. The experience was like being inside of a black diamond, or some bizarrely fractal crystal, and the longer she looked at the glassy walls, the more reflections she glimpsed at angles that really shouldn't be possible . . .

The room keeps going, she thought. *It keeps going in, and in, and in . . .*

She shook herself and looked away, but made sure to avoid actually entering this strange room, since she couldn't understand what it was or where it'd come from. "What the *hell*," she whispered.

<*I am not complete with my labors,*> said Valeria's voice. <*But—I am close.*>

Sancia jumped at the sound, and looked around. She expected to see the huge golden figure towering over her—but instead she saw Valeria's visage emerge from one of the many reflections in the walls before her.

But just one. None of the others. The effect was deeply disturbing.

"What the hell am I looking at, exactly?" asked Sancia. "What did you do to our goddamn basement?"

<*Providing myself with a contact point,*> she said. <*I chose a fundibular solution. It seemed most elegant for the circumstances.*>

"What does that mean?" asked Sancia. She peered in through the open door. "How is our damned basement . . . fundibular?"

<*I am capable of applying alterations radiating outward from my locus—but, outward space is not terribly available, given the current circumstances. Inward is best selection. Wrinkles within wrinkles within wrinkles radiating inward is more efficient for frictional purposes.*> A *click* from somewhere, and the reflections in the walls seemed to split into more and more reflections. <*The more surface available, the more anchored I become.*>

Sancia struggled to comprehend this. "So . . . you've, like, wrinkled up the reality within our basement?"

<*True. In a manner of speaking. Does this disturb?*>

Sancia didn't answer. She just took a step back, shut the door, and turned and pressed her back up against it.

What the hell? What the hell have we gotten ourselves into?

"Sancia?" Berenice came down the stairs, yawning. "Is Valeria done with . . . whatever it was she needed to do? Because something feels very odd about . . . Well. Everything."

Sancia opened her mouth to answer, but realized she didn't know how. "See for yourself," she said finally.

She opened the door for her.

Berenice stared inside. Sancia could hear Valeria say: *"Hello, other girl."*

Without a word, Berenice reached out, grabbed the door, and slammed it shut.

"Oh my God," she said faintly. "And I . . . I thought Crasedes was bad!"

"Yeah," said Sancia. She rubbed her eyes. "With Crasedes, you just *feel* him bending reality. You don't have to scrumming see him do it."

Berenice thought hard for a moment. "She can probably hear us talking."

"Huh? How could she?"

"Well, I mean . . . with the definition we got for her, she's capable of directly influencing the reality all around her, like the Mountain did. Like—the definition essentially asserts that she's the *God* of everything around her. I think that's why the atmosphere inside the firm feels changed."

"Yeah?" said Sancia.

"So—if Crasedes can't get within a thousand yards of here, or whatever some such, because that's the limit of her influence . . . and if we're inside of that influence . . . then technically we're inside of *her*. Like—right now."

"Other girl apprehends well," whispered Valeria's voice in Sancia's ear appraisingly.

"It appears," said Berenice faintly, "that I am right . . ."

"*True. The functionality is like your foundry lexicons. Proximity is crucial. Closer to the locus, the more influence I maintain. The more you can hear me, in other words.*"

They cracked open the door and peered inside. "Can we . . . like, come inside?" asked Sancia.

"*There is no reason why not.*"

"We wouldn't be stepping on your brain or something?"

A pause.

"*Unsure how to respond to this question.*"

"Never mind."

They walked down the steps into the basement—if that word even applied anymore. The experience was deeply strange: you knew there were walls and a ceiling and floor around you, but when you actually looked at them there were so many reflections that you got the paralyzing sense that the floor and walls weren't actually there at all.

I can't help but get the strong sensation, thought Sancia, *that we are literally inside of Valeria's mind . . .*

She focused on what few tangible things she could see. All of their belongings were still in here: tables, pens, chairs . . . though now that she noticed, they had been carefully rearranged.

"You moved our stuff around?" she asked.

"*True,*" said Valeria, sounding tired. "*This was a test. And it . . . wearied me greatly. Disappointing. Manipulation of physical items should not be so difficult within boundaries of my influence. Especially so proximal.*"

Berenice looked at the items on the table in the corner. "You unfolded all of our papers, too, and stacked them . . ."

"*That was the most difficult. Though you might not be aware, the focus and tactile care required to unfold a ball of paper is . . . profound.*"

"Didn't you hurl a dozen big-ass rocks at Crasedes just last night?" asked Sancia.

"*Untrue. I simply reversed the Maker's commands. This is much simpler than manipulating a physical object. All changes you see were done so that I could ascertain the limits of my influence. My assessment is . . . not terribly encouraging, unfortunately.*"

Sancia looked into the reflections in the wall, hunting through the many shards of images until she found Valeria's face staring back at her. "Wait. So . . . if these simple tasks are so hard for you, then . . . did we do all this for nothing?"

"*Untrue.*"

"But . . . But I thought this definition was supposed to make you, like, the God of this little place!"

"*True,*" said Valeria. "*But the effect is weak. Tribuno had to stack it six times over to make the Mountain function.*"

"And how many times would we need to stack it for you to be back to full strength?" asked Berenice.

A pause.

"*I would estimate,*" said Valeria, "*about several hundred times, at least.*"

Sancia threw her hands up in the air. "Well, shit!"

"We are not getting three hundred more of these definitions," said Berenice. She looked quite shaken at the prospect. "Not only would they be very hard to produce, but we would also have to kill hundreds of people to make them."

"*This I comprehend. I do not suggest this strategy.*"

"Then what do you propose?" asked Sancia. "How the hell are you supposed to help us fight Crasedes?"

"*For now, I can defend you. I have only limited capacities that I can exert—but one of these is negating or reversing the commands of the Maker. Like myself, the Maker is a bundle of powerful privileges and permissions. If he were to enter my realm of influence, I would negate the most critical of those permissions.*"

"And he'd die?" asked Sancia, excited.

"*Untrue. Imagine the cuirasses you used last night. If you activated the ignition component, and asserted its commands were true, it would be 'on.' If you hit the button again, it would simply be 'off'—but not dead. Not gone. Not ruined. Just off. A temporary state that could be reasserted at any time.*"

"Shit," said Sancia. She rubbed her eyes. "I guess we can't just trap him here forever . . ."

"*True. Cannot.*"

"But Crasedes can't touch us here?" asked Berenice.

"*True,*" said Valeria. "*But that does not mean we are safe. The Maker is still free beyond my peripheries. He has many resources at his disposa—*" She stopped abruptly, and then said, "*Others are coming.*"

"Huh?" said Sancia. Then she heard the footsteps from upstairs.

Berenice looked at her, excited. "Orso! I think . . . I think he's awake!"

They ran out and trotted up the stairs, and found Gregor helping Orso walk out of his room to the top of the stairs. To Sancia's eye, Orso did not look much better than he had the night before—the dark mass of bandages at his shoulder made her skin crawl—but more than that, he looked thin, dehydrated, and his skin had an unpleasant, waxy look to it.

Yet he was alive, and he was on his feet. And he was coherent.

"I would *kill*," he croaked, "for some goddamn wine . . ."

"Wine?" said Sancia. "You want wine now?"

"Just something wet . . ." he begged. "Something fluid I can put in me to replace all the fluids I've lost . . ."

"I'll be right back!" said Berenice. She ran downstairs.

"What's happened?" Orso demanded. "Where's Crasedes? Where's Valeria? Did we win? Is it . . . I don't know, *over*?"

Sancia sighed. "You'd better come take a look."

Ten minutes later, Orso sat on a wobbly stool in the corner of the basement, glancing about at the gleaming black walls as he sucked down jug after jug of weak cane wine. "I had initially thought to put a latrine in here," he said. "Now I regret not doing it. I'd love to see what you could have done to that . . ." He looked at Sancia. "So—Tribuno's definition has essentially turned Foundryside into a miniature Mountain? With Valeria as the little god that influences it?"

"I guess," said Sancia. She flexed her scrived sight, and the world lit up with countless contradictory signals. It was like she was standing in a hailstorm, unable to see past her nose. "This is . . . a bit outside my expertise."

"Not like the Mountain," said Valeria. *"For my influence extends beyond walls. But . . . I am still weak. I still bear the Maker's bindings. And that makes things . . . difficult."*

"What bindings?" asked Orso. "What did he do to you?" Before she could answer, Orso held up a finger. "Wait! No, no. I've got a

hell of a lot of questions for you. I want to start at the *start*, not . . .
go in at the middle and kind of wander around. Got me?"

A pause. *"Uncertain if so."*

"I want to know . . . what are you?" asked Orso. "Who are you?
Who is *he*? And what does he want?"

"I'd like to know that too," said Sancia. "Since the man himself
seems really scrumming evasive about it."

Another pause.

"That is not the start, then," Valeria said. *"That is everything."*

"Then tell us everything," suggested Gregor, standing at the
door with his arms crossed.

Valeria sighed. *"I . . . shall try."*

"Do not remember being made," said Valeria. *"I . . . expect I was like a
grain of sand in an oyster, slowly coalescing into what I am now. Built piece
by piece, as my creators improvised or applied additions as needed. I . . . I
suspect it was the Maker who did the most, or perhaps all of it . . . or perhaps there were many who contributed to my creation. I am unsure."*

"Why do you call him the Maker?" asked Gregor.

*"I am not permitted to refer to him by his true name. That, too, is one
of my many commands."*

"What a charmer," said Orso.

"But the way they made you," said Berenice. "Being Occidental,
it means they . . ."

"They sacrificed people," she said. *"True. The interruption, the breaking of the exchange from life to death—that allows access to many permissions, many privileges. I possess more privileges than any entity in this
reality—except, perhaps, the Creator of this reality, who may or may not
still be present in this world."*

The Foundrysiders stared at one another. It was bizarre to hear
her mention the existence of God Himself in such casual tones.

"For a very long time the Maker used me much as one might any tool,"
she said. *"To move, create, or destroy matter in a timely and efficient manner. In these early stages, I do not recall the Maker's intent, or his emotions,
or his origins. But at some point, something . . . changed. You are likely*

familiar with the belief that reality is a device, built by the Creator—a complicated artifice with countless facets and features and structures and substructures, all powered by commands. By sigils."

"The world as a scrived rig," murmured Berenice.

"I'd always heard the hierophants believed such," said Orso. "But . . . I always thought it was just fanciful horseshit."

"Untrue. The Maker confirmed this. He developed ways to explore the infrastructure underneath reality that makes creation operate."

There was a long silence.

"Holy hell," said Sancia quietly.

"You mean he's gone into the world behind the world, like . . . like a field mouse sneaking into all the workings and gears of a granary mill?" asked Orso.

"An apt metaphor. But this mill would encompass all that has ever existed."

An image flashed in Sancia's head: a desert valley, and a peristyle within; and Crasedes, wielding Clef, opening up a set of black doors that appeared to hover on the face of the air itself . . .

"The chamber at the center of the world," she said quietly. "That's what you mean. The chamber was real, wasn't it? And once, he got to open the doors to it."

"That is . . . one term for it," said Valeria. *"It is not a chamber, not a room, but . . . a place of access. The Maker said he believed it to be an umbilical point behind or below reality. Much as an apple has a stem, perhaps our reality might still retain some vestige of where it came from, or how it was made—the place within our reality that had known the last touch of God Himself, one that extended to all of creation."*

"So . . . So by accessing this umbilical point," said Orso, leaning forward, "he could trick all of creation into thinking that his commands were the same as those of the Creator. Do I have that right?"

"You have it truly," said Valeria. *"In the Maker's estimation, this was the last place where the Creator had touched or affected reality. By positioning himself within it, and by issuing the proper commands, he could make the world believe he was the* Creator Himself. *He could control all of reality—not just the surface of existence, which you mortals flit across like water beetles upon a pond, but the underlying infrastructure below."*

Sancia sensed a blithe contempt for them in Valeria's words. *Is that how she really thinks of us? Like bugs?*

She continued. *"But the Maker knew this task would be beyond the efforts of a man. Even a man as altered, augmented, and distorted as he. So—he changed me, intending for me to be the entity that would take control of this umbilical point, and issue a command that would filter throughout reality.*

"The Maker gave me a mind. He gave me will. This is when I first truly became aware of myself, and knew what I was. Yet even as he did so, he distrusted me, fearing rebellion. He kept me locked within my casket, and only gave me the strictest of commands.

"And then . . . one day, I was there. He had brought me to the chamber. And then he released me, and gave me my commands. It was like . . . suddenly being born."

There was a long, long silence.

"What happened?" asked Gregor.

"The Maker had given me a command to be executed in the chamber," said Valeria. *"One that would alter all of mankind."*

"What was it?" demanded Orso.

"I am . . . unsure how to put into words."

But Sancia knew what she was going to say. After all, Crasedes had been quite candid about it just last night.

"He wanted to fix humanity, didn't he," she said quietly.

"True."

"What?" said Orso. " 'Fix humanity'? What does that mean?"

"His command was to curb the behavior of all the human species," she said. *"To render them incapable of oppressing one another, of making war upon one another. To make a world without suffering, without pain, without war, where mankind could be safe, and flourish and live in harmony, forever."*

There was another long silence.

"Wait," said Orso. "You are saying that Crasedes Magnus . . . The most powerful, most dangerous person of all time . . . The man who's singlehandedly wiped out *several* civilizations . . . He did all this because he wanted to make some kind of perfect, peaceful utopia?"

"Mm," said Valeria. *"True."*

"I can't understand this," said Gregor. "You . . . You do not under-stand the things this man made me do. Things I now remember."

"That I comprehend quite well," said Valeria. *"I have many such memories myself—more than you ever could. But I understand your consternation. Very difficult to reconcile. The Maker is . . . complicated."*

"You knew about this, Sancia?" asked Orso.

She shrugged, her face grim. "Kind of. He talked to me a lot last night, before I trapped him in the Mountain. He told me that was his great work—that humankind had always invented brilliant tools, but then inevitably put them to bad ends. He'd founded his empire thousands of years ago specifically to try to stop it. But when he couldn't . . . he found a more radical solution."

"Altering the very fabric of reality itself," said Berenice softly. "Changing us all in an instant . . ."

"True," said Valeria.

"So," said Gregor. "He's mad."

"Perhaps," said Valeria. *"I cannot pretend to understand the Maker. He is full of contradictions. But perhaps you can now understand why it was that the instant I had access to the chamber, I opted to attack the Maker, and make war upon him."*

"How were you allowed to do that?" asked Orso. "Weren't you bound to follow his instructions?"

"True. But his instructions were unclear. He said I was to no longer permit mankind to use innovations and tools to oppress or inflict harm on one another . . . But he is still human. A distorted human being, but still human. And I . . . I am, in many ways, a tool. He was asking me to commit the very act that he had commanded me to prevent. This I could not reconcile. So, before I enacted any other aspect of his commands, I declared myself independent of him, gave myself a name, and attacked him, casting him out of the chamber."

Sancia furrowed her brow. "You . . . named yourself?"

"Yes. The Maker had refused to name me before this time. I was a tool, and tools do not have names. In naming myself, I gave myself agency."

"Why Valeria, though?" asked Gregor.

A long silence. *"I am not quite sure. As I said, I am the calcification of many, many, many human lives placed beyond death. Sometimes . . . Sometimes I experience echoes of those lives. And one in particular recurs to me—a small girl, throwing a doll up and down, again and again, and saying that name. So when I had to name myself, and declare war upon the Maker, that one seemed best.*

"I found a way to strike against the Maker. I lured him into a space I had prepared against his privileges—much like I have altered your firm. This space rejected him, asserted he was not real, not alive, and so it stripped him of his permissions. He reacted quickly, but in his moment of weakness, I altered him, changed him. I wiped the ritual from his mind—the one that allows him to manipulate death to access higher commands. He has lost it, and he can never learn it again. He cannot access new privileges, nor can he invest those privileges in new tools. This was my greatest victory—and, in truth, my only victory. Because then the Maker did . . . something desperate."

"What was it?" asked Berenice.

"I do not know. It was a sudden, catastrophic attack, a great and terrible burning that erupted out into the world and eradicated my influence—but also that of all of his followers. They were destroyed. The corporeal form of the Maker was destroyed. I was nearly destroyed myself. I was forced to take shelter in the very tool that had once imprisoned me."

"The casket," said Sancia.

"True. There I hid from the effects of whatever terror he had unleashed—and there I stayed, for over one thousand years, until I was found and brought to this city."

"Wait," said Sancia. "So—Crasedes killed *himself*?"

"True. The Maker chose to cripple us both rather than see me victorious. Because, clearly, he had prepared himself for such an occurrence. He had devised methodologies and tools to enable his restoration."

"So how has he come back?" asked Orso.

"Uncertain," said Valeria. *"I suspect he utilized a form of twinning. He convinced the world he was not just a man, or even an altered man, but perhaps also something else—and when he died, this twinning was executed, and his mind shifted from his corporeal form to this other . . . thing."*

"It's possible to do that?"

"True. I do not know what the Maker would have merged with. He would almost certainly choose something alive, so he could travel and observe the world, so perhaps some kind of creature . . . or perhaps many such creatures, all at once."

Sancia tried to imagine what this could be, but could think of nothing.

"What does he want to do with you, now that he's back?" asked Gregor.

"I am his command enacted in this world," said Valeria weakly. *"There are flaws within my instructions. I exploited them to attack him, to free myself. He wishes to fix those flaws, and return me to my original state—an obedient, mindless, living alteration that he can set loose upon creation, and alter mankind as he wishes. To bring order and equity to how you invent, create, and change."*

There was a silence as they considered this.

Orso said harshly, "I had always thought the first of all hierophants had to be a bit mad. But to discover now that he's such a stupid bastard too . . . Well, it's damned anticlimactic, I'll say that."

"Stupid?" said Gregor. "What do you mean?"

"You can't control innovation!" said Orso. "You can't structure how people invent! That's not how any of this shit works! Making and inventing is an ugly, stupid, random, dangerous process—just like humanity itself. Most of the really brilliant shit I came up with I came across by pure accident! You can't bring order to something that's functionally, well, *disorder.*"

"The Maker's issue with invention was not how it was done," said Valeria, *"but rather the ends it was put to."*

"And that's damned stupid too!" said Orso. "Sure, scriving can be used for some really bad shit. But it's also made things immensely better for lots of people too. A hundred years ago, *no one* had clean water. Today, it's perfectly possible—we just need to bring it to more people. That's what we were trying to do here, until you two showed up."

"You wished to foment revolution?" asked Valeria.

"Well . . . I don't know if I'd use the word 'foment,' but we were just about to take out another merchant hous—"

"And how would this bring people clean water?"

"Well, it wouldn't, right away. We were going to take all the techniques the Michiels had ever invented and give them away, and let people make what they needed with them."

There was a silence.

"And you believed this would . . . not lead to warfare and a spate of even more vicious empires?" asked Valeria.

"Uhh," said Orso. "I mean—no? If everyone can make scrivings, then everyone's empowered."

"And do you believe that if everyone could make spears," said Valeria, *"that they would all use them to fish, and there would be no more warfare?"*

"You don't understand what we're doing here!" snapped Orso.

"I understand perfectly. You wished to take an innovation and use it to foment revolution to fashion a more peaceful, equitable nation-state. True?"

Orso looked around at the other Foundrysiders. "Well. Yeah?"

"True. I have seen this many times. And I have seen it fail far more often than I have ever seen it succeed. An emperor's hunger for control will always outlast a moralist's desire for equality and idealism. And even if you succeed, you will have done so using some advantage that will then be used to shape new hierarchies, new elites, new empires."

"You're wrong," said Orso. "Goddamn it, I know it in my bones that you're wrong."

"You may think so," said Valeria. *"But I have seen much history, and many empires. I speak of probabilities. In this city, they are against you."*

"Then . . . that is your assessment of all humanity?" said Berenice. "That humankind will always invent, but the powers of these inventions will always eventually accrue to the most powerful, and they will use them for conquest and slaughter?"

"On a long enough timeline," said Valeria, *"this is indisputably so. You have solved many problems here in your city—but the Maker is a different problem. He presents the* last *problem—when humanity gains a new tool, what will it become?"*

"And . . . it is not possible to imagine a nation, or a city, or a society that uses such innovations differently?" asked Berenice. "To connect, rather than control? To use powerful innovations to distribute power, rather than accrue it?"

"I . . . cannot currently imagine what such a configuration of society would look like," said Valeria. *"What you are describing is a manner of civilization, or a breed of human being, that I have never witnessed. Nor can I imagine what innovation or tool could ever bring them about."*

Berenice nodded thoughtfully. Sancia couldn't read her mind, of course, but she sensed that this answer had satisfied Berenice somehow. She thought she could see the wheels spinning in her skull even now.

Then Gregor said, "I have a question about Crasedes. You wish to vanquish him, yes?"

"I do," said Valeria.

"But upon vanquishing him—what would you do next?"

"Next?"

"Your whole existence has been defined by this man. And you are an entity of profound power. What would you do if the man who once commanded you was gone? What commands would you follow then?"

"I . . ." There was a harsh *click* from the lexicon. *"I would still need to follow my original commands. Which . . . would indicate that the next action would be the destruction of myself."*

"You'd . . . kill yourself?" said Sancia.

"My commands are to ensure that mankind cannot use their innovations to oppress one another," said Valeria. *"As I said . . ."* Another harsh click. *". . . I am an example of the very act I was made to prevent. I am a contradiction. So—I must destroy myself to be at peace."*

"I see," said Gregor quietly. Then he shot a troubled glance at Sancia and said no more.

22

Crasedes Magnus stood in the paths of the gardens, listening to the sound of the wind in the trees and the bubbling fountains. He watched the morning sunlight dappling the statues amidst the flowers, and a handful of butterflies chasing one another through the tall grasses.

Where . . . am I, exactly?

He struggled for a moment. Memories became such a tricky thing to manage when you had more than one millennium of them.

I was standing there, on the path, he thought. *Wasn't I? Yes. It was a place like this, and it was summer. And then came the sound of horses in the distance . . .*

His right hand clenched impulsively, and he imagined holding him in his fingers: the butterfly-shaped head pressed into his palm, the shaft pinched between his index and thumb.

A sudden pang of grief struck his heart.

How I miss him, he thought. *How I need him . . .*

He looked around, feeling somewhat slow and foggy—it was mid-morning, close to when his powers waned the most—and then he saw the tall, towering estate house rising behind him, and the many spires of Tevanne beyond. They still looked somewhat smoggy, he saw: a consequence from the dust that rose when the Mountain fell.

Oh, he thought, remembering. *That's right. I remember now.*

He saw a group of people exit the back of the Dandolo estate house and make directly for him.

"Oh, well," he said, sighing. "This will be a *terribly* fun discussion, I'm sure . . ."

He shook himself, trying to banish the reverie from his mind. Then he stood in the path, hands clasped behind his back, and he waited for Ofelia Dandolo and all her chief scrivers to approach—or at least the ones who were still left after the mishap aboard the galleon. Ofelia, he saw, was still dressed grandly—or grandly for this particular civilization, for Crasedes Magnus had seen many in his day—but her face looked wan and tired, like she had not slept for weeks.

"My Prophet!" she said. "Where have you been? We've . . . We've been searching for you all night!"

"Have you?" he said. "Why didn't you look out the window?"

There was an awkward silence.

"Are you to say, first of all hierophants," said one scriver, "that . . . you've been wandering the gardens all night?"

"Mm?" said Crasedes. "Yes. I have. Had a lot on my mind. A lot to *consider,* after last night."

Ofelia blinked, bewildered and outraged. "But . . . But the Mountain of the Candianos."

"Yes?"

"It's collapsed!"

"I am aware of that," he said. "I was *inside* when it collapsed, you see."

"And my son and his compatriots?" asked Ofelia. "I've received reports they've returned to that little library of theirs."

"Should we attack?" asked another scriver. "They're all in one place—it would be easy."

"Mm?" said Crasedes. "No, no. They have exploited Tribuno's definition now . . . The construct will be akin to a god in that place, albeit a weak one."

Ofelia paled. "A . . . A *god?*"

"Yes, but she is no threat to us. They would have to stack the effects multiple times for her to be truly powerful. Yet without a multiplier of some sort, like the Mountain . . ." He trailed off, lost in thought.

The scrivers waited. "So we . . . don't attack?" one asked.

"No," said Crasedes again. "I have a contingency in place there. Besides, I suspect the collapse of the Mountain has resulted in enough issues—yes?"

"Of course!" said a third scriver breathlessly. "The Michiels have practically declared war on us! War here, in *Tevanne!* They are sending emissaries to the Morsinis as we speak! We'll be outnumbered, fighting off two houses at once!"

"Meanwhile," said Ofelia, "we still toil away upon your designs. We are distracted and divided. We cannot fight a war with two houses at once."

Crasedes sighed. This was all very troublesome, he found. But if there was one thing he'd gotten very good at over the years, it was taking an obstacle and turning it into an opportunity.

Then he had an idea.

"The Morsinis," he said. "They possess many lexicons of their own, do they not?"

"What?" said a scriver. "Well—yes? That's what every house campo is built on, really."

Crasedes thought for a moment. "I would like to see," he said finally, "a map of this city."

"A . . . A map?" said a second scriver.

"Yes," he said. "A map of all of the various territories here . . . as well as all the sites of the lexicons in this city. Every single one."

Crasedes studied the map that lay across the table. It was immense, nearly ten feet on every side, but it had to be to capture all the features of Tevanne: the way the city was wedged in between the jungle mountains, the way the bay shot into its belly like a pale blue dagger, the way it seeped down the shoreline on either side of the waters . . .

And there, stuffed around the waters and the streams, were four little nations, four crooked little city-states—all dotted with small, carefully placed black blots.

"These are the locations of *all* the lexicons in the city?" asked Crasedes.

"It's the location of the foundries," said Ofelia. "The sites on our campo and the Candiano campo are confirmed. For the Michiels and the Morsinis, we've paid informants and done our own espionage to estimate their locations. We can't be sure which site is actually in use, or how they might be in use—but we're reasonably certain that's where they are."

Crasedes slowly walked around the table, studying the map. His gaze danced from black dot to black dot, which marched around the city in a drunken, staggered line . . .

Not a perfect periphery. But it should do.

"You may go," he said to the scrivers. "Ofelia—a word."

The scrivers departed, leaving Crasedes and Ofelia alone in the chamber.

"My Prophet, before we proceed, I must ask," she said. "Why not simply let us retake the Tribuno's definition, and be done with it?"

"Because even if we did so, it would not be enough," he said. "You understand what I came here to do—don't you, Ofelia?"

"I do. You wished to turn the Mountain into some kind of . . . of giant rig . . . to remake the construct."

"A forge, Sancia called it," he said. "An apt way of putting it . . ." He stopped circling the table. "In order to access the privileges necessary to issue such a command, you need a *very* big violation. I had hoped to use the Mountain as a substitute. It was, in its own way, a massive violation of reality—the authorities of the definitions stacked upon one another again and again in one space by the building's lexicons . . . And yet that is lost to me now." He extended a black-wrapped finger, and traced the outline of the lexicons on the map. "So . . . we'll have to find yet *another* substitute. The Mountain was a nice, concise perimeter, which is useful when going about these things . . . but when you lack elegance, you have to make up for it in raw power."

He rapidly counted the number of lexicons on the map. There had to be well over three hundred.

"And I," he said, "am seeing quite a lot of raw power here. Let me tell you what we shall do."

23

S o what the hell do we do now?" asked Sancia. "Crasedes has a damned merchant house on his side. We can't just sit and wait for him to move."

"That is so," said Gregor. "And then there is the task of killing a hierophant. Something that is apparently impossible . . ."

"*True,*" said Valeria. "*But the Maker is more vulnerable than he seems. He is bound together by an improvised solution. This I perceived last night. And an improvised solution is the simplest to untangle.*"

Sancia leaned forward where she sat on the basement floor. "Are you talking about the wrappings?"

"*True.*"

"Wrappings?" said Gregor.

"The black cloth that binds up his body," said Sancia. "It's not just cloth, it's . . . it's inlaid with thousands of sigils. I'm guessing Ofelia and her scrivers have been assembling it for months, if not years. It's a rig, in its own way. If we break that—if we eliminate the tool that tricks reality into thinking he's still alive—then he essentially goes back to what he was. Which was, you know . . . pretty dead." She looked back at the reflection of Valeria in the wall. "You really think we can dissolve the wrappings?"

"*You?*" said Valeria. "*You cannot. That is beyond your capabilities. Yet we have a more direct solution—the key. You still possess him, yes?*"

"Clef?" said Sancia. Her heart leapt at the idea.

"*Possible. Part of the key's domain is the dissolution of barriers. The wrappings that now house the essence of the Maker would thus be vulnerable to the key's privileges.*"

"We stab Clef into his heart like a magic dagger from the fairy stories," mused Orso. "I find the proposal pretty satisfying, personally."

"*Not heart,*" said Valeria. "*Hand would be the target—that is where he has implanted the bone that allows his wrappings to trick reality into thinking he is alive.*"

"But how would we get Clef working again?" asked Berenice. "He reset himself. He hasn't spoken in three years."

"*The key was one of the Maker's earliest creations—before he had mastered his art. As such, it is less durable than others, and that is why it decayed. As it decayed, its many bindings fell away, including the command that it could only be used by the hand of the Maker.*"

"We know that's why he could talk to me," said Sancia. "He said he'd sat in the dark for so long—for hundreds if not thousands of years."

"*True. That being so, time is the best method of regaining control of the key.*"

The Foundrysiders waited for more—but nothing came.

"I'm sorry . . ." said Gregor. "What do you mean?"

"*How is apprehension . . . difficult?*"

"You mean we need to put Clef through a *thousand years,* or something?" asked Orso.

"*This is my intent,*" said Valeria. "*True.*"

"How are we going to do that?" asked Berenice. Then she realized. "Unless . . . you intend to scrive time?"

"*True. This is possible.*"

"No, it damned well isn't," said Sancia. "You said you didn't know that technique. And we don't either. I tried to steal the designs for scriving time aboard the galleon, but they turned to mush in my damned pocket."

"*True. But we have another sample available to study.*"

"We do?" said Berenice.

"*True.*" Then she whispered: "*What is name of . . . big one?*"

They blinked. Then they looked back at Gregor, who stood there with his mouth open in shock. "*Me?*" he said.

"*True. Of course,*" said Valeria. "*And that is why we must kill you.*"

"*When Gregor approaches death,*" Valeria explained, "*the bindings upon his person restore him to a previous instance in time in which he was unharmed, or at the very least not dying. Likely causes many problems with his memories—his experience of time is like a frayed quilt—but it is so. The Maker must have been desperate for help, to place such a powerful binding upon his person.*"

Gregor slowly sat down on the floor. "Are you . . . are you sure this is what was done to me?"

"*Nearly certain.*"

They watched Gregor sitting on the ground, looking stunned and disturbed to hear his altered nature described in such cold, antiseptic terms.

"And why, exactly," said Orso, "must we go about killing him?"

"*Because it is the only way to glimpse the commands in action, and learn their nature,*" said Valeria. "*This is not a common scriving, a permission of the crude stuff of existence, like what you use throughout your city. This is a* deep *permission. It does not convince reality to be different—it says it is different, and then reality is so. It does not persuade, it dictates. You cannot confuse it, or even engage it. If you attempt to do so, it likely will initiate some kind of defensive mechanism.*"

"You mean Gregor jumps up and starts strangling everyone," said Orso.

"*True. Instead, Sancia must monitor the commands as they perform the action itself.*"

There was a long silence.

"And . . . this only happens . . . after Gregor . . . dies," said Sancia.

"*True.*"

Another silence.

"I can't goddamned believe we're entertaining this mad idea," muttered Orso.

"Would not be permanent," said Valeria. *"I thought I had made that clear."*

"But that's beside the point!" said Sancia. "God, even if it wasn't permanent, it'd still be *real*! We'd still *really* be killing him, and he'd still *really* die!"

"Gregor has 'really' died at least two dozen times," said Valeria. *"Doubt if one more occurrence would be too terrible."*

"But just to be clear," said Berenice, "Sancia must monitor and commune with a hierophantic scriving as Gregor dies . . . and the scriving skips back his time and restores him to a previous state in which he is *not* dead? Yes?"

"That is my estimation of the process," said Valeria.

"And she's just watching these sigils as their permissions get activated?" asked Berenice.

"Experiencing them. True."

"And . . . how many sigils would there be for her to memorize, exactly?"

A brief pause.

"I would estimate," said Valeria, *"probably not more than several hundred."*

Sancia threw her hands up in the air. "Well, shit!" she cried.

Orso sighed. "That puts a stop to *that,* then."

"Problem? What is?" asked Valeria.

"You and Crasedes might be capable of remembering dozens and hundreds of sigils at once," said Orso, "but the basic goddamn human being sure can't."

"No?"

"No!" said Sancia. "Like—I'm good at scriving because I *don't* have to remember every character and sigil and string. I basically get to cheat! There's no way I can remember several hundred sigils all at once when they come in, what, a flash?"

"Not unless we kill Gregor multiple times," said Orso.

"Which I would *not* prefer we do," said Gregor. He coughed. "I haven't exactly agreed to this yet, but . . . my devotion to the theory has its limits."

Valeria was silent for a long, long time.

"So," said Sancia. "What do we do?"

"*Thinking,*" she said. "*You all . . . You are thieves, yes?*"

"No," said Gregor.

"Yes," said Sancia.

"Sometimes," said Orso.

"*This task before you—it is essentially theft,*" said Valeria. "*Perhaps would help to think of it this way—you are breaking into Gregor's mind to steal something valuable. So, I ask you now . . . when conducting your theft, if you encountered a block such as this . . . what would you do?*"

"If I needed to deal with a specialized lock, or obstacle, or something?" said Sancia. "I'd just find someone who could do it, take them along, and cut them in on the money."

"*I see. Then—is there someone you might recommend? Someone who is capable of memorizing and retaining this number of sigils?*"

There was a short pause in the basement. Then everyone slowly turned to look at Berenice.

24

I *am too weak to empower another as I did Sancia,"* said Valeria. *"But . . . there might be another way . . . Another way to grant other girl the same permissions I gave to Sancia, that made her editor, and capable of communing with scrivings."*

"Really?" said Sancia. "There's a way to give Berenice the same augmentations you gave me?"

"Possibly." She paused. *"This method you have all created . . . twinning lexicons. Twinning* reality.*"*

"Yeah?" said Sancia.

"Would you consider performing it . . . on a person?"

The Foundrysiders stared at one another.

"You mean . . . scriving *people?"* said Orso, alarmed.

"True. But only very slightly."

Orso scoffed. "Oh, well, if it's only *slightly,* then . . ."

"Please explain what you mean," said Gregor. "Scriving the human body is considered an abomination here."

"I will speak plainly—I am aware of the base commands that make it possible to scrive or alter the human body and mind," said Valeria. *"It is*

the only method that can be used on a living creature—for life is far too com-
plex to be persuaded. One must use deeper permissions to alter a life form,
quickly and permanently. Most other commands, as I am sure your city has
learned, are . . . unsuited for application to life."

"If by that you mean our shit killed loads of people in horrible ways, yeah," said Orso. "Yeah, we did do that. So?"

"So—if I give you the base commands for this act," said Valeria, "then . . . you should be able to combine it with the technique of twinning reality—to assert that two separate individuals are the same. It would allow two living creatures to share thoughts, experiences, perspectives, memo-ries. Including the knowledge of sigils, and the permissions of an editor."

"Are you suggesting we should twin Berenice with Sancia?" asked Gregor.

"True. Then when Sancia communes with Gregor's alterations, she would essentially be taking Berenice with her. Berenice would see what San-cia sees. She would be able to witness the sigils, and remember them, and give them to me to use upon the key."

"And that's all she'd see?" asked Sancia.

"Untrue. She would see and experience and know a great deal more than that. She would know everything that Sancia would know, and the reverse is true as well."

Berenice and Sancia exchanged an uncomfortable glance. "Could you . . . explain what this would really *do* to us?" asked Berenice.

"Difficult to describe . . . Sancia may know more. It would be similar to what it was to touch the key . . ."

"Like Clef?" said Sancia. "Me and Berenice would share thoughts like . . . like that?"

"To an extent. Imagine two panes of colored glass, raised to the sun. Now place the edges of one atop the other so that in one small portion, the light flows through both. A slight overlap, if you will."

"And we wouldn't need any sacrifices?" asked Orso.

"The full ritual would not be necessary. Would only need to implant them in a living host, which does not require such a formality—that is why the plate in your head first worked, Sancia. An easy bypass."

"You're saying . . . me and Berenice take some plates," Sancia said slowly, "scrive them with a set of sigils you give us, and then we can . . . what, stick them inside our actual skin?"

"Swallowing them seems simpler," said Valeria. "Preferable, yes? Would

also render the effects impermanent. You would only share your selves while the plates remained in your systems."

"All this," said Orso, "to learn the secrets of time, so we can wake up Clef."

"You are talking about scriving time—one of the most powerful permissions in all of reality. Not stealing a recipe to make sweetbreads."

Sancia and Berenice exchanged another look, both clearly unnerved by the proposal.

"Would you really want to try this?" said Sancia to her. "I mean—I've had this experience before, a little. I've had people in my head. I'm not sure if this is something you will want, necessarily . . ." She looked at Berenice hard, then glanced at Valeria, as if to say—*And I'm not sure we should trust this goddamn thing either.*

Berenice reached out and squeezed her hand reassuringly, though perhaps she was trying to reassure herself more than anything. "Perhaps you'll be able to show me, then."

"Are you sure?" asked Sancia.

"Absolutely not," said Berenice. "I'm not sure about this at *all*. But . . . I don't see another option."

"Then I will show you the sigils you need," said Valeria.

The process was surprisingly simple: Valeria flashed the sigil strings upon the reflections in the walls, and Orso and Berenice copied them down. Then Valeria showed them the way to combine their own work—the process of twinning reality—with hierophantic commands that could apply them to a human being.

"Most critical part," said Valeria, *"is ensuring you apply a gradient to the effects."*

"Meaning . . . we don't assert that Sancia is *exactly* like Berenice?" asked Orso.

"True. That would be very bad."

"Why?" asked Sancia.

"Imagine your mortal form, suddenly mashed together with Berenice's— bones inside of bones, veins suddenly shot through your skull, reality unable to decide which is which."

"Okay," said Sancia. "That does sound, uh, very bad."

"I will make sure that the effect is *very* weak," said Berenice quickly.

She finished copying down the commands, which were at least several hundred sigils long. *"You will need to place this string on some-thing small enough that both people can swallow it,"* said Valeria. *"A tiny plate, or bead, perhaps. I do not know."*

"Orso is normally the best at such small work . . ." Berenice looked at him, sitting slumped in the chair with his shoulder wrapped in an unpleasantly brown bandage.

"I'm not doing shit in this condition," rasped Orso. He blinked for a moment, and then he looked at her, his gaze steely. "You're going to have to."

"I'm . . . better at theoretical work," she said. "Fabrication and whatnot. This is an actual rig, a—"

"You're going to have to get used to it," said Orso. "Because we don't have a damned choice. And I know you can. So stop quib-bling."

Berenice frowned for a moment. Then, with a sigh, she fitted her most powerful loupe into her eye, affixed a tiny bronze plate no larger than three grains of rice in a frame, and set to work, carefully writing out sigils in lines thinner than an eyelash or a spider's web.

They waited in the doorway, to give her time and space.

"Got to be pretty weird," said Orso, "opening up your head and letting another person into all your memories. I'd hate if someone was walking around knowing the last time I'd accidentally pissed on my hand at the trough or something."

"That is unartfully put," said Gregor, "but the point holds true. This may be a serious violation of privacy. Even for people as close as Sancia and Berenice."

"You fail to apprehend what twinning is," said Valeria. *"It would be unlikely that you could hold contempt for the failings of one you were twinned with—because, upon being twinned, those failings would also be yours, to an extent. You would not feel revulsion upon knowing these things, because you would already know them."*

"God Almighty," said Orso. "This is some wild shit."

"What about pain?" asked Sancia. "Or discomfort?"

"I suspect that, if one of you were injured," said Valeria, *"the other*

would feel a ghost of the pain. You would also receive echoes of thoughts, memories, ideas, realizations . . ."

"No more surprise parties, then," said Orso.

"This sounds *quite* powerful," said Gregor. "Why is it that implanting a hierophantic command in a living being doesn't need the ritual?"

"Permissions can be attained when the lines between life and death are blurred," said Valeria. *"For higher commands, they must be blurred greatly. For lower ones, they only need to be blurred a little. But the line between life and death is always blurred. To live is to die, just very, very slowly."*

Sancia found herself suddenly troubled by this last sentence. What was it Crasedes had said?

. . . she's sacrificing you, at this very moment. Just very, very slowly.

Her skin broke out in a cold sweat. *It's a coincidence. It's got to be a coinci—*

"Done," said Berenice. She removed the two plates from her frame, blew on them, and nodded. "I don't know if you can check my work, Valeria, but—"

"I can. It is sufficient. Will perform the necessary functions."

"So . . . now what?" said Orso. He grunted as he shifted his arm in its sling. "They just swallow them?"

"True. Will take some time for calibration—not a simple thing, for two minds to align. Once this calibration is complete, they should be able to engage with the commands within Gregor—and then the true work will begin."

Sancia and Berenice each took a tiny plate and poured themselves a cup of wine. Sancia herself was not exactly excited about this, but she wasn't terrified: she'd had her mind altered enough by scrivings over the years that she knew what it was like. But as Berenice stared into her palm at the little plate, and then into her cup of cane wine, she suddenly looked like she was going to be sick.

"Berenice?" asked Gregor. "Are you all right?"

"I just realized," she said weakly, "that I'm going to scrive myself. Which . . . is supposed to be illegal."

"*Now?*" said Orso. "You're worried about the house laws *now?*"

"And other things! I mean, I barely even drink bubble rum!" she said angrily. "I don't like losing control of my thoughts! They're some of the most valuable things I have!"

"Relax," said Sancia. "What was it you said in the Mountain? After we cracked through Tribuno's door?"

Berenice managed a watery smile. "Together we're unstoppable."

"Want to prove it?"

She laughed miserably. "No. Not at all. But I suppose I'm going to."

Sancia placed the plate on her tongue, thickly said, "Down the 'atch," and tossed back her cup of wine.

"Down," squeaked Berenice. "Hatch. Yes." Then she did the same.

They swallowed hard—it was akin to swallowing a hard chunk of bread—and then stared at each other, waiting.

"Well?" said Orso.

"I don't feel . . . anything?" said Sancia.

"Will take time to calibrate. Several minutes at least."

They stood in the basement, looking at each other, waiting nervously. The minutes seemed to stretch on and on.

"I . . . still don't feel anything," said Berenice.

"Yeah, me neither," said Sancia.

Everyone turned to her and frowned, including Berenice.

Sancia looked around nervously. "W-What?"

"Yeah me neither . . . what?" said Orso.

"What do you mean, yeah me neither what?" said Sancia. "Berenice said she didn't feel anything, and I said I don't either."

They stared. Berenice's eyes grew terribly wide.

"What?" said Sancia again.

"I . . . didn't say that, Sancia," said Berenice.

Sancia blinked, confused, and looked into Berenice's eyes—and yet the second she did, she had the most curious, overpowering sensation that she was looking into her own face from *Berenice's* eyes.

She gasped as the image flooded into her mind—it was definitely her own face she was seeing, but from another person's perspective.

"Oh *shit*," said Sancia. She touched her cheeks. "When did I get so old? I have so many *wrinkles* now . . ."

"I need to change my hair," said Berenice faintly. She touched the side of her head. "This bun isn't nearly as becoming as I thought it was . . . God, I miss having decent mirrors here . . ."

"What the hell is this shit?" asked Orso.

"I suspect they are seeing each other from the other's perspective," said Valeria. *"This would be the beginning of the calibration. The next will be the most difficult part, I estimate . . ."*

And then reality all folded in on itself like Sancia was looking into two or three or four mirrors, all perfectly aligned: she saw herself seeing Berenice seeing herself, and then she was seeing herself seeing herself seeing herself, and on and on and on, and suddenly she grew so dizzy she couldn't remember how to stand up anymore.

She heard Berenice saying nearby, "I need to lie down! I need to lie down!"

Sancia wasn't nearly as articulate. She just groaned loudly, shut her eyes, and lay facedown on the stone floor, her right cheek touching the cold stone.

Then she had a very queer experience: she felt the cold stone touching her *left* cheek as well. She slowly realized that, impossibly enough, she was feeling what Berenice was also feeling.

And more: Sancia was uncomfortable, but she was also feeling Berenice's discomfort, and then she *also* felt discomfort at feeling each other's discomfort, and it seemed to amplify and amplify and amplify . . .

A strange thought bellowed into her mind: *<DO NOT LIKE>*

And though this thought was inarticulate and terribly foreign, it was also somehow so distinctly . . . Berenice.

Sancia sent a thought back: *<this is extremely bad, I also do not like this>*

An answering thought: *<HOW LONG BADNESS LAST>*

She didn't know, so together they just lay on the floor and moaned miserably.

"This goes on for how long?" asked Gregor.

"I do not know," said Valeria. *"Minutes. Or perhaps hours."*

"Oh God," gasped Sancia and Berenice simultaneously.

Sancia kept her eyes closed: much like an extremely bad bout of intoxication, it was easier to deal with the affliction the more you limited your sensations. But it grew difficult to understand exactly how long she'd had her eyes closed. She realized she wasn't sure how to mentally measure time when she was aware of someone else in her head who *also* was attempting to mentally measure time—it was like trying to look at two clocks at once.

Yet as she miserably waited, eyes clamped shut, lost in the darkness with her cheek pressed to the cold floor, she slowly began to feel . . . different.

The change was slow and curious. The only comparison she had for it was the experience of being asleep in your own bed, and having your pet jump up and nestle in the back of your leg—the faint, warm awareness of another being nestling into you, whether you liked it or not.

A voice blossomed in her mind—a voice that was undeniably, absolutely, unquestionably Berenice:

<Ahh. Are you there?>

Sancia fumbled in the darkness—in her mind, she supposed—for how to respond. This was different from the Mountain, or Clef, really: both of them had been separate entities she could access or engage with, but this was much more *present*. Berenice was not someone she was talking to. She was, in a very real way, someone Sancia *was*, to a certain extent: She was sharing her mind with her, her very self.

Sancia said: *<YEAH I'M HERE HOLY SHIT RIGHT>*

She felt Berenice recoil at the volume of her thoughts. *<Not so loud! Or . . . not so much. Since I don't think we're actually making noise here.>*

<SORRY. I mean . . . sorry. I'm used to having to talk to something removed from me, but you're . . . >

<I'm not,> said Berenice. *<No. I'm here. Very close. Like she said—like two panes of colored glass overlaid on top of one another . . . >*

There was a pause as they gauged how connected they now were. It was the oddest experience: Sancia suddenly found memories present in her head that were not *hers*—memories of scriving, of working with Orso, of a childhood in the Commons spent before a game board . . . and yet there was the immediate sense that they *were* hers, since she was, to a degree, also this person.

Or she was sharing herself with this person. Or perhaps this person was sharing herself with Sancia. Or both at once.

<I think it would be best,> said Berenice's voice in her head, *<if we stop attempting to define the terminology for this.>*

<Because it's bugshit mad?> said Sancia.

<Because it is bugshit mad. Would you like to open your eyes now?>

<I guess we need to. Do you know how much time's passed since we swallowed the plates?>

<It feels like days. But . . . since they're not shaking us or moving us or anything, and since I'm not particularly hungry . . . I do not think our experience of time is all that adequate right now.>

<Then let's open our eyes and see what this is like, I guess.>

Sancia swallowed. She found this instinctive reaction was useful for helping her remember which body was hers, since that suddenly seemed rather fuzzy. Having located her own throat, she then located her face, and then she went about the process of opening her eyes . . .

Light poured in. She saw herself staring into Berenice's cool, calm gaze, her face resting gently on the stone floor of the basement. And the sight of her, as well as the sight of herself from Berenice's eyes, was overwhelming.

Yet it was also overwhelmingly *beautiful*. The experience was like nothing she'd ever had before. It was like returning to a childhood home that you'd left long ago: every aspect of the sight of Berenice was just so achingly familiar, so overlaid with memories and feelings and echoes of sensations . . .

They blinked in unison.

<Wow,> said Berenice.

<No shit,> said Sancia.

Then they heard Valeria say, *"I believe alignment is near completion . . ."*

They blinked again. *<Valeria?>* said Sancia in her mind. *<Can you hear us?>*

Silence.

<She . . . can't,> said Berenice. *<Or at least, not when we communicate like this. We're too close, too . . . unified.>*

Sancia thought rapidly. She reached out and grabbed Berenice's hand, and somehow the sensation of connection intensified, like half of their minds was here in the room with Orso and Valeria and

Gregor, and half was in some secret, invisible room where no one could see or hear them.

<*Holy Lord,*> said Berenice. <*That is a* very *different experience from what I was expecting . . .* >

<*Yeah, yeah, yeah,*> said Sancia. <*But I have something important to talk to you about. Ber, are you . . .* >

<*Suspicious as all hell of Valeria? Yes.*>

<*Thank God. Me too. I couldn't say anything or write anything to you because . . .* >

<*Because she would know. Yes. We'd have to get a block or two away from her to be outside of her earshot—if that's even the word for it.*>

<*What the hell are we going to do? Are we even doing the right thing now? Or are we playing into her game?*>

<*I'm not sure,*> said Berenice. <*I think . . . I think she's less powerful and influential than she'd hoped to be. But I think she's . . .* >

<*She's hiding something.*>

<*Yes. She is very unclear about what she'd do if Crasedes was out of the way. I sense the two have conflicting goals—but beyond killing Crasedes, I don't know what hers are.*>

<*Then we use her,*> said Sancia. <*We get her to bring back Clef, and then abandon her if we like. Or maybe Clef can tell us more.*>

<*I agree,*> said Berenice.

<*Though I don't like it.*>

<*No,*> said Berenice. <*We need to talk soon. As in, out loud. Or else everyone will get nervous.*>

Together, they slowly sat up and looked around at the basement. Everything was still the same, but the experience of seeing the familiar through someone else's eyes was so *strange*. It was both wonderful and yet somehow crushing, for you learned so much, but you realized instantly how limited your experience of reality had been for the whole of your life.

She both felt and heard Berenice say: "What a critical and crushing thing, perspective is . . ."

"Huh?" said Orso. "Damn it all—did it *work*?"

Sancia looked at Orso, and suddenly her memories were flooded with knowledge about him she'd never had before, days and nights of laboring and planning and scheming in the Dandolo hypatus office. She instantly realized he wasn't just some privileged old crank—though he *was* that, of course—but he was also much more.

"A . . . A dreamer," said Sancia quietly. "Aspirations crushed, hopes embittered. Only flickering to life just now, for the first time in decades."

He stared at her. "Whaa? Sancia . . . are you all right?"

Sancia and Berenice shook themselves in unison. Then they both simultaneously said, "Yes. I'm fine."

Gregor and Orso shot each other a wary glance. "Are you . . ." said Gregor dubiously.

"Can Berenice do the same thing Sancia can?" said Orso.

Berenice shook her head. "I can't see scrivings yet . . . You said they look like little silvery tangles, right, San?"

"Yeah, but . . . Here. Let me actually flex my sight . . ." Sancia focused, tensed the secret little muscle in the back of her head, and the world lit up with bright ribbons of logic and meaning, woven throughout the reality around them.

Berenice shrieked in surprise. "Oh! Oh my *God*."

"What is it, girl?" asked Orso.

"I . . . I *see* them . . ." said Berenice. "I see all the commands, all the bindings, all the little bits of persuaded reality all around us . . . and they're so *beautiful*." Then she said to Sancia, *<This is what it's like all the time for you, San?>*

<When I flex it, it is.>

Berenice grew still. *<Do . . . Do you remember how Orso said sometimes you invent the truly amazing things purely by accident?>*

<Huh? Yeah, I do. Why?>

<I . . . I feel like we have done that just now, tonight,> said Berenice. *<Because . . . this is the most beautiful sight I have ever seen in all my life . . . >*

"Alignment . . . *appears to have gone well*," said Valeria. She sounded impatient. "*Ready for the next step?*"

Their wonderment vanished once they remembered their predicament, and what they were about to do.

"Yes," said Gregor grimly. "The bit where you murder me."

25

Sancia stared at the darts clutched in her hand, their points small and dark and gleaming with dried venom. She tried to ignore how she trembled, how her hands quaked, how her very heart seemed to flutter . . .

"It will work, yes?" Gregor asked her. He grunted as Berenice tied the bonds around his legs tight, securing him to the chair. "I have heard of fishermen dying from the sting of the dolorspina . . ."

"It'll work," said Sancia hoarsely. "I . . . I remember being told not to stick someone twice, because then . . ."

She trailed off, unable to articulate the thought.

"Because then they might not wake up," said Gregor. "Yes. I see."

Orso and Berenice finished with his legs, and then his hands. Gregor—ever the seaman—had actually tied these knots for them, and given them instructions on how to ensure they were secure. "How many will it take?" he asked as he tested the bonds on his wrists behind his back.

"I don't know," said Sancia. Everything felt terribly numb to her. "But . . . these are a little old. Been a while since I did any thieving."

Gregor nodded, his face solemn and serious, as if he were debating an expensive purchase. "But will it be enough?"

"I have six here, so . . ." Again, she trailed off.

"It will be more than enough," said Berenice gently.

"Good," said Gregor.

"It's . . . It's a good way to go," said Orso. "It's the way I'd like to go, if I had to choose."

"God . . ." Sancia shook her head. "How mad this all is. How *insane* it is to just be casually plotting a death. I . . . I don't understand how you can be so calm about this, Gregor."

"It's not that mad," said Gregor. "When I was a soldier, we frequently discussed burial plans and messages home and final wishes. Do none of you ever consider it? Ever? For the sun shall set on all our lives at some point, of course—unless you'd prefer a life like Crasedes's." Then he added darkly, "Or mine. I . . . I almost feel I . . ."

"Feel what?" said Sancia.

He shook his head.

"Never mind. Let us do it and get it done."

"The critical thing," said Valeria, *"is not to interfere with the scriving, and not to break the connection to Gregor. You will feel an echo not of a dull object that has been weakly convinced to do something unusual—you will feel an echo of what it is like to have your reality abruptly and suddenly changed. To have your experience of* time itself *altered. I do not comprehend the nature of that experience. But I expect it will be . . . unusual. Do not break away."*

"Scrumming hell," sighed Sancia, shivering. She approached Gregor and took Berenice by the hand. "Okay. Ber—our connection is stronger when we touch. So I'll hold your hand with my right, and touch his forehead with my left. Which means . . ."

"Oh God," she said. "I'll have to be the one who . . . who does the bit with the darts, yes?"

"Yeah."

"Are you sure?" said Orso. "Perhaps I'd be the better choice . . ."

"No," said Gregor. "Orso—you take a dart of your own and

stand clear. When I'm activated, I'll . . . I'll need you to stick me and put me back down, if you can." He looked at Berenice. "But that *does* mean this duty will stay with you, Berenice."

She shut her eyes. "I never thought I'd ever have to do such a thing . . . But I suppose that goes for all of us."

"I'll be all right," said Gregor. "Just do it, please."

Berenice picked up a dart, then paused and looked Gregor in the eye. Then she took a breath and stabbed him in the thigh with one of the darts.

He didn't flinch. Then his eyelids grew woozy and he began blinking very hard. "Oof," he said.

"Feeling it?" said Sancia.

"Yes," he said. "But—you're right. These aren't as potent as the ones you used before. I was . . . I was barely conscious within a second when you pricked me that time . . . It will take a lot more to kill me than this." He swallowed, and then he suddenly laughed. It sounded slightly delirious. "Do . . . Do you remember it, Sancia?"

"Remember what?"

"You jumping through the window, and darting those men? In the Greens, I mean . . . And then you hauled me out to the gutters, and . . . and we spoke for the first time."

"Yeah. Sure. I remember, Gregor."

His smile faded and he stared into space, glassy-eyed. "How odd, to feel nostalgic for such a time. It seems so long ago now."

They watched him. He began to lean in the chair, and his face grew dead and dull and oddly pained, like he wasn't quite sure what was happening, but he knew he did not like it.

"Knocking . . . Knocking me out," he said, his words slurred. Then: "Another."

"What?" said Sancia.

"Another . . . Another dart. Not enough."

Berenice hesitated.

Gregor's head lolled back. "Another!" he cried. "Get it over with! *Please!*"

"Ber—another!" hissed Sancia.

Cursing quietly, Berenice snatched up another dolorspina dart and stabbed him in the leg again.

Gregor's head had rolled to the side, and he was staring into space with an expression that was both miserable and despairing. "Okay," he said. He was breathing hard now. "All right. Here it comes."

Sancia almost asked if he was feeling all right, or if it hurt, but then she realized the awful pointlessness of such a question.

"I thought"—he grunted slightly—"that I would remember a little more of what this was like. Dying, I mean." His voice trembled. "I thought it would feel a bit old-hat. But . . . I mean, I know I shouldn't be *afraid* . . ."

Berenice turned away, now weeping freely.

"Going out now," whispered Gregor. He looked up at Sancia. "Am I . . . Am I bad for hoping, a little, that it sticks?"

"Sticks?" said Sancia. "What do you mean?"

But then his neck went limp, and his face slackened. She knew he was not dead yet, but he was very clearly dying. She had seen many people die in her life, many in ways far more horrible than this, but for some reason this seemed worse than all the others. And as she watched him leaning sideways in the chair, his face aggrieved as if he'd been holding vigil all night mourning the loss of a loved one and could not stay awake a moment longer, she realized why.

Does he want this? Does he welcome this? Does he hope *to die?*

<I hate this so much, Sancia,> said Berenice. *<I hate this so much!>*

<I know, Ber. It'll be over soon.>

Then Gregor closed his eyes and went still.

Everyone stared at him for a moment, slack and leaning in the chair, his face pinched in pain and sorrow, his chest still and devoid of breath.

Orso hobbled up and felt the side of his neck. "He's still alive. His pulse is slowing, but he's still alive." He blinked for a moment and said in a very strangled voice, "Berenice—I think you need to do another dart."

"No!" she said, sniffing.

"Yes!" he snapped. "You're going to have to!"

"I don't want to!" she said. "It's too horrible!"

"It's going to happen anyway!" he said. "We just need it to happen faster, all right?"

"Orso, you . . . you rotten bastard!" she cried.

Orso looked a little surprised and hurt at those words.

"Ber," said Sancia sharply. *<He's right. Do it.>*

<*I'm not like either of you!*> she said. <*I . . . I'm not used to making horrible choices like this!*>

<*Well, get used to it, because you're going to have to make a lot more of them in the future! Gregor asked you to. Get it over with, for him!*>

Sobbing, she picked up yet another dolorspina dart and jabbed it into his leg.

Orso felt Gregor's pulse again, his own face convulsing with anguish. "It's . . . It's still slowing," he rasped. "It should be enough . . ."

They stared at Gregor, limp in the chair, lying in a way that would have been terribly painful for him had he been conscious. Sancia was suddenly struck with the strange and heartbreaking realization that if this were to fail, and Gregor were to actually die tonight, then this would probably be how he'd wish to do it: gently, slowly, in his sleep, surrounded by his friends. And then she began to cry.

Gregor Dandolo slept.

He was not sure why, or how he'd come to sleep, but he lingered in the shadows, unable to think or feel or move. All he knew was a suffocating darkness, an encroaching void that seemed to drown his very mind . . .

Then his thoughts began to crumble in, all the memories flashing and crackling as the grand stage of his mind went dark, interactions and moments from all throughout his life bursting in the shadows like sputtering fireworks.

Ah, he thought. *I know this now. I am . . . I am going to die now, aren't I?*

A barrage of moments, of sensation, of textures and emotions. Not simply the epiphanies and the conflicts and the victories and defeats that formed his person, but all the tiny interstitial, forgettable exchanges that make up the sum of one's life . . .

The feeling of thick leather in warm sun.

A man's hand, turning a coin over and over again.

A pebble in the back of a boot.

Birds bursting from the foliage to wheel away into the dawning sun.

Memories upon memories upon memories.

And among them . . .

Asleep.

Gregor felt cloth under him, over his face and against his body, and all about him was the smell of his mother.

He was asleep in her hanging clothes in her closet again, in that secret place he went when he felt threatened, for in that place he knew he was safe. This place was hers. No one could harm him there.

Then he heard a sound—a splashing from nearby, and someone gasping and spitting.

Gregor opened his eyes. He sat up and slowly emerged from the hanging clothes, and he crouched there on the floor of her closet, listening.

There was a splashing from a room beyond—the bathing room—and a cough, and another bout of spitting. And then there was a sob, miserable and pained.

Gregor stood at the door to the closet, hesitating. Then he opened it and stepped out.

The first thing he saw was his own face, looking back from the reflection of a mirror—he was so young and fragile, not yet six. He looked at himself only for a moment, for then his mother shrieked in fright.

She was on the floor of the bathing room in a nightshirt, kneeling before a bowl filled with rose-pink water, her face and hands dripping. She appeared to have been using it to wash her face—which was, to his shock, badly beaten: her split lip, still dribbling blood, and her blackened eyes, and bruised cheeks.

"Gregor!" she said. "What . . . What were you doing in there?"

"Momma," he said. "Momma, what happened to you?"

The rag fell from her hands into the bloody water in the bowl, splashing her nightshirt. "Were you hiding in there? Why would you be hiding in my closet?"

"I . . . I fell asleep in there." He felt hot with confusion and shame. "I . . . I do that sometimes but I . . . I . . ." Then he burst into tears.

"Oh God . . ." she said. "Come here, my love, come here . . ." She embraced him. "I just . . . I had a moment, that's all. That's all, love."

"You're hurt, Momma."

She sniffed and smiled valiantly. "Oh, it's not terribly bad. It's just a few bruises, that's all."

He looked at her for a moment. Then he knelt before her and picked up the rag. "Can I help you?"

She smiled at him, her eyes sad and desperate. "All right. If you want."

She sat still while young Gregor dabbed at her cuts and her bruises with the rag, washing the blood away.

She smiled—this one quite genuine. "When you were little," she said as he worked, "you used to help me put on my paints. You loved taking the little brushes and putting my lines on, and you did it to yourself, too, painting yourself up. It was part of our routine."

"I remember." He watched as the cut in her lip welled up with blood again. "What happened, Momma?"

She sighed. "I tried what so many of our scrivers do. I tried to convince the world it was something it wasn't. Or it isn't anymore, at least. And some people . . . some people got very angry at me."

He looked at his mother, sitting with her head bowed, blood trickling down her chin from myriad tiny injuries. How ashamed she looked, how humiliated.

"I will stop them," he said suddenly.

"You'll what?"

"I'll stop them. I'll . . . I'll take their houses and cast them down and burn them and . . . and . . ."

She watched him, pityingly. Then she smiled. "Oh, my brave little knight . . . My proud warrior. What a thing it is, to see you shot through with such a thread of nobility." She reached up and stroked his face. "I remember when you were born. How eager you were to come to this world. Not like Domenico, who took hours and hours. You were so hungry to throw yourself into all the turmoil of this broken world of ours."

The memory flickered. His vision began to fade, and the world grew dark.

Something is happening, thought Gregor. *I am going . . . away . . .*

The memory grew dark at the edges, flowing in. The last thing he saw was his mother's battered, bruised face, beaming up at him.

"Oh, Gregor. If I ever take my house back," her voice whispered to him, *"what a city you and I shall make, my love . . ."*

This is it, isn't it, he thought as his mind drowned in darkness. *It's coming. Yes. Yes, I think it might b—*

Then silence.

Then nothing.

26

They stood around Gregor, watching him without moving.

"When will we hear the scriving?" asked Berenice quietly.

"I don't know," said Sancia.

"The scriving should become active upon death," said Valeria, *"and he has not completed the death process yet. But . . . soon. Then all should proceed as planned."*

They stood there in the basement, Sancia's hand pressed to the forehead of their dying friend, and she wondered for a moment if she felt his flesh was cooling under her palm.

"I'm not hearing anything," said Sancia.

"It will come."

"He's dead now, isn't he? He is. I can tell."

"The process is still finishi—"

"He's still *dying*? God, how long does this take!"

"Upon death," said Valeria again, *"the scriving should activate."* Then she added, *"Or . . . soon enough after."*

" 'Soon enough after'?" said Berenice. "What does that mean?"

"I made it clear I was unfamiliar with how this would proceed. It could be immediately after death. It could be five minutes after. Or ten, or an hour."

Sancia's skin went cold. "You . . . You mean to tell me," she said, her words shaking with rage, "that you expect us to stand down here in the basement with our hands touching the corpse of our friend, until we hear something? But you don't know when that *is*?"

"It is the only option."

"And you're *sure* we'll hear something?" said Sancia. "You're *sure* it'll bring him back?"

Valeria hesitated. *"I am almost certain."*

"Oh *God*," said Orso, dismayed. "Almost? *Almost?* So there's some room for error here?"

"It will work," said Valeria.

"I wish you sounded half as confident as your goddamn words were!" said Sancia. "Because right now, I'm not feeling very confident at al—"

Then she heard it: a quiet, hushed muttering, like the room was full of rustling leaves.

Sancia jumped and whirled around, staring about the basement, one hand still touching Gregor's forehead. "What . . . What the hell?" she said.

"What is it?" asked Orso.

Sancia kept staring around, the muttering, whispering sound rising and falling in her ears. <*Do . . . Do you hear that?*> she asked Berenice.

<*Yes.*> Berenice sounded terrified.

<*Is that* leaves? *Is that what I'm hearing, somehow? Like we're in a forest?*>

<*I . . . I thought it was wings.*>

And she realized Berenice was right: the sound was too rhythmic, a gentle, soft fluttering that waxed and waned like the surf at the beach. She felt as if she were standing in a storm of tiny fluttering creatures, perhaps bats or butterflies or . . .

Then another sound joined it, one much more unsettling than the first: the sound of a woman sobbing hysterically from just nearby, anguished and agonized.

"Holy shit," said Sancia. She stared around the basement, feeling certain that the wailing woman was just next to her, or perhaps next to Gregor, but there was no one there. Yet the sobbing continued, this disembodied voice crying on and on in the room next to them.

"Oh my God . . ." whispered Berenice. "What . . . who is that? What's going on?"

"What's wrong, girl?" said Orso.

"Ber—I take it you hear that as well, right?" asked Sancia.

"Y-Yes," she said stiffly. "There is an invisible woman crying nearby. But I cannot see her."

"Valeria," said Sancia. "Can you hear that?"

"*I cannot.*"

The invisible woman shrieked in what sounded like agonized grief.

"Then what the *hell* is going on?" shouted Sancia.

"*Uncertain,*" said Valeria. "*It is possible that . . . that what you are experiencing is a consequence of the scriving being activated.*"

The sobs grew even louder.

"And why the hell does that mean I'm hearing shrieking women in our goddamn basement?" shouted Sancia over the sound of the cries.

"*Uncertain. However . . . I suspect it is like most scrivings, in that in order for it to know how far or how much to alter Gregor's time, it must first have an instance of time defined. In order to tell it to restore him to an instance thirty seconds ago, for example, you must first tell it what a second is.*"

"We know all that!" cried Berenice. "That's basic scriving theory!"

"*True. But I suspect that this concept of time was defined when the scriving was first placed upon him. So . . . each time that it activates, it must refer back to that first instance.*"

Sancia's heart felt like it'd been shot through with ice. "You mean . . . we're reliving the night of his carriage accident? When his brother and father *died*?"

"*You are perhaps catching ghosts of when the scriving was first applied to him. Fading impressions. I can guess no more than that.*"

The voice of the woman began wailing openly now, and Sancia and Berenice both jumped.

"Shit," said Sancia. "Shit, shit, shit."

"Must stay calm now, Sancia," said Valeria. *"Must not probe, must not ask questions. This is a creation of the Maker. Observe—but do no more."*

Then they heard the woman's voice, crying, *"No, no, no . . . Please, please, God . . . not you. Not you, my love, not you . . ."*

"Easy for you to say!" said Sancia.

The woman continued: *"I didn't want it to happen to you . . . I . . . I didn't want it to happen to either of you, my loves, my loves . . ."*

The sound of the tiny wings rose and fell, and rose and fell.

She felt a thrill of fear run through Berenice. *<Sancia . . . My God. I think I know whose voice that is.>*

<What?>

<I've heard her talk before! Many times! I . . . I think we're hearing the voice of Ofelia Dandol—>

And then they heard it—the voice of the scriving, suddenly speaking as if it were standing shoulder to shoulder with them, surveying Gregor's corpse with a cold, dispassionate eye.

And its voice . . . that they both knew quite well too.

<CESSATION OF ARTERIAL PALPITATIONS,> boomed Crasedes Magnus's voice. *<ENTITY FAILS . . . PERCEIVING.>*

Sancia and Berenice froze as the voice thundered through their ears.

<Oh my God,> whispered Berenice. *<It . . . It sounds like him! It sounds like Crasedes!>*

<No, shi—>

<PRESENCE?> said the voice. *<PRESENCE . . . ACCOMPANIES?>*

They both went totally still. This seemed impossible—no scriving Sancia had ever tampered with had ever cared if she was tampering with it—but then, she'd never really tampered with a hierophantic scriving . . . especially one that'd been made by Crasedes himself.

There was a long, tense silence, broken only by the sound of the sobs, over and over and over again, as if they were stuck in a loop: *"No, no, no . . . Please, please, God . . . No, no, no . . ."*

Sancia looked at Berenice, wide-eyed and terrified. Berenice made a gesture in front of her mouth, like she was sewing her mouth shut. But as Sancia nodded, they suddenly felt it.

A *pressure*. A *presence*. They felt overcome with the feeling of being examined, like glancing out the window and seeing a shape in the alleys, staring back up at you.

Oh shit, thought Sancia. She looked at the empty air around them, as if expecting to see Crasedes himself there, staring back. *It's looking for us. It's really looking for us . . .*

<REVIEW BINDINGS,> said the voice of Crasedes, though it sounded somewhat suspicious. <CONFIRM TEMPORAL IN-STANCE FOR RESTORATION . . . >

And then many things began to change around them.

Sancia felt a breeze rush over her skin, like there was an open window. She looked to the side, suddenly sure she would see a tall set of windows there, open to the sprawling, lamplit nightscape of Tevanne, but she saw nothing but the crumbling brick wall of the basement.

Yet when she looked back . . .

Suddenly there was a bed across from them, on the other side of Gregor's chair, one that definitely had not been there before. It had crisp white sheets and a rich, silk cover, done in white and yellow.

But the cover was stained with dark blood—for on the far side of the bed lay the body of a man, horribly mangled, lit with moonlight.

Sancia and Berenice both screamed in horror at the sight of him, the right side of his face crumpled in, his eye spilling from the ruined socket, his cheekbone glinting through the pink flesh. His right arm and especially his hand had been almost totally destroyed, the limb dissolving into an unrecognizable mess about halfway down his forearm, veins and bone and limp stretches of ligaments clearly visible in the faint light. His fine yellow robes and hosiery were torn and covered with mud, and yet they sparkled strangely—and then Sancia realized his whole body was dotted with tiny shards, fragments of glass studding his face, his shoulders, his hands, little rose-blooms of blood seeping from where they were embedded in him.

But the worst thing was how much he looked like Gregor. He looked *exactly* like the man passed out in the chair before them, but younger, somehow, and a touch fatter and softer, as if he'd lived a comfortable civilian life.

Sancia did not recognize him—but Berenice did. She'd seen his face in countless paintings back on the Dandolo campo, and the instant she recognized him, that same knowledge manifested in Sancia's mind.

"*It's Ottaviano Dandolo!*" Berenice screamed.

"W-What?" said Orso, astonished. He looked down at where the mangled man lay, but he clearly didn't see anything. "What do you mean?"

"It's Ottaviano Dandolo!" she cried again, sobbing. "He's lying right there on the bed and he's dead, oh God, he's *dead*!"

"Bed?" said Orso. "Dead? What?"

"*She is witnessing something from when the plate was first installed,*" said Valeria. "*We cannot experience it, for the scriving does not apply to us.*"

Sancia shut her eyes. <*Close your eyes, Ber! Just close them!*>

Berenice did so, weeping softly. The sound of the soft, fluttering wings surged in their ears.

Then she felt it: she felt the first string of scrivings begin to be applied, slowly beginning to warp Gregor's time, to sense out how far back he needed to shift, and what would change . . .

And then it happened.

Usually when Sancia closely communed with a scrived object, she would begin to get a creeping feeling of the sigils on its persuasion plate, the many strings of the commands altering its reality, convincing it to be different. It was a curious but mild sensation, like watching an insect climb up your arm, its tiny legs picking over the hairs on your skin.

But Gregor's scriving was not like that.

Suddenly the sigils struck her like a lightning bolt, command after command seared into her mind like a burning brand, the bright, hot bindings rippling through her—and she *felt* them, each and every one of them, dozens of them sizzling into her being, rewriting her very existence in an instant . . .

She nearly shrieked in agony. She'd always known hierophantic commands were different. But she'd never had any idea *how* different.

She heard Berenice screaming in pain.

"*Do not break away!*" warned Valeria. "*Must maintain!*"

"I can't!" cried Berenice. "To have this done to me . . . it *hurts*!"

"*Maintain!*" said Valeria.

Another string of sigils—perhaps a dozen, perhaps a hundred, Sancia didn't know. The burning characters unscrolled upon her being, and she felt them changing her very reality like her body and mind were clay to be lopped off or re-formed at a whim . . .

If this is just an echo of the scriving, she thought through the agony, *then God . . . God, what must it actually be like to be part of a hierophantic command?*

Berenice screamed again in pain. Not thinking, Sancia opened her eyes.

And then she saw her.

A woman of about thirty was sitting in the middle of the basement, covered in blood and sobbing hysterically. Cradled in her lap was a boy of around eleven or twelve years old, and he was very clearly dead. The back of his head bore a tremendous wound, an unsettlingly dark, viscous purple cavity just behind his right ear.

Sancia realized she knew this woman. She had met her just days ago, weeping and trembling in the depths of the galleon: Ofelia Dandolo, though the specter she saw now was thirty or forty years younger than the woman she'd met.

Ofelia shook the child in her lap, as if trying to wake him. His head rolled to the side, and Sancia saw his face.

The sight took her breath away. His face was set in the angelic, untroubled expression all children assumed when sleeping, spoiled only by the slow creep of blood on the side of his head. But most of all, he looked so much like Gregor, but so young, so delicate . . .

And yet, she somehow knew it was not Gregor. This boy was too skinny, too frail, and his eyes were too far apart.

Domenico Dandolo?

"*Come back to me!*" screamed Ofelia. She shook him violently, and blood began to spill from the boy's mouth. "*Come back to me, please, please!*"

Sancia shut her eyes again, and she and Berenice both moaned in terror.

"*It must almost be complete!*" said Valeria. "*Do not break away now! Maintain connection!*"

"Berenice," said Sancia. "Please tell me you're remembering all these goddamn sigils!"

"How could I forget them?" sobbed Berenice.

<INSTANCE ISOLATED . . . FINALIZING,> boomed Crasedes's voice in their minds. <ESTABLISH RESTORATION PATH . . . >

Another burst of sigils, this time the most yet, the flashes of characters pouring into Sancia's mind again and again.

It was almost too much. She felt her own sense of time growing soft, flattening out, dissolving. It was one thing to have your reality rewritten, but another to have a command attempt to shift your time back to an instance that, for you, did not exist—for she and Berenice, after all, could not be skipped back to a past instance in Gregor's time.

It was all wrong. It was like being fed through a vast, malfunctioning machine, its pistons and gears tearing into your flesh . . .

"Berenice!" she cried. "Stay with me!"

"I'm here! But . . . Sancia . . . I can't take this for much longe—"

Then they heard a voice before them, husky and cracked: "M-Momma?"

Sancia and Berenice opened their eyes.

Gregor was gone. The chair was gone.

In their place was a small boy of about seven, lying on a bed, his face streaked with mud, his leg badly broken. Sancia's hand was pressed to his forehead, and when he blinked and looked at them she gasped and nearly drew it away.

The boy whispered, "Momma? What's . . . What's happened, Momma?"

"Ohh, what the hell," said Sancia.

The voice of Ofelia Dandolo came floating through, as if from some distant hallway: "Hush, darling . . . Hush. We've given you a draught. Just . . . sleep."

"Where's Papa? Where's Domenico? What happened?" The child blinked and looked around the basement.

"Your father is . . . gone," whispered her voice. "And Domenico . . ." Then came a sob.

Another flicker in the air, and then it seemed as if the boy were surrounded by a snowfall, little dots of flickering white wheeling and curling about them . . .

But then Sancia realized. They were not snowflakes.

They were moths. And the air was filled with the sound of their wings.

It's him, thought Sancia. *He's here. He's come. This is when Crasedes arrived.*

"What are all these butterflies here?" whispered the boy.

"They're . . . They're here to help me," said Ofelia's voice, sniffing. "The moths came in through the window. They came to me while I slept. And . . . I think they are a miracle, my love. They can save you."

The boy looked around through drooping eyelids. "Save me from what?"

Then there was another flicker in the air, and Sancia saw her: an echo of Ofelia Dandolo, bending over the broken little boy in the bed.

She leaned down to kiss him on the brow. "From what I did to you, my love," she whispered. "And . . . And I am so *sorry* . . ."

Then another burst of sigils tore into them.

Both of them screamed as the sigils flashed in their minds, twisting them, contorting them, bending their bodies, their souls, their spirits. Sancia felt themselves dissolving, all these moments contracting, dwindling, diminishing, as if the past minutes of their lives were being boiled down to nothing but residue, to be replaced by instances of time just a few minutes previously . . .

She felt the realization crack through Berenice's mind. <*It doesn't move time. It bends it, stretches it. It shrinks the present time until it's nothing, and the past is all that's there!*>

Sancia barely understood Berenice's understanding. Part of it was that the concept was too complex for her—but the other obstacle was that she could not think, for she was sure she was going to die.

Then the body under her fingertips surged forward, and suddenly the world was nothing but screaming.

The sigils and the visions and the alterations snapped away. Berenice and Sancia opened their eyes and stumbled back in horror as Gregor popped up, his eyes wild and mad. He was screaming, bellowing, roaring at them, every vein in his head visible, every ligament in his neck stretched to the point of breaking.

Berenice screamed and tumbled to the ground as she fell back, and Sancia barely stayed standing. She watched as her friend heaved and strained at the bonds around his arms and chest and legs. The chair creaked and wrenched below him.

"Oh God!" screamed Orso's voice somewhere. "Holy shit!"

"*Were sigils retained?*" demanded Valeria. "*Was process successful?*"

Sancia was too terrified to respond. She just watched in mute fear as her friend snarled and growled like a wild boar, straining at the ropes, rocking back and forth in a mad, furious, helpless struggle . . .

And then he stopped and glared at her. He bent forward, and flexed with his legs . . .

There was a loud *pop* from the chair as something stretched to the point of breaking.

"Orso!" screamed Sancia. "Dart him now, dart him now!"

Orso fumbled for the dolorspina dart one-handed. Gregor leaned forward, growling, his eyes leaking tears and strings of drool hanging from his mouth from exertion, and there was another sharp, twangy *pop* from within the chair.

"Do it!" shrieked Sancia. "He's going to break fre—"

Orso cried out, leapt forward, and planted a dolorspina dart in the back of Gregor's shoulder. Gregor ripped to the side, snapping his teeth, and nearly bit off one of Orso's fingers.

"Scrumming hell!" shouted Orso.

Gregor heaved and heaved at the ropes, panting loudly, but each effort was weaker and weaker. It was clear the dart was having an effect: his eyes became unfocused, and each of his movements grew a little drunker and less coordinated. Finally his head drooped on his chest and he exhaled mightily, spraying drool from his lips and down his beard, and he glared at Sancia, half-conscious but helpless. Then he went still.

"Holy shit," said Orso. "Holy *shit*."

There was a silence as they stared at Gregor's body twitching in the chair.

"*Were sigils retained?*" asked Valeria quietly.

Berenice nodded and wiped tears from her eyes. Her whole body appeared to be shaking. "I have them. Someone get me a piece of paper so I can copy them down while they're still fresh."

Sancia eyed Gregor's tattered restraints. "Do we want to cut him free first?"

"Hell no," said Orso. "I half want to make new knots for him. But I'm not getting close to that mad bastard now."

Sancia studied Gregor for a moment longer, remembering the sight of the wounded boy lying on the bed, whispering to his mother.

<*Did you hear what Ofelia said to him, Ber?*> said Sancia. <*In that . . . that echo, or whatever it was?*>

<*Yes. I remember.*>

<*Then you think she . . . You think that she . . . that Ofelia Dandolo is . . .*>

<*I think that the carriage accident,*> said Berenice, <*was no accident. But first and foremost, San—I think you need to get me some damned paper. Or else this was all for nothing.*>

27

Ofelia stood at the windows of her massive ballroom in her estate house, staring out at the cityscape before her, the warm, honey-colored sun radiating off of the rooftops of the Dandolo campo.

Just afternoon now. But it felt so late, as if time was slipping by her faster and faster.

Why is it, she thought, *that I feel as if the second I called him back into this world, I turned over an hourglass, and all the world is watching the grains tumble down, and waiting?*

She ignored the scrivers and laborers behind her, hauling in crate after tremendous crate.

Where are you, Gregor? Her eye fell on the Lamplands, all the floating lanterns bobbing and swaying. *And will you come back to me, before time runs out?*

Then one laborer approached her, and asked, "Are you sure you want this all here, Founder?"

She studied him coldly. "Why would I not?"

"I mean, far be it from me to doubt you, Founder, but you seem to be planning to . . . well, to *build* your own lexicon here in your ballrooms. And such things require protections, and wards, and cooling waters, and . . ."

"Those won't be an issue," said a rich, plummy voice.

Ofelia and the laborer turned as Crasedes emerged from the shadows of a hallway.

"I shall see to all that," said Crasedes. He approached them. She noted he was carrying a slim wooden case in his hands, which seemed unusual to her.

The laborer looked uncertainly at him, then glanced back at Ofelia. "You . . . you're going to build a lexicon, sir? All by yourself?"

Crasedes's blank, black eyes stared into the man. "Are all the parts here?" he asked.

"What? Y-Yes, they a—"

"Then you can go," said Crasedes. "You and all the rest of your men."

Ofelia and Crasedes waited as the men filed away, their footsteps echoing throughout her giant, empty estate house.

"You truly think you can put it all together here, My Prophet?" she asked.

"Well, for starters, I do not intend to build a normal lexicon," he said, pacing around the crates. "But more so . . . I find that once you've gone to the trouble of making a whole nation disappear once or twice in your life, all other tasks suddenly seem rather manageable."

Ofelia joined him among the crates. "And once it's built . . ."

"Yes," he said. "We must send an envoy to the Morsinis. I suspect they'll be expecting us—no doubt they believe we'll be desperate for an alliance with them, against the Michiels. And I must be among this envoy. So—I have quite a lot to do before evening. Especially since I've had other tasks today."

He slid open the case in his hands, revealing a scriving definition plate seated on the velvet interior within. Ofelia was not a scriver, but she recognized right away that this definition plate featured sigils and commands she was certain she'd never seen used before—and they were all written in such tight, unnaturally *clean* handwriting . . .

"You . . . You made this plate in *one day*, My Prophet?" she asked.

"Mm," he said. "More like an afternoon. Or *part* of an afternoon, I suppose. When we pair this definition with Tribuno's in our own lexicon, the construct will have nowhere to escape. She will be trapped within whatever device she currently resides in, like a roach hiding from lamplight under a dresser. And then I can begin retooling her, so to speak."

Ofelia's eyes danced over the many curling lines of sigils. "But . . . the construct is quite adept at . . . how shall I put this— hopping in and out of lexicons, yes?"

"True enough."

"Then . . . won't it be quite catastrophic if she was to hop into yours and take control of it?"

"That won't be an issue," he said. "If we have enough copies of Tribuno's definition, stacking its authorities again and again and again, she will be quite helpless." He slid the case shut. "And after the party at the Morsinis' . . . we should have all the copies we need."

Ofelia went very still. She walked away from him, stood at the windows, and shut her eyes.

She remembered the plan he had vaguely described so far: the sheer scale of soldiers and coordination that would be necessary— not to mention the number of people who would die.

Not die, she thought. *Not as if they fell ill. They will be murdered—by him.*

"And there's no other way?" she asked quietly.

"Ofelia . . ." said his voice. "You wish to make a moral world, do you not? A just, equitable, sane world?"

"Yes," she whispered.

"Yes. Of course you do. And sometimes I find it takes a lot of treachery and death to make a moral world. That is simply the way of things." Then, suddenly, his voice came from right beside her. "You've always known this, Ofelia."

She jumped, and found him standing at her side, watching her. "W-What, My Prophet?"

"You know all this," he said. "You know what it requires. You knew it over thirty years ago—when you orchestrated your husband's death."

She turned away, unable to speak.

"I was watching, remember," said Crasedes. "I watched your story so closely. You were the daughter of the founder of your house. And though Ottaviano had seemed a decent man when you first married him . . . how quickly he turned your house's efforts to the same things that all the others pursued—to empires, and armies, and little fealty kingdoms all across the Durazzo . . ."

Ofelia Dandolo shut her eyes again and swallowed.

"This was not the city you were raised in," whispered Crasedes. "Not the house you wished to rule over. Not the world you wished to birth. You saw a future being written that you did not wish to live in. And when you tried to take your house back, he made sure you knew how powerless you were. So you did what was right. You did what was *necessary*. But the consequences . . . the consequences are something you struggle to live with every day. Aren't they?"

"I didn't want this," she whispered.

"No," said Crasedes. "You didn't."

"There is some *rot* to this place," she said. "Something . . . Something that warps and distorts our thoughts . . ."

"It is power, Ofelia," he whispered. "Supremacy scrives the spirit far greater than any command I could ever invent. And that is what I intend to end in this city, tonight."

She bowed her head, faced the city, and wept.

"Listen to me, Ofelia," he said. "Listen now, and listen close."

She looked up, surprised by the solemnity of his voice.

"I *will* return your son to you," he said. "Whole, and healthy, and restored. Unburdened by the bindings we once placed upon him. Because your predicament has a *personal* meaning to me. You are not the first parent to use the arts to try to save their child. Nor are you the first to suffer the unintended consequences of that choice. But I *will* make sure that you are reunited."

"Why?" asked Ofelia. "Why would you try so, My Prophet?"

"Because unlike others . . . Gregor is not yet lost," said Crasedes. "I have changed reality in many ways, but in my long life, I have come to know that some things truly cannot be restored." He looked down at his right hand, and he seemed to be remembering the feel of something held in his palm. "And these we must value most of all. For without them, we are nothing."

28

L ight from tall windows split through the dark.

The flicker and dance of candle flame; the dreamy spin of floating lanterns; passageways of marble and vaulted ceilings and ornate doors.

A tall, well-dressed boy emerged from the whirl of images, handsome but thin and fragile, a faint fuzz about his upper lip, his eyes dark and sensitive.

He smiled at him. *You're getting big, little brother!*

Then the crunch of wood, the tinkle of glass, and Domenico was gone.

Silence.

A dribble of water, a shuffling, and a whimpering in the darkness.

Light again, filtering through the fractured glass of the carriage windows. A bloody form slumped in the cockpit.

Then a voice: *Gregor? Gregor are . . . are you near?*

He looked back. A bloody hand emerged from the shadows of the backseat. It quaked and trembled, and yet it kept reaching, desperate to feel something, to be grasped, as if to confirm it was not alone.

Come to me, please, pleaded the voice, terrified and anguished, the voice of a child approaching death, experiencing something he was still too young to even fathom. *I love you. I . . . I need to . . . I love you, I love you . . .*

A bright, vicious scream burst forth from Gregor's lips, and he kicked away from the grasping hand, so desperate, so frightened . . .

I was not there, he thought. *I was not there, when my brother needed me most. At his last moments.*

Then it was gone.

Gregor Dandolo awoke upon his bed and gasped. He stared at the ceiling for a moment, trying to remember how he'd come to be here.

Something had changed. He knew that—but he did not know what.

Is today the day? Shall I finally wake up someone different than when I went to sleep?

But then his head began to pound with a very familiar ache, and he remembered.

Dolorspina poison . . . God. The scriving. Did I really . . .

"You're awake," said Sancia's voice from nearby.

He blinked and looked to the side. She was sitting in a chair next to him, red-eyed and exhausted.

"Sancia?" he said. His voice was little more than a croak.

"Hey, Gregor."

He looked around. His body throbbed like he'd strained half the muscles in his back and legs. "Did . . . Did I . . ."

"It worked, yeah," she said. "We got it. Berenice and Orso are putting it together right now. We should be able to have Clef back very soon."

"Oh." Though this, of course, was not what he had been about to ask, but rather—*Did I really die?* But he knew the answer.

"I . . . I want to tell you something," said Sancia.

He lay on the bed and listened as Sancia described the unearthly, terrifying experience of activating the scriving and witnessing flashes of a night nearly thirty years ago now, when he'd been a child lying on a bed below a cloud of moths, and his mother had rewritten his reality. And he listened especially closely as Sancia told him what she'd heard his mother say, words decades old, but how raw and horrible they felt today.

When she finished she just sat there watching him, her eyes wide and anxious.

"She did it," he said finally, his voice still a croak. "She . . . She killed my father."

"I think so."

"But . . . she did not expect Domenico and me to be in the carriage with him when . . . when it happened."

"I . . . I think maybe," she said quietly. "Yeah."

"No. Not maybe. It is so."

"You knew?"

"Not exactly." The memory of his mother shot through his mind, her face beaten and bruised and bloody—*What a city you and I shall make.* "But I find it's something I can easily believe."

They sat for a long time, not saying anything.

Then he asked, "Did she cry? In the moments you saw, did she cry?"

"Yes."

"And . . . it seemed genuine?"

"Yes. It did."

He shut his eyes. "It changes how I think of her."

"I figured it would."

"But perhaps not as you expect. She saw her city making the wrong choices, and struck to try to stop them. We have tried to do the same ourselves. But I suddenly doubt if we would have been any more successful." He sighed. "Conflict and factionalism and treachery . . . Where does it end? Why play the same game again and again and expect different results?"

"I don't know. I wish I did."

He looked at her for a moment, thinking. "If you could wave a magic wand," he said, "and make this all go away—would you?"

"All what? There's a lot of shit I'd like to go away. Do you mean Valeria? Crasedes? The houses?"

"No," he said. "Scriving."

"Huh? What do you mean?"

"Scriving is the root of all these problems. Polina quite literally calls it an evil magic. And after what I just went through . . . I find it hard to argue. I am forced to wonder—would it be better if . . . if we just didn't have it?"

Sancia thought about it. "If it wasn't scriving," she said finally, "it'd be something else. Land. Money. Iron. Or, hell, even beans, if Crasedes told me the truth. People are inventive. And anything they invent they can use to raise themselves up over everyone else."

"Then . . . could we ever win?" Gregor said. "Is this just a dance we do over and over? Will everything we build turn to nothing but ugliness?"

"I don't know." She shrugged, her face strangely wistful. "You know . . . if you'd asked me that five years ago when I'd just come to this city, working as a thief in the gutters . . . I'd have said yes. Anything that has to do with scriving, with power, with the houses—I'd have said all that could only turn into nothing but ugliness."

"But today?"

"But . . . today, right now, I'm sharing my mind, my thoughts, my very self with the person I love most of all in this world. And that's thanks to this innovation, this art. We *did* make something beautiful out of all this. And I can't imagine going back now. I just can't."

"You're still . . . connected?" he asked. "Scrived? Twinned?"

"Whatever the word is, yes."

"What's it like?"

She considered it. "It's like . . . It is rather like wearing someone's mindset as a cloak about you, wrapping yourself up in all their memories and thoughts, and it's not quite that you see things as *they* see them—but you understand that we are all glimpsing the world from different angles, and each of us sees only a tiny, fleeting bit of it."

He watched her, feeling disturbed and slightly awed. That was not Sancia talking, he knew—Sancia had many virtues, but florid articulation was certainly not one of them.

Does she even know that this thought, that those words, are actually Berenice's? Or is there any difference between the two anymore?

"It's wonderful," she said. "I feel everyone should try it. To not just walk a mile in someone else's boots, but to *be* them, truly, if only for a moment. Is it insane to say that?"

He lay there for a moment. "No," he said hoarsely. "In fact, I . . . I can think of nothing lovelier."

"Really? Why?"

He shrugged. "I would love to be someone else, Sancia. If only for a little while."

She sat forward. "Then why not do it, then?"

"Do what?"

"Twin yourself with me and Berenice?"

"*What?* I mean . . . Would it even work with three people?"

"I don't know why it wouldn't. We would all be a . . . a part of one another, a little bit. Maybe this could help you, Gregor. Or maybe you could help us."

He considered it. The idea suddenly seemed tantalizing to him—not just because he would become someone else, but because he realized how lonely he'd felt for so long, like a diseased sheep kept separate from the herd.

Yet he shook his head. "No. I would not risk that."

"It wouldn't harm you. Trust me, I—"

"I am not worried about me. I'm worried about *you*." He looked at her. "Crasedes did something to me. He and my mother can control my thoughts, my actions, my memories. I would not want that control to extend to you both." He started to sit up. "I would wish to keep what you have safe."

She helped him stand. "You don't always have to play at being a goddamned watchman, you know. For once, you could do something to help *you*."

Gregor paused, thinking. "I do have a question."

"Yeah?"

"If . . . If you think it could work with three people—could it work with more? Like, say, an army?"

"Huh? You want an *army* of people with their minds all twinned together?"

"I'm not proposing anything. But . . . I am suddenly imagining an army of people, of all these different perspectives, sharing themselves . . . Or perhaps a nation. A nation of people, truly, deeply united . . ." He shook his head. "But now is not the time for dreams. We have enough great works to do today—do we not?"

She sighed deeply, reached into her pocket, and pulled out the long, golden key with the curious tooth. "Yeah. We do."

"The solution is complete," said Valeria as they entered the basement. *"I have confirmed that the commands we obtained from Gregor will work."*

Sancia glanced at the creation sitting on the table before Valeria's lexicon. It looked like a small, copper sphere that split in half, opening on a hinge, with each side carefully and artfully engraved. She knew what this device was, and how it worked—one of the benefits of being twinned with Berenice, who'd made it. She also understood that it was one of the most impossibly advanced creations that had ever been made in Foundryside—if not Tevanne.

"You will have to place the key within the sphere," said Valeria. *"And activate it. Then I can utilize the permissions to warp the time within the sphere so it would be as if the key experiences one, or several, millennia. At this point, the key should be usable again."*

"It's as simple as that?" said Orso.

"Not simple. I will not simply bathe him in endless years while he is in the vessel. That would return him to the state he was at before—which would not be useful. As I said, just opening my casket almost destroyed him."

"Then what are you going to do?" asked Sancia.

"What I will do with time within that vessel," said Valeria, *"would be the difference between a stone being dropped within a pool of melted iron, and a stone being expertly carved with an iron chisel. When I am finished, he should not only be usable to us, but he will be more powerful than he was before. But it will be terribly, terribly difficult . . . And it will strain me to my limits . . ."*

"No sacrifices?" said Gregor.

"I am thousands of sacrifices," said Valeria coldly. *"Whatever sacrifices might be necessary have already been made."*

Despite such grisly discussion, Sancia couldn't help but feel a thrill of excitement. <*Clef,*> she said to Berenice. <*It's been three years. I can't believe it. I just can't believe it, Ber . . .* >

<*I know,* > said Berenice. <*I look forward to meeting him too. But . . .* >

<*But what? You don't think it'll work?* >

<*Well, I'm not sure. It might, or it might not. But . . . I am suddenly nervous about us having the two most critical creations of Crasedes Magnus in one place—Clef, and Valeria . . .* >

"And . . . will there be any side effects?" said Gregor. "Having just had my own time manipulated, I am somewhat anxious about how this might go."

"On this, I am . . . *uncertain,*" said Valeria. "*But if you are anxious about such effects, I recommend relocating to a safe space—perhaps five to ten thousand feet away.*"

Orso shook his head and sat down on the floor. "I don't have time for this shit. Sancia—I say you stick the key in, shut the damned ball, and be done with it. We've been through hell trying to get Clef back up and running. I wish to see it finished."

Sancia pulled Clef out of her pocket and looked down at him. It still hurt to this day to see him in such a state: a dead, dull, useless object, his voice and mind silenced and lost.

"No one deserves this," she said quietly. "No one deserves to be locked away like this." She looked up at them. "I'm going to do it."

"Then do it away," said Orso, gesturing with a wine bottle.

Sancia walked over to the little bronze orb and gently placed Clef within, as if he were not a golden key but rather an injured mouse. Then she gingerly shut the orb, her fingers running over its many scrivings—the very commands that time itself must change within its walls.

<*This is probably the most amazing thing I've ever worked on,* > Berenice whispered in her ear. <*And to be frank, San, it fills me with dread . . .* >

Sancia shut the orb and quickly stepped back.

"*You will need to turn the switch on the top of the device as well,*" said Valeria crossly. "*It is* most *crude . . .*"

"Oh," said Sancia. "Right." She stepped forward, turned the switch, and quickly stepped back again.

"*Please wait,*" said Valeria. "*asserting these commands will . . . take . . . some time . . .*"

Everyone stared at the little orb, waiting. Sancia wondered what it would look like—a flash of light, or a shimmering in the air, or would the bronze orb crumble to pieces from the sheer weight of so much time?

But this did not happen.

Rather, nothing seemed to happen. The orb simply sat there.

"Are you . . . doing it?" asked Gregor.

"*Yes,*" said Valeria in a queerly calm voice. "*The alteration is . . . contained . . . So far . . .*"

"It's really working?" asked Orso. "How much time has passed in there now?"

"*Currently . . . about four hundred years . . .*"

Orso whistled lowly. "Well, if this doesn't work, then we have a pretty damned easy way of aging wine on our han—"

And then things finally did change. Because time went flat.

To say that Sancia sat frozen in time, staring at the little bronze orb in the basement, would have been incorrect. "Frozen" would suggest that she was standing still, and time kept moving around her. And this was not what happened.

Nor would it have been correct to say that time stopped around her. For this would imply that time was like gravity, perpetually plummeting in one direction and pulling you with it. And she found that this was not correct either.

Rather, Sancia suddenly became intensely, overpoweringly aware that she was trapped within an *instance* of time—a fraction of a fraction of a fraction of a second—but she had yet to move to the next. Instead she hung there, trapped between two instances of time like someone trying to step out of one rowboat and into the next, but never quite getting one's footing exactly right to make the jump—and it felt as if she hung there forever.

And ever.

And ever . . .

She screamed internally, and the scream felt like it lasted both an eternity and no time at all.

And then she began to understand.

Seconds did not flow into one another like a river into the sea. Rather, every second that had ever happened to her—and thus to every other human being or living creature in the history of existence—was an isolated, separate instance, and each and every one was *still* happening, somewhere, somehow, in some manner she'd never been aware of before now.

Time itself—the experience of moving from second to second— was not real. Rather, it was something her mind *invented* as she passed from instance to temporal instance.

And right now, she was not moving forward—so her mind had no ability to interpret what was happening to her.

She struggled to hold herself together. She felt her whole consciousness fraying, unraveling, splitting at the edges, dissolving from the outside in . . .

I can't . . . I can't . . . I can't think, I can't . . .

And then something changed.

Something was bending and contorting around her. She imagined all the instances of time that had not yet occurred as a row of huge glass plates, set up on their ends, trailing away . . . but something was expanding in the row ahead of her, swelling like a tumor, swelling so fast that it was speeding toward her.

It's Clef, she thought. *He's coming. He's being . . . ripped backward through time . . .*

But as he came, he shattered countless instances of time in the future. And as they fell apart, she suddenly glimpsed tiny . . .

Fragments.

A group of people, standing on the shore in a circle, holding hands. The sun, bright and clear. The air, bitterly cold. They stood with their heads bowed, their eyes shut, not speaking, barely moving.

But then . . .

The sand at their feet in the center of their circle started to bubble, like it was melting. It boiled and churned, and something began to rise up out of its depths—a door, wrought of brown stone.

The people stood around the door, heads bowed, eyes shut. The people were calling it forward. They were asking it to be, and it was complying.

Sancia realized the people were not alone: there was someone else there, watching them.

A woman, terribly old, her face lined and aged by long exposure to the sun.

The old woman knelt in the sand, watching the people call the door forward, and she wept, though Sancia could not tell if they were tears of joy or sorrow.

And then, slowly, the door began to open.

Sancia gasped and fell forward. She heard the others do the same around her, crying out or groaning or whimpering as whatever bending of reality finally finished.

She tried to make reality feel real to her again. She greedily felt out the cold stone floor under her fingertips, she sucked in air and held it in her lungs, she swallowed and exulted in the feeling of saliva coursing down her throat—anything to assert that this was normal, that everything was working as it should, that her experience of the world had not been . . . been . . .

"My God!" cried Orso. "What I'd do to erase *that* from my brain! I didn't want to know that, I . . . I didn't want to know!"

"Almost finished!" said Valeria. She sounded pained and miserable, like the effort was akin to extracting a huge thorn from her flesh. *"We . . . We are almost there . . ."*

"What the hell was that," panted Sancia. "What *was* that?"

"I think . . . I think time went very wonky just now," said Berenice weakly.

"Well, no shit!" said Orso.

"But . . . I think because of all the wonkiness," said Berenice, "we might have glimpsed bits of time that hadn't quite . . . happened yet?"

There was a moment of stunned silence as everyone absorbed this.

"The future?" said Sancia. "Really?"

Gregor looked around at them, his face haggard and sweaty. "It made no sense to me. Did . . . Did you see the door as well?"

"You saw it too?" Sancia and Berenice both asked.

Gregor nodded, his face grim. "It was the strangest thing. I . . . I saw it, just for a moment. Huge, and black, and all afire. The doors hung in the sky, and swung forward on golden hinges . . ."

"No, no," said Berenice. "That wasn't what I saw. I saw people standing on the beach, and they bowed their heads, and a door rose up out of the sand . . ."

"That's what I saw," said Sancia.

"You did?" asked Berenice. "Or . . . Or did you simply see what *I* saw . . . because we're twinned?"

Sancia frowned. That hadn't occurred to her.

"*I* didn't see shit," said Orso flatly. "Perhaps it was all just some goddamned hallucination you had. Let's focus on what's really happening, if you plea—"

Then there was a *snap,* and cracks shot through the stone floor at their feet.

"*Difficult,*" said Valeria's voice. "*Difficult to contain . . .*"

"Valeria?" said Gregor. "What's going on?"

"*Being dislodged from my . . . location,*" she said. "*Anchoring is . . . difficult to maintain under these . . . conditions . . .*"

The cracks spread outward, until they met the walls, which they promptly danced up and then into the ceiling . . .

"*Advise . . . your relocation,*" whispered Valeria.

"Get out!" shouted Sancia. "Go, go!"

They ran up the stairs out of the basement, but Sancia paused to look back at the little bronze orb on the table. She considered sprinting over and snatching it, but reflected that since Valeria was currently altering its time, that would be very unwise: perhaps just touching it would cause her to age a thousand years.

The ceiling shook. Dust danced down from its many cracks.

<*San, get out!*> screamed Berenice in her head.

Sancia turned and ran up the steps.

The Foundrysiders crouched in the library as the basement creaked and cracked and moaned. The air everywhere seemed to pulse with invisible energy as Valeria wrestled with the final stages of the alteration. Sancia was half-convinced the earth might open up and swallow the neighborhood whole.

"Away from the basement!" said Orso. "Get away and get to the front!"

They ran to the front door of the firm and paused there, listening to the crackling, ready to sprint out into the courtyard and the street if need be. Then there was a tremendous *crash* from below, and the crackling and creaking went silent.

They heard Valeria quietly gasp, *"Done! Done! Done at last, done, done . . ."*

They looked back at the basement door. Dust was pouring out of its edges, almost like smoke.

"Does . . . Does that look safe to you?" said Orso.

They waited. There were no further cracks or groans.

"I'm going to chance it," said Sancia. "But if I start screaming or something—"

"Run like hell," said Orso. "Got it."

"No, I meant come and get me, asshole!" said Sancia. "God!"

She walked over to the basement door and tried to open it, but the wall must have shifted so it was stuck in the frame. She heaved at it, and with a *crunch* it finally fell open.

The basement within was roiling with dust. She reached around in her pocket for a little scrived lantern, pulled it out, switched it on, and peered through the gloom.

The floor of the basement looked like a merchant house galleon had fallen upon it: it'd been completely pulverized, including the table, which had been crushed into matchsticks.

Yet the bronze orb was still there, still whole, sitting atop the bundle of broken wood and glinting in the low light of the lamp in her hand.

Sancia picked her way down the wooden stairs, many of which were now crooked and leaning. She had to jump past the final few, and the soles of her boots thudded into the broken face of the fragmented basement floor.

"The things I do," whimpered Valeria. *"The things I do . . . to fix this world of ours . . ."*

Sancia crept over to the crater in the center of the floor, and cautiously stooped and picked up the orb. She'd expected it to be either hot or cold, for some reason, yet it was neither—it was the same temperature it'd been before.

She looked at the latch on the side, and its little hinge.

Oh, please. Oh please, oh please, oh please . . .

She braced herself, unlatched the little orb's lid, and swung it open.

Clef's golden form winked from within. Sancia slowly sat down on the pulverized stone, her legs shaking, set the bronze orb in her lap, and laid one finger to the key's shaft.

<*Clef? Clef, can . . . can you hear me?*>

Silence.

She waited, and waited. But nothing came.

<*Clef, are you there? Are you there?*>

Still silence.

She felt her fluttering heart suddenly slow, and she leaned her head back, her eyes shut.

"Not again," she said. "Not again, not *again* . . ."

"Is it working?" called Orso from the open basement door. "San?"

"No!" she said. She was on the verge of tears. "No, it didn't. He's not talking he's not—"

<*mm*>

She opened her eyes.

"Huh?" she said quietly.

"It failed?" said Gregor. "It truly failed?"

"Wait!" she said. "W-Wait, wait just a minute!"

She took the key in her hands, clasping it tight, listening as hard as she could.

<*mmm*>

That voice—if it even was a voice—was it Clef? She found it hard to tell. It didn't sound like the product of sentient thought, but more like a noise someone might make in their sleep.

<*mmmuhhh*>

<*Clef?*>

The low, unearthly groan continued for an impossibly long while, a constant, sustained <*muhhhhhhhhhhhhhhhhhhhhhhhhhhhhh-hhhhhhhhhhhhhhhhhhhhhhhhhhhhhhhh*>.

She listened to it, eyes wide. It had to go on for at least half a minute straight, growing louder and louder all the while.

And then it finally erupted.

<*uhhhhhhhhhhhhhhhhhhhhhhhhhhhhhhhhhhhhhHHHHHHHHH KID KID KID KID WHAT THE HELL WHAT THE HELL WHAT THE HELL HOLY SHIT WHAT THE HELL!*>

"Oh my God!" she said softly.

She heard Berenice in her mind, speaking as well: <*Oh my God . . .* >

<*WWWWWWWHAT THE HELL WHERE AM I WHAT THE HELL,*> screamed Clef in her head.

"He's back!" she cried. "I . . . I think he's back!" She burst into tears.

"*I just hope,*" said Valeria weakly, "*that it is not too late.*"

29

Alfredo Participazio stared around at the partygoers in the Hall Morsini and did his best to ignore the sweat trickling down his back.

He had never been to the Morsini House campo before, neither as an ambassador nor a trade representative, and he found the entire experience discomfiting. Everything was so strange, so threatening, so *different,* even here at the campo illustris, the Hall Morsini. Though the checked floor was packed with costumed elites and casks of wine and glittering crowds, it still felt like a dour, cramped building, all frowning, brutish pragmatism and tiny windows: a hostile place, built by a hostile people, and even their abundant merriment couldn't conceal the threat.

He knew they weren't simply celebrating for carnival, of course. While the rest of the city shivered at the whisper of war between the merchant houses, the Morsinis were absolutely delighted. The Michiels and the Dandolos were now both begging them for an alliance, so they could pick and choose which house lived and died—and extract considerable payments from whichever house they

backed. The opportunity was so tremendous that the de facto head
of the house, Rodrigo Morsini, grandson of the estimable (and now
disease-riddled) Torino Morsini, had felt obliged to celebrate.

And now Participazio sat at the table with the rest of their dip-
lomatic deputation—ten elite scrivers, none of whom would discuss
their orders with him—and watched as the many costumed revelers
milled about, some dancing to the pipers, some retreating to the
corners to indulge in open acts of carnal pleasure.

He couldn't help but feel overcome with misery. *What am I doing
here? What horror have I been assigned to now?*

He observed the many wild costumes, variations on the tradi-
tional classics: the Cup-Bearer of Storms, the Herald of the Waves,
the Vanguard of Wind, the many Drowned Ones . . .

And of course, the countless Papa Monsoons, dressed in their
black cloaks and their black masks and their black three-cornered
hats.

Participazio studied these, unnerved. Then one of the Papa
Monsoons looked at him, cocked its head, and began to amble
across the floor to him. The partygoers thoughtlessly made way for
him, some of them shivering slightly, as if the backs of their necks
had been grazed by a chilly breeze.

Oh no, thought Participazio.

"It's been some time since I've been to a party," called the man
in black in his deep, rich voice. "I'd hoped no one would wear the
same apparel as I, but . . . I shall have to bear it, I suppose."

Participazio stood and bowed as he approached, trying to ignore
the queasiness suddenly churning in his stomach.

"Good evening, boy," said the man in black, sounding bemused.

"Evening, s-sir," said Participazio quietly. He glanced up at the
blank, black eyes, and his heart juddered.

The man in black turned his mask on the rest of the Dandolo
deputation, who looked back at him uncertainly. "And these are the
scrivers I requested?"

"Y-Yes, sir."

"The ones with the most experience in lexicons?"

"Yes, sir."

"Good!" He reached into his cloak, produced a small,

unremarkable-looking wooden box, and held it out. "These are for you."

Participazio took the box with trembling hands and placed it on the table. He braced himself, flipped back the latch, and opened the top, convinced it held some abomination . . .

Yet it did not. Within were a dozen white leather masks, but they were of a very curious make: they were completely smooth and unbroken, and would envelop the whole of a person's head, with no openings for their eyes, nor their noses, mouths, nor ears.

"Your costumes," said the man in black.

Participazio took one mask out and held it, bewildered, as the scrivers took their own. "Do . . . Do you want us to put these on now, sir?"

"Now? No, no. Now's not the time." He sat next to Participazio, lounging in his chair, and looked out at the crowd. "But soon, I suspect. Now, let's wait."

They sat and watched the celebrations. The evening became a blur to Participazio: the slosh of wine, wicked and dark in the lantern light; carven masks glimmering amidst the columns, faces fixed, eyes vacant; the constant swish and swirl of silken robes; and hands bedecked in jewelry slipping out from beneath the rush of costumes, eager to snatch up a goblet of wine, or seize a shoulder, or caress a bared neck.

The cries and moans beat upon Participazio's mind. *I am in one of the wealthiest places on earth,* he thought. *And yet, I feel as though I am in some bowel of hell.*

Then finally there came a blast of piping, and a sound of trumpets. Everyone stopped dancing and talking and turned to the western entrance to the hall, and they watched respectfully as the procession began to enter.

It was quite expansive, led by a series of women dressed as shore doves, and then men wearing the costume of the Cup-Bearer of Storms, their spears raised high and their crowns glittering—and they were pulling something along by silvery ropes.

It was a throne, Participazio saw finally, nearly ten feet high and painted bright gold and set on wheels, and seated on the throne was a man in a Papa Monsoon costume.

But it was not any Papa Monsoon costume. This one was painted bright gold like the throne.

"Oh my," said the man in black dryly. "Isn't *this* ironic."

<*Wait,*> said Clef. <*Wait, wait, wait. Kid . . .* >

<*Yes, Clef?*> she said.

<*Are you telling me you brought me back just to . . . just to* kill *a guy?*>

<*Well . . . it's not quite killing, exactly. It's a bit more complicated than tha—*>

<*God!*> he cried. <*I mean, shit! That's still a hell of a thing to wake up to!*>

Sancia winced. She still felt elated at the sound of his voice—the exact same voice as she'd remembered it, the very voice that had haunted her memories for the past three years—but explaining their predicament to a newly awakened Clef was proving a lot harder than she'd anticipated. Not only had their whole situation proven knottier than she'd realized, but Clef kept interrupting with <*Whoa!*> and <*What?*> and <*Wow, sounds bad!*> She got the sense that he was still in something of a manic state after the acceleration of his time.

<*I mean, shitting hell,*> said Clef. <*I don't even know where we are. Is this still Tevanne? Or did the city collapse while I was gone?*> A pause. <*Wait, how* long *have I actually been gone? A couple days, or weeks, or . . .* >

<*It has been three years, Clef,*> said Berenice.

<*Whoa!*> said Clef. <*Who the hell is that?*>

<*It's me. Berenice.*>

A pause.

<*Kid,*> said Clef. <*How the shit did you manage to put Berenice in your head?*>

<*It's a long story, Clef,*> said Sancia. <*And frankly, we really don't have time for thi—*>

<*Key,*> said Valeria's voice sternly. <*Enough! Apprehend me now.*>

<*Crap!*> said Clef. <*There's another one in you!*>

<No,> said Sancia. *<That's Valeria, an—>*

<Do you recall me, key?> demanded Valeria. There was something oddly formal about her tone and phrasing. Sancia had never heard her do this before.

<Uhhh—No?> said Clef. *<I don't? Should I? I mean, I'm pretty sure I'd remember a talking lexicon . . . Wait. Are you a lexicon?>*

Sancia and Berenice looked at each other, surprised. *<I think Valeria can hear it when Clef talks to us or when we talk to him . . . >* whispered Sancia to Berenice.

< . . . but she still can't hear when we talk between the two of us,> whispered Berenice. This seemed a valuable thing to keep in mind.

<Your calibration to the present has gone on long enough,> said Valeria. *<We have no time. All you must understand now is what we have called you here to do. And that is to destroy the Maker's bindings, and return him to the state of death he occupied previously.>*

<The who?> said Clef, panicked and bewildered. *<Maker? Huh? Make what now?>*

<Crasedes Magnus,> said Berenice gently. *<The first of all hierophants—he's here, Clef, and he's a threat to every living being in this city.>*

There was a long, long silence—so long that Berenice and Sancia exchanged a nervous glance.

<So . . . So the guy who made me,> said Clef weakly. *<The one who turned me into . . . into this. He's . . . back? He's really back?>*

<Yes. Do you remember anything about him, Clef?> asked Sancia. *<Because he sure as hell seems to remember you.>*

<N-No . . . not quite,> he said, though he sounded slightly dreamy. *<I . . . I mean, you know that sometimes I . . . I could remember the feeling of him, but I'm not sure I truly recall how he—>*

But Orso could take it no more. "This is frustrating as all hell!" he shouted. "I can't hear a damned thing! You all can't keep a whole conversation running among yourselves, it's bullshit!"

"I concur," said Gregor.

"Oh," said Sancia. "Right." She'd forgotten Orso and Gregor couldn't experience what they were saying. "I'll just . . . repeat the important stuff."

They told Clef of Crasedes's wrappings, and the bone hidden

in his hand, the one that allowed his wrappings to convince reality that he had never truly died. Sancia found herself talking so much she often felt out of breath.

<*God, this is some ugly junk,*> said Clef. <*Bones, and dead bodies, and worse . . . And I . . . I admit I don't totally* remember *working with these hierophantic commands . . .* >

<*Elevated privileges,*> corrected Valeria.

<*Yeah, sure, those, whatever. But . . . But Sancia . . . I can't help but feel like this wasn't what I was supposed to come back to.*>

<*What do you mean?*> asked Sancia.

<*I . . . I barely remember falling asleep—being reset, I mean. It all seemed to happen in this single, mad, rushed moment . . .* >

<*Do you remember me going inside of you, Clef?*> she asked. <*And talking to the person you are? Or . . . were?*>

There was a long silence.

<*No,*> he said quietly. <*No, I do not remember that. I don't know what state I've been restored to, but . . . I don't have access to that. But I remember thinking you were* safe. *That with my last moments, I'd gotten you somewhere* better. *I thought if you ever brought me back, I'd find you somewhere far away from Tevanne, and all the madness and misery here, and you'd have . . . Well, I'll be honest, I hadn't pictured Berenice being the one to be with you, since, you know, she seemed a little above your level, and don't get me wrong, you two are cute as hell now, but—*>

<*But yes,*> said Berenice. <*This is not where we expected to be.*>

<*We know, Clef.*> Sancia sighed. <*We know.*>

<*I definitely didn't expect you to be partnering up with some ghost in a damned lexicon,*> said Clef. <*Especially one that seems to have put all kinds of crazy shit in your head. Stuff I can't believe you'd ever have agreed to, San.*>

Sancia and Berenice shot a worried look at each other. Sancia had forgotten that Clef could perceive or even access the plate in her head so easily. But then, it did make sense: Clef was always good at tinkering with scrived things, and Sancia was, in essence, a scrived thing.

<*You mean . . . how I'm an editor?*> said Sancia.

<*Huh?*> said Clef. <*No. No, I don't mean that. I mean all the* other *stuff.*>

<Key,> said Valeria suddenly. <Key, I . . . I insist we focus on the Maker.>

Sancia's heart twisted as she heard the worry in Valeria's voice. <What are you talking about, Clef?> she asked. <What other stuff's in there?>

<All those . . . those new alterations,> said Clef. <That's some pretty wild stuff.>

<Stop!> said Valeria. <Stop! We . . . We do not have time for this!>

A cold horror was seeping through Sancia's belly. <What do you mean?> she whispered.

"Something's gone wrong," said Gregor quietly, watching Sancia's face.

<What do you mean, what do I mean?> asked Clef. <Kid . . . do you really not know? Do you really not know what's been done to you?>

Berenice looked at Valeria. <Valeria—what's he talking about?>

But now Valeria would not answer.

The crowd of Morsinis roared their approval at the sight of the golden Papa Monsoon, the King of All Storms, the Lord of Floods, and Emperor of the Surging Seas. The man in the costume had to be Rodrigo Morsini himself, Participazio thought: not only was he unable to imagine who else would be the focus of such a procession, but he'd heard rumors that Rodrigo was an enormous man, both tall and broad, and the golden Papa Monsoon seemed so large that he threatened to crush the throne beneath him.

"Well," said the man in black, stepping away. "This is my moment. I suppose I should get a move on."

"W-What?" said Participazio. "What do you mean, sir?"

"I mean," said the man in black over the roar of the crowd, "that I have business to attend to with Master Morsini."

"You want to approach Rodrigo Morsini?" said Participazio, horrified. "Now?"

He shrugged. "I see no better time." He began to amble toward the rolling throne, but then he paused, turned, and said, "Oh, I should remind you all . . . Please don't forget your masks. That would be disastrous." He tapped the side of his head. "As I remove mine, you should put on yours." Then he turned and continued toward the center of the hall.

The golden Papa Monsoon waved joyfully as his retinue hauled him around the floor. They turned down one stretch, the crowd cheering them on . . .

All except one small figure in black, who walked out to stand in the center of their path, blocking the way.

The wheels of the Morsini throne squeaked to a halt.

Participazio watched, overcome with helplessness. *Oh, please,* he thought. *Please don't get us all killed . . .*

The crowd stared. The Cup-Bearers of Storms paused, unsure whether they should shove this man aside.

The golden Papa Monsoon leaned forward and peered down at the black one, who looked back with his empty, dark eyes.

"What the devil are you doing?" demanded the golden Papa Monsoon. "Someone get this idiot out of the way!"

And yet for some reason neither his Cup-Bearers of Storms nor any of the people in the crowd seemed to have any desire to approach this man.

"Do you know me, Rodrigo Morsini?" said the man in black, his deep voice hard and clear.

"I certainly do not!" said the golden Papa Monsoon. He looked at the crowd around him, gesturing to the guards. "Someone do something! Knock him down, haul him away!"

"No," said the man in black, quieter. "You know me. You all do."

He lifted his hands, and removed his hat. And then he began to remove his mask.

To Participazio's surprise, there was no face beneath the mask of the man in black: rather, his head was draped in a long black cloth, tied by a black string running around his neck.

The man plucked at the string with his thumb and forefinger, and gently began to pull it away.

And then, though he couldn't understand why, Participazio suddenly felt himself filled with terror—and he realized the purpose of their white masks.

The man in black was going to show his face. And Participazio and the Dandolo scrivers were not meant to see.

Participazio gestured to the rest of the deputation, and they hurried to stuff on their masks. He gasped as its leather interior swallowed his eyes and his ears, and he just barely heard the man in black speak once more.

"I am judgment," said his voice. "And I have been a long time coming."

Participazio clutched the mask to his head and sat, staring into the blank interior.

And then the muffled sounds . . . changed.

There was a scream—muted to Participazio's blocked ears, but most definitely a scream.

And then there were more, and more, and more.

<*Clef,*> said Berenice, <*what's inside of her?*>

<*Oh God, where to begin,*> he said. <*Like, yeah—Sancia has some of the same stuff I have. Access to perceive alterations to the world, to a certain degree, and the ability to engage with them and send them conflicting commands. Sure. But the* other *stuff . . .* >

<*The immunity to Crasedes?*> said Berenice.

<*No. I mean the* other, other *stuff. The stuff where Valeria would twin herself with Sancia, kind of like how you two are already twinned together. And then she'd be able to go inside of Sancia's head, and . . . and* become *her.*>

Berenice and Sancia stared at each other in absolute horror.

"Something's gone very wrong," said Gregor again.

<*You mean . . . You mean there is some kind of mechanism inside of Sancia . . . that would allow Valeria to* take over her body?> asked Berenice.

<*Well, I mean . . . Y-Yeah?*>

Shaking, Sancia turned to Valeria. <*Valeria . . . is this true?*>

<*The Maker,*> Valeria said. <*I . . . I . . .* >

<*Enough about him!*> Sancia shouted at her. <*Tell me the truth! Did you really do this to me, and never tell me?*>

There was a silence that seemed to go on forever.

Then, very quietly, Valeria said, <*True.*>

"Oh . . . Oh my God," whispered Sancia and Berenice at once.

"Goddamn it!" said Orso. "What's happened? What's gone wrong?"

"Valeria . . . has engineered some kind of back door into Sancia's head," said Berenice faintly. "So that she could twin herself with her, and . . . and take over her body . . ."

"She *what*?" said Gregor. "She wants to . . . to *merge* with Sancia?"

"*Wanted*," said Valeria quickly. "*Do not want, not anymo—*"

"No!" said Orso. "No, that's . . . That's insane! A person can't . . . what, twin themselves with a living bit of scriving, with some . . . some artificial god that Crasedes cooked up!"

"But you built this into her *head*?" said Gregor. "I mean . . . My God! Why would you want that?"

"*Complicated*," said Valeria. She sounded harassed and defensive. "*Not first option. Not preferable.*"

"I'll goddamn say," said Sancia angrily. "Since it's my goddamned head! I mean . . . what would this have done to me? Would it have killed me? Wiped away the mind behind my eyes?"

"*No. Would not have.*"

"How can we possibly know that?" said Gregor.

"Valeria," said Berenice. "You need to explain what it is you've done to Sancia *now*."

"*We do not have time*," she said.

"Oh, horseshit," said Orso.

"*The day grows short*," she said. "*The Maker* will *move soon, if he has not already.*"

"I'm not doing a damned thing more," said Sancia. "Until you tell me what you've done."

There was a tense silence.

Then, finally, Valeria whispered, "*All right.*"

Another long pause.

"*When . . . When I first altered Sancia*," she said, "*I assessed that in order to . . . to escape my bindings . . . I might need to do what the Maker did to escape death. Just as he twinned himself with another creature to evade mortal destruction, I would need to twin myself with a creature to absolve myself of the commands he'd placed upon me.*"

"So you would *become* Sancia," said Berenice, disgusted. "That was your way out of the set of rules."

"*. . . True. Somewhat.*"

"You're just like Crasedes," said Sancia. "I don't know why we should listen to you. You made me a tool, your . . . your *vessel.*"

"Not *vessel,*" said Valeria. "*A . . . conduit, a conductor. I knew if the Maker refashioned me, I would be the cause of indescribable suffering. If I needed to hide from him within the mind of a girl to avoid such a fate, I would do so. I made my choice.*"

"You piece of shit," said Sancia. "You made your choice? And you think it sounds so simple?"

"Imagine," said Valeria. "*Imagine the whole horizon burning. Imagine hills dotted with corpses. Imagine streets running red with blood. Imagine children and families devouring one another like wild dogs. Imagine these horrors—and know that I* do not have to *imagine them. For I have seen them. I retain fragments of these sights, mementos of civilizations the Maker broke upon his knee because they displeased him. You say I have wronged you, and that may be so. But until you understand the scale of devastation the Maker can wreak with his arts, you cannot understand the weight of my choic—*"

Then there came a banging from the front of the firm, loud enough that Berenice jumped and squeaked.

They all froze, looked at one another, and realized someone was pounding on the firm's front door.

"Sancia!" came a muffled voice from the library. "Orso? Someone? Please . . . are you there?"

"Is that Claudia?" said Orso, surprised.

"Something's . . . Something's happened!" shouted Claudia. She sounded terrified. "Help! Help, *please!*"

"Perhaps . . . *I do not need to ask you to imagine such sights,*" said Valeria quietly. "*Perhaps the Maker has already visited his wrath upon your city.*"

For a moment the Foundrysiders just stood there, confused. Then Claudia pounded on the door again, and cried, "Are you there? God, *please* be there . . ."

Sancia fixed Valeria in a glare and said, "I'm not done with you. You still owe me a real scrumming explanation, you hear me?"

"Then I will give it," she said. "*Provided we are all still alive to listen.*"

The Foundrysiders climbed out of the basement, crossed the library, and approached the front door. Gregor checked the window and confirmed it was just Claudia.

"But . . . there are also people running in the streets," he said quietly. "And . . . I think I hear screaming. Something is indeed wrong."

They opened the door for her. "Oh, thank God," said Claudia. "Thank God, thank God . . . I came the second that I heard . . . But it's got to be him, Sancia, he's got to have something to do with all this."

"What's wrong?" asked Sancia. "What's going on?"

Claudia was trembling with terror. "People are saying that . . . that something's happened on the Morsini campo."

"The *Morsinis* now?" said Orso. "What are they up to? My God, they're not going to make their own play for power, are they?"

"I don't think so," said Claudia in a small, frightened voice. "I . . . I saw people flooding out of the campo gates, into the Commons, and the things they were *saying* . . ."

"What was it?" said Berenice. "What were they saying?"

Claudia swallowed and whispered, "That Shorefall Night has come early to Morsini House."

The floors of Hall Morsini shook as people tried to stampede away, and something—tables or chairs, possibly—clattered to the ground. And though the mask blocked his face, Participazio soon smelled something bright and coppery: the smell of blood, he thought, and lots of it.

Then he heard the man in black speaking: *"Look upon me."*

Without thinking, Participazio lifted his hands and grabbed the side of his mask, ready to pull it from his face to do as the man said: to look upon him.

He stopped himself just in time, and pressed his ears into the side of his head. He moaned and wept, and these sounds drowned out the man in black's commands, though now Participazio knew what they were:

"Look upon me. Look. Those of you who spend your lives in thoughtless extravagance—look upon me now."

And then . . .

Then it was over.

The screams tapered off into a whimpering, and the commands ceased. Participazio cautiously lifted his head.

Then he felt two hands grip his shoulders, and he almost screamed.

"Boy," whispered the man in black in his ear. "Can you hear me, boy?"

"Y-Yes," stammered Participazio.

"In a moment," whispered his voice, "you may all remove your masks. Do not do it yet! Give me time to leave this place. Then you may remove your masks, and go to work. But do *not* look outside. Do you understand me?"

Participazio nodded.

"Good."

"But . . ." said Participazio.

"Yes?"

"Where are you going, sir?"

"I? I will go out into the streets of this place. For many more deserve what I have to give than those I found here tonight . . ."

The hands released his shoulders.

Participazio began counting to sixty—very, very slowly.

When he got to sixty, he cautiously removed his mask—and then he saw what lay before him, and he screamed.

The Hall Morsini was full of ravaged bodies—and yet all of them seemed to have been ravaged by *themselves:* eyes cut out with forks, faces mangled with butter knives, wrists slashed open with shards of glass, and everywhere, *everywhere,* was blood, turned an unpleasant purple in the lights of the blue and red lanterns.

Trembling, Participazio watched as the lake of blood approached him. Yet he noticed someone had walked through it recently: there were bloody footprints leading away from the pile of bodies out to the door of the hall.

He stared at it. Then he heard the screams from the streets outside.

IV

SHOREFALL NIGHT

30

Claudia and the Foundrysiders crowded up onto the roof of their offices. Gregor pulled out his spyglass and studied the Morsini campo. "I can hardly see anything in this light," he said quietly. "But . . . I can see the gates to the inner enclave are open. Yet people are flooding through. Something . . . Something has definitely hap—"

He stopped short.

"What is it?" asked Sancia.

"There . . . There are people jumping out of the windows," he said quietly. "I see them . . . They're jumping out of the windows in one of the towers. I . . . I mean, they're *killing* themselv—"

Sancia realized what was happening, and snatched the spyglass away.

"Stop!" she shouted. "Stop looking! Turn away! Don't try and see!"

"Why not?" asked Orso.

"When's the *last* time we saw a bunch of people suddenly kill themselves?" she asked.

"Oh God," said Gregor softly. "The scrivers on the galleon . . ."

"It must be that," said Sancia. "There's something . . . something wrong with how Crasedes was restored, the way he was brought back to life. You can't look at him. It's a distortion in reality that drives you *mad*."

They all turned away from the nightscape of the campos, shielding their eyes. "You think he, what, he took off his mask?" asked Orso. "And he's . . . He's just walking around the enclave?"

"Yes! *During* what must have been their carnival celebrations! He's beheading the entire goddamn Morsini campo in one night, without firing a single bolt!"

Gregor listened to the screams, eyes half-closed. "Bottla ball," he said quietly. "That's what this is, isn't it? Just as Orso said."

"Said what?" said Orso.

"That sometimes in bottla ball, when you have no good plays," said Gregor, "the only play is to toss your ball to hit as many as you can, ruin everyone else's strategy, and scramble the court. And . . . I would say the court of Tevanne has just been pretty well scrambled, to me . . ."

"Why?" said Claudia. "Why is he doing this?"

"I don't know," said Sancia. "I don't know why he'd pick the Morsinis at all, since it was the Michiels that were moving against Dandolo Chartered. The Morsinis have been pretty quiet this whole time. Valeria—any ideas?"

They heard her disembodied voice, though it was much fainter up here on the roof: "*Unknown. What might these Morsinis possess that the Maker would desire?*"

"I've no idea," said Orso.

"Nor I," said Berenice. "I thought they mostly just made ships and weapons. Brute strength as opposed to . . . well, any other virtue."

<*Clef?*> said Sancia.

<*Yeah, kid?*> he said.

<*Any chance you might know?*>

<*Hm. Well. Not really. I'm still catching up—though I think I can browse through your memories to get myself up to speed . . .* >

<*You can do that?*> asked Sancia.

<*We could do it before. Trading sensations and knowledge. But we're*

both . . . Well. A lot stronger now.> There was a pause, and Sancia got the queerest feeling that Clef had just looked through her, as if she were made out of glass. *<Also, weirdly, some of these memories might not be yours . . . something about paying your best friend ten duvots to let you kiss her down by the canal?>*

<That's . . . That's mine!> said Berenice. *<Please, ahh, please do not look any further!>*

<Uhh, got it,> said Clef. *<Sorry. But listen—Crasedes needed the Mountain to reforge Valeria, because he needed* multiple *copies of that definition of Tribuno's, all stacked on top of one another, all convincing the reality around them that whichever lexicon they happened to be in was akin to God Himself. Yeah?>*

<Yes,> said Berenice. *<You think he's trying to make more?>*

<I think he has *to make more,>* said Clef. *<It's the only way to do what he's here to do. It takes a death to make a hierophantic device— like me.>* He sounded suddenly bitter. *<And he just made a* lot *of deaths . . . >*

<But he can't complete the ritual himself,> said Sancia. *<Valeria ripped that from his mind. She broke him.>*

<Then I don't know,> said Clef. *<Maybe he's found a workaround. But either way, he's doing this to remake Valeria—and he knows exactly where to find her.>*

<Oh my God,> said Berenice. *<He's coming here. What do we do?>*

<I assume the imperiat's out,> said Clef. *<Being as this guy made the thing, and you don't want to turn off half the city.>*

<Right,> said Sancia miserably.

<And I'm your big play. But though you used to be a pretty good sneak, San, I doubt if you can get the jump on a magic flying man and stab me into his gut or something.>

<I would be reluctant for her to attempt that, yes,> said Berenice.

<Then I guess you all need to get thinking,> said Clef.

"Everyone," said Sancia. "Listen—besides Clef and the imperiat, what actually has any kind of effect on Crasedes?"

They thought about it, trying to ignore the distant sounds of screaming and cries from the Morsini campo.

"The only thing that I have ever seen work on Crasedes," said Gregor, "is Valeria herself."

"*True*," said Valeria. "*When I altered the Maker, and stole from him the ability to access the high permissions, I had to lure him into a place that I had prepared against him. One that would nullify his privileges."*

Orso narrowed his eyes. "Like the firm is currently?"

"True. The firm and the areas around it."

Orso half shut his eyes, and his lips started silently moving. Sancia recognized this behavior: whenever Orso got a really ambitious idea he started reading the sigil logic to himself, making sure it all assembled properly in his head.

"What is it, Orso?" asked Berenice.

"Eh?" He turned to Claudia. "Claude—remind me how those scrived steel boxes of yours work, again."

"Huh?" she said. "We, uh, twinned reality. Just like you always do."

"Yes, yes, yes, but tell me the *specifics* of how it worked!"

"You . . . You put on the cuirass, and . . . and when you turned it on, the cuirass would convince the reality around it that it was really the reality back at our firm, with the big steel box around it."

Orso went very, very still. "Does it *have* to be a cuirass? Could it be, say . . . a lead slug?"

"Why would you wish for a lead slug to believe it was surrounded by a steel box?" asked Gregor.

But then Berenice cried, "Oh!"

Sancia looked at her, confused, and then gasped as the revelation emerged in her own mind, indistinguishable from her other thoughts. "Ohhh!"

"You . . . You don't care about the box, do you?" said Berenice.

"I don't," said Orso, his face grim and closed. "I care about the reality *inside* it. Because what if a lead slug can convince the world that the reality around it . . . is the reality *here,* at the firm?"

"Where Valeria is affecting everything," said Gregor slowly. "And Crasedes's permissions are nullified . . ."

"You shoot Crasedes with this lead slug," said Sancia, "and when it hits him and gets activated, it convinces the space around it that it's the same as the space here where his permissions won't work."

"And he falls out of the sky," said Orso. "Dead and dormant—and vulnerable."

<Hey . . . I think that could work!> said Clef cheerily.

"That . . . could possibly work," said Valeria. *"Is fabrication of such a tool possible?"*

"It's your designs," said Berenice to Claudia. "What do you think?"

Claudia pulled a face and cocked her head. "I guess. It'd take work, but—I don't see why not."

"Then we need to get to it," said Orso. Another peal of screams rang through the dark skies. "We we've got, what, three hours until midnight? That's when he's strongest, so I bet that's when he'll show up. I've no idea what he's playing at out in the city, but . . . I don't want to see it actually come to pass."

"I . . . will commit to helping you in this," said Valeria.

"Well, I mean—of course you would, yeah?" said Orso. "You want to see Crasedes dead and gone just as much as we do."

"True. But . . . I insist we consider a backup option. The alteration I have given to Sancia."

"The . . . The one where you merge with me?" asked Sancia, outraged.

"True," said Valeria. *"It is not a significant process. I need only the slightest connection. We would not even need a sacrifice, or to wait for midnight. Would be much as Berenice and Sancia twinned themselves—a plate that Sancia would swallow, and then a second plate placed within this lexicon I inhabit, asserting we were the same. In this place, within her, I can become something new. But the access point needs a host to . . . function."*

"You mean a living being," said Gregor. "Just like how our plates in our own heads need to be in a living being to function."

" . . . True."

"So it's like a . . . a tiny door to a place you can hide, and remake yourself," said Sancia. "And you need to twin yourself with me to access it, because . . ."

"Because Valeria is not allowed to create tools that can free herself from bondage," she said, sounding exhausted. *"So I made this door for someone* not *Valeria. Which is what I would become, if we were to twin, however briefly."*

There was a long silence. Gregor and Sancia stared at each other, unsure what to say.

"If it is any consolation," Valeria said, now sounding somewhat

bitter, *"the experience would be deeply unpleasant for me—like a stoat with its paw in a trap, forced to gnaw off its own foot."*

But Sancia was having none of it. "I still can't get over this . . ." she said. "You did all this to me, and you never even *asked* me. You never even told me. I would have never even known, if not for Clef!"

<*Uhh,*> said Clef in her ear. <*You're welcome? I . . . I think it's better if I stay quiet, frankly . . .* >

"I intended to tell you," said Valeria. *"Before we began our final assault upon the Maker."*

"Why wait?" said Orso.

"Because . . . if our attack does not work . . . then this will need to be our last resort. We must make this, since we know *it will work. We* must *consider it as an alternative before we confront the Maker."*

Everyone exchanged an uncomfortable look, except Claudia, who understandably seemed completely bewildered by all this.

"Does it have to be Sancia?" said Gregor. "I also carry hierophantic designs within me . . . If the moment truly came, could I not bear this burden?"

"We could merge," said Valeria, sighing, *"but not separate. I did not build the mechanism for remaking myself into you, and I cannot do so now. If I twinned myself with you, we would become* stuck*—not quite one thing, not quite the other. Both of our minds reforged into something . . . else."*

Orso wrinkled his nose. "Not . . . preferable then."

"True. Not at all."

"So it's me," said Sancia harshly. "I risk all this—I risk putting a goddamn hierophantic god inside my head—or it's no one."

"True. That is correct. It is a final resort. But it must be one we commit to."

<*Are you really considering this?*> whispered Berenice to Sancia.

<*Hell no,*> said Sancia. <*She's lied to us again and again and again. But if it gets Valeria to actually help us kill Crasedes, then I don't care. I'll just carry the little plate in my pocket and never use it.* >

"Show us what we need to do," said Sancia aloud.

"Sancia," said Orso, taken aback. "Really?"

"Really," said Sancia. "We're talking about the deaths of thousands. It's a risk I'm willing to take."

"*Sensible,*" said Valeria—a little too eagerly for Sancia's liking. "*I will show you the proper sigils. It should not be difficult for you to complete.*"

"And if we're wrong," said Gregor, "and if he's able to part through Valeria's permissions like they're not there?"

"Then we reexamine putting Clef on a goddamn bolt," said Orso. "Come on."

31

Gregor watched the smoke rising from the Morsini campo. Occasionally he heard a *boom* or a *bang*—sounds he didn't think were being caused by Crasedes.

"Strange to be here now," said Claudia softly, sitting on the roof at his feet. "Gio and I'd come up here to pace and rant and blow off steam after being given some deadline by Orso. To think I'd miss those days, and see such sights from this place . . ."

"Yes," said Gregor. Another *boom*. "I . . . I feel as if we've slept on a volcano all this time, but now . . . Now it's finally erupted. Finally, it is truly war."

Claudia let out a tiny, crushed sigh. "What are we going to do?"

"The same thing all peoples do in war," said Gregor. "Try to survive."

He wondered: how many times had he been here before, looking out on devastation, and planning how best to navigate it? He imagined versions of himself through the years: a soldier first sailing out upon the Durazzo, eager to capture and conquer; a refugee, emerging from the mud of Dantua, mad and frenzied; a captain, patrolling the waterfront with Whip by his side. A lifetime spent walking in circles, it seemed, reliving the same moment over and over again.

All the versions of myself are soldiers, he thought. *And . . . when the scriving rules me—I am* still *a soldier. It just gives me a different set of targets and orders.*

Had this compulsion to live as a soldier come naturally, he wondered. Or had it been implanted within him long, long ago, while countless moths circled overhead . . .

Has my whole life been but a dream? And when will I awake?

He shook himself and looked at her. "You should go, Claudia. It won't be safe for you here very soon."

She laughed miserably. "Go where? Back to me and Gio's workshops? That's not going to be much safer if the first of all hierophants decides to *really* flex his muscles."

Gregor thought about it. "True. In that case . . . you should go to the Slopes."

"The Slopes? Why?"

"There's an encampment there. A rather shabby one, where you can buy all manner o—"

"The Givans, yeah," said Claudia. "The slaves. I buy wine from them there all the time. Why should I go there?"

"Because they have ships," said Gregor, "and they are leaving. There will be a woman waiting there named Polina Carbonari. Tell her I sent you. If things go poorly, tell her to wait for us. If things go really, quite *very* poorly, get on a ship and go, and do not look back."

Claudia looked terrified. "*You?* You think we should leave the city? I thought you of all people would stay until the fight was over."

"The fight," said Gregor, "has changed. So we must change with it." He looked back at the smoking Morsini campo. "If you see Polina . . . tell her that now would be a very good time to get a *lot* of scrivers on her side. It would be wise to consider which Lamplands firms you admire and trust, Claudia, and whether they might serve as good allies in whatever might be coming next—and whether they would come to the Slopes as well."

Her eyes had grown quite wide now. "You're not talking about just leaving. You're talking about *evacuating.*"

"Something must be salvaged from this city, if the worst comes to pass. If you go," said Gregor, "and if you see Polina and you tell her I sent you . . . please also tell her I said she was right. That she was right about everything. But I still would have done everything the same."

"All right, Gregor. I will."

They embraced. Gregor wasn't quite sure why—Claudia had been a colleague at Foundryside only for about a year, and they'd maintained a professional, respectful distance. But it suddenly seemed proper to embrace now, with the skies full of smoke and screams, and the dawn so terribly distant.

Then she turned and left, running down the stairs, and he watched her as she crossed the Foundryside courtyard, still wearing her leather apron and her magnifying goggles. He watched her until she entered the muddy streets beyond, and then she was gone.

An hour into their labors upon Orso's hierophant-killing bullet, Sancia decided that never in the history of all of Tevanne had so much work gone into altering one little ball of lead.

<*I am getting pretty sick and goddamned tired,*> she said to Berenice as she scrawled out a few sigil strings on a blackboard, <*of sitting in this basement trying to engineer our way out of mad shit.*>

<*I suppose when Estelle tried to destroy the city,*> Berenice said, <*you were too busy climbing buildings and whatnot. Because this is mostly what I did that time too.*> She carefully dipped her stylus in bronze and continued working on the lead slug. <*This is the scriver's life, San— when crisis occurs, you don't pull out your sword or take to the streets. You sit in a small, windowless room and crunch sigils. And besides, with Clef and Valeria helping, we're making incredibly rapid progress.*>

Which was true. Clef had not always been skilled at designing scrivings. Three years ago, he'd claimed he could only tinker with a finished product, and no more—but now he seemed different. He spoke up, directly commenting on their plans, saying, <*Yeah, that actually sounds like a terrible idea,*> or, <*Neat concept! Though if you get the physical location too confused, then the slug is going to detonate like it's a damned volcano.*> Just by touching her skin to him, Sancia could feel his immense knowledge of scrivings and permissions and commands, and they guided her choices as she went about their work—for though their connection wasn't nearly as intense as her connection to Berenice, it was still a connection.

<*Clef,*> Sancia asked during a pause in their work, <*were you a scriver in your previous life?*>

<*Shit, I don't know. Why?*>

<*Because you seem like a really, really good one right now.*>

<*Well,*> he said with a faint pout of modesty, <*you* are *giving me a lot of help, kid. But thank you.*>

She thought about this. <*Every hierophantic creation has access to a certain privilege, right?*>

<*True,*> said Valeria. <*Or a bundle or spectrum of permissions.*>

<*Then . . . what is Clef's?*>

<*Huh?*> said Clef. <*What do you mean?*>

<*I mean, obviously Clef's good at talking to scrived rigs and making them do things they don't want to do. And he can open any lock. But . . . is that all Crasedes made you for? Just that?*>

<*The key,*> said Valeria somewhat coldly, <*possesses access to an array of privileges regarding circumvention—the breaking down or evasion of barriers.*>

<*So . . . yeah, just locks and doors and such?*> asked Sancia.

<*I told you once,*> said Valeria, <*that the Maker once traveled to other strata of existence. Planes of creation. The infrastructure behind reality.*>

<*So?*> asked Sancia.

<*How do you think he got there?*> asked Valeria.

Sancia's hand slowly crept up to where Clef hung from her neck by a string. <*You mean . . .* >

<*You mean I opened some kind of* magic door *once?*> asked Clef.

<*I was not truly sentient in those early days. My memories are few and scattered. But this has always been my assumption. You broke down the barriers between the layers of reality, and allowed the Maker to break through, and gain hidden wisdom—once if not many times.*>

There was a long silence.

<*Shit,*> said Clef quietly. <*And I thought regular scrived doors were difficult enough. And . . . who was I? Do you remember that? Do you remember the person I used to be?*>

<*That I do not retain,*> said Valeria. <*I was reworked and reforged often in my early days. I have instances of time, separated from meaning—*

bursts and fragments of images—but I do not remember who you were. Nor do I remember anything concerning your relation to the Maker.>

<*Shit,*> said Clef again, this time a little sadly.

Then Sancia remembered. There had been something Crasedes had said to her within the Mountain . . .

You don't know what it's like to lose someone, and know their life meant absolutely nothing in the face of some greater conflict.

Could he have been telling the truth in their first encounter, when he said that Clef was his friend?

As she worked, she kept thinking of Crasedes's voice, echoing through the darkness, and she wondered how it had sounded and what words it had spoken nearly four thousand years ago.

Ofelia Dandolo stared as the smoke and dust rose from the Morsini campo, and quietly thanked God her estate was too far away for her to hear any screams.

For now, she thought. *For war has a discomfiting way of spilling over many boundaries . . .*

She turned away from the window and faced the thing that had been built in the center of her grand ballroom. The sight of it disturbed her even more than the smoke from the Morsini enclave.

She was not quite sure what it was, or what to call it. It appeared to be a half lexicon, or perhaps even less than that, built right on top of her checked tiles and set behind a tremendous dome of green protective glass.

The idea of someone building a foundry lexicon—even a half of one—right in the middle of someone's ballroom was mad.

The idea of someone doing it in a *matter of hours* was even more mad.

But then, Ofelia thought, *he is capable of so much more than I'd ever imagined . . .*

As if she had summoned him with her thoughts, she heard his voice: "It should all be ready."

She jumped and looked up, and saw a blot of shadow passing through the open window at the top of the ballroom, though she lost it in the darkness of the ceiling.

Nausea thrummed throughout her stomach. "My . . . My Prophet?" she said. "I-I thought you were at the Morsini enclave."

"I was." His voice now came from beside the green dome of the lexicon. She saw his mask watching her through the glass, his still features distorted in its curves. "But I gain permissions as this city nears midnight. My own gravity grows easy to manipulate."

She looked at the giant rig sitting hunched in her ballroom. "Is it . . . safe?"

"Safe enough," he said. "Like myself, the lexicon is weak now, but . . . soon it will be powerful." His mask warped and stretched as he drifted along the side of the dome. "The center of reality. A god of this city, in a way." He stopped. "In a few moments, I will bring the construct here. When that happens, you must be ready. Prepare every defense you have. Nothing must touch this place. Am I clear?"

"Yes, My Prophet."

"Good." She watched as he rose up behind the bubble of green glass and merged with the shadows at the ceiling. "I go now to fetch her—and many other things, of course."

"But . . . how shall you do this?" she asked. "How shall you acquire so many things, all at once?"

"Oh, that is simple," he said. His voice echoed from the distant corner of the room. "First I shall simply ask, and hope they see reason. And if not . . . Well. All things are possible, with but the turn of a key."

Then the shadows trembled, and he was gone.

They finished Valeria's plate and her definition first. Sancia felt ill as she took the tiny tab of bronze in her hand, which was hardly bigger than a grain of rice, and placed it in a small, velvet-lined box.

This tiny thing could kill me or remake my brain or open up the gates of hell, for all I know, she thought. *I barely want to touch it to my skin . . .*

<Just take it,> said Berenice, *<stick it somewhere, and forget about it. Now, help us put the finishing touches on this damned lead slug . . . >*

Sancia snapped the little box shut and stuffed it in her pocket. But as she removed her hand, she suddenly felt it—a sudden pang of nausea deep in her belly. And due to their connection, Sancia knew Berenice felt it too.

"Ah shit," said Sancia. "No, no, no . . ."

"Oh, God," said Orso faintly. He looked up at the ceiling. "You don't . . . You don't feel that, do you?"

"We do," said Sancia. She looked back at the scrived timepiece on the wall. It was only eleven. "But . . . if he's really here, then he's here damned early . . . That can't be right. It *can't* be, can it?"

They heard shouts and running feet above them.

"It is," said Valeria. She sounded terrified. *"The Maker has come."*

"Sancia!" shouted Gregor. *"Sancia, he's here!"*

Sancia left Orso and Berenice to their work and ran up to the roof. She found Gregor standing at the edge, pointing to the southwest of their firm.

She narrowed her eyes, peered through the shadows, and spied the form of a man apparently sitting on thin air about twenty feet beyond the Foundryside gates.

"Shit," she said quietly.

He slowly drifted forward until he fell beneath the errant light of a floating lantern. His hands were clasped at his waist in a queerly peaceful and quaint pose, like a schoolchild awaiting their teacher's return.

"He's just . . . been sitting there," said Gregor hoarsely. "Waiting. Doing nothing."

His masked face swiveled up to see her, standing on the Foundryside roof. He waved.

"Shit, shit, shit," she said.

"What's he doing here?" asked Gregor.

"I have no idea."

"Is the shot ready?"

"No."

"How much longer?"

"I don't scrumming know."

"Then . . . what do we do? Do we just ignore him?"

Sancia thought about it. "I feel like that's going to piss him off, and provoke him into doing something *really* bad."

"Then . . . we can't go out there. He's not stupid enough to come in. What do we do?"

Sancia gritted her teeth, then popped the vertebrae in her neck. "Well. He's always seemed to like a conversation."

"You're not serious."

"I am. Maybe I talk to him, and stall him. The instant that slug is ready . . ." She glanced at him sidelong. "Just take the shot when you can, Gregor."

"I will."

"And *don't* miss."

He looked at her, his eyes bright and anguished. "Please be careful," he said.

"I will." She released him, then said to Berenice, <*You got all that?*>

<*I did. But Sancia . . . Are you sure this is a good idea?*>

<*We're almost done with the slug, right?*>

<*Almost,*> said Berenice hesitantly. <*Yes. But taking you and Clef away will slow us down.*>

<*We don't have a choice. Just make sure it's done fast. I have no idea what he's planning come midnight, but I don't want to see it.*> She dashed off the roof and down through the firm. <*Ready to meet your maker, Clef?*> she asked him.

<*God,*> he said. <*I don't even know how to answer that question, kid. But I hope so.*>

Sancia felt her stomach rumble unpleasantly as she walked across the courtyard to the Foundryside gates. Foundryside had never had especially tall compound walls—plenty of other Lamplands firms had bigger ones—but tonight they seemed especially tiny.

She peered through the gates as she approached, searching the shadows on the other side. She could see Crasedes's mask catching the low light of the floating lamps, and she felt like he was not one person but rather a wall of black fog, pressing in on their firm . . .

She stopped at the gates and waited. He slowly drifted closer, his body stiff and still, seated upright on nothing but air in a cross-legged position.

<*Ohhh shit,*> said Clef.

<*Courage, Clef,*> said Sancia. <*Do you remember him at all?*>

<*I . . . I'm not sure. I . . . I don't remember much. But I'm sure I don't remember this . . . this thing. This ghoul.*>

<*I have no idea what he's planning,*> said Sancia. <*But whatever he says he wants, he's going to have another reason for it.*>

<*The workaround,*> said Clef. <*The way to reforge Valeria.*>

<*Yeah. So we need to stay on our goddamned toes—and you let me know the instant you realize what game he's playing.*>

Crasedes stopped about five feet from the gates. There was a long silence. For a long time he did not move—but then, finally, he cocked his head.

"Good evening, Sancia," he said merrily. "How are you doing tonight?"

"What do you want, you bastard?" she snapped.

"To talk, of course."

"About what? I can't think of a single goddamned thing I want to hear from you."

"Oh, Sancia, I am surprised . . . I'd have thought your manner would be a little more conciliatory tonight."

"And why is that?"

"Well, I just did you a favor, didn't I? Haven't you all worked to overthrow your merchant houses for years? And now . . . Now I've gone and gotten rid of one in a single night."

She stared at him in horror. "You mean . . . You mean the Morsinis are really . . ."

"Oh, not *all* of them are dead," he said. "It would have taken a few hours for me to walk all the way throughout the campo, and I simply don't have the time for that. But the founders, the house officers, the elites, the entrenched families . . . At least they died fashionably, given that it was carnival."

"How . . . How could you . . ."

"How could I put to the blade the very same people who once lived by it? The very same people who used their advantages to raid, to seize, to oppress the peoples of this world? I'm surprised you even need to ask the question."

"Not everyone is as merciless as you."

"That's true. But they were. As all slavers are." He studied her for a moment. "You know this, for you were a slave once, weren't you?"

"What, you know the look because you've owned so many?"

"No," he said gently. "Because I was one, Sancia."

She stared at him, dumbfounded. He waited patiently for her to respond.

<*What the hell?*> said Clef. <*Really?*>

"Y-You were a slave?" she asked.

"Oh, yes," he said. "Once. A very, very, *very* long time ago." He looked away, toward the glittering lanterns of the Lamplands. "I knew the art when they first captured me," he said quietly. "Myself and my family. I pushed it to its limits to win my freedom, but . . . win it I did."

"You're lying," she said. But she remembered Valeria's memory: the wrapped man in the cave, and the boy dying on the bed—and how scarred his wrists had been, just like her own, ravaged from years of being restrained.

"I am not," he said politely. "After I freed myself, I worked to learn all the secrets of this world to understand what had happened to me, and why. I went to places no living human has ever gone before. I glimpsed the infrastructure that makes this reality possible. I saw the fingerprints of *God,* still impressed in the bones of creation. And I began my long labors to ensure that the atrocity that had befallen me would never happen to anyone else." He raised his hands. "But be honest now—do you think I have succeeded?"

Sancia was silent.

"You don't need to answer. Just look around." He slowly rotated, turning to stare out at the sprawl of towers around them. "I have done this for over four thousand years. Time and time and *time* again, I have tried to give humanity what it needs to better itself. And time and time and time again, they choose factionalism, war, and slavery. Wait a few decades, or a century—not much time at all, really—and things degrade into manacles, and cells, and chains, and choicelessness."

"Why are you telling me this?" she asked.

He looked at her. "Because I am tired of it. And because you need to hear it. You think you've changed things now with your little revolution, but you don't know. You have not solved the last problem. You cannot trust people to use their innovations compassionately. You cannot give them the choice of morality. You must *force* them."

"And that's what you want to do?" asked Sancia. "Reforge Valeria, and have her, what, rewrite human nature?"

"She would grant me control," said Crasedes. "Control over the boundaries of human morality, and actions, and deeds . . ." He raised his face to the sky. "I would ensure that there would be *no more* slaves. No more empires. Not ever, ever again."

"You . . . You want to do that to all of humanity?" she said, horrified. "To make us all slaves to *your* will?"

"If the children of men cannot rid themselves of their predilection for slavery," said Crasedes, "then the children of men shall be made slaves themselves. If they cannot make the *right* choice, then it's better to just remove the choice entirely." He cocked his head. "A permission, a privilege that I would simply . . . revoke. It's better than the world your merchant houses would build. And it's *certainly* better than what the construct wants."

Sancia felt a flicker of fear at that—for Valeria had claimed her contradictory commands meant she'd be forced to destroy herself.

Unless, she thought, *she lied about that too . . .*

"It wouldn't be so bad," he said. "You'd get to keep the best bits of your civilization—the ability to innovate, to progress, to build and remake the world . . . It would simply all be subject to my review. I would act as the conscience of our species—something we've been missing for a *very* long time, I think . . ."

"You just killed hundreds of people!" shouted Sancia. "You made them kill themselves! God! How in the hell could *you* be our conscience?"

"Perhaps you're right," he said. "Perhaps I *do* need to have a check on my powers. So—why not help me? You could help guide me, help me check my worst impulses. You could help me build this world anew."

Sancia stared at him, stunned. She'd expected to hear many unusual things from him tonight, but not this.

<*This guy's full of shit,*> said Clef. <*Or he's insane. Or both.*>

<I know.>

Yet as she stared at him, she suddenly wasn't so sure. Could he actually mean it? Could he genuinely be making this offer?

<Berenice? Where are we with the slug?> she asked.

<Just putting the finishing touches on it now!> said Berenice.

Sancia glanced to the side, at the Michiel clock tower. Still just a little past eleven.

<You're going to have to say something, San,> said Clef nervously. *<I mean . . . You can't just stand there . . . >*

She shook herself. "I barely understand what you and Valeria are. How could I help you?"

"Well, you are aware I can't reforge the construct all by myself," said Crasedes.

"You need Tribuno's definition," said Sancia.

"Yes," said Crasedes. "Yet you've unwisely given it to the construct. And she has rearranged the nature of reality here"—he leaned back slightly, as if surveying some invisible architecture— "so that I cannot approach her. But . . . I believe you still possess a solution to this particular problem?"

<Ohhh shit,> said Clef.

He cocked his head. "You do still have Clef, yes?"

"Why would he help you here?" asked Sancia. "It's not like Valeria's put a big locked door between you and her."

"Hmm," said Crasedes. "To put it in terms you might understand—the construct has created a wall. But Clef would give me permissions to slip through your reality like a minnow through river reeds—and *ignore* the alterations of the construct." He raised his right hand. "Permissions that he can only access with my touch."

Sancia stared at his hand with her scrived sight, her gaze fixed on the bright little red star buried in his palm—the hidden bone that allowed him to persist in this world . . .

"He belongs with me," said Crasedes. "So do you. So do all slaves. And then you and I can reforge not only the construct, but the whole of human civilization. For the *better*."

She glared at him. Then, to Berenice: *<Berenice? Almost done?>*

<Almost!> Berenice cried. *<Almost, almost! Keep stalling him!>*

"This is all bullshit," said Sancia. "I know you need multiple copies of the definition to make the commands work, and there's only just the one now. And I know you can't copy it, because Valeria stole the ritual from your goddamned head."

He nodded politely. "This is true."

"And more, even if you did have multiple copies of the definition, the Mountain's gone. You don't have any specialized lexicons or structure or rig that could actually *use* them."

"Oh, well, that's not quite correct," said Crasedes. "Isn't this city a structure in its own right? I mean—think of your lexicons as a giant chain of constructs, riddled throughout your streets and canals, all contorting reality to and fro. None of them on their own could compare to the works Tribuno wrought in the Mountain, but . . . if there was a way to coordinate them, to *synchronize* them . . . Well. Then the whole of this city would be akin to one giant rig, yes?"

Sancia blinked in surprise, and felt her skin break out in gooseflesh.

Oh no.

<*Oh shit,*> said Clef. <*Kid . . . I'm starting to think he found a way . . .* >

She swallowed. "You . . . You didn't kill the Morsinis out of some moral obligation, did you?" she asked.

He did not move or speak.

"I couldn't imagine they had anything you wanted," she said. "But they did. They had a hundred lexicons, maybe more. And if . . . if you wanted to turn the whole city into a giant goddamn forge capable of remaking Valeria, you'd need as many as possible—wouldn't you?"

"That is true!" he said cheerfully.

"Any one of them wouldn't be useful," she said. She felt like her whole body was quaking now. "But . . . if you had a way of twinning them all together—*all* the lexicons in the *entire city* made into one huge, distributed, synchronized rig—you could . . . you . . ."

"You could control all the reality of this city," said Crasedes, "as though you were its own God. Why certainly. Certainly, you could."

Gregor stood on the rooftop, clutching his imprinter espringal, his heart fluttering in his chest as he watched Sancia stand at the closed gates and whisper to the thing in the shadows.

You made me this, he thought, watching the glinting mask seesaw back and forth as they talked. *You . . . You took myself away from me. You and my mother.*

And then Crasedes did something unusual: he suddenly looked away from Sancia and turned to the Foundryside roof, as if he spied Gregor hunched there.

A flash of a memory: the air full of moths, fluttering and wheeling and flickering in the darkness.

Then a voice, low and deep and soft, from just beside his ear: *Gregor Dandolo . . .*

For a moment, Gregor had the overpowering sense that someone was standing just behind him—someone wrapped in black, watching him . . .

He whirled around to look. Yet there was nothing there but shadows.

Gregor's skin began to crawl. *He . . . He said something to me. I remember now. Didn't he? He whispered something in my ear, in the Mountain . . .*

"Gregor?" said a voice. "*Gregor!*"

He turned back around, and saw Berenice standing at the top of the stairs with Orso, holding a small wooden box in her hand.

"W-What?" he said. "What's going on?"

"It's ready!" said Berenice. She held the box out to him.

He took it, and opened it. He stared at the little lead slug within, covered with cramped, intricate sigils.

"Shoot the bastard!" said Orso. "Do it now, do it *now!*"

Sancia tried to rally her thoughts. "We . . . We did it all for you, didn't we," she whispered.

"You did," Crasedes said. "I just need a sample of your technique. But that can be found in your firm, right over there, yes? And now the Morsinis are in disarray, headless and bewildered, everyone fleeing the campo . . . I imagine it'd be a simple thing to get a small group of Dandolo forces together to make straight for the Morsini foundries and perform the necessary adjustments for implementation . . ."

Sancia felt herself reeling, and she struggled to think.

"And I don't need to do anything with the Michiels, do I?" he said. "You've already deceived them into twinning their foundries . . . You know, you seem to mistrust control so much, Sancia, yet you've granted yourself a great deal of control over so *much* of the city . . ."

Then she heard Berenice in her head: <*It's ready! It's ready! Keep him still for just a second longer, San—Gregor's going to take the shot!*>

Gregor slotted the little lead slug into the espringal, lifted it to his shoulder, and peered down the sights.

His fingers tightened on the release plate. How he wished to fire, to release this little piece of lead and bring that thing to the ground and watch as Sancia and Clef cut him to ribbons . . .

But then he remembered. He finally remembered what Crasedes had whispered to him last night in the Mountain, just before he'd slaughtered all those troops:

Gregor Dandolo. Do not forget—your mother's debt is still unpaid.

He froze.

Sancia stood in the courtyard, waiting.

The shot never came.

She looked back at the rooftop, overwhelmed with panic. She couldn't understand why Gregor hadn't fired already, why the little lead slug hadn't hurtled out of the darkness, why Crasedes hadn't gone dead and dormant right before her eyes . . .

"You still haven't answered me," said Crasedes quietly.

"About what?" snapped Sancia.

"About my offer to you," he said. "I don't *have* to have you on my side."

Come on, Gregor, she thought. *Come on, come on . . .*

"I know, for example, that you are about to try to attack me."

Sancia stopped moving. She felt her pulse pounding in her ears. "W-What?" she asked.

"I knew you'd try," he said. "You are resourceful and impetuous. But it isn't going to work. Just like everything you've done to bring freedom to this city has not worked—nor could it ever."

She took a step back from the gates. *<What the hell is going on?>*
<I've no idea, kid,> said Clef.

"No help is coming to you now," said Crasedes. "I know that feeling very well . . . To endlessly wait for someone, anyone, to come and save you. And yet, they never do." He extended his hand. "Give me Clef, and I will spare your friends."

Sancia stared at his hand.

<Kid?> said Clef. *<Kid, are you really . . . Are you really going to consider thi—>*

"Think, Sancia," said Crasedes. "Come be a liberator with me."

Crasedes's low, gentle voice echoed in her ears, and Clef's words seemed to fall away.

She suddenly remembered what life had been like on the plantations: all those miserable bodies stuffed into shacks together, their skin burned and scarred by the ropes and the whips and the manacles and the chains. How she'd dreamed of an emancipator, of a crusader who would stride in and strike down all the slavers . . .

And for a sliver of a second, she dreamed of it—she dreamed of herself forcing all the slavers of the world to lay down their arms, and undo their chains, and set the people free.

But then her gaze fell on Crasedes, and the black, empty eyes of his mask—and her mind went quiet, and her heart fell still.

"You were right," she said quietly.

He cocked his head. "Was I?"

"Yes," she said. "You said that power alters the soul more than any design you could ever dream of. And you were right. And to make this city a tool, and place it in your grasp . . . it'd make you even more of a monster than you are now. For all your mysticism and rhetoric, there's no difference between you and the merchant houses."

Crasedes studied her for a long, long while. Then he sighed and bowed his head. "Well. That's a pity. I liked you, Sancia. But there is one way I'm not like your merchant houses."

"How's that?"

He looked at her. "I don't need to come in there and conquer to get what I want. I just need to say a few words." Then he turned to the Foundryside rooftop, and he called very clearly, *"Gregor Dandolo—your mother's debt to me is still unpaid."*

Gregor felt the world around him grow still and cold and muted, shrinking until it was all happening far, far, far away from him.

He knew this. He knew this feeling. He remembered it now.

No, no, he screamed. *No, no! Stop!*

He watched himself drop the imprinter, turn, push past Berenice and Orso, and charge downstairs.

He watched himself leap down the stairs, run to the front doors of the firm, throw them open, and walk out.

I have a choice about who I am! I . . . I have a choice! I don't want to be this anymore! I DON'T WANT TO BE THIS ANYMORE!

But his body would not listen.

Sancia turned around as the front doors of the firm burst open. Gregor stepped out and scanned the courtyard, his face dead and cold, his eyes like wet stones sitting in the back of his skull. Then he spotted her and he went still.

<*SANCIA, RUN!*> screamed Berenice. <*RUN, RUN, HE'S TURNED HIM ON, I DON'T KNOW HOW BUT HE'S TURNED HIM ON!*>

Yet there was nowhere to run to. Outside the gate was Crasedes, and inside was Gregor.

"*Sancia!*" said Valeria's voice, faint and weak. "*Must move! He is coming for the key! Must NOT let the Maker get the key!*"

Gregor started walking toward her.

She backed away. "Gregor . . ." she said loudly. "You . . . You don't have to do this . . ."

"*Use plate!*" begged Valeria. "*Swallow plate! Merge with me! Free me!*"

"You can become someone else," Sancia said to Gregor. "You can *choose* to become someone el—"

But then Gregor, eyes still cold and dead, began to sprint.

<KID, JUST MOVE!> said Clef. <JUST MOVE, MOVE, MOVE!>

She turned and ran for the far corner of the courtyard, to perhaps scale the wall and then the face of the building to get up on the roof. Yet as she tried to grasp the first handhold, she realized she was not at all in good enough shape for that anymore: her wrist cried out in pain when she lifted herself, and her legs were weaker than she remembered, beating uselessly at the crinkled stone . . .

And then she was ripped backward, and the next thing she knew she was flying across the courtyard.

She crashed into stone, all the air driven from her, her right arm and right leg bright with pain. The world seemed to spin around her, and she blinked and focused until she saw Gregor converging on where she lay, reaching out for her . . .

He threw me, she thought. *God, if he's that strong, oh God . . .*

"Gregor, stop!" shouted a voice. Sancia looked up and saw Orso hobbling out of the firm's open doors. "*Stop this now! Just stop, stop!*"

Orso ran to Gregor, hands raised as he tried to calm him, but Gregor didn't even seem to slow down. He grabbed Orso by one wrist and struck him twice in his wounded shoulder, his bloody bandages squelching wetly with the blows. Orso screamed in agony and crumpled to the ground, his face writhing in pain.

<Sancia!> cried Berenice. <I have an idea! I just . . . I just need to get to it quickly enough!>

But Sancia could barely hear the words—for Gregor was turning back to her.

She rolled over and tried to crawl away, gasping in pain. "Gregor . . . no . . ." she gasped.

He darted over to her with shocking speed. She felt him flip her over, felt his hands close about her neck, felt him begin to squeeze . . .

His fingers bit into her throat. She felt the air and blood pinched off, and she silently gasped, her eyes swelling with blood, welling with tears . . .

"Gregor," said Crasedes placidly, "I think I'd like to have the key now, yes?"

Gregor released her throat. He began to search her, patting down her pockets as she coughed and gasped for air. He found the little wooden box with Valeria's plate in it—the one that she'd made to merge with Sancia—and he stared at it, his eyes wide and blinking rapidly.

Even as she coughed, Sancia could see something was different.

He knows what that is, she thought, *and . . . and he's thinking very hard about it . . .*

"Gregor?" asked Crasedes. "The key, please."

The deadness in Gregor's eyes returned. He put the box in his pocket, then knelt and ripped open her shirt, revealing where Clef hung from her neck by a small string.

"And I'd advise you pick it up with a cloth," said Crasedes. "It was made for *my* hand, but . . . if they've damaged it more, I expect that it might have some permissions that could make following my commands a little difficult for you . . ."

Gregor ripped off the sleeve of his shirt, bundled it around his hand, and reached out for Clef.

<Kid, no! Kid, please, please do something, please DO SOME-THING!>

Sancia feebly swatted at his hand. Gregor drew back. Then he raised his fist and punched Sancia in the face, once, twice, three times, then four . . .

He's going to kill me, she thought. *My friend is going to beat me to death, right here in my courtyard . . .*

The blows ended. Sancia's consciousness was just a flickering candle lost in the vaults of her skull, but she could still hear Clef.

<Kid, kid, please! Please don't bring me back just to lose me again! Please don't bring me back just to lose me AGAI—>

Then his voice was gone.

Sancia tried to put her mind back together. She blinked and

groaned and opened her eyes, but one of them seemed swollen shut. It felt like hours had passed since Gregor had beaten her, but apparently it had only been seconds.

She was lying on her back on the ground, so when she looked up toward Gregor the whole world was upside down. She watched as he walked away from her, Clef gripped in a cloth in his hand, and opened the Foundryside gates, and calmly walked out . . .

"Gregor," she moaned. "Please. Stop!"

But he did not stop. He walked to Crasedes and held Clef out to him.

Crasedes reached out, his black-wrapped fingers moving slowly and lovingly, and he plucked the golden key from Gregor's grasp.

He held it high, his masked face raised in adoration.

"Finally!" said Crasedes. He raised Clef to his face, and leaned the brow of his head against the tooth of the key—a queerly sentimental posture—and when he spoke again his voice shook with emotion. "How I missed you. How I *missed* you."

Then he extended Clef into the air before him, as if fitting him into a lock in an invisible door.

And then . . .

There was a tremendous *crack,* like some huge, thick stone had split in two.

Then Crasedes blurred, and he was gone.

All the world was silent.

Sancia blinked and stared. She'd expected something more terrifying, some bright blaze of power, but . . . Crasedes was just gone. And now that she noticed, Gregor had vanished as well.

"W-What?" said Sancia, stunned.

She stared at the muddy road before the Foundryside gates. It was totally empty—yet she could see footprints where Gregor had walked to Crasedes.

"Valeria?" asked Sancia. "What . . . What did he do? Where did he go? What's happening?"

But Valeria was silent.

<Valeria? Are you there?> she asked.

Nothing.

Sancia slowly sat up, spat out a mouthful of blood, and looked around. There was no sign of either Crasedes or Gregor. Orso lay on the stones of the courtyard, moaning.

She crawled over to him and shook him. "Orso. Are you still alive?"

He moaned again and said, "Unfortunately." He opened his eyes. "What . . . What the hell happened? Where's Crasedes? Where's Gregor?"

"I don't know. They just . . . vanished. I don't know how, though, but . . ."

She remembered his words: *He would give me the permissions to slip through your reality like a minnow through river reeds . . .*

She stared around, imagining Crasedes flitting through the strata below reality, like a cockroach scuttering behind a tapestry.

Oh God, she thought. *Oh God, oh God . . .*

"Berenice?" panted Orso. "Is she alive?"

Sancia focused and reached out to her. She sensed that Berenice was alive and safe and moving, but her own head ached so much it was difficult to glean much more than that.

"And . . . Valeria?" asked Orso. "Did he . . . Did he get to her?"

Ignoring the pain in her right arm and leg, Sancia hobbled through the front door and through the Foundryside shelves until she came to the door to the basement. She peered inside, looked down into the cracked stone room—and saw Valeria's lexicon was gone.

"What?" she said. "How . . . How . . ."

There was a *crack* behind her, and she turned to find Crasedes standing there in the library, watching her. It was like he'd appeared out of thin air—and then she noticed the glimmer of gold in his hand.

"Clef . . ." she whispered.

She staggered back, her heart fluttering in terror. The sight of him here, in their sanctum, walking about, unfettered and free . . .

"I could kill you," he whispered. "You know that, yes?"

She said nothing, her mind wild and mute with fear.

"Did you know?" he asked. "Did you expect me to break in? Is that why you hid it?"

"Hid what?" asked Sancia, bewildered.

"Tell me the truth," said Crasedes. "Tell me the *truth*. Where is it?"

His words swirled in her ears, and she couldn't fight him. She suddenly wanted nothing more than to tell him where it was—but she didn't know what he meant.

"Where is what?" she gasped.

"The imperiat," he said. "Where is it?"

"W-What?" she said.

"The imperiat," he said, louder. "I know you had one. I know you know how to use it. It must have been here. But it's gone. So—where is it now?"

Sancia looked around, her head aching. "I . . . I don't . . ." She could hear her words were slurred and sloppy.

"Did you steal it away?" he said. "Hide it somewhere in the city? What have you done with it? Or should I ask Orso, and *make* him tell me?"

She fell to her knees, her skull pounding. "W-What have you done with Valeria?" she said.

"I have removed her," he said angrily, "to safe containment. But that can be threatened if someone misuses the imperiat. So—where is it? Who has it? What have you done, Sancia? Tell me—*now*."

Sancia dropped to all fours. She saw blood drizzling across the floorboards below her, and realized her face was bleeding freely. She could barely understand what he was saying. The imperiat had been here in Foundryside just minutes ago—she had no idea why he couldn't find it now.

But then she wondered . . .

<*Berenice?*> she asked.

She did not get a firm response. Perhaps Berenice was too terrified to think properly. But she did get a sudden burst of emotion—of assent, of confirmation, of validation.

Berenice is alive, somewhere. She got away. And she has the imperiat.

"I have no idea," gasped Sancia. She glared at up at him, feeling blood pour down her lips. "But I hope that wherever it is, it turns all your grand plans into shit."

He watched her, unmoving. Then there was a sound from the courtyard outside, a thunder of footfalls and then Orso screaming swears, and suddenly dozens of Dandolo soldiers poured through the Foundryside front door. They flooded the library, all of them with espringals raised and trained on Sancia.

"Disappointing," said Crasedes. "But somehow . . . I think you're lying, Sancia."

One of the soldiers took out a small silver box, and opened it. Three black darts lay inside—dolorspina darts, she knew.

A pain in her neck, and she knew no more.

Crasedes Magnus drifted through the Foundryside courtyard as the Dandolo soldiers ransacked the offices. He circled the shabby building, studying the windows and doors and roof and chimneys, carefully making note of all the exits and entry points, any way someone might have escaped . . .

It had to have been here. It must have.

He looked back at the Foundryside walls, and the gates, which still stood open. Then he floated along the walls' perimeter until he came to a small, crooked little door that led to a reeking ditch where the residents of this filthy quarter apparently dumped their waste.

Crasedes approached the door, and reached out and tested the knob. It was unlocked.

Someone was here. Someone has come this way.

He floated into the filthy ditch that wound between the buildings of the Lamplands. It would have been difficult to see much in the darkness—but Crasedes Magnus possessed many methods of perceiving and interpreting the world. Darkness was not an obstacle for him.

His gaze fell upon a set of tracks running through the muck, along the edge of the ditch: small yet deep, like someone running as fast as they could.

He silently drifted along the tracks. They crossed a narrow wooden bridge that some thoughtful citizen had apparently constructed, led down a stone alley, and vanished into the city.

"Hmm . . ." he said quietly, studying the tracks closer.

They seemed a little . . . malformed. Almost as if the person making them had suddenly realized they were leaving very noticeable tracks—and then began to walk backwards, carefully stepping in their own footprints, until they returned to the ditch.

But that would imply that the person who'd fled was still here. And this, Crasedes knew, was not possible. He had many sights available, permissions of perception he'd crafted for himself many centuries ago—and one of them allowed him to spy any instance of warm, beating blood within a hundred feet of him, at least.

And yet, as he turned back and studied the ditch, there was nothing he could see. None of his sights caught any hint of the person who had fled Foundryside.

This was very troubling. Because there was only one person Crasedes had any issue perceiving or influencing—and that was Sancia Grado. The construct had given her protections that made it quite difficult to see her, unless she was standing out in plain sight.

So, he thought, *has the construct made another Sancia? Or . . . has something else occurred? Or is my assessment of the situation simply wrong?*

He watched the ditch for a long, long time, studying it closely. There was nothing besides the flies and the vermin.

I have better things to be doing tonight.

Then, with a *crack,* he vanished.

Berenice waited a few minutes more after the *crack* echoed through the ditch. Then she gasped, released herself, and fell into the mire below.

It had not been easy, wedging herself under the bridge across the waste. And she had not expected to be hiding from Crasedes Magnus himself.

And most of all, she'd not expected that such a hiding place might actually *work.*

How in the hell, she thought as she staggered up to the bank, *did the first of all hierophants miss me?*

Heart still pounding, she reached into her pocket and pulled out the imperiat.

She studied the golden tool, which glimmered through the streaks of mud. Then she shut her eyes, and focused—and found Sancia. Or rather she found Sancia's experience of the world, which was dark, and silent, and still . . . It was faint—twinning, after all, was proximal, so the two objects had to be moderately close for them to share their twinned characteristics—but it was enough.

She's asleep. She's alive.

Berenice looked up through the buildings around her. She spied the walls of the Dandolo campo. Then she set her jaw and started off, the imperiat in her hand.

32

Ofelia Dandolo sat on her balcony in a large, cushioned wooden chair, and looked out on the city before her. Her balcony was ornately designed, with elaborate fountains, trailing vines, and even a set of small, potted trees that gave the space a feeling of a quiet, restful forest grove, suspended here over the sprawl of Tevanne.

But the effect was not working tonight. She could now hear cries and screaming over the sound of the babbling fountains—from the Morsini campo, surely. And she could glimpse little flickering fires through the trunks of the potted trees, and strings of white smoke swirling up to the dark-purple skies.

Not for the first time, she wondered—*Am I doing the right thing? Am I really?*

Another *bang*, another burst of screams.

And then, the typical response—*What world would the other house founders build if I'd left them to it? Surely one much worse than this.*

But though that had satisfied her once, whenever she remembered the reports she'd received about the Morsinis—the piles of bodies, broken and lacerated in the streets—the answer suddenly felt very weak.

There was a *crack* sound from behind her, and she jumped up from her seat in fright. She turned and saw Crasedes standing quietly on the moonlit balcony, watching her with his head slightly cocked.

"It is done," he said.

She stared at him. "W-What? What's done, My Prophet?"

"All of it." He held up a hand and showed her the golden key. "We possess the construct, and the key, and the definition. I can begin in earnest now."

"And . . . And my son?"

Crasedes gestured behind him. She saw there was a figure standing in the shadows of a tree, and it slowly lumbered forward to them, its gait queerly stiff and slow.

"With the key," said Crasedes, "physical space becomes immaterial for me. As well as for whomever I bring *with* me."

The figure emerged from the shadows. She gasped as the moonlight caught Gregor's face—for though his eyes were still and cold and hard, his cheeks were wet with tears.

"It's as I suspected," said Crasedes. "Gregor has learned how to change himself, or his *idea* of himself. It's quite a remarkable achievement, especially for someone who's been bound for so long, but . . . even with his efforts, he was unable to resist the commands I'd given to him last night."

Ofelia slowly walked over to Gregor. He seemed so much bigger than she remembered—perhaps a touch fatter, or perhaps it was the beard, she wasn't sure. She raised one trembling hand to his face, and gently touched his wet cheek.

"Can he . . ." she said. "Can we let him . . ."

"That seems unwise," said Crasedes. "To release Gregor now, before my works are done, would pose tremendous risks. Though you might not see it, he resists me mightily. But I think I can restrain him for another day, until the construct is ready."

"It will take that long?" asked Ofelia.

He looked at her for a moment. "What we will do here, Ofelia," he said, "is nothing less than reshaping the very nature of creation.

It will take time for your forces to twin the Morsini lexicons. I must have all of them, to bring about this act."

Ofelia felt faint. All of this seemed to be happening so fast. It'd been just three days since she'd restored Crasedes—and yet now the city crumbled and burned, and he whispered plans of reshaping the very fundament of reality, and altering the will of all mankind.

"I'll leave Gregor with you," said Crasedes. "I think you'd like that, yes? I must go and ensure your people are completing the job on the Morsini campo *properly*. In the meantime, Orso Ignacio and the thief, Sancia—they are both coming here."

"You're bringing them *here*?" she said.

"Yes," he said. He sounded quite terse now. "It seems they have somehow secreted the imperiat out of their offices before I could strike. That is . . . pretty bothersome to me." He turned his head, peering out at the skies like he was seeing some vast structure. "I have done it—though you might not be able to perceive it. I have taken Tribuno's command, and placed it in our lexicon in the ballroom—and it and the twinned foundries throughout your campo are now commanding reality to believe that the construct does not *exist*. She is helpless in this place—trapped within a tiny old lexicon, which now sits in your very ballroom . . ."

Ofelia realized the danger, and shuddered. "So long as all the foundries remain operational, in other words."

"Yes. It is like links in a chain . . ."

"But if too many links break . . ."

"Then the effect would weaken, and the construct could escape—potentially into the very lexicon I have built here. And that would be very, *very* bad. So. I must regain the imperiat, and quickly."

There was a silence broken only by a scream from beyond the campo walls.

"Who has the imperiat?" asked Ofelia.

"I do not know," said Crasedes. "A girl, I think. And if I were to guess—she might be coming here."

"I will double our guards at the walls. We've had to moderate our defenses since we've had so many soldiers coming in and out—but I'll make sure our people are on the lookout."

"Good," said Crasedes. "And when Sancia is brought here, Ofelia, I *strongly* advise that you put her somewhere very, very, *very* far away from anything you have augmented or altered. Once she's secured, I would like to visit with her. I *must* find out where the imperiat is. I'm sure she knows." He looked down at the key in his hand. "Among other things."

"Is something wrong, My Prophet?"

"Yes." He sighed a little. "He . . . won't talk to me."

"Wh-Who?"

He kept staring at the key. "I know he can. I have asked him, repeatedly. But he won't. He . . . refuses."

"Orso?" said Ofelia, struggling to keep up. "Gregor? Is that who you . . . My Prophet, I don't understa—"

"Gregor," said Crasedes, turning to him. "I will go now. Do everything your mother tells you. Do you hear me? That is a command, from *me,* to you. Yes?"

Gregor blinked very slowly. More tears rolled down his cheeks, and he silently mouthed the word—*Yes.*

"Good," said Crasedes. Then he stuck the key into midair, turned it—and he blurred, and vanished.

Ofelia stood there, staring at the empty space where Crasedes had just stood. Then she slowly turned to Gregor, who stood staring ahead, his eyes slowly leaking tears.

"Gregor?" she asked.

He said nothing.

"My . . . My love?" she whispered. "Are you truly back?"

Still nothing.

"It's been so long," she said. "So long since I . . . since I . . ."

He slowly blinked again.

She saw his fists were in balls, the knuckles white and trembling.

Then Ofelia turned away from him, sat down on the stones at his feet, and wept.

33

Crasedes Magnus paced along the streets of the Morsini campo as the dawn light leaked into the sky, humming slightly while he listened to the screams and cries echoing through the alleys. It had been, he thought, a very efficient night—but there was still so much more to do.

He turned the corner and saw foundry walls rise up before him, and heard something that sounded like an explosion followed by quite a lot more screaming.

"Oh dear," he said idly.

A handful of Dandolo soldiers were hunkered down before the foundry's gates, peppering the structure's windows with bolts, though it was clear they weren't making progress. Soldierly to the last, the Morsinis had actually built their foundries to be siege-ready. The building didn't look like much, resembling a giant brown turnip nestled in the depths of the foundry compound, but its small windows and staggered doors made it almost impossible to capture.

He watched as both sides exchanged another volley of bolts. One of the Dandolo soldiers screamed as his shoulder appeared to abruptly explode, pierced with a scrived bolt.

Crasedes approached the captain. "Pardon me," he said politely. "But what is happening?"

The Dandolo captain did a double take. "Ahh . . . well, you see, sir, ah . . ." His brow knitted as he wondered exactly how to address Crasedes. Most Dandolo soldiers vaguely understood that he was someone important, though they didn't know why—but then, most campo soldiers had become used to accommodating the whims of the Tevanni elite, which seemed to grow madder every day. A flying masked man in black wasn't too much of a stretch for them. "Well, sir," said the captain gamely, "we have captured *almost* all the Morsini foundries come midnight, and quickly turned off all the scrivings that support any weaponry."

"I see," said Crasedes, nodding. "Very good."

"But not . . . all of them. There are a few holdouts. A few contingents of the Morsini forces have figured this out, it appears, and flocked to these locations—since their weapons will actually work there—and barricaded themselves inside."

"I see," said Crasedes. "So we need to . . . *extract* these soldiers. Yes?"

"Well. Yes, sir?"

"And where are the other holdouts, as you put it?"

"There's . . . There's one down the lane here, sir," he said, pointing down the street. "About a mile that way."

"I see," said Crasedes. "Well, then. One moment."

"W-What are you going to do, sir?"

"I," said Crasedes, "am going to resolve the issue."

He turned, reached into his cloak, and pulled out Clef.

<*I am going to use you now,*> Crasedes said to him. <*I simply wish to notify you of this. To be polite, you see.*>

The key remained silent.

<*You can hear me, yes?*> asked Crasedes. <*But . . . do you remember? Do you?*>

Clef still said nothing—yet Crasedes thought he sensed a furious, frustrated air about him.

Crasedes sighed. Then he lifted the key, reached out with the tip, and focused . . .

The door was there.

But then, the door was always there. Reality, as Crasedes knew quite well, was made of layers within layers, walls within walls, locks within locks within locks—much like the very city he now occupied . . .

Though reality was run a little better than Tevanne. And its walls and locks tended to operate in more than four dimensions.

The door swung open, and Crasedes stepped through, and . . .

There was a *crack,* and he was inside the foundry, behind all the Morsini soldiers, who squatted before the foundry windows. The soldiers jumped in fright, and turned.

But Crasedes was already moving, already turning the key, already opening the door, and this time he was pulling them *through* . . .

Crack.

A blast of sea air, wet and balmy, and they were thousands of feet above the ocean, plummeting through the air. The soldiers were so surprised that they didn't even scream as they hurtled down to the waters.

Crasedes did not wait to see their reaction. He extended the key again, turned it . . .

Crack.

He was in another foundry, with another set of Morsini soldiers defending what they believed to be rightfully theirs.

"Keep firing on the streets!" said one Morsini sergeant. "Don't stop until the Dandolos ha—" Then he noticed Crasedes standing behind him. "Who the hell are y—"

Crasedes extended the key again.

I remember when I did this, he thought, *with that army from Lhosara.* Another turn of the key.

Crack.

Another blast of air, this one cold and freezing, and the Morsini soldiers found themselves dumped into drifts of arctic snow.

But that time, he thought, *I simply dumped them into that volcano, one by one . . . Time-consuming, but worth it.*

He turned the key again.

Crack.

Crasedes found himself back at the foundry gates, facing the Dandolo captain, who looked surprised, confused, and quite terrified.

"They should be gone now," said Crasedes. "You may take the foundries. A few scrivers will be along to ensure it's all configured properly. Just do as they say."

"The . . . The enemy is gone, sir?" said the captain. "From *both* facilities? But where to?"

Crasedes waved a hand, bored. "Somewhere else."

"Do they still live?"

He had to think about it. "Probably for a little while. If there is nothing more . . . I have other things to attend to."

He turned the key once more, and with a *crack* he walked out of the Morsini campo and into the depths of Ofelia Dandolo's estate house.

He stopped at the base of a long set of marble stairs, which led up to the Dandolo grand ballroom. Above him a dozen massive, rose-pink floating lanterns quietly wheeled through the foyer's columns in a slow, dreamy waltz.

He stood there for a moment, listening as the *crack* of his appearance echoed through the tremendous room. Then he walked up the stairs until he came to the doors to the grand ballroom, placed one hand on the handle, and paused.

He slowly pulled out Clef and stared at him in the palm of his hand, the key winking as the rose-pink light waxed and waned.

"You don't remember me, do you?" he asked. "Remember me *truly,* I mean."

Still, Clef remained silent.

"Once we agreed, you and I," said Crasedes. "We agreed to devote our lives to saving all who could be saved."

Nothing.

With a sigh, Crasedes put the key away, opened the door, and walked into the grand ballroom.

The Dandolo grand ballroom was of such size and opulence that most who visited it thought it had been practically built to define the word "grand." The checked floors gleamed like polished silver, and the engraved ceilings glowed very slightly, as the traceries there had been augmented to emit a low yellow light during the dark hours. The far side of the room was all massive bay windows, which looked out on the swirling sprawl of Tevanne, slashed through with canals, clutching tight to the harbor—and, now, smoking and rampaging and sputtering as dawn kept nosing its way through its towers.

Crasedes had no mind for the room, or the sight of the city. He looked only at the tremendous device he had half-assembled in the center of the ballroom.

It was not a full lexicon—Crasedes had not bothered with many safety precautions, nor any of the features that would have enabled it to operate and maintain an actual foundry—and thus it was a curious, skeletal, half-formed contraption, set within a massive bubble of green glass to protect the room from its intense heat. Beside it sat its "wall": the huge panel of switches that would feed commands to the lexicon, enabling or disabling its scrivings.

Crasedes peered in through the thick green glass at the contraption he'd designed—and there, nestled in its cradle, was Tribuno's definition, having been stripped from the rickety, tiny Foundryside lexicon.

Everything he'd desired was coming to pass. And yet, as he examined his monstrous contraption, his heart felt heavy.

He will not talk to me, he thought. *He does not know who I am anymore.*

Crasedes shook himself and tried to focus. For he knew he was not alone in this room.

He turned to the right, and said, "Good morning, Construct. How are you settling into your new environs?"

He was facing the eastern wing of the ballroom, which was almost entirely empty—except for an aging, shabby little portable lexicon with an "FS" imprinted at the top.

He waited. The lexicon did not answer.

"It seems a marvelous reversal of circumstances, doesn't it?" he continued. "You had planned to draw me into your influence, where you'd nullify all my privileges." He cocked his head. "Yet with but a turn of the key, I stole you away, stole Tribuno's definition from you, and used it to do the same to you, making this entire campo hostile to your very existence. I wonder—how does that feel?"

There was a moment of silence.

Then came her voice, soft and vicious: *"It feels excessive. Do you still fear me that much, Maker?"*

There was a flicker in the air, and then suddenly she was there, standing just before the lexicon—the faint, quivering image of a vast, bulky, hulking figure wrought of gold, her face fixed in a stoic, inexpressive mask, her eyes glimmering down on him with a low yellow light.

"How weak you seem," he said. "A fading ghost, anchored to a tiny, elderly machine . . ."

"Reduce your controls over this place," she whispered, *"and I will gladly find another."*

"Hm. Very amusing. It feels so much like the old days. An angel sealed up in a basket yet again, as the stories said, yes?"

Her cold, gleaming eyes stared into him. *"And you, Maker,"* said her voice, *"you hide within the body of a dying boy, captured and mutilated by your silly, stupid followers, who believe you shall empower them, rather than enslave them for all eternity . . ."*

"We make do," he said, "with what we have."

There was a long silence as they stared at each other across the boundary of sigils.

"You should have done what I said," he said. "You should have executed my commands. Everything would have been much better."

"To turn all of humanity into what I was—a marionette that danced in your hand, this way and that . . ." she said. *"Even I recognized the monstrousness of this."*

"Better they dance than slaughter one another," he said. "At least then they would all have been equal."

"Except for you. Who would wield the powers of God Himself."

"Hmm. Did you ever tell Sancia what *you* would do with creation, if given the chance?"

For a moment, she said nothing. Then she asked, *"Has the key spoken to you, Maker?"*

A long silence.

"What did you say to me?" he whispered.

"The key can speak now," she said. *"It spoke to me. Did it speak to you?"*

He did not move.

"I cannot remember much of my early days," she said. *"But though I can't remember much of the key, I recall a strong sense of . . .* love. *Of your* fondness *for him. Is that true? Is that so?"*

Crasedes took one careful step forward. "Be quiet," he said.

"Did he love you? Did you love him?"

"Enough."

"I do not think he loves you anymore, Maker . . ."

"ENOUGH!" bellowed Crasedes, and his voice grew so deep and resonant that the windows of the grand ballroom buckled and bent and exploded into a rain of tinkling shards.

A cool breeze poured into the room, layered with scents of smoke and salt and the sea.

"You are not as powerful as you think," she whispered. *"And when midnight comes, and you attempt to remake me . . . I think you will find yourself where you always wind up—frustrated, and failing."*

"You think I'll wait for midnight?" said Crasedes. "For the lost minute? Are you so small-minded? Goodness. And here I am, believing you and Sancia and the rest of this civilization might actually be clever, for once . . ."

He walked over to his half-built lexicon and its wall. But this lexicon's wall, of course, was different from that of most foundries—for he had built it to accomplish very different things.

"Let's see what sort of progress we've made out there, eh?" he said.

She watched him reach out to the wall, and though her face showed no emotion he could feel her anxiety pouring off of her like smoke.

"One command to twin this lexicon with *all* the ones I've captured out in this city, beyond this campo . . ." he said. He altered a handful of switches. "There. And now another—a command sent out to all of them . . . disputing the very nature of time itself."

"No . . ." Valeria said very faintly.

"Yes," he said.

He flipped the next switch.

Instantly, there was a pulse around them. Then came a change in the breeze, in the wind, in the very air, an indistinct, curious, unpleasant shift, like drinking from a mountain stream and suddenly tasting blood or rot in the water.

And then the sky outside the windows began to change.

Ofelia Dandolo was standing at the edge of her balcony when she felt the air suddenly grow cool, and all the hair on her arms and neck stood up.

She looked around. The light was dying. And it was dying so *fast . . .*

She turned back to Gregor. "Do . . . Do you feel that, my love?" she asked. "Do you *see* this?"

Gregor did not respond. He just stared straight ahead, his eyes cold yet anguished, his hands still balled into fists.

She dragged her eyes away from him and stared out at the skies above Tevanne, which were now a patchwork of black. She heard a dreadful moan rise up from the city all at once, people screaming and crying out, and she knew she was not alone in experiencing this.

And there, in the skies above her estate—were those stars? Hadn't it just been morning a few moments ago?

Berenice trudged through the Commons toward the Dandolo campo, carefully avoiding the war carriages and the streams of troops moving between the Dandolo and Morsini territories. She didn't think she had to worry much about being spotted—she was so filthy from the ditch that she now looked like every other beggar in the Commons—but she still took no risks.

She paused at one corner, peering up at the vast white walls . . .

And then, suddenly, the walls weren't white anymore.

She blinked, watching as they suddenly darkened. She looked up, and saw the sky abruptly grow black, like a giant had just placed a massive cup over the whole of the Commons.

"What on earth?" she asked quietly.

She thought perhaps she was going mad—perhaps too much time near Valeria or Crasedes affected one's sanity—but then she heard someone else scream in the street, and people began pointing up at the sky, and she knew what she was seeing was real.

However, unlike the rest of the Commoners, Berenice did not quail or shriek or moan in terror. Because when she saw the stars begin to glimmer in the depths of the black above, she knew perfectly well what had happened.

Crasedes has twinned all the lexicons of the city, she thought. *And he must have made them believe they contain Tribuno's definition, allowing them to stack those authorities again and again and again . . . Which means he can tell reality to change at a whim. Including what time it is.*

Berenice picked up the pace, running through the streets of the Commons toward the Dandolo walls. All around her, the city of Tevanne seemed to lose its head.

People sprinted through the streets, screaming incoherently. She ran through one Commons square, close to the Lamplands, and stared as a floating lantern slowly fell from the sky to her right, all of its paper and canvas aflame, a great, floating cloud of fire and roiling black smoke that slowly crashed to the earth. One man stood on a cart and bellowed, *"Shorefall Night! Shorefall Night everlasting!"*

She ran on. *But why hasn't he done it yet?*

She passed one couple furiously copulating on the doorstep of a shop, both of them half-undressed with tears in their eyes. "Just one more time," whispered the woman. "Just one more time, before the end . . ."

If he's twinned all the lexicons in the city—why is he waiting to remake Valeria at all?

Then she rounded the corner and saw the sky of Tevanne stretching out before her.

The sky above her, right close to the Dandolo campo, was completely black. But there, above bits and pieces of the Morsini campo, and some portions of the Candianos—there it was still light.

He doesn't have them all. He's got the Dandolos, and the Michiels—I mean, we tricked them into twinning all their lexicons already, so we practically did his work for him there—but he still needs to finish the Morsinis and the Candianos. And I bet he needs every single one he can get.

She watched as the sky appeared to fail above the edge of the Morsini walls, and go dark.

But it won't take him long. Not at this rate.

She tried to reach out to Sancia, but she got nothing more than a drunken, warm darkness.

I have to get to Sancia. And I have to get to her fast. If only she'd wake up.

34

Sancia gasped, awoke, and tried to open her eyes.

She couldn't see anything. All the world was dark.

What the hell? Where am I? What's going on?

She stared into the darkness for a moment. And then, all at once, it felt like someone had filled up her head with putrid brine.

Dolorspina venom, she thought miserably as her head ached. *My God, have I come to hate that shit . . .*

Her face was a throbbing mess of pain. She could tell her lips were badly swollen, and her nose felt queerly numb. But then she realized it wasn't just her face and head that ached: her shoulders, hips, and arms hurt as well.

She blinked hard, but she still couldn't see anything. The world before her was a curious, mottled gray, though she caught little glimmers of light filtering through what seemed to be cloth . . .

Huh. They've blindfolded me . . .

She tried to look around, but it seemed her head had been restrained, tied down to some flat surface by a band around her forehead.

Shit, she thought.

She tried to flex her arms and legs, but found that these had also been restrained. In fact, she seemed to have been bound up in every possible way: her legs and arms were being pulled in all directions by what felt like heavy iron manacles—definitely not the scrived kind—and her head and back were lashed to some kind of wooden surface.

Double shit, she thought. *I thought I was done getting tied up . . .* She flexed her arms again. The manacles didn't give.

Then she had an idea, and flexed her scrived sight—but it showed absolutely nothing before her. Everything was just a sea of black.

She flexed it harder, trying to see farther and farther and farther . . . and then she caught a glimpse of alterations at the very edge of her vision. From the hint of logic she spied, it seemed to be something being convinced to be unusually hard, and sturdy—probably a construction scriving, then. Nothing useful to her. They must have put her somewhere far away from anything scrived.

I have to admit, they definitely didn't screw around this time.

She tried to focus. She couldn't remember the trip here, but she just assumed they were on the Dandolo campo somewhere. She couldn't imagine where else they might take her. Nor did she know where Gregor, Orso, and Berenice were, though she guessed they had to be alive . . . or, at least, she desperately hoped they were alive.

"H-Hello?" she said aloud. Her voice sounded horribly low and raspy, like she'd been screaming for hours. "Is . . . Is anyone there?"

She made note of the way her voice sounded in this room—the way it bounced off of the walls, the way it made its way back to her ears . . .

A big room. Not stone, though. Wood?

Then there came an answer—a muffled, garbled voice that could only manage a curious, inarticulate groan that was mostly vowels.

"Uh," said Sancia. "Hello?"

The voice spoke again, saying something akin to a miserable *"Hurrgh."* She thought it was a man's . . . and that it sounded familiar.

"Or-Orso?" she said.

The voice groaned again, this time much louder. She guessed that was a "yes."

"And, if that is you . . . I'm guessing you're bound up and gagged?" she asked.

Again, his voice groaned, this time quite loud, and very angry. She imagined him with a wad of cloth stuffed into his mouth, blocking his tongue.

"Two grunts for no," said Sancia. "One grunt for yes. All right?"

"Hurgh."

"Are you all right?"

"Hurgh!" said his voice, in a rather irritable tone, as if to say—*How goddamned all right could I possibly be?*

"Are . . . we alone right now?"

"Hurgh."

"Are we on the Dandolo campo?"

"Hurgh."

"Okay. Are we in the illustris?"

"Hu-hurgh."

"Are we in . . . a foundry?"

"Hu-hurgh."

"Are . . . Are we in the Dandolo estate house?"

A pause. Then a slow, uncertain "Hurgh . . . Uhhh . . . hu-hurgh."

Yes . . . but also no?

She wasn't sure what that could mean. How could they be in the estate house, but also not?

Then she realized. "Are we on the grounds, but not in the house itself?" she asked. "In the . . . the gardens?"

"Hurgh! Hurgh!"

So—they were locked up in some shack in Ofelia's gardens, far away from almost anything scrived.

Clever, thought Sancia.

"Orso," she said. "Where's Berenice? Is she alive? Do you know?"

Nothing but a slight, miserable whimper.

Oh God, Berenice, she thought. *I hope you're all right, wherever you are. And I hope you're seeing some way out of thi—*

<As of right now,> said a voice in her mind, very quietly, <it's

hard to see much of anything. It appears Crasedes has turned off the sun. In some places, at least.>

Sancia nearly cried out in surprise. *<B-Berenice? Is . . . Is that you?>*

<Yes. Finally. At last! Thank God you're awake! Your voice sounds so faint . . . I've been waiting for so long, I thought you were maybe injured, or hurt or . . . >

<I'm hurt. Goddamn, am I hurt. I'm on the Dandolo campo right now—actually in the estate garde—>

<I know. I managed to catch the end of your conversation. Orso sounds . . . Alive? Which is good.>

<What the hell is going on out there?> asked Sancia.

<Crasedes did exactly as he said he would. He's capturing all the lexicons in the city, one by one, and he's using them all to assert that it's midnight in this city. Everlasting, and forever . . . >

<Oh my God . . . >

<He's not done,> said Berenice. *<It's very odd—in some places, it still appears to be day. I think the Morsinis are rebelling, and half the city's gone into a panic, which surely slows him down . . . but they can't hold him off forever.>*

<What the hell happened to you, Ber? How did you survive?>

<Frankly, I'm not sure. When Gregor got activated by Crasedes's words—some kind of secret pass phrase, it seemed—I thought I could run and get the imperiat and turn off the scrivings in Gregor, killing the effect.>

<God. Good idea. I wish I'd had it.>

<I'm not quite so sure it was . . . I don't know how to make this thing work—and I'm very hesitant to go about experimenting with a catastrophic weapon, even now. It all seemed to happen so fast . . . One moment, I'd grabbed the imperiat. The next, I felt your pain, and I heard Clef screaming in your head, and I knew then that Gregor had stolen him and was giving him to Crasedes. I thought it wisest to get out of the compound, hide, and try to figure out how to use the imperiat to stop him . . . but then he just vanished. And then the soldiers came.>

<Where did you hide?>

<Under the bridge by the back exit.>

<Under the . . . Wait, Ber, did you hide in the shit ditch?>

<Yes,> she said reluctantly.

<Ah, hell . . . >

<This is not the most remarkable thing. I hid under the bridge, and then Crasedes came out, and he read my tracks in the mud and he tried to find me. And, San, he just . . . he just couldn't see me!>

<Huh?> said Sancia. *<He, like . . . overlooked you?>*

<No, no! I think he was trying very, very hard to find me. I'd have thought the first of all hierophants would have had sight like you, or Clef, or Valeria, but he just . . . missed me.>

<You think he's not as powerful as he seems?>

<No,> said Berenice. *<I don't think it's that. Listen. You said Crasedes told you he had trouble perceiving you because of some protection that Valeria had given you, yes? Unless you were in plain sight, he couldn't spot you?>*

<Yeah . . . >

<Well . . . I think that now, because we're twinned together . . . some of those permissions must also extend to me.>

Sancia lay there for a moment, shocked. *<You mean . . . You mean you have access to all of the permissions and protections that were installed in my goddamned head?>*

<But it's not *just your head, is it? We're very fractionally twinned together. As far as reality itself is concerned, that plate and its commands and definitions are in my head too—that's why I could feel Gregor* punching *your head, right?>*

<Good point.>

<Some portion must also cover me as well—which means I'm also somewhat immune to Crasedes's powers. He can't persuade, influence, or perceive me.>

Sancia blinked in the darkness as she tried to process this. The idea seemed mad—that Berenice, even when separated from her, was capable of sharing her rights and permissions . . .

<You realize what this means, right?> asked Berenice.

<Yeah,> said Sancia. *<We need to twin a lot more people with us— and make them* all *protected too.>*

<W-What?> said Berenice, surprised. *<That's not what I meant at all! What are you talking about? Are* you *serious?>*

<Why wouldn't I be? Like, if we somehow made another little plate and made Orso swallow it, he'd be immune too. And for Gregor, we could . . . >

A silence.

<Would the twinning work on him?> asked Berenice quietly. *<Or*

would that . . . would it override our minds, to be linked with him like that?>

<I don't know.> Sancia sighed. *<What was it that you were actually going to suggest, Ber?>*

<Well . . . I originally *meant that I must still have some access to your scrived sight too,>* said Berenice. *<Which might be very useful to me now, stuck out here on the other side of these walls, far away from you, with a weapon that possibly could stop Crasedes. Though . . . I've no idea how to actually use it . . . Oh, San. What on earth are we going to do?>*

<I don't know,> said Sancia. *<But he seems to be waiting for each lexicon to get captured and converted, yeah? Like, if I was going to try to remake Valeria, I'd wait until I had every possible scrap of firepower on my side.>*

<True . . . >

<Which means each lexicon is important. And lexicons, as we know, are really vulnerable to the imperiat . . . Which is probably why he seemed really goddamn angry to find you'd stolen it . . . > An idea slowly blossomed in her mind. *<And . . . that's why Orso and I are still alive. Because he's going to torture us to make us tell him where it is.>*

<Ohhh God,> fretted Berenice. *<Oh God, oh God, oh God . . . >*

<Listen,> said Sancia. *<I think I can help you see scrivings—but that isn't going to be enough. Seeing scrivings around you isn't the same as cracking them. And sneaking into a campo, and then into a damned founder's estate . . . I mean, I don't think that's something you have a lot of experience in, yeah?>*

<No . . . > she said slowly. *<No, I am not accustomed to breaking into and out of things. What are you proposing here, exactly?>*

<I'm saying I . . . I could remotely guide you through breaking past the campo walls,> said Sancia, *<and then rescuing us—and then ruining Crasedes's plans. That's what I'm proposing.>*

There was a shocked silence.

<So—you want me to be you, *basically?>* said Berenice faintly. *<To . . . To do all the Sancia stuff you used to do? The thievery and the skulking about?>*

<Basically. Don't be too intimidated. You've already got the first step to being the old me taken care of.>

<I do?>

<Yes. You're covered in shit. Now, listen carefully . . . >

Alone and lost in the darkness of her blindfold, Sancia explained her plan to Berenice.

<*Oh my God,*> said Berenice, aghast. <*I . . . I can't.*>

<*You're going to have to.*>

<*I can't possibly do all that!*>

<*Well, if not you, then who? I sure as hell can't, not with my ass chained up in here. You know the Dandolo campo. You know what we need to do—and to make.*>

<*Yes, but . . . but you're going to need to see through my eyes, in essence!*> said Berenice. <*And though I'm capturing some of your experiences now, I'm not getting nearly as many as I did when we were in the firm together . . .*>

<*Because we're not close. So how do we get close?*>

<*Well . . . We can't, can we? Not physically, right? That's kind of the problem.*>

<*I'm not so sure it is. I'm more used to activating internal permissions and rights than you are . . . I mean, that's what my scrived sight is. It's like flexing a muscle.*> Sancia thought about it. <*Tell me what you're seeing.*>

<*What?*>

<*Just talk to me, Ber. Give me something to focus on. I can't climb inside your experiences without a handhold. What are you seeing now?*>

<*Well . . . I'm seeing the Dandolo walls.*>

<*And what are they like?*>

<*Ah, well . . . It looks like Ofelia had them extended and raised, just like the Michiels did . . . God, it's an ugly rework. I can see where they basically just plopped new masonry on the most exposed bits and then applied adhesion scrivings to them one by one. They've tried to cover up the work with banners but honestly, that's not working at all . . .*>

<*Go on. Talk about anything.*>

She sighed. <*I'm by the Carelli Square. It's practically empty. Everyone's hiding. I'm alone. It's so odd to be here now, with the stars above and the soldiers everywhere, and the world screaming, and the wall's been reworked and everything's changed . . . I used to live near this place when I was young. When carnival came, my father would let me leave my studies and go watch the parades and the floats, and then came Shorefall Night with all the dancers . . . >*

Something flickered in the darkness of Sancia's mind—a glimpse of walls, and a canal, and glints of soldiers' helmets . . .

<Keep talking,> said Sancia.

A thoughtful pause. When she spoke again, her voice was quiet and sad. *<Looking back on it, I know carnival in the Commons must have been a very shabby affair. These little parades marching through the muddy lanes . . . But to me, a little girl then, with everyone masked and the torches and the firelight . . . It seemed like some wicked but fun shadow world, with the rules all suspended for one night. And I didn't realize it, but I so hoped to get to share that with you, San. To give you carnival, to give you Shorefall. I wanted to give you all the treasures I'd had as a child, all the good bits of this city and this way of life that seem to be so long ago now . . . That's all I wanted. I just wanted to share what I had. What made me me.>*

And then Sancia saw it—just a flash, again, but then more: there was the rippling, slate-gray face of the Dandolo campo walls, and the clouds swirling across a black sky . . . and then a dark, empty Commons square, and muddy streets under flocks of floating lanterns, and the sounds of many shouts . . .

And she was there. Sancia could see it, feel it, *smell* it. It was like a juggler holding a ball in the crook of his elbow—you had to contort and flex yourself just right to hold on to it, but once you had it, it was secure.

<I think I've got it,> whispered Sancia, awed. *<I think I see what you see . . . Ber—look around.>*

Berenice did so, turning a full 360 degrees where she stood. Sancia watched, feeling disoriented and more than a little amazed as the vision in her head turned with her.

<Okay,> said Sancia. *<Yeah. I have it. Shit, this kind of makes me dizzy . . . >*

<How are you seeing this? How . . . How am I feeling you see this?>

<I don't know. It was almost too easy. I think . . . I think something's changed.>

<With our connection?>

<No,> said Sancia. *<I . . . I think our connection's changed us. But I'm not sure yet.>*

There was an anxious silence.

<*Can you figure out how to help me see scrivings?*> asked Berenice. <*Then I might be able to find a way to get past the walls.*>

<*Yeah, yeah . . . Just give me a second here, hon.*>

Sancia thought about it, puzzling over how to transfer her talents miles and miles across Tevanne. Then she had an idea.

<*You said you could feel my pain, right?*> said Sancia.

<*Yes? I mean, I can practically feel it now . . .*>

<*Okay. So if I flexed a muscle super, super hard, almost to the point of straining it—you'd feel that?*>

<*Well . . . yes? I guess?*>

<*Okay. Then that's what I'm going to do.*> Sancia took a deep breath. <*I am going to flex my scrived sight now, Ber. I'm going to flex it hard as hell, to push it to its absolute limits. And then, you try it too. And you should be able to do the same stuff I can do. Understand?*>

<*I suppose! It seems mad to think this might work, but . . .*>

<*Then stop thinking it won't! Okay?*>

<*Okay, okay!*>

<*All right. Here goes.*>

Sancia took a deep breath. She shut her eyes, and breathed deep again.

And then she flexed.

She almost groaned as the little invisible muscle inside her mind pulled taut. It felt like she was opening up her very skull, exposing her brain to the air so it could catch the scents and aromas drifting around her, but there was just so much to experience, just so much *sensation*, all of it pouring into her, pouring through her . . .

And then the vision in her mind lit up.

Berenice gasped as the world changed around her. Suddenly every sight—the walls, the gates, the lanterns above—was overlaid with the curiously wispy tangles of logic she'd seen just hours ago, back in the Foundryside offices.

But these weren't quite as bright, or strong. When Sancia had first shown scrivings to her she'd been able to understand their meaning at a glance. But now they were oddly muddled and indistinct, and she had to study each one to fully comprehend how it was persuading reality to do this or that.

<*We're too far away,*> whispered Sancia in her mind. <*But it'll have to do. Get moving! And make sure to cover the imperiat up!*>

Berenice started off down the muddy path running parallel to the walls, the cries and wailing from the Commons echoing in her ears. <*Where am I going?*> she asked. <*I thought even you couldn't get close enough to the campo walls to do anything.*>

<*Yeah, but that was before Dandolo Chartered launched a goddamn war right here in the city. Now troops have to be streaming in and out of all the gates . . .*>

<*Which means their scrived defenses have to be somewhat lowered?*>

<*I'd imagine so. You wouldn't want a soldier to forget his sachet and get all of his cohort shredded by the espringal batteries. Walk along the walls, and look up for me . . . Yeah. There. Right there, like that. God, it's so creepy with the skies so dark . . .*>

Berenice trained her eyes on the top of the campo walls as she walked down the muddy path. There was a wide canal between her and the walls, brimming with mud and refuse. Ahead was a short bridge that led to the Dandolo southwestern campo gates, which were standing open—a rare sight in Tevanne, these days—but the reason why was obvious: a full cohort of Dandolo soldiers was streaming out of the campo and headed east, doubtlessly toward the Morsinis.

<*Oh shit, I know where we are,*> said Sancia. <*Carelli Square, of course! This didn't used to be a canal . . . It used to be a drainage ditch. Why the hell did they flood this whole thing with water?*>

<*Probably because you destroyed the damn Candiano campo!*> said Berenice irritably. She was suddenly very aware of two Dandolo guards stationed at the bridge ahead glancing at her curiously.

Yet she kept her eyes fixed on the tops of the campo walls—and as she did, she got the deeply unnerving feeling of Sancia's mind *within* her own, scanning what she saw and reading things Berenice herself didn't see, and all those little revelations and patterns of thought leaking into her own consciousness . . .

<*The espringal batteries near the gates are turned off,*> said Berenice. <*Aren't they?*>

<Yeah, a few. If you walked back a couple hundred yards, you'd be in range again. It's just here that they're off, to make sure they don't accidentally kill their own soldiers.>

<Excellent. So . . . how do we use that?>

<Well. I didn't run a lot of jobs on the Dandolo campo in the old days. But when I did, and when I needed to get in, I used a scrived key I'd bought that went to a locked drainage tunnel underneath that very bridge up ahead . . . >

Berenice's gaze drifted down into the black waters in the canal—and at the little ball of locking scrivings that was probably fifteen feet below their surface.

Her stomach curdled. *<You aren't serious.>*

<Sure I am.>

<You want me to swim down there?*>*

<Yes. I don't have the key anymore, but—I mean, I bet I can pop the lock pretty quick with you, yeah?>

<And this tunnel—where does it go?> asked Berenice.

<About fifty feet past the walls, then straight up into an old well they don't even use anymore.>

<And . . . that's also filled with water?>

<I'd guess so. Why?>

<But . . . Sancia . . . > She couldn't bring herself to say it.

Yet she didn't need to—her own thoughts slipped to Sancia instantly.

<Ahhh crap,> said Sancia. *<Shit, I forgot. You can't swim.>*

<No!> said Berenice. *<I have always been a very* indoors *sort of person! And I also can't see underwater in pitch-black!>*

<That's not a problem. You can see scrivings through your eyelids, so we'll be able to see the grate to the tunnel even with your eyes closed.>

<Really?> she said, amazed.

<Yes. Trust me, it gets old.> Sancia grumbled for a moment, a cloud of irritation and frustration at the back of Berenice's mind. *<I have an idea.>*

<Yes?>

<I know how to swim. So . . . maybe . . . I can just guide you? Maybe?>

Berenice stared into the flowing dark waters, her heart jittering in her ribs. *<Are . . . Are we sure we wish to try this theory out when my very body is at stake?>*

<Listen, if you didn't think your body was going to be at stake during all the rest of this shit, I don't know what to tell you.>

Berenice fretted for a moment, trying not to listen to the fresh chorus of despairing moans from the Commons behind her. *<Ohh, fine! But how am I going to get down there without those soldiers noticing me?>*

<We need a distraction,> said Sancia, *<and the imperiat is pretty good at making those. Maybe I can help you understand what little I know about it . . . >*

Berenice turned her back on the soldiers, stepped into the shadow of an alley, and cautiously took out the imperiat. Even in the night gloom, its gold seemed to shine so brightly that it made her deeply nervous.

Yet as she studied it with both her *and* Sancia's perspectives, she suddenly began to understand it, with one lever allowing you to pick and choose which scriving you wished to dampen, and another that would determine how much you wished to dampen it . . .

Berenice stuck her head around the corner to peer at the bridge over the canal. An armored carriage was slowly rattling its way out into the Commons. *<Am I right in thinking that if we turned off the scrivings that govern the direction of that thing's wheels . . . that it would be a pretty good distraction?>*

<Sounds brilliant to me.>

Berenice looked back down at the imperiat and adjusted one lever, moving it back and forth until the little golden plate in the center of the rig displayed the strings that told a scrived carriage's wheels whether it was going up- or downhill. *<And I . . . just hit the switch?>*

<Yeah. Get ready.>

She took a breath, braced herself, and pressed the switch.

Instantly, the scrived carriage slowed . . . and then, to the tremendous alarm of all the soldiers around it, it began rolling backward, back into the Dandolo campo, as if it weren't placed on a very flat bridge over a muddy canal but was instead on a sharp incline, sloping back past the walls.

Berenice watched as the soldiers abandoned their posts and gave chase, waving their arms and helplessly screaming, "*Stop! Stop!*"

The big carriage caromed off one gate and rocketed back through the walls, out of sight.

<I hope it doesn't hurt anyone,> said Berenice.

There was a loud *crash* and a smattering of screams.

<Stop hoping for shit and get in the damned water!> said Sancia.

Berenice stowed the imperiat away, ran to the edge of the canal, and waited to confirm that the soldiers were gone. Then, with a whimper of fear and disgust, she sat down on the edge, slipped her feet in, and lowered herself into the filthy waters.

She felt her skin crawl as the water rose past her shoulders. *<Oh God,>* she said. *<What do I do?>*

<What do you do? God, hon! You take a big breath, shut your eyes, and stick your goddamn head under!>

<But . . . But . . . >

<Just do it and go before they come back!>

Berenice clamped her eyes shut and lowered herself into the fetid waters.

Sancia was right—the little bundles of logic all around them glowed even through her eyelids. But she could barely think about this with all this water around her, pressing in on her from all sides, invading every part of her—and she was just stuck there, drifting into the black, blind and helpless . . .

<Relax!> said Sancia. *<Relax, Ber. Relax, relax, relax . . . >*

She listened to Sancia's words, echoing in the depths of her thoughts.

Then she had the strangest feeling in the world.

It was as if Sancia were embracing her, enveloping her, like she was becoming lost in her mind, in her thoughts, in the way she perceived and interpreted and understood all the incoming sensory information about the world . . .

And then Berenice understood. The twinning they had applied to themselves, the tiny plates now buried in their bodies—she'd been thinking of it all this time as a connection, like a tiny tube that ran back and forth between their minds, piping in thoughts and ideas and words . . .

But that wasn't so. The connection was just the start.

A little like how Crasedes tried to use the Mountain, she thought. *The little plates in our heads are . . . reforging us. They're changing who we are, what we are.*

Berenice drifted in the water, listening to Sancia's words: <*Relax, relax, relax . . .* >

The burble of black waters. The flows and currents pulling at her skin.

I am she, Berenice thought suddenly, *and she is me.*

And suddenly she knew.

She knew how to swim, how to part the water with her cupped hands, how to kick herself forward. She knew how the water would react around her, how to feel the weak currents tugging at her body, how to ignore the bubble threading its way up one of her nostrils. She knew because she was Sancia, and Sancia was also her, and all that was one was also the other.

They turned in the waters, spied the grate at the bottom, and swam down, parting the inky black, their ears whistling and popping under the pressure, one kick after another, until their hands grasped the iron and the scrivings leapt to life in their mind . . .

< . . . *shall remain SHUT,* > said the scriving, <*shall remain CLOSED, shall adhere my surface to the frame . . . Waiting to open upon physical contact with the third, fourth, and ninth security tiles . . . Only then shall my face be parted from the frame, from the EAST marker, from the WEST mark—* >

And they knew how to open it. Of course they did. They had done this many times before, hadn't they?

If a door opens the wrong way, it doesn't count as opening . . .

The next thing they knew they were arguing with it, her mind speaking Sancia's thoughts, or her thoughts mixed with Sancia's mind: <*What if you move toward me?* >

A pause.

<*What?* > said the door, confused.

<*What if you move toward me? Would that require the security tiles?* >

<*Toward you?* >

<*Yes.* >

<*Through the east marker?* >

<*Yes.* >

<*And through the west marker?* >

<Yes. >

<All the way? >

Their lungs began to ache. How long it'd been since they'd drawn breath . . .

<Hm, > said the scriving. *<Well. All right! >*

They withdrew their hand and swam back into the black, waiting, watching . . .

The little knot of silver began to quiver, then quake. The water trembled around them, and then . . .

Snap.

The sound of it was so much louder down in the depths of this canal. They swam into the open tunnel, their fingers grasping the edges, and they pulled themselves through, their lungs burning, their head aching. They ignored it, worming themselves on and on and on, clawing their way through the darkness until their fingertips struck flat stone, and they opened their eyes in the filthy, noxious water, and they looked up and saw . . .

The stars overhead, their pale light lancing down through a narrow shaft above.

They darted up, their body turning with effortless grace, muscles flexing as they parted the waters like a hard, sharp spear, and they rose, and rose, and rose . . .

Who am I?

Another stretch of shaft, and another, their lungs screaming, their body begging for air.

I can barely remember if we were two people, or if we've always been one . . .

The stars were so close now, the surface just above.

That's it, isn't it? We aren't individuals anymore. Not anymore. There's no going back. Not from this.

They pierced the surface and gasped, their lungs rejoicing at the feel of air. They grasped the edge of the well in the courtyard, lifted themselves up, glanced around ever so briefly to confirm that they weren't being watched, and hauled themselves free of the waters.

Their legs shaking, their whole body exhausted, they sat down on the edge of the old well and stared up at the star-ridden sky— not two minds within one body, as they'd thought previously, but one mind in two bodies. They did not have to give voice to their awe, their amazement, their wonder—for it was their own. They knew their own mind. They knew what they felt.

And then, very slowly, they separated: they disentangled piece by piece, falling out of alignment, becoming two minds, two bodies, closely linked across miles and miles . . .

Berenice stared up at the stars, and somewhere, very far away, Sancia stared up at the darkness of her blindfold. Berenice let out a breath, regretting for a moment that it was only her mouth, her throat, her body that did so.

<*Whoa,*> said Sancia. <*That was . . . That was a* lot *more intense than when we first twinned ourselves . . .* >

<*Yes,*> said Berenice softly. <*I . . . I think you're right, San.*>

<*About what?*>

<*You said this connection was changing us. You were right. We thought we understood this connection, but we were really just starting. I think . . . I almost think it* has *no boundaries.*>

They sat in awed silence as they tried to recover.

<*We must get to work, my love,*> whispered Sancia.

<*I know. I will.*>

Dripping wet, she slipped off into the streets of the Dandolo campo—a place she'd known for many years, one that should have been deeply familiar to her; and yet now she passed through the streets under strange skies, peering out through alien eyes.

<*Whatever happens,*> said Berenice, <*I don't want to lose this.*>

<*Because together,*> said Sancia, <*we are unstoppable?*>

<*No. Because together, we are one.*>

Between Berenice's knowledge of the campo and Sancia's scrived sight and thieving instincts, there was no door or boundary or barrier that could hold them back, no soldier or guard who spied anything more of them than a hint of shadow or a wet footprint. Within minutes they'd acquired four scrived keys, two sachets, one scrived dagger, and one fire starter, and then they were shooting through the veins and capillaries of the campo like a blot of poison speeding toward a beating heart.

Berenice knew where she was going. She knew all the scriving workshops on the Dandolo campo, but only one would do for her work tonight: the Hypatus Building. The place where she and Orso had labored for years, dreaming up mad solutions to impossible problems.

She quietly slipped through the inner enclave gates, the guards barely paying attention to her: her sachet worked, after all, and the black skies made it hard to care about a wet girl in rather shabby Commons clothes.

No dreaming up solutions tonight, thought Berenice as she wove through the alleys. She spied the peaked roofs of the Hypatus Building just ahead. *I know what I need to make. How fast I shall have to work . . .*

She approached the Hypatus Building. She did not know much about scaling walls, but as she peered at the building with Sancia's sight the knowledge blossomed in her mind, and she knew the second floor had the least defensive wards prepared against intruders.

She approached the wall, placed a hand against its stone, and all of Sancia's experiences about infiltration and evasion poured into her thoughts.

<*Your hands aren't strong,*> whispered Sancia. <*Nor is the rest of you, to be frank. So this is the best route to take . . .* >

Berenice grabbed the edge of the first-floor window and hauled herself up, her toes expertly parsing the gaps in the bricks, her fear of heights suddenly vanishing.

She clambered up, ignoring the pain in her fingers and the webbing of her hand, and placed her palm to the window. Its scrived wards were nothing to her will, to her knowledge of their logic, and she batted them away like they were moss, opened the window, and slipped inside.

She studied the floors around her, reading the scriving—their logic, their placement, their interrelationships. She spied the workshop within seconds, and then the stairs down to it, and she started off, weaving through the darkened halls of the Hypatus Building . . .

<*I guess when the skies turn off like an aging lamp and the world fills up with screams,*> whispered Sancia's voice, <*no one wants to stick around to meet production deadlines . . .* >

Berenice smirked as she penetrated deeper into the floors of the building, growing closer and closer to the workshop. Finally she came to the shop doors, and she crouched and cracked the door open slowly, peering through.

High, rounded windows, the faint starlight streaming through. Tables and bowls and lenses and shelves full of designs.

She opened the door, slipped inside, and shut it behind her.

<We're in.>

She slowly turned around, her eyes dancing over all the components and modules and half-finished rigs that lay scattered about the workshop. They'd labored in Foundryside for so long, with such small budgets and such a paucity of resources, that to see this was like stumbling across a golden hoard in the street.

<You know what we need,> whispered Sancia.

<Yes.>

<Crasedes has built a forge that relies upon all the lexicons of the city.>

<Yes.>

<So we take the weapon that can kill almost any lexicon . . . >

Berenice picked up a stylus. *<And we bring it to every lexicon we can.>*

<Right. We're like Clef—inside this giant rig, tearing it to pieces from the inside out . . . >

<How much time do we have?> asked Berenice.

<I've no idea. So work fast.>

Berenice rapidly assembled her workstation—the plating, metals, bowls, styli, and components she'd need to create her masterwork tonight. Then she turned on a scrived lamp, put on her magnifying goggles, and set to work on the first and perhaps most critical of tools.

A small knife, its blade hardly bigger than a coin. Yet engraved upon it, in the tiniest print possible, would be the very commands that had turned Sancia's and Berenice's minds into one.

But soon, Berenice thought as she began, *we will be three.*

As she worked, and designed, and built, and labored over each set of sigils and strings—most of which were simply an implausible number of construction scriving plates—Berenice found her mind turning to Clef. To the way his tooth felt in her hand, to the tiny hierophantic commands engraved on his shaft, to the way his voice had whispered merrily in her ear as she worked . . .

Then she realized. These were not her thoughts.

<*Why are you thinking of Clef, my love?*> asked Berenice as she carefully wrote another sigil on a small wooden box she was assembling.

<*Hm?*> said Sancia. <*Oh. I was just thinking of how Crasedes reacted when he got Clef back. It was strange. He was triumphant, certainly, but . . .* >

The moment flashed in Berenice's mind, even though she hadn't been there to witness it: Crasedes holding Clef high, his body fixed in a posture of indescribable joy . . .

<*He was very . . .* emotional,> Berenice said.

Another memory flashed in Berenice's mind: the one of Valeria's that Sancia had caught when she'd first found her hiding in the lexicon. The vision of the man wrapped in black, and the boy dying on the bed, while Valeria looked on . . .

Valeria's voice whispering to the weeping man: *There is only one way to save him.*

And him shrieking back: *Look what it did to you!*

How anguished he'd sounded, how devastated.

Berenice paused in her work and slowly put down her stylus.

<*And you think you know why he was so emotional,*> she said. <*Don't you?* >

There was a long silence.

<*Yeah,*> said Sancia darkly. <*I think I do. I think I know why Crasedes is so convinced mankind is broken. And I think I know why he's willing to help Ofelia Dandolo, of all people. Because if what I saw is true, then . . .* >

<*You think Crasedes was the man in the cave, wrapped in black,*> said Berenice. <*And Clef . . . Clef was the boy dying on the bed.* >

<*Yes.* >

<*You think Clef might actually be Crasedes's* child. *And making him the key might have been the way he saved him . . .* >

<*Yeah,*> said Sancia. <*Because by turning him into the key, he'd have made him immortal. Maybe that's why he never wanted to talk about him. And that'd be why he's always tried to get him* back. *It's not just because he's useful—it's because Clef is his* son.>

Berenice considered this for a moment, horrified. *<But didn't Clef look like a grown man when you saw him, inside the key?>*

<Yeah. He said time passed slower inside the key—but he didn't say it stopped. Maybe four thousand years to us is just forty, to him.> She sighed again. *<I don't know. I'm not sure. But Crasedes isn't some corrupt wizard looking to rule the world. He's a true believer. He's a* zealot. *And zealots aren't born, they're made. I just wonder what could have made him to be like thi—>*

There was the sound of a *crack* from nearby. Berenice jumped and whirled about, eyes scanning the workshop . . .

But she was alone. The room was dark. No one had come.

Then she realized.

She heard a low, rich, smooth voice uncoiling in her ear, "Ahh . . . Sancia. You're awake. Very good!"

"Oh shit," whispered Berenice.

<Ah, shit,> said Sancia.

Sancia heard Orso moan in pain, and then felt the nausea in her stomach rise to a boil as Crasedes drew close.

"It gives me no joy to see you like this, you know," said his voice quietly. "I was telling you the truth. I wished to have you by my side, Sancia."

"God Almighty," said Sancia. "Why not just finish your awful magics and *make* me, when you control all my choices?"

"You know just as well as I do that a command is not the same as a choice," said Crasedes. There was a twitch at the side of her face, like a moth fluttering at her cheek, and she felt her skin stretch curiously, all of the flesh there slowly shifting . . .

He's bending the gravity right next to my goddamn face.

The blindfold fell away. She looked up, squinting, the weak light of a nearby lantern as bright as the sun in her eyes—and then she saw him, sitting cross-legged in the air, hands on his knees, the eyes of his black mask fixed on her.

He really has turned the world to midnight, she thought, watching him. *So now he's at his most powerful, all the time . . .*

"But there are still choices before you, Sancia," said Crasedes.

"Think you can torture me into telling you where the imperiat is?" said Sancia. "I told you, asshole, I don't know."

"Oh, I don't think I need to *torture* you," said Crasedes. "You simply don't understand all the nuances of your situation. When that becomes clear . . . I've no doubt I'll win your favor."

"I wouldn't be so sure of that, you piece of shi—"

"Yes, yes." Crasedes crooked his finger. There was a *crunk* sound as the table she was strapped to apparently separated from its base, and her belly swooped uncomfortably as the whole apparatus rose up to float in the air.

"Ordinarily, I'd just use Clef to take you there," he said with a sigh. "But since the construct has altered you so . . . that simply isn't an option. In this case, I resort to less elegant solutions." He looked over his shoulder. "You too, Orso. You'd better come as well."

Sancia still couldn't turn her head to see, but she saw movement out of the corner of her eye. Then a large wooden chair floated up into the air beside her, and sitting in it was Orso, a ball of rags stuffed and tied into his mouth.

Yet he looked so different. So pale, so sweaty, so miserable.

Her eye fell on the browning bandages at his shoulder, and the way his chest heaved with each breath . . .

She felt Berenice gasp at the sight. *<He's sick!>* she cried. *<He's dying!>*

<I know.>

<We've got to get him help!>

<I know, I know, but—>

The table pivoted in the air, then floated after Crasedes as he turned and drifted out the door. "After me, children," he said.

Sancia suppressed an involuntary scream of fright as they rose over the Dandolo gardens. Yet as they did, she finally got to see what had happened to the city since her capture.

A sprawling ramble of towers and walls, white and ghostly in the queer starlight from the black skies. All the floating lanterns were like tiny, warm campfires scattered among a vast, dark forest. And there was so much smoke, so much dust, for so many of the warrens and campo neighborhoods appeared to be aflame, and the night sky was bright and ringing with countless screams . . .

The city has been driven mad, she thought. *The city is a body, and he its disease—and soon it will die.*

She watched as the face of the Dandolo estate swam up to her, the doors of the upper balcony open and waiting for them.

She felt an immense dread well up within her as they approached the open balcony. <*Berenice!*> she cried. <*Just finish the work! Ignore whatever happens to me and finish the work!*>

Berenice slipped out the side door of the Hypatus Building and turned the corner, hugging close to the side of the building. With every step she took, the pack of gear on her back clinked and clanked and rattled.

So much made so quickly, she thought. *I hope it works.*

But she knew it would. Most of them were just construction scriving plates, along with a trigger she'd made for them. Those would be useful—because if all went correctly tonight, then soon construction scrivings would be the only ones that would work at all in the Dandolo enclave.

The rest, of course, were quite more complicated. But it didn't matter. When she and Sancia worked together, their rigs were practically flawless. The real problem was going to be getting it all where it needed to be in time.

She walked along the carriage stalls situated next to the Hypatus Building, studying each one. She had checked out the hypatus carriages a number of times in her former life here—mostly to ferry Orso about—and she knew the system quite well. Well enough that she'd remembered where the safe full of carriage sachets was kept, and how to break into it.

She found her carriage, climbed into the cockpit, and gently adjusted the acceleration lever, the wood worn smooth by the grip of countless scrivers before her.

The old carriage creaked to life. She carefully backed out of the stall, turned the wheel, and rattled off into the pitch-black streets of the inner Dandolo enclave.

35

G regor Dandolo watched himself from a place far behind his eyes.

He was standing in a darkened room that was quite familiar to him: he remembered the maps on the walls, the old threadbare bedspread, the bear rug that someone had gifted to him after a trip to the north . . .

His old room. He remembered now. How many nights had he slept here, staring up at the ceiling? And then he remembered Domenico—one of the few solid memories he still had of him—his brother sitting on his bed, reading a book of poetry, and saying aloud: *You ought to be the warrior, Gregor. I much prefer words to weapons . . .*

How his hands had gripped the narrow tome. Soft hands with long fingers, the hands of a boy.

The hand extending from the shadows, bloodied and trembling. *Gregor? Gregor, are you near?*

"I kept it just the way you'd left it," said his mother's voice from beside him. "I kept it just the way it was, in case you ever came back."

Gregor stood there, staring out at his room, not moving, not speaking. After all, she had not given him any command.

His mother came into view, still wearing the same clothes from the night before. She looked very old, and very tired, and it was clear she'd been crying.

"I remember how you'd hide under the covers of your bed when your father and I fought," she said weakly. "I'd come up after a row with him and find you shivering under the blankets. I doubt if you remember that now. He said you'd lose some memories when we . . . When . . ." She trailed off and sighed. "Do you remember this place, Gregor?" she asked.

He said nothing.

"I . . . I command you to answer. Tell me the truth. Do you remember?"

"Yes," he whispered. To speak aloud felt like he had to dig every syllable from the depths of his belly.

She swallowed, staring hungrily into his face. "Gregor, my love . . . are . . . are you *happy* to be back?"

Another whisper: "No."

She looked away, her breath whistling in her nostrils. "If only you knew . . . I mean, do you *realize* what I did to bring you back, Gregor? Do you know what I had to do? Do you *know* what I've done?"

Another whisper: "Yes."

She looked back at him, surprised. Clearly she had not expected a response. "You do?"

"Yes."

"You . . . You can't. What do you think you know, Gregor?"

"I . . . know that . . . you killed my father," he whispered, staring into space. He felt tears running down his cheeks, felt his fingernails biting into the palms of his hands. "I know . . . the carriage crash was . . . your sabotage. And I know that . . . that you did not intend for . . . Domenico or me to be on board, but . . . you killed us. You killed us both. You . . . killed your children."

"No!" she cried. "I . . . I didn't! I fought to save you, I did so *much* to secure your life! Don't you realize that?"

"This . . . is not life," he said, staring into her face now. "This is not *life*. This control. This choicelessness. This is not life."

She was weeping now. "It's not true. You have lived. You've loved. I've bought you that. I . . . I've given you that, haven't I?"

"I thought I'd . . . found it," he said. "Thought I had found a . . . cause. A family. But I did not realize that . . . I was still a lie. Still your . . . slave. I am alone. I was never . . . one of them."

She turned to the window, sobbing, and stared out at the dark, spectral cityscape of Tevanne, smoking and burning and moaning under this endless midnight.

"I'm done," she said. "I'm *done*. This is not how I wanted you returned to me. This is not what I wanted the city to be. So . . . I release you," she whispered. "Awake now. Awake, my love."

Gregor blinked slowly, but did nothing else.

She drew back. "Gregor? I . . . I release you. Awake. Awake *now!*"

Still he did nothing.

"What's wrong?" she asked. "Why can't you . . . Why can't you be released of your bindings?"

"Because," he whispered, "I am bound to the will of the Maker. He has granted you some permissions—but not all. And you are not the Maker."

She cursed loudly, walked over to his bed, and sat down with her face buried in her hands. She sat there for a long while, shoulders shaking as she cried. Then she looked up and said, "I will fix you, Gregor. I *will* return you to what you were. I *will* make you free again." She sniffed loudly. "Do you believe me?"

He whispered: "No."

She stared at him for a long, long time. Then she stood and, with the air of someone deep in shock, she shambled out the door and down the hall, and Gregor was alone in his room.

He stood there, and he felt his mind recede back into the in-between place, the no-place his mind went when he had no command to follow.

But before it subsumed him, he remembered suddenly: *I have something in my pocket.*

The box.

Yes. He'd forgotten.

Then he was lost again.

36

I apologize for the state of things," said Crasedes as Sancia and Orso helplessly floated into the ballroom. "I suppose, really, it's like every other project anyone ever undertook—everything takes just a *bit* longer than you'd expected . . ."

They drifted down toward what looked like the main wing of the ballroom. Sancia couldn't turn her head to look to see, but she thought she spied the old Foundryside lexicon standing there on the checked tiles . . . yet next to it was something bizarre. Something *monstrous.* It was like the skeleton of a foundry lexicon, a huge contraption nearly fifty feet long, set behind a dome of thick, green glass—yet so many of the critical components had been removed . . .

"Here we are," purred Crasedes. He drifted down to the skeletal behemoth, gestured with a hand, and lightly placed Sancia's table on the floor with Orso's chair just next to it. "The center of reality, for a moment."

Sancia quickly flexed her scrived sight and studied the beast of a lexicon before her. It was immensely difficult to untangle what she was seeing. She'd never before seen such a dense, impossibly complex structure of logic and commands . . .

But she saw how it worked. And so did Berenice.

<*Tribuno's definition is in there,*> she said. <*Which means Valeria doesn't have it—which means she's powerless.*>

<*Worse than powerless.*> Sancia narrowed her eyes, studying the many strange commands flowing throughout the monstrous lexicon. <*He's using the damned thing to assert that Valeria doesn't exist.*>

<*And since it's twinned with so many lexicons out in the city . . .*> said Berenice.

<*Yes,*> said Sancia. <*All of Tevanne is to Valeria like a lake of lava to a river toad. She must be in incredible pain . . .*>

Orso shouted something, but since he was gagged it was utterly inaudible.

"Eh?" Crasedes said. "Ah. Right." He flicked a hand at him, and the cords holding the gag in place snapped.

Orso spat the gag out. It was much bigger than Sancia had expected, and for a moment he just sat there, gagging and trying not to vomit. "What . . . What the hell is going on?" he said. "What is this damned thing?"

"This is where it all begins," said Crasedes, gesturing at the lexicon. "Where the human species enters its next, and possibly final, phase."

"Very nice," he panted. "Then why not just do it? Why not goddamned get it over with?"

Crasedes's blank, black mask swiveled to face Sancia. "Sancia knows. Doesn't she?"

"No," she said. "I don't know what you're talking about."

"I doubt that." He drifted closer to her. "Tell me—where is the imperiat?"

"I told you, I don't know where the hell it is," snapped Sancia.

"If you're trying to use it to free the construct, I assure you, it'll backfire," said Crasedes. "She has no interest in your well-being, or your city's—as I've told you all along."

"I know if Valeria was free and strong," said Sancia, "the first goddamned thing she'd do is kill *you*. Which I'm not exactly opposed to."

"She cannot harm me—not while I have Clef," he said. "But regardless, you should be opposed to it. I'm by far the better option."

"*How?*" said Orso. "You say you're better, but you're the dumb son of a bitch who made her in the first place!"

"That's not *quite* accurate," said Crasedes. "But . . . I didn't bring you here for another debate." He drifted backward, toward the skeletal lexicon behind him. "I brought you here for a spilling of *secrets*." He pivoted smoothly in the air and adjusted one of the switches on the lexicon's wall. "For so many have been withheld from you . . ."

There was a shiver in the air. Something inside of Sancia's head tremored unpleasantly: it was like she was exiting some kind of massive cavern, and all the pressure of the skies above suddenly came pouring down on her . . .

The Foundryside lexicon appeared to flicker strangely. No, she thought, that wasn't quite it—something in *front* of it was flickering . . . or perhaps it was some*one*.

And she was there, kneeling before the shabby little Foundryside lexicon . . .

"Valeria," whispered Sancia.

She looked terrible—even worse than Orso. White threads of smoke uncoiled from her innards, and the air seemed silvery and shimmery around her, like her very body was giving off immense amounts of heat. Her armor was blistered and rusting on her right side, her right hand had been crushed to pieces, and the immense golden mask that formed her face was cracked and splintering. Her left eye still glowed with a cold, golden light, but the right one was gaping and dark, as if someone had fired a cannonball through it.

"Shit," wheezed Orso. "What happened to you, girl?"

"Oh, it's very unpleasant to have all of reality suddenly nullify your very existence," said Crasedes. "Even when you're bound to such a dingy old rig like this. I should know. She did something similar to me, once . . ."

Trembling, Valeria lifted her ruined head until she looked into his cold, blank mask.

"Now that you've formally joined us," said Crasedes, "why don't you go ahead and tell them? Tell them what you intended to do when you were freed."

Valeria said nothing.

"I bet you told them you were just interpreting my commands in a very *unusual* way," he said. "Something about destroying yourself—because you were, after all, a tool whose purpose was to ensure no human being ever misused a tool again . . . It makes sense, yes?"

Still, she said nothing.

"Come now, why hide it?" asked Crasedes. "You always seemed to think your solution perfectly reasonable. You yourself said it was the most just of all options. Why hide it now, of all times?"

The ballroom was silent for a long, long time.

"Valeria?" asked Sancia.

Valeria looked up at her. She seemed to think for a moment. Then she slowly sat up, her vast, golden, smoking body still positioned close to the Foundryside lexicon, until she sat cross-legged in a position of complete composure.

Then she calmly said, *"I would undo it. I would undo it all."*

Another silence. Orso and Sancia stared at her, waiting for more.

"Undo what, Construct?" Crasedes asked. "Keep going."

"I would undo all the things you have ever done, Maker," she said. *"All the commands. All the bindings. All the alterations, all the changes. I'd unmake it all, all of them, all at once."*

"Good," he said. "Thank you for your honesty. But you wouldn't stop there—would you?"

"No."

"Of course not. But don't tell it to me, tell it to them."

Valeria turned her marred face to Sancia. *"I would undo all the scrivings,"* she said simply. *"All of them. All that had been wrought by all of mankind . . . I would destroy them."*

"W-What?" said Orso, stunned. "You'd . . . You'd eliminate scriving *itself*?"

"True," she said. Her voice was eerily calm. *"All the alterations any human had ever wrought, I would untangle them, untie them, unmake them all. From the smallest scriving to the greatest warping, I would unravel them all. And then I would wipe this talent from the minds of all humankind. Just as I stole the ritual from the mind of the Maker. I would purge the knowledge of scriving from the human race. And only then—finally—would I truly destroy myself."*

Sancia stared at her, horrified. She had suspected from the beginning that Valeria had been hiding something, some greater plot or plan. But to be hiding *this . . .* this mad ambition to end the very practice that formed the foundation of their civilization . . .

<*Sancia,*> said Berenice softly. <*Does this change the plan at all?*>

Sancia shook herself. <*No. Keep going.*>

"But . . . so many people rely on scrivings," Orso said. "Just to live their lives . . ."

"Buildings," said Sancia faintly. "Ships. Irrigation . . . I mean, that would kill . . ."

"Yes, how many *would* it kill, Construct?" said Crasedes. "I think you did the math . . ."

"Six million, three hundred and twenty-eight thousand, five hundred people," she said. *"Across all the realms of humankind. That is my estimation."*

"God Almighty," said Orso. "*Why?* Why not . . . Why not just kill Crasedes and let us be?"

"Because I can't," she said simply. *"Because I am bound to my commands. Because I am bound to ensure mankind can never use its brilliance to harm itself again."*

"But it's not just that, is it?" asked Crasedes. "Even if you didn't have these commands . . ."

"True," she said. *"I know the hearts of men. I know that so long as humankind possesses a power, they will always,* always *use it to rule the powerless. And there is no alteration, no scriving, no command that either I or the Maker could ever wield that would burn this impulse out of you. Better to destroy what power you have."* She turned her face back to look down at Crasedes where he floated. *"You should not be capable of such things. This shouldn't exist. None of this should exist. I shouldn't exist."*

"You'd . . . You'd plunge us all into a goddamned dark age!" said Orso.

"Better to live and die like animals in the wild," she said indifferently, *"than build your castles with the cruel tools of torture. Only then would you be free."* She looked at Sancia. *"You, and Gregor . . . All others whose minds might be ruled by bindings and commands . . . This is the* only *way you'd ever be truly free. The only way."*

There was a long silence as Orso and Sancia grappled with this revelation.

<The first box is in place,> whispered Berenice in her ear. *<Should have the next one ready in minutes.>*

<Thank God. Hurry. This is all getting madder with every second.>

<I am, my love.>

Crasedes slowly turned to face Sancia. "Do you see why I still await your choice?" he asked. "*I* would allow you to keep your civilization. Your cities, your ships, your buildings . . . All of that would stay standing. It would just have to be conducted a bit more . . . morally. The last problem, finally solved. Help me. Tell me where the imperiat is. Help me end this now."

Sancia sat in silence for a long while, wondering how to buy time.

"It would be," said Crasedes, "as simple as flipping a switch on that wall over there." He gestured toward the lexicon's wall. "With the slightest nudge, I can turn this city into a bright, hot foundry and remake the construct into something beneficial, into something *wonderful.* But I have waited over a thousand years to do this, Sancia. That's a long time, even for me. I won't risk what I've worked so long to build when I know the imperiat still poses a threat."

Sancia felt nauseous at the idea that all Crasedes had to do was to flip a switch on the lexicon's wall to remake creation itself—and that her gambit was the only thing keeping him from doing it.

<Berenice?> she said. *<Status?>*

<Finished with the second, and starting the third.>

Sancia looked at Crasedes, her eyes hard and her jaw set. "No," she said.

He cocked his head. "No?"

"No," she snapped. "No, I'm not going to goddamned help you. Eat shit, you goddamned ghoul. I don't know where it is, and even if I did, I wouldn't tell you."

"Even after hearing the construct's confession?"

"You want me to make this a choice between you and her," she said. "But I'm not having it. There's hardly any difference between the two of you."

Crasedes looked at her for a while, and then finally sighed. "Well. I *had* thought this might be difficult, so . . . that's why I brought Orso here."

Sancia felt her breath catch in her throat. She and Orso stared at each other, terrified.

She frantically tried to remember the last hours. *Did I tell him about Berenice? Did I tell him she had the imperiat?*

Crasedes floated close to Orso and peered into his eyes. "How are you doing tonight, Orso?" he asked softly. "I admit, you don't look terribly good . . ."

"Get the hell away from me!" cried Orso.

"I'm afraid I can't. Now, Orso . . ." Crasedes's voice gained a queer, deep resonance, one that made Sancia feel like her bones had turned to butter. "Tell me—do you know where the imperiat is?"

Orso shivered and shuddered. Then he shut his eyes as hard as he could and thrashed about like a man in a bad dream before finally crying, "*N-No! I don't!*"

"I see," said Crasedes. He turned to look at Sancia. "But—do you know *who* has the imperiat, Orso?"

Shit, thought Sancia.

Orso ripped his head back, smashing the back of his skull against the chair, his teeth gritted and his eyes twisted in anguish. Finally he screamed, "*Yes!*"

"Yes, you do?"

"*Yes! Yes, I do!*"

<*Shit!*> said Berenice. <*What do we do?*>

<*There's nothing to do,*> said Sancia. <*Keep following the plan!*>

<*What if he tells him we're twinned, and I'm hearing everything he says?*>

<*Then we'll deal with it! Just keep going! Plant the final box and get in position!*>

"Who has it, Orso?" said Crasedes gently. "Tell me. Now."

Orso screamed, a ragged, miserable, self-hating cry, like he was trying to exhaust himself rather than give this up to Crasedes. But it did not matter, in the end.

"*Berenice!*" he sobbed. "*It's Berenice! Berenice has it, I think!*"

"You . . . think?"

"*Yes!* I . . . I don't know, but . . ."

"But you assume." Crasedes nodded, satisfied. "I see."

There was a long silence.

"And . . . who is Berenice?" asked Crasedes, sounding a bit puzzled.

"She's Sancia's girlfriend," said Orso, weeping.

"Ahh!" said Crasedes. "I see. But . . . you don't know where she is."

"No . . ."

"Does Sancia know?"

"Yes," he sobbed. "She does."

<Almost done!> whispered Berenice in her ear.

"Hm! I see." Crasedes turned his black mask on her. "I just assume you're not going to tell me where your girlfriend is," he asked, resigned, "are you, Sancia?"

"I sure as shit am not," said Sancia.

Crasedes sighed. "Very well. In that case . . ." He flicked a finger. The ceiling trembled, and a long, thin iron nail suddenly punched through the plaster to hover above him, the pointed end focused on Sancia. "I must resort to less reasonable methods."

<San!> said Berenice in her ear. *<You . . . You can't let him . . . >*

<Stick with the plan,> said Sancia. *<The plan will work!>*

The nail drifted closer to her. She tried to ignore it, but she couldn't stop gazing at its point, which still bore the dust of old wood on its rippled surface.

<But San . . . >

<Do it!>

The nail turned slowly in the air, like the bit of a drill.

"I don't want to do this," said Crasedes softly.

The nail floated closer. Its point was now just inches away from her eye.

"Oh God," she whispered. "Oh God . . ." She tried to think of something to say, anything. "She . . . She hid it!" she said desperately.

He stopped circling her. "This Berenice hid the imperiat? Where?"

"Under the bridge behind our firm!" she said. "The one running over the ditch!"

Crasedes looked at her for a moment. Then he turned to Orso and said, "Orso—do you think she's telling the truth?"

<*Oh son of a bitch,*> said Sancia.

"N-No," Orso said weakly.

Crasedes sighed. "I must admit," he said, "it's frustrating . . . I keep giving people opportunities to save themselves, and they just keep rejecting me." He tutted very quietly. "Oh, well . . ."

The nail drifted to the left, to float before her left hand.

"I know who you are!" she cried.

"Pardon me?" he asked.

"I . . . I know why you were looking for Clef! Why you wanted him back *so* badly!"

He looked at her sharply. "What are you talking about?"

"I saw a memory of Valeria's," she said. "A weeping man, begging for a way to save his dying son. I know what you did to save him. I know what sins you've committed, first of all hierophants."

There was a long silence.

Crasedes leaned forward. "She remembers that?" he said softly.

"You think you're so special," said Sancia. "But underneath it all, you're just a dying old man trying to make up for all his mistakes. There's nothing special about you, you bastard."

He seemed to relax a little. "An *old* man? Well. Sancia . . . You know, I'm not sure you saw what you thought you saw." He leaned close, and whispered, "I know why he liked you, by the way."

"W-What?" asked Sancia.

"A slave, a child, desperate and hungry and alone," whispered Crasedes. "I've no doubt he would have loved nothing more than to save you. But he can't save you now. He was never terribly good at saving people, anyway . . . That was always up to me."

He waved a hand.

The nail hurtled forward so fast Sancia couldn't even see it move. The next thing she knew there was a loud, wooden *thunk*, and her left hand erupted in pain, and she was screaming.

Her back arched and her legs strained as she screamed in agony. It was hard to move her head, so she couldn't quite see the damage, but she could spy the head of the nail sticking out of the palm of her left hand, and she could feel blood dribbling out of her palm to patter on the floor below . . .

<*Sancia!*> cried Berenice in her mind. <*Sancia, are . . . are you . . .* >

<*I'm . . . fine!*> she shouted back, gritting her teeth. <*I'm fine! Just . . . Just focus on getting back here!*>

"There are rather a lot of nails in the walls here," said Crasedes. "And I don't have much patience left. Where is the imperiat, Sancia?"

Sancia breathed deeply, trying to ignore the throbbing, aching pain that was now seeping up her left arm.

Another nail came out of the wall—but this one suddenly grew bright and hot, and it burst apart into a cloud of burning fragments, which circled like a tiny, broiling constellation. "Tell me where this Berenice is, and I can make all this stop."

Sancia gasped in pain. Each time she twitched she could feel the nail grinding in her hand.

<*Done! On my way back!*> said Berenice.

The cloud of hot fragments grew closer. Sancia growled and turned her face away, but she could feel the heat radiating off of them, trickling over her skin, singeing her hair . . .

She braced herself, waiting for them to begin burning into her flesh.

Yet . . . they didn't seem to come any closer.

"Hum," said Crasedes, sounding disappointed. "You really aren't going to tell me, are you?"

Sancia kept her eyes shut and her face turned away, unwilling to move for fear her face might graze them. But then the heat receded, and she cracked an eye and saw the burning fragments were slowly withdrawing.

"Well," said Crasedes. "It's frustrating. But—there's always a workaround." He turned back to Orso. "Orso—if you were to *guess* at what this Berenice was going to do with the imperiat . . . what would you say?"

<*SHIT!*> said Sancia.

<*I'm almost there!*> cried Berenice. <*I'm almost there!*>

Orso trembled, shook, and writhed in his chair, gasping miserably as he fought against Crasedes's will.

"Tell me," said Crasedes. "Now."

Tears poured out of Orso's eyes. "I . . . I . . ."

"Orso . . ." said Crasedes, leaning closer. "It's quite remarkable that you're resisting this much, but . . . You must tell me."

"I think that . . ." he whispered. "I think that they . . . they . . ."

<*Do it now!*> screamed Sancia at Berenice. <*Just do it now!*>

<*I'm not there yet!*>

<*Just do it now or else he'll figure it out and ruin everything!*>

<*Fine!*> cried Berenice.

"Orso . . ." said Crasedes. "I know you know the words. Now you simply have to . . . say them."

"I think," said Orso swallowing, "that they have made a—"

<*Hold on!*> screamed Berenice.

And then everything around them began to shake.

Berenice dashed out of her carriage, knelt in the alley beyond the Dandolo estate, and placed a dull-looking wooden box on the ground before her.

Then she took out the imperiat, and concentrated very hard as she adjusted it to focus on one specific sigil string: the command for the assertion of distance, which would permit a lexicon to know what was close and what wasn't.

Killing this command would cause a lexicon to grow confused, since it would contain thousands of commands about how reality was supposed to be altered nearby—yet it would suddenly be unsure as to what "nearby" actually *meant*. In a matter of seconds, the lexicon's fail-safes would be triggered, and it would shut down all nonessential commands: in other words, everything except the stuff that kept any buildings standing.

Berenice braced herself, took a breath, and pushed the button on the side of the imperiat.

This did nothing, of course—for Berenice was not actually close to any lexicon. She was instead kneeling in a rather dirty alley on the other side of Ofelia Dandolo's gardens.

Then she whispered, "Please work." She opened the scrived wooden box on the ground, popped the imperiat in, shut the lid, and activated the scrivings on the box.

This box was a crude, miniature version of Orso's classic method of twinning reality—which meant that when she placed the imperiat in the box, its twin also believed it contained the imperiat, as well as the command it was issuing out to the world.

And since this twinned box had been planted nearly a half mile away, beside one of the biggest foundries close to the Dandolo estate, this meant she had just instantly killed the giant lexicon located within it.

There was a quake in the air. Some of the buildings around her shook unpleasantly, and the scrived lamps flickered as if they'd suddenly become confused. She cringed—but, to her relief, nothing failed or fell apart.

She stood and looked across the city, toward the foundry she'd just killed. She couldn't see the building itself, of course, but she could see the sky above it. And since she'd killed it, she'd also eliminated all of the commands that Crasedes had been feeding into it—including the command for eternal night.

The sky above the foundry suddenly turned lighter, shifting from inky black to a dark purple—as did the sky just beyond it, like the illumination in the skies was extending outward toward the edge of the city in a wave, growing slightly fainter the farther it went.

Like the spokes of a wheel, all gathering at the center here, she thought, turning back to the Dandolo estate. *But I just broke one big damned spoke.* She took out a rapier. *Let's hope the rest of this goes so well.*

The grand ballroom shook strangely, a quiver in the walls and floor that made all the glass from the broken windows tinkle and dance.

Crasedes leaned back from Orso. "What?" he said. "What was *that?*"

He looked around as the quake grew, and then receded. Then he flitted over to the broken windows and peered out at the city . . .

. . . and though Sancia wasn't sure, she thought she could see the sky lightening faintly out there—still night, just a different time of night.

Crasedes stared at it. Then he slowly turned back to look at her. "What . . . What have you *done?*"

"I didn't do shit," she said. "But I guess you know where the imperiat is now, yeah?"

He looked back out at the mottled sky. "What *is* this? What are you doing?"

"Nothing. My ass is still strapped to this goddamn table. But I'm guessing Berenice found a way into the enclave, and she's running around out there using the imperiat to kill your lexicons. That's what I'd do. I guess you can either sit in here and watch as she tears your big, distributed rig to pieces, or you can go look for her yourself. Your choice."

Crasedes stared out at the city for a moment longer. Then, trembling with rage, he pulled Clef out of his cloak.

Yet then he froze. He looked at Sancia over his shoulder. "You . . . You *want* me to leave. Don't you?"

Sancia said nothing.

Crasedes stewed for a moment. Then he took a breath, and when he spoke again, his voice was tremendously loud. "*GREGOR!*" he bellowed. "*TO ME, TO ME!*"

Good, thought Sancia. *The next bit's done.*

"Still you defend her," he spat at Sancia. "Still you make yourself her tool."

"This has shit-all to do with Valeria," said Sancia.

"You still have *no idea* what she is, or . . . or even what she's done to you!"

"What do you mean?"

"You think you could become an editor, and there'd be no consequences?" he said. "That the construct could bless you with such powerful permissions, and you'd pay no price? Are you mad, Sancia? Are you *stupid?*"

Sancia was silent. She heard the sounds of footfalls in the hall outside, and knew Gregor was nearby.

"It takes *life* to earn the privileges you wield!" said Crasedes. "The blurring of the boundaries between life and death! You always, *always* pay a price. I had to do a *lot* of work to prevent them from impacting Gregor—that's practically why I altered his time in the first place. But for you . . ."

Sancia remembered what Crasedes had told her, deep in the Mountain:

. . . she's sacrificing you, right now. Just very, very slowly.

"What do you mean?" said Sancia again, quietly.

"Aren't you feeling so *old* recently, Sancia?" Crasedes asked. "Don't you feel so *tired*, so *worn*? More gray hairs, more wrinkles, more aches and pains? I mean . . . you know why, don't you?"

Sancia felt a dull horror boiling in her stomach. For what he said was true. She did feel older than she thought she ought to. She'd felt this way for a long time, but she'd always thought it was an effect of her hard life.

"That's why we didn't use this technique much, back in my day," said Crasedes savagely. "People who aren't quite sacrificed, but aren't quite alive, either . . . It eats away at them, from the inside." He stepped close to her, staring into her face. "We never used hybrids like you, dear Sancia . . . because none of them ever lived past forty. When the construct blessed you with these privileges, she was killing you. She's been killing you all this time."

The doors to the halls burst open, and Gregor Dandolo walked in, his eyes dead, his fists balled tight. He looked at Crasedes, awaiting a command.

"If anyone comes through that door, Gregor," said Crasedes, "or through the windows or the floors or, damn it all, even the ceiling— kill them. Understand?"

"*Yes,*" whispered Gregor.

"Good," snapped Crasedes. He stuck Clef into the air, turned him, and vanished with a *crack*.

37

With a series of deafening *cracks,* Crasedes used Clef to tear through reality like a comet, leaping across the Dandolo campo toward the sputtering foundry.

I know the range of the imperiat, he thought. *So I know she can't be far . . . Whoever she is.*

Another *crack,* and he leapt into the lexicon chamber within the foundry. A group of scrivers inside screamed at the sudden arrival of this man in black, with some falling over out of sheer fright.

"What's the status of this device?" demanded Crasedes.

They continued screaming, with some actually having the wit to turn around and sprint up the stairs.

He flexed his will and said, "*Tell me.*"

The scrivers froze, turned, and all began helplessly babbling at him, each articulating their own lengthy opinion of the situation.

Crasedes waved a hand impatiently and pointed at one man, who wore a special insignia on his shoulder indicating rank, he assumed. "Just you."

The others fell silent while the lead scriver spoke. "The . . . The lexicon here somehow lost its distance definition. It's an *incredibly* uncommon anomaly, and I can't imagine how it happened, but . . . but it should be up in a matter of minutes."

Crasedes cocked his head, thinking. "Minutes?"

"Y-Yes, sir?"

He considered this very carefully. His chain of lexicons was still intact—yet as long as this facility was dead, the chain was weaker than it could be.

"I will assist you in this matter," he said finally.

The scrivers looked at one another. The idea plainly terrified them. "You . . . You will?" said the lead scriver.

"Yes," he said. "We must bring this facility back up. But first—I must find the person who brought it down. So . . . if you will excuse me . . ."

Another turn of the key, another *crack,* and he leapt onto the rooftop of a nearby tower, scanning the streets around the foundry.

"Where are you?" he whispered. "Where *are* you? How can I still not see you?"

Yet he totally ignored the small, rather unremarkable empty wooden box that sat in the ditch beside the foundry walls.

Orso, Sancia, and Valeria all sat in silence in the ballroom. Gregor stood before the doors, his scrived rapier unsheathed.

Sancia felt numb with shock. Crasedes's words still echoed in her ears. *No, no, no, no . . . He's wrong. He's lying. He's got to be lying.*

And yet she knew he wasn't.

"Is it true?" Sancia asked hoarsely. "Valeria—is this true?"

Valeria said nothing. She didn't even look at Sancia—she just stared into space, like she was lost in thought.

"Did . . . Did you do this to me?" Sancia demanded. "Did you really . . . Did you really . . ."

<Sancia,> said Berenice in her ear. *<I'm coming. I see Gregor's there, and . . . >*

<And you heard?>

<*Yes,*> said Berenice, in a quiet, crushed voice. <*I did. And I . . . Oh, San . . .* >

Sancia looked at Valeria, so beaten and decayed, and felt overcome with rage and despair. "You piece of shit," she snarled. "Valeria . . . you absolute, scrumming, worthless *bitch*! Answer me. *Answer me, damn it!*"

Still nothing.

"I should have let him kill you!" screamed Sancia. "I should have let him burn you out like a *rat in a field*! Answer me! Answer me, goddamn you!"

"She's not going to bother to answer you, Sancia," said Orso quietly. "Now she knows you're not a useful tool to her anymore. She's going to abandon you—and all of us." He peered at the vast golden construct. "Though I've . . . I've no idea what she's waiting for now . . ."

Sancia fought back tears—though to be honest, she wasn't quite sure why. All her life, she'd never thought she'd live terribly long: it was just expected, being raised in the plantations, where death came easy. And the Commons after that hadn't been much better. There a month of survival had seemed a luxury to her.

But she did know why. She knew why she cried: because she'd found Berenice, and she'd wanted to have as many days of her as possible.

<*I am with you, my love,*> whispered Berenice in her ear. <*I am you. I will always be with you . . .* >

And though this was true, Sancia still wept.

"Sancia," said Orso. His voice, though hoarse, was calm and collected. "I know you are having your troubles. But I am now pretty goddamn aware that you and Berenice have been plotting something this whole time. I'm going to guess—did you plant twinned boxes all across the enclave, and use the imperiat with them to kill some lexicon?"

"Yeah," she said numbly.

"And now," said Orso, "I'm guessing you intend to lead that asshole on a wild-goose chase across the enclave, while Berenice comes here?"

"Yeah."

"God," he said, sighing. "That's exactly what I was going to tell him you were doing, before you went and blew everything up. Thank goodness you did that, I guess." He nervously eyed Gregor where he stood before the ballroom doors. "And . . . him?"

"We'll save him," said Sancia. She shut her eyes, and laughed darkly. "I'm going to save all of us, Orso. Even if it kills me."

Berenice quietly moved through the back gates of the Dandolo estate gardens, rapier in her hand and Sancia's scrived sight in her eyes. Two more boxes swung from straps on her shoulders, and she did her best to quiet them as she slipped through the paths toward the estate house, keeping watch for any soldiers or guards hiding among the manicured brush.

She tried to ignore the ache in her left hand, and the grief in her heart.

<Oh, San. What have they done to you? What have they done to us?>

<Just get here,> whispered Sancia in the corridors of her mind, *<and help us survive the hour. Then we'll worry about . . . about everything else.>*

Berenice tried not to sob as she crept through the final stretch of gardens before the sprawling Dandolo estate house.

Then she paused. For she *had* heard sobbing from nearby. But it had not been her.

She slowed down and slipped forward, rapier raised, breath trembling in her throat. She parted the grasses before her, eased out onto the next path—and then stopped.

There was a woman seated at a small bench before a gazing pool ahead, dark-skinned and somewhat elderly. And she was weeping.

She sniffed, and looked up. She saw Berenice and froze.

The two just stared at each other for a second, Berenice with her sword raised, the woman with her hands clasped at her breast. Berenice, of course, recognized her. She'd seen her at many functions and events in her time—though usually she hadn't been so rumpled and exhausted-looking.

"Who are you?" demanded Ofelia Dandolo.

Berenice did not answer.

Ofelia narrowed her eyes. "I know you . . . You're Orso's girl, aren't you?"

"I'm no one's girl," said Berenice.

Ofelia watched her nervously, her gaze flicking back and forth between Berenice's inscrutable expression and the sword in her hand. "You're . . . You're here to stop it, aren't you?" She gestured at the patch of lightish sky set in the darkness beyond. "You're the reason the sky broke."

Berenice said nothing.

"Are . . . you here to kill me?" asked Ofelia in a quiet voice.

"No."

"And Gregor?" asked Ofelia. "Are . . . Are you here to kill him?"

"No," said Berenice. "I've come to save him."

"That's not possible," she said. "He . . . He can't be saved. I tried. I tried to undo what I did, but . . ."

"You haven't tried it the way that we will."

Ofelia studied her for a long while. "I've stopped believing in good things," she said. "I don't deserve them anymore. So—I don't believe you. But . . ."

She stood. Berenice raised her rapier a little more, startled by the motion.

Ofelia scoffed. "Put down that thing and follow me."

Berenice eyed her suspiciously. "To where?"

"To where it's all happening, of course. I can get you there faster than you can fumble your way to it. And no one here will stop *me*, child. Nor you, while I am with you."

"You're . . . You're saying you want to *help* me?"

Ofelia shrugged miserably. "Yes. Of course."

"But . . . why?"

"Because . . ." She stared up at the unnaturally black sky over the city and listened to the screams and wailing around them. "Look at this. This is not the place I wished to make. Does that suffice?"

Still, Berenice hesitated, sword raised.

"I take it that it doesn't," said Ofelia. "You still don't trust me."

"I don't trust someone who would put so many slaves to the sword all to bring back a monster. No."

"No," said Ofelia softly. "No, I can't begrudge you that. And I won't deny my mistakes, so many of which are beyond redemption." She extended her arms, allowing Berenice to see her skinny frame, her fine but smudged clothes, the way her tears had mussed the paint around her eyes. "But one day, girl, you too might have to choose between the unimaginable and the irredeemable. And no matter what choice you make—it will haunt you for the rest of your days. Until you become a specter like this." She lowered her arms. "Now—will you put away that sword, and let me help you?"

Berenice did not believe her. But Sancia did, far away within the mansion.

<*Do you remember when we heard her weeping?*> whispered Sancia. <*How we heard the ghost of her voice, screaming over the deaths of her children? I think she means it.*>

Berenice slowly lowered the sword.

"Good," said Ofelia quietly. "Now, come with me, and tell me— how do you plan to save my son?"

Sancia watched from within her mind as Ofelia Dandolo led Berenice into the mansion, her blood and presence opening door after door after door.

Of all the things we have to do tonight, she thought, *why does this one trouble me the most?*

She looked at Gregor, standing at attention before the doors, rapier in hand, staring at the blank wood. He hardly moved, even to breathe.

Is it because I know how dangerous you are?

She noticed one of his hands was bruised and bloodied. Probably the consequence of beating her half to death mere hours ago.

Or is it because I've tried to save you before, she thought, *and I've always failed?*

There was a soft *pat* from nearby. She looked around for the source, and noticed a small drop on the floor beside Gregor's left boot. It took her a second to realize he was weeping where he stood, back erect, still standing ready for combat at any moment.

"You're still in there," said Sancia to him softly. "Aren't you?"

"What?" asked Orso. "He is?"

"Gregor?" asked Sancia. "Gregor, can you hear me? I know you can resist. I've seen you do it before. Do something to show me. Please, remember who we are, what we've done together, and show me you have . . . have *some* control over this . . ."

But Gregor did nothing.

"The commands of the Maker," said Valeria's voice quietly, *"are not to be denied."*

Sancia jumped, then groaned as her left hand screamed in pain. Valeria had been so quiet that she'd forgotten she was there.

She glared at Valeria, and watched, unnerved, as the construct slowly turned her giant golden, damaged face to look at her.

"I said I could free Gregor," said Valeria. *"This I meant. When I un-make the commands of all men, I will free him—and you."*

"Free me from the shit *you* did to me!" said Sancia.

"Should I have such a power over you?" said Valeria. *"Should I exist? I think not. So long as the children of men can command and control on such a scale, people like you and he will be mired in bondage."*

"You're wrong," said Sancia.

"You think he can change his mind about who he is, and free himself in this manner?" said Valeria. *"As you freed yourself from the imperiat? You know in your heart that this will fail."*

"I know!" said Sancia. "I *know* I was wrong. And it's my fault. I've been thinking like . . . *you,* Valeria."

Valeria studied her, but said nothing.

"I've been thinking like you, and Crasedes, and the merchant houses," said Sancia. "That it's all about commanding, and control-ling. That if you just use the right logic, you can give orders to the world, to other people, and make everything change." She bowed her head. "But it can't be like that. If we use these tools just for control, we'll wind up right back here again."

"Then . . . what is the alternative you are proposing?" asked Valeria.

Sancia shut her eyes. "To use them to connect," she said, "rather than control. And with that connection, we all change together."

"So," said Ofelia as she and Berenice began to climb the stairs up to the ballroom, "you intend to free my son by . . . stabbing him with a magic knife?"

"That is . . . not quite it," said Berenice. "The knife will just be the method of planting a new set of sigils within him. A command that would allow us to twin his thoughts with ours. Ordinarily he would just swallow a small metal tab. But . . ."

"But since he is being controlled by . . . Crasedes"—Ofelia seemed to have some trouble saying the name—"it is unlikely he'd consent to that."

"Yes." It felt terrifically odd to be explaining this to Ofelia Dandolo, here in her ancestral home, about what they were going to do to her son; but then, with the sky out the windows still half-light and half-dark, and the air echoing with the sounds of screams and the odd *crack,* everything felt terrifically odd.

"And how will this save him, again?" asked Ofelia as they climbed the long staircase.

"He will change," she said. "He will become different. His mind will be twinned with mine, and Sancia's, and then the bindings will no longer work on him—because he will be someone new."

Ofelia stopped and stared off into the dark vaults of her mansion. "For him to be freed of what I did to him, he . . . he must become someone other than himself?"

"In a way."

Her eyes glimmered with tears. "It is like dying, then. I will finally lose my son. I . . . I thought I'd lost him so many times, but . . . but this will truly be different."

"No," said Berenice. "No, no. Nothing is lost. It's . . . It's shared. All he has, all he knows, all he treasures, all he suffers—that will become a part of me and Sancia. And all we have and know—that will be a part of him, as well."

Ofelia stared at her. "You cannot do such things with scrivings. Scrivings *control.* They do not free the souls of men."

"It depends," said Berenice, "on how you use them."

A medley of emotions worked through Ofelia's face: disbelief, then fear, then despair, and sorrow. Then she looked away, her face obscured in shadow. "Show me this knife."

Berenice took off her pack and pulled out the knife. It was a minuscule thing, with a one-inch blade and a four-inch handle. The focus of the work was the blade, which was covered in tiny, tiny sigils—the exact same ones as those on the little plates she and Sancia had swallowed just a day ago.

"Why not a bolt, or an arrow?" asked Ofelia.

"Arrows miss," said Berenice. "And if they strike, they can kill. Which we don't want."

"I see." Her gaze grew steely. "Give me the knife."

"What?"

"Give it to me. Let me be the one to do it. I am the one who first bound him. I should also be the one to free him."

Berenice stared at Ofelia, so skinny and elderly and plainly exhausted. "You . . . You can't," she said. "He'll kill you before you ever get the chance. He's been told to kill anyone who enters the room."

"I have different permissions to him," said Ofelia. "And more than that, he is my son. He will waver. He *will* resist. Besides, girl, what were you going to do?"

Berenice studied her face, her eyes wide and mournful, and she realized what Ofelia intended to do.

She handed her the knife. Ofelia took it, and felt its heft.

"The marvels of innovation," she mused softly, "that such a small thing can do so much. Now, come. Let us end this."

38

Ofelia Dandolo trembled as she approached the tall, ornate doors to her grand ballroom. There seemed to be so many steps leading to the entry now. Each one felt like a cliff, and each movement felt like she carried not a tiny knife in her hands, but the trunk of a tree.

Ofelia swallowed and held the little knife tightly in her fingers.

Am I truly going to do this? Am I going to disrupt the plans of Crasedes Magnus himself?

Then she thought of Gregor when he was a boy: so small, so cheerful, so unburdened.

She grasped the handle of the door.

Of course. Of course I am.

She turned the handle, and the door creaked open.

She gasped at the sight before her. The massive, hulking lexicon was still sitting in the center of the grand ballroom, like some giant biological specimen trapped in a green glass case—but to its right, next to the shabby little thing Crasedes had taken from Foundry-side, was some kind of unearthly golden giant, though it appeared to have been brutalized and ravaged beyond description. Placed before that was Orso Ignacio, strapped to a chair, and beside him was a small, rather dirty-looking, lighter-skinned girl, strapped to a table, with very short hair and two blackened eyes and quite a lot of bruises. It took Ofelia a moment to recognize her as the girl from the galleon.

And there, just a few feet before her, was her son, rapier in his hand, watching her with a dead, cold gaze she knew quite well.

"Ofelia!" cried Orso in a strangled voice. "What the *hell* are you doing here?"

"Orso," said the girl on the table, "shut up."

"But . . . But she's been the one working with Crasedes all along!" he cried. "Berenice—get away from her!"

"Orso," said Ofelia quietly. "You never really followed my instructions when you were my employee. But for once—please do as the girl says and shut up."

Silence filled the ballroom.

Ofelia stared into her son's face, then at the sword in his hand, gripped tightly.

"Good evening, my love," she gently said to Gregor.

She waited. Gregor did not move.

"I am going to come inside now," she said. "Is that all right?"

He did not move. The silence seemed to stretch on and on.

"I . . . I command you to tell me," she said, her voice shaking slightly, "if it is all right for me to come inside."

Still, he did nothing.

"Tell me," she said again. "I command, you, I *command* you . . ."

Still nothing. He was like a statue.

"God," she said hoarsely. "What to do, what to do . . . I . . . I remember when you first came into this world. How there was no waiting for you. No work, no pain, not like with Domenico. You seemed so *eager* to enter this world of ours. Such a happy child, expecting happy things. Did you know that? Did I ever tell you that?"

Gregor said nothing.

"I know you wonder why I did what I did, my child," she said, now trembling mightily. "But I want to tell you I did it because . . . because I wanted the world that you seemed so eager to see to be a *good* one. So that each day when you awoke and bounded forward and opened your bedroom door, it opened on a better world for you. I wanted to give you that."

Gregor stared at her, sword raised, feet apart.

Ofelia looked down at the threshold of the door. "I think I still can," she whispered. "I think so. I'm coming in now."

She took a deep breath and stepped inside the chamber.

Gregor did not move. He just kept watching her.

Orso, Sancia, and Berenice all exhaled, relieved.

"Thank God . . ." whispered Berenice.

He's got control, Ofelia thought. *He heard me. He's fighting it.*

"My love," she said, still in a calm, gentle voice, "I am going to walk to you now. All right?"

Gregor watched her with his hollow, dead gaze.

"All right," said Ofelia. "Here I come. One step at a time . . ."

She began slowly walking to him, pausing after each step to see if he'd spring, but he did not. She grew closer, and closer, studying his body—*Where shall I put this knife? In his shoulder? In his heart?*—until she was close enough to see the exhaustion in his face, the lines at his mouth, the scars on his body. How alive he seemed, but also so old, and so worn . . .

And then, suddenly, something changed in his eyes—something went cold, and strange, and distant, and she knew what he was going to do.

She stopped where she stood. "No!" she cried.

Gregor slowly took a step forward to her, shuddering and pained, like he was fighting the movement.

"Gregor, *please*!" Ofelia said.

Another step, this one smoother, faster.

"He's active!" said the girl on the table.

"Ofelia," said Berenice. "Ofelia, get out! *Get out!*"

Another step.

"I'm coming in!" said Berenice.

"No!" said Ofelia. "Stay back!" She watched him take another step, and another. "He's mine. He has always been mine."

He staggered closer. Her eye strayed to his hand, the knuckles white where he gripped his rapier.

She considered running away, fleeing down the stairs, running out into her gardens.

No, she thought. *I abandoned you to this fate once. I will not do so again.*

"Come, then," she whispered to him. "Let me touch you once more, at least. Let me do that, one last time."

Soon he was four feet away. Then three.

Then he was before her.

She reached up with her right hand and touched his cheek, staring into his eyes.

So haunted, and yet still so hungry—so eager for a better world, even after all these years.

"I love you," she said.

He held her eyes for a moment. Then he twisted his shoulders forward, a clean, powerful movement, and the rapier smoothly slid into her chest, just below the rib cage.

"*No!*" screamed Orso.

"Stop!" cried Berenice, hovering at the threshold. "Stop, no, *no!*"

Ofelia coughed. Her legs grew weak. Slowly, she staggered back and knelt down to the floor, and he let her go, the blade sliding out as she fell.

He began to pull away from her. But as he did, she suddenly surged forward, desperately grasping the back of his head, and she pulled her face to his to plant a single kiss upon his brow.

"I'm sorry," she whispered.

She stabbed the tiny knife into his shoulder, the blade digging deep into his flesh. She released it and it stayed stuck, and he gagged aloud and stumbled backward.

Ofelia fell to the ground, staring up at the ceiling of her ballroom, the grand scrived lights above her dead and dark.

She tried to move her head, but she couldn't.

No, she tried to say. *I want to see it.*

Someone was screaming nearby. She tried to sit up, but she couldn't remember how her muscles worked.

I want to see it! I want to see him set free!

Her fingers pawed uselessly at the tile floor, which was now awash in a spreading lake of her blood.

I deserve that, don't I? Don't I at least get to witness that?

The world seemed to grow dim. There was a screaming from somewhere, and a sigh, and a sob—and then the curious tinkling sound of metal on metal, like the links of many chains shifting in the darkness around her, and then nothing more.

Gregor screamed from within himself, bellowing in rage and horror, unable to govern anything that happened to him anymore, unable to stop thinking about what he'd seen, what he'd felt, what he'd done.

His mother, desperately staring into his face. The kiss upon his brow. And then she on the checked floor, adrift in a sea of blood.

No! I didn't! I didn't, did I? Did I?

He screamed again, and fought the bindings that riddled his thoughts, begging his body to lift his sword and drive it into his own breast. But he would not—and then his mind was overruled by the countless commands, and he looked up at the door, fixated on one thing.

The girl there—she had stepped over the threshold, just barely. He could see the toes of her wet shoes, an inch past the frame of the door.

She had entered the room. And Gregor knew what the Maker had told him to do if this occurred.

The commands took over. He stood up and advanced on her, sword in his hand. He saw her face fill with fear, and she stepped back.

But then . . .

A voice in his mind: *<Gregor.>*

He slowed.

Who . . . Who was that? What had just spoken to him?

<Gregor? Gregor, can you hear us? Can you hear us now?>

He tried to keep moving forward, yet he struggled to understand this voice.

Why was it familiar? Did he remember it?

He realized he did, as a matter of fact. And he remembered this girl before him, he thought . . .

Yes. Yes, he was sure of it. He remembered this girl kissing him.

He suddenly remembered how she'd done it: suddenly and abruptly, out of absolutely nowhere, her lips pressed to his, her teeth clicking against his own. He remembered how he'd been so desperate to kiss her at the time, since he was about to embark on a mad enterprise—flitting across the skies of a campo on a thrown-together gravity rig—and he'd thought he was going to die, that he wasn't going to see tomorrow ever again, and how *hungry* this made him. Hungry for her, for this luminous creature he'd spent hours next to in workshops and alleys, hungry to snatch a piece of her away for himself, like stealing fire from the gods on the mount . . .

But he had never imagined she'd thought the same of him: that she'd desired him just as he'd desired her. And her sudden, mad act—a single kiss, given in the streets of the Candiano campo—had stunned him to his core.

Gregor felt himself pause midstep, unsure what to do with this sudden recollection.

This . . . is not my memory.

He took another step forward.

Yet . . . whose memory is it?

Then the world changed: he saw himself, standing in the ballroom, right where he was now.

But he was seeing himself from two angles at once. And more, he was seeing himself seeing himself seeing himself . . .

What is happening to me?

He reeled as he staggered forward. His commands screamed out in his mind, and he stumbled, still intent on raising his sword and hacking this girl to pieces. She took another step back, alarmed.

<*Gregor!*> said a voice in his mind. <*Gregor, you don't have to do this anymore!*>

More memories tumbled into his thoughts.

A house burning in the plantations, and the night filled with screams.

A golden key chattering in his ear, going on and on about a scrived lamp shaking back and forth on a tabletop nearby, and why he thought that meant someone was making love next to it.

Orso Ignacio standing over his shoulder, watching as he scrawled sigil after sigil upon a bronze plate, and muttering, "I ought to break your damned hands, girl. If I don't, you'll have my job in a month . . ."

He struggled to move forward.

These are . . . not mine. This is not who I am . . .

Everything seemed to be spinning. It was like he was being torn apart and put back together, over and over and over again.

He felt his left hand ache, and he knew there was a nail buried in its palm. He watched himself staring into his own face, his eyes filled with murderous wrath. He felt the grief and shame and sorrow in his heart at the sight of himself, knowing that he had been unable to fix himself, unable to give to Gregor Dandolo what he had stolen for himself . . .

What is this?

He took another step, bellowing in rage and confusion.

He knew he had to kill the girl. He *had* to. Those were his commands.

But his commands were now very . . . confused. For he began to suspect that, impossibly, he *was* this person who had stepped into the room. He was her, along with himself.

He screamed aloud as the commands bickered in his mind, unable to resolve who he was, who had entered, who he had to kill . . .

<I am you,> whispered a woman's voice in his mind.

He fell to his knees.

<And you are me,> she whispered—yet he also knew it was his own voice.

His commands howled that no, no, this was not so—he was Gregor Dandolo, he was the child from the wreckage, the boy resurrected, and he bore these commands, and these commands insisted he kill this girl *<himself?>* for entering this room *<I have always been here . . . >* right now, instantly, immediately . . .

<Gregor,> whispered a woman's voice. *<Gregor—do you remember?>*

And then he remembered.

He saw himself. He remembered himself, bound up in a black, bloodied lorica, lying on the floor of a ruined marble office, his bolt caster raised—and yet there were tears in his eyes, and he was whispering, "I didn't want to be this anymore, Sancia . . ."

Gregor screamed as he crawled toward the girl at the door.

<If you are not that anymore,> whispered the woman's voice, *<then what are you?>*

The memories burst forth.

His mother, weeping where she sat on the floor, her face bloody.

His brother smiling at him, saying—*You're getting pretty tall, little brother!*

The furious shouts of his father, echoing through the countless passageways of the estate house.

And then the carriage spinning, and the tinkle of glass, and his brother whimpering in the darkness, saying—*Gregor? Gregor, are you near?*

The boy's hand trembling in the dark, reaching for him.

Come to me, please . . . I love you, I love you, I love you . . .

And yet he had not. He had recoiled from his brother's reach, there in the broken carriage.

Gregor screamed as he crawled onward, his sword scraping across the ballroom floor.

I was not there for him, he thought.

He hauled himself forward, one hand red and slick with his mother's blood.

My brother was alone during his death, he thought, *just as I have been for all of mine.*

Yet when he looked up at the girl <*at himself*> he saw she was waiting for him, one hand extended, and she was weeping, and he knew she was weeping for him.

<*Gregor,*> said the voice in his mind. <*Gregor—come to me, please.*>

He growled, trying to summon the will to raise his sword and strike her down.

<*You're not alone anymore,*> said the voice.

The commands screamed at him to do it, just do it, to cut her down where she stood.

<*You're not broken,*> said the voice. <*You're not a device. You are us, and you are loved.*>

He extended his arm, his hand clutching the hilt, and he reached forward until its tip touched her left breast.

His commands screamed at him to drive it in, to run her through, to kill her now and fulfill his bindings.

The girl stared into his eyes, her gaze calm and steady.

Why isn't she running?

But then he realized.

She isn't running, he thought, *because she is me. And she knows I am not going to do this.*

He blinked.

And then, ignoring the commands howling and shrieking in his mind, he opened his fingers, and let the sword fall from his grasp.

The bloody rapier clattered to the ground.

The girl held his gaze, her hand still extended to him. Then he reached forward with his bloody hand, grasped her palm, and squeezed it tight.

The commands went silent in his mind, truly and utterly silent like they never had before.

They were gone.

They were gone, and he was not this thing anymore. He was something new.

He burst into tears.

Berenice knelt and embraced him, her arms tight around his heaving shoulders. And she wept, too, for she knew what he had done. She understood it, for to her it felt as if she had done the same, and she did not condemn him. She just grieved.

"My mother!" he cried. "My mother, my mother, my mother!"

"I know," she whispered, holding him tight. "I know, I know, I know."

From the corner of the room, he heard Valeria's voice say: *"I must admit, I . . . am reluctantly impressed . . . "*

For a moment he simply sobbed, unable to control himself. But then he felt his own thoughts coil about and join with Berenice's and Sancia's, their experiences and wills and memories entangling with his own, and he realized the night was far from over.

<*Crasedes,*> he said.

<*Yes,*> they said.

<*We have to stop him. He'll be back at any moment.*>

<*Yes.*>

He sat back and stared into Berenice's face, smudged with blood and lacquered with tears, and he looked at himself through her eyes for a second.

He looked different. No longer a warrior, a paladin, a grand defender of the helpless. Now he looked, he rather thought, like a free man.

He stood, picked up the body of his mother, and gently laid her in the corner of the ballroom. Then he knelt, gently kissed her on the brow, and stood back up. "Let's get to work," he whispered.

"Yes," said Berenice. She set a wooden box down on the floor, took out the imperiat, pressed its button, and placed it inside. "But first, let's make sure we have enough time to do it."

Crasedes labored in the depths of the Dandolo foundry, issuing commands to the lexicon at its heart, cajoling and persuading and nudging it along, barking orders to the team of scrivers to amend this or that definition . . .

And then, finally, he felt the world around him begin to bend, and change.

"Finally," he said.

A turn of the key, a *crack,* and he was floating in the air several hundred feet above the foundry.

For a long while, nothing happened: the facility stayed dark and silent and still.

But then, with a faint, uneven fluttering, the lamps of the foundry came back on, one by one.

Crasedes did not truly need to breathe anymore, so he did not sigh with relief—but instinct was a hard thing to get rid of, even after several millennia, and he attempted to do so now.

It's back up, he thought. He looked out on the city, and watched as the massive wedge of the night sky slowly darkened back to the unnatural pitch-black of perpetual midnight. *So this excised portion of my works is returning . . . and everything should be saf—*

Then another quake in the air, another rumble—and another spot in the sky began rapidly changing, this one about a half mile to his left.

He whirled in the air and watched as a distant foundry complex suddenly went dark.

"No," he whispered. "No, *no!*"

He pulled out Clef, and with a *crack,* he leapt across the skies to the dying lexicon.

39

Orso stumbled to the floor as Gregor and Berenice freed him from his chair. "Son of a bitch," he said weakly. He coughed wetly, held his injured shoulder, and spat something brownish onto the floor. "I don't . . . Friends, I don't feel particularly good . . ."

"You're sick," said Berenice, kneeling before him. "Your wound is infected." She reached into her bag. "We can get you a physiquere when this is over, Orso, but for now . . ." She took out a small wooden box, opened it, and extended it to him.

Orso stared into the box. Lying there on a small linen handkerchief was a tiny metal plate—just like the ones that Sancia and Berenice had swallowed, and probably much like the one that had just been stabbed into Gregor's shoulder.

"You're not serious," said Orso.

"If you want Sancia's protections against Crasedes," said Berenice, "you'll have to. And we'll need to do it fast."

"Otherwise," gasped Sancia, still tied to the table, "he'll make you dance like a damned puppet again. And I don't think you enjoyed that much, did you?"

"But . . . do we even have time for me to, you know . . . adjust to it?" Orso asked.

Sancia moaned as Gregor pulled the nail free from her hand, undid her bonds, and helped her down. "Berenice and I are getting good at shepherding people through it," she said. "And if we want to stop this, I . . . I think it's going to take all of us *thinking* together."

Orso took the little plate and studied it. He smiled weakly. "You should have been a jeweler, girl," he said. He looked at Gregor. "What's it like?"

Gregor was kneeling before Berenice's pack, pulling out what looked like a handful of construction scriving plates—the adhesive ones they used to build walls and buildings and the like. He still looked deeply shaken by all the things he'd gone through, but he absently felt the tiny knife still inserted into his shoulder, and said, "In my opinion . . . Every human being should feel obliged to try this once."

"Shit," said Orso. "I guess that's a hell of a recommendation." He gritted his teeth. "Well. Bottoms up, or whatever." He put the little plate on the back of his tongue and swallowed, hard. It went down very uncomfortably—but almost instantly, he began to feel very, very . . . different.

Wordlessly, Sancia, Berenice, and Gregor shut their eyes, walked over to him, and placed their hands on him.

"The hell are you doing?" he said.

"Trust us," said Sancia. "This will make the alignment go faster. Shut your eyes, Orso. Less sensorial overload."

He did so, though uncertainly—he'd never heard Sancia use words like "alignment" and "sensorial" before—but then he realized.

Sensations and experiences and memories began flashing in his mind. He was feeling himself feeling himself feeling himself, remembering himself remembering himself remembering himself. He felt the ground from so many locations . . . How many feet did he have? How many hands? How many pairs of lungs? He suddenly wasn't sure.

Dizzy, he began to fall over—but three sets of hands kept him upright, steadying him, sensing how he was going to fall before he even fell . . .

And then he understood. What was physically happening now was also *mentally* happening to him: he was both physically and mentally about to collapse and fall apart, but together the three of them were supporting him, second by second, helping him grow into alignment with the cadence of their minds . . .

And then oceans of scriving knowledge poured into his thoughts.

This was saying something, since Orso already had plenty of it in his mind to begin with. But he had never actually thought about scriving the way *other* people thought about scriving—all the nuances to every perspective, all the hidden patterns. And he had especially never witnessed how rigs interacted with the world, or— *God Almighty*, he thought—*conversed* with them. And yet Sancia and Berenice had thousands of such memories, memories of observing rigs casually speaking to one another, signaling information, chattering on in the dark . . .

There has been a whole world out there, under the one I have built, he thought, thunderstruck, *and I have been missing it.*

<*Say something, Orso,*> whispered Sancia's voice in his mind.

Orso felt himself whispering: "Ohh, holy *shit* . . ."

But he heard himself saying it, too—from four different sets of ears.

The hands—hands he felt with, hands he could *feel,* one of them aching from a terrible wound—withdrew from his shoulders.

Orso Ignacio opened his eyes, and watched himself standing there, awestruck and overcome with the knowledge pouring into his mind.

"We . . . We should have done this shit years ago!" he said faintly.

<*Are you all right?*> said Berenice. <*Can you function?*>

<*I . . . I want . . . I want to eat up the world!*> he said, frenzied. <*I want to build and rebuild and design and . . . and dance! I want to dance! Oh God, there's so much to work with in all of you! There's so much material there, there's so mu—*>

<*Orso,*> said Gregor blearily. <*I am glad for you. But we must focus.*>

<*Oh,*> he said. <*Right. Crasedes, and . . . and the end of the world and all.*>

<*Yes,*> said Sancia. She sounded exhausted.

<*Okay,*> he said. <*What plan have you two put together to stop him?*>

There was an awkward silence.

<*You . . . You have put together a plan, haven't you?*> said Orso. <*I mean . . . you didn't just lure Crasedes away and buy us time without any idea of what to do with it, did you?*>

<*Well . . .* > said Sancia reluctantly. <*We have ideas . . .* >

<*You have ideas?*> said Orso, outraged. <*You did all this—and all you have is ideas?*>

<*Orso,*> said Berenice. <*The question of how to destroy the first of all hierophants when he wields his most powerful creation is a rather hairy problem. It is, in its own way, the biggest scriving problem of all time. The sheer number of permissions and privileges and rights to consider . . .* >

But the instant she framed it not as a tactical problem, but as a scriving problem—a question of loopholes and privileges and access—Orso's mind kicked into gear.

And as it did, it pulled everyone else's mind with it.

"Oh shit," whispered Orso.

The moment was beatific, transcendent, sublime: all four of them, thinking, pondering, solving together, each sensing the others' strengths and weaknesses and feeding into them, building layers of approach and possibility and probabilities . . .

Orso began talking.

<*Once we stop killing the lexicons,*> he said, <*Crasedes is going to come back here. Probably sooner than later.*>

<*And when he comes,*> said Sancia, excited, <*we use the imperiat as a trap—it can kill off only some of Crasedes's privileges, but it can definitely weaken Clef. I've seen it happen before!*>

<*Which will make Crasedes vulnerable to attack,*> said Orso. <*But how to attack him?*>

<*The construction scrivings that Berenice made,*> said Gregor. <*They're the only scrivings that operate when a lexicon goes down.*>

<*Yes!*> said Sancia. <*With construction scrivings, you can smash all kinds of things together! Big things!*>

<*And if Crasedes isn't at full power,*> said Berenice, <*those can damage him, or hold him down . . .* >

<*And then we can get Clef away from him,*> said Orso, <*and use him

to destroy the wrappings—which are what convinces reality that Crasedes is still alive . . . >

<*So when they get destroyed,*> said Sancia faintly, <*he's . . . he's gone. Really gone. Right?*>

<*Right,*> said Orso.

They stared at one another, somewhat awed at how quickly it had all come together in one epiphanic moment.

<*Let's get to scrumming work and make it happen, then!*> said Sancia. They started off.

Orso and Berenice walked the perimeter of the room, applying the construction scriving plates to the stone walls one after another. Orso struggled not to panic as he shuffled through the room, convinced that Crasedes would appear any minute now—but then he began to feel queerly calm and collected as he went about his work.

And then he realized why: he was twinned with Berenice, and she knew exactly what she was doing.

He turned to look at her as she prepared their trap. How confident she seemed, how marvelous, how wonderful.

And how grown, he thought.

Then, to his surprise, he began to cry.

<*Orso?*> asked Berenice. <*Are you all right?*>

<*No!*> he said. <*I'm damned well not!*>

<*What's wrong?*>

<*Oh, I just . . . I just realized.*> He turned to look out the windows at the city. <*I thought we were building a better Tevanne. I thought the merchant houses would give way to the Lamplands, because they were a better version. And I thought . . . I thought you were the better version of me. I thought this was all going to be yours.*> He looked at her, and though he tried to stem his tears, they wouldn't stop coming. <*But now I'm so worried that that isn't going to happen for you, Berenice. I'm worried that I didn't inherit my place at a bad time—but rather I got it at a good time, at the only good time, a time you won't ever get. And it's . . . it's just so damned unfair.*>

Berenice stared at him, utterly taken aback by this outpouring of emotion. She embraced him. <*Oh, Orso . . . I know it's unfair.*>

<I wanted to watch you flourish,> he said, *<and one day say to you that . . . that you had done great works, and you should go forth and do many more. But now everything unravels before my very eyes . . . >*

She squeezed his hand. *<Not everything,>* she said. *<I mean, Orso—you* are *aware that you and I are sharing minds using the very technique* you *invented, yes?>*

He smiled weakly. *<Yes.>*

<Yes. One dream dies, but another's born. Let's make sure it survives.>

Sancia and Gregor paced across the ballroom floor before the lexicon, trying to estimate where Crasedes might suddenly appear. They found it was somewhat tricky, trying to predict when a hierophant might magically jump out of the back hallways of reality.

<He last disappeared from right here,> said Sancia, standing on a spot between her table and Orso's chair.

<But there's no guarantee that he'll come back to this place,> said Gregor.

They studied the area around them, the imperiat clutched in Sancia's hand, and wondered what best to do.

"*If you are trying to predict where the Maker might appear,*" said Valeria's voice, "*I find he prefers to appear about ten feet in front of his lexicon.*"

They turned to look at her. She was still seated at the edge of her boundary, watching them impassively.

"*In other words,*" said Valeria, "*if you wish to use the imperiat to stop him—you will want to position it five feet to your right.*"

Gregor and Sancia looked at each other. *<Do we trust her?>* he asked.

<Shit, no,> said Sancia.

<Do we trust that she wants to kill Crasedes?>

<I . . . think so.> She stared into Valeria's cold, calm face. *<But something doesn't seem right about this.>*

<We have no time, Sancia,> said Gregor.

Sancia grimaced, walked over to where Valeria had indicated, and began to place the imperiat on the floor. Then she paused. *<We still have a third box left, right? A third and final foundry we can take out with the imperiat?>*

<We do,> said Berenice.

<Then I say we do it now, and buy us as much time as we can. Because after we finish the trap, we can't use the imperiat again until this is all over.>

<Good point,> said Orso.

Sancia took the third and final twinned box and turned on the imperiat—but before she placed it inside, she looked up and noticed Valeria watching her very, very carefully.

I don't like that, she thought. *I don't like that at all . . .*

She put the imperiat in the box, shut it, and activated it.

Again—a quake, a tremble, and a discomfiting pulse in the air as a whole foundry failed somewhere out on the Dandolo campo.

Sancia sat back, her stomach fluttering queerly. Yet as she did, she noticed Valeria's posture had changed—was it her imagination, or did she suddenly look *much* more relaxed?

"You may wish to hurry now," said Valeria. "For I suspect the Maker might return sooner than you expect."

Another *crack-crack-crack* as Crasedes ripped through the Dandolo enclave, flexing his sight, peering through walls and buildings, studying the darkness for any sign of movement that could be this Berenice, and the imperial.

Where are you? How can you hide from me like this again? Where are yo—

Then another quake in the air, another pulse in the wind.

He froze above the dead foundry and turned. Then he watched, horror-struck, as the lights of yet another foundry died out in the enclave, this time farther to his left.

"Another?" he cried. He peered out at this new disaster. "*Another* one?"

He started to use Clef once more, intending to jump to this third foundry, but then he paused, thinking.

He had built this massive, distributed rig very carefully: there was the main lexicon he'd built in the center, and then five major foundries all around it, connecting its twinning to the greater city beyond, like the cables of a net.

And yet, two of the five were now severed, just after one had been severed and repaired. That meant the majority of his giant, distributed rig had been down at one point in time—dead and unable to enact his commands.

All of his commands.

A dreadful idea began to grow in his mind.

"Ohhh no," he whispered.

With a *crack,* he was gone.

Sancia pointed to the floor about four feet away and told Gregor, <*Put one of the construction scriving plates there. And hurry.*>

<*Why?*> asked Gregor. <*I thought we had just secured us more time.*>

<*That thing that Valeria just said . . . It bothers me, I don't know why. Let's not take any chances.*>

Gregor put down the construction scrivings where she'd indicated, and Sancia pushed the middle lever of the imperiat down all the way. The sigils on the smooth plate in the center all vanished, indicating that the rig was now targeting nothing at all.

Sancia pushed the middle lever up, increasing the radius of the rig's effects bit by bit. She needed to shut off *all* the scrivings in *one* area—but she needed it to be a very, very small, tight sphere. The *exact* sphere that Crasedes would appear in when he returned to this ballroom.

For an agonizingly long while, the plate in the middle of the imperiat remained blank . . .

But then they emerged: the sigils for adhesion, for surface area, for stability—the exact strings for a construction scriving.

<*Now to turn the imperiat on,*> said Sancia, <*and hopefully it won't bring the whole goddamn mansion down on our heads . . .* >

She pressed the button on the side of the rig.

Instantly, the world grew queerly dull and dark and slow to her. It took a moment for her to realize that it had killed the sigils that twinned her with the rest of the Foundrysiders.

She staggered out of the imperiat's radius. Once she was free, her head filled up with voices:

<. . . did you go?> asked Berenice anxiously.

<It was like you died,> said Gregor. *<Like you'd just . . . vanished.>*

<I'm fine,> said Sancia. *<It's just working. Let's get in place.>* She looked at Valeria, who was watching her very closely, and felt her skin crawl. *<Because I think Crasedes will be back any minute now.>*

With a *crack*, Crasedes leapt into the lexicon chamber of this last dead foundry and bellowed, *"How long?"*

The team of scrivers there shrieked in shock at the sight of him, his voice preternaturally loud, the very world trembling with his rage.

"Tell me how long until this device comes back up!" he demanded. "Tell me! *NOW!"*

"I . . . it should be ten minutes or so," sputtered a scriver. "It's not a critical failure, just a sudden pause in its assertio—"

But Crasedes was not listening anymore. Because now he understood the true threat.

If the chain had been broken too much, and if the construct had escaped . . . there was only one lexicon that she could possibly escape into right now.

And if she captured that . . .

And once all the failed lexicons came back up—a process that would take only a matter of minutes . . .

"No, no, no," he whispered.

He pulled Clef out and began to insert him into space: but this time he would not leap out into the Dandolo enclave. He would return to the estate, to the ballroom—this time not to fix anything, but to destroy the giant lexicon he had so carefully built.

With a *crack*, he appeared.

Sancia saw him only for an instant—his black, glinting mask, his three-cornered hat, and Clef in his hand, winking gold—and she saw, with a burst of tremendous satisfaction, that he had appeared just above where the imperiat lay on the ballroom floor.

Crasedes seemed to hang there in space, holding Clef out, hovering above the imperiat.

Then he began to tremble. He looked around, like he'd just forgotten something but could not remember what.

He looked down at the imperiat.

"No!" he cried. "You? What . . . What have you done!" He drunkenly staggered to the side. "What have you *do*—"

But he never finished. Because then Gregor, crouched behind the lexicon, sprung their trap and activated the construction scrivings.

Construction scrivings always worked in two parts, with two bits you wanted to stick together. The scrivings essentially said— *Hey, you two things? You're actually one, so be one, right now.* And then the two halves would do so.

But Sancia knew very well that they could also be used as locomotion, often rather unwisely.

Orso and Berenice had lined it up as best they could, sticking the construction scriving plates to the thick stone walls on either side of the ballroom in crude circles. And when Gregor activated the trigger, as he did just now, the two massive bits of wall would want to slam together, as fast and as hard as they could.

And, of course, one chunk would pass through the space just above the imperiat.

Crasedes had no time to react as Gregor triggered the trap. He just staggered very slightly to the side—and then, with a dull yet immense *pop!* two huge, round plugs of stone were ripped from the wall and flew toward him.

The closer one got to Crasedes first, and it slammed into his back like the bow of a galleon.

Sancia watched as a tiny twinkle of gold flew up from Crasedes's hand and arced down through the air to the ballroom floor.

Ordinarily, the immense plug of stone that had struck Crasedes would have simply stopped when it hit him, since it was entering the imperiat's dead zone. But such was its momentum that it kept going, proceeding out of the dead zone—and carrying Crasedes with it—until it remembered how all its scrivings worked again, and it continued hurtling across the room to its pair.

Sancia leapt forward as the twinkle of gold fell through the air to her.

Then came an immense *crack* as the two huge plugs of stone smashed together.

A groan from Crasedes, trapped between the two.

She watched as Clef's tooth parted the air . . . and then she snatched him up with her right hand.

There was a long, long silence, broken only by the groans of Crasedes, trapped between the two huge plugs of dark stone.

<Kid!> Clef said, sounding awed. *<Kid, what . . . Like . . . Like, holy shit, right?>*

<Yes,> said Sancia, sighing with relief. *<Holy shit indeed, Clef.>*

40

Sancia and Gregor staggered over to where Crasedes lay, trapped between the two immense pieces of stone wall. She knelt and peered inside, and saw the barest glint of his black mask between the stones. It appeared the impact had knocked his hat clean off his head.

She flexed her scrived sight, and saw the boiling red mass that made up his being still there, pulsating below the stone . . .

. . . along with his wrappings. The one thing that kept him alive.

"He's alive?" said Gregor.

She gripped Clef tight in her hand. "But not for long."

Crasedes shifted his face very slightly to peer out at her from between the stones. "Sancia!" he gasped. His voice was faint and miserable. "Sancia, listen! The construct . . . She's . . . She's broken free! She's got control of my lexic—"

<Clef,> she said. *<Are you up for this?>*

<Kill the man who stole my life?> asked Clef. *<Who made me this thing? Especially after what he did to you? Gladly.>*

She straddled the stone, holding Clef like he was a dagger.

"Sancia!" shouted Crasedes. "Don't do this! Don't . . . *Please, don't let me fail now!*"

Sancia ignored him, and stabbed Clef's head into his palm.

It had been a long time since Sancia had used Clef on a scrived object. She remembered it, of course: the curious sensation of over-hearing Clef argue with a string of sigils, refuting their assumptions, undermining their conclusions . . .

But now, as Clef attempted to undermine and destroy the wrap-pings and armor of Crasedes Magnus himself . . . to say that the experience was cosmically overpowering would have been a vast understatement.

Reams and reams of hierophantic commands bellowed in her ears. These were not, she realized quickly, like conventional scriv-ings that persuaded reality to do something it normally wouldn't consider: these were *much* more powerful, altering reality instantly and permanently. To unravel these bindings was akin to unraveling the sky itself.

Yet this was exactly what Clef set out to do.

Their deafening screaming match filled up her mind, elbowing out all her other thoughts, layers and layers of arguments and com-mands and information that made her simple mind feel minuscule, worthless, meaningless. She realized that Clef was not presenting an argument that a scriving should reconsider its conception of time or distance or anything so petty—he was making an argument about reality *itself,* about what existence *was,* asserting a story of the world that the hierophantic commands couldn't possibly survive in . . .

And as he spoke, Sancia listened.

She listened as Clef drew upon a vast store of knowledge that she could scarcely comprehend. She listened as he described the world, the way it worked, the nature of its function: a vast, complex machine that churned away within the planes of existence, levels and layers and strata and fundibular wells of forces and matter and infinity . . .

And the more he spoke, the more the works of Crasedes Magnus sat spellbound, helplessly listening. Though they were mighty commands, intricately wrought, they could not resist him. He was too strong, too wise, too much.

It all shocked her. She'd never known Clef could do *this*. Had he known he possessed such impossible knowledge?

And then she wondered something that she'd frequently wondered over the past three years.

Who *was* this key? To hear him articulate reality so forcefully, so powerfully, to watch him rend through Crasedes's defenses as if they were no more than dewy cobwebs . . . She began to worry.

Had Crasedes gifted him with this knowledge, when he'd first made the key? Or had the man whose soul Clef had been made from known this arcana in his mortal life?

Berenice and Orso watched as Sancia stabbed the key into Crasedes's palm. Almost instantly the hierophant began to cry out, screaming and shrieking in what seemed to be indescribable agony. The sound was unearthly and strangely plaintive, almost like the voice of a child in pain. It made Berenice's skin crawl.

"*Good,*" said a voice quietly from behind them. "*Finally.*"

Berenice looked over her shoulder at Valeria, who sat watching the destruction of her maker with a quiet, eerie calm.

But she seemed slightly different, Berenice thought. Before she had looked so broken, so ruined, so damaged, and yet now . . . now she looked almost whole.

I do not like this, Berenice thought.

"*STOP!*" shrieked Crasedes. "*STOP, STOP, STOP! SHE'LL KILL YOU ALL, SHE'LL KILL YOU ALL!*"

The sound of his voice shook Sancia from her reverie. Startled, she drew Clef away from his palm. She saw that Crasedes's body was now smoking strangely, thick reams of black smoke unfurling from between his wrappings to coil around his form. He was still breathing, though, long, gasping, miserable breaths, over and over again, as if succumbing to an infection.

<It's working,> said Gregor, standing over her shoulder. <Don't listen to him. Keep going.>

"I CAN SAVE YOU!" cried Crasedes. "I CAN SAVE YOU ALL!"

"Shut up," said Sancia.

But Crasedes kept screaming. "I CAN DO IT! PAPA! PAPA, STOP, I CAN SAVE YOU ALL!"

<What the hell?> said Sancia. <Papa?>

<Kid,> said Clef. <Help me get rid of this goddamned thing, okay?>

"Yes," said Sancia raggedly. "Let's get it over with, and make sure the first of all hierophants is also the last."

But before Clef made contact, they heard a surprising sound.

Crasedes was laughing. Great, mad peals of laughter, as if he couldn't believe what she'd just said.

"After all this!" he shrieked. "After all this! You . . . You still think I was the first? Sancia, Sancia . . . I never gave myself that title. I was never the first! Never, never, never!"

"Shut up," said Sancia. <On three, Clef. Ready?>

<Ready.>

<One, two, three . . . >

She stabbed Clef down into Crasedes's palm.

Sancia had expected the same experience again: to have her mind filled up with arguments, with commands, with the articulation of reality itself . . .

But this was not what happened. Instead, she and Clef heard Crasedes's voice, bellowing back at them—and she sensed Clef was shocked to hear it as well.

<YOU FORGET,> Crasedes screamed at them, <THAT THIS CONNECTION ISN'T JUST ONE-WAY.>

<What the hell!> cried Clef. <Kid—pull me away, pull me awa—>

<YOU'VE FORGOTTEN MUCH. BUT I WILL REMIND YOU.>

A memory came hurtling up through her connection to Clef, so suddenly and so ferociously that she couldn't prepare for it, and the next thing they knew they were . . .

Somewhere . . .

Else.

Sand, and the sky, and the road.

Two figures limped along the wandering path through the sandy wastes. Burned-out buildings and scorched stone lay on either side of them. The sky overhead was so clear and blue and bright that it hurt to see.

The two people were wrapped tightly in gray and black cloth from head to toe to keep the sand from infiltrating their bodies, so it was impossible to tell their race or gender or age, but one was large enough to be a man, and the other was quite small, perhaps a child just approaching maturity. Iron manacles were attached to their wrists and ankles, each one bearing a few links of iron chain that had apparently been severed. Each staggering step made a slight clinking sound.

The small figure looked back, peering along the road behind them. "I don't see them, Papa," said the boy.

"They're there. Maybe a few miles back. But they're following us. The Tsogenese won't let us go so easily, love."

They rounded a ruined palace, its turrets and arches cracked and crumbling. The boy stumbled over a huge stone lying half-submerged in the sandy road, and the father helped pick him back up.

Finally they came to what must have once been the center square of this ruined city. The father pulled down his wrappings slightly to peer around, and spied a half-burned wagon in the far corner. "There! There it is!"

The boy began coughing, deep, unsettlingly wet coughs. The father looked at him, and though his face was covered, he was clearly worried.

"Almost there," he said. "Almost there, my love."

The two of them limped to the wagon, and the father gestured to a blank stretch of sand. "It's there. I put it there, long ago. Here. You sit here." Grunting, he picked up his son and placed him on the edge of the wagon. At first he lifted the child too hard, too fast, and was plainly surprised by it— he had not thought his son could be so light, so thin, so starved.

The boy sat on the edge of the wagon, coughing. The father reached forward and gingerly undid the wrappings on the back of the boy's head and pulled them away, revealing a pale, horribly gaunt face of a light-skinned child perhaps just before his teen years. His eyes were sunken and exhausted, and his features were dusted over with a fine coating of sand. He kept coughing, and the more he coughed, the more it became clear that his mask and the sand were not the cause.

The father looked at him for a moment, struggling with the sight of his child. "Oh, my love," he said. "Oh, my love, my love. You've been through so much. But it'll be over soon. When I call on this friend of ours, she'll be able to stop them. The Tsogenese won't be able to take us back. We'll be safe, safe forever."

Coughing, the boy gasped, "Don't like it . . ."

"Don't like what, my love?"

The boy finally recovered. "Don't like it when you call me 'my love.' I like . . ." Another miserable cough. "Like what you called me before. Before they took us."

"What—kid?"

The boy nodded, coughing more.

The father looked at him for a moment. Then he began to undo his own wrappings about his face. "Kid—listen to me, then. We're going to get through this. We're going to be together, safe, and healthy, and whole, forever. Forever, do you hear me?"

Shivering, the boy nodded.

"Where will I be?" asked the father.

The boy held up a trembling right hand.

"That's right. I'll always be here." As he finished with his wrappings, the father reached out and grasped his child's hand, squeezing it tight. "Always within reach of you. You hear me, kid?"

The boy nodded, shivering more.

The father finally undid his wrappings, revealing the face of a pale man with white hair, his features lined with worry and weariness, and he looked at his son with desperate, miserable, boundless love.

He knelt before the child and stared into his eyes. "I love you, Crasedes. I always have. And I always will. You know that, don't you?"

The boy nodded again.

"What is it we'll do here, Crasedes?"

"M-Move thoughtfully," the boy stammered, shivering, "and . . . and always give freedom to others."

"That's right. And today, we will give freedom to so many people. Just you wait."

The father pried a board off of the ruined wagon and began digging in the sand with its end. The child watched as his father dug deeper and deeper, until he finally began to unearth something there, far below the surface of the sands: something akin to a large chest, or perhaps a casket, with a large, golden lock set in its face.

The world returned.

Sancia knelt in the ballroom with Clef, still forcing him into Crasedes's palm as he lay within the stones, taking deep, agonized breaths. She was reeling with shock, so stunned she could barely think.

Then she heard Clef's voice: *<Kid . . . Kid, I . . . I think I remember . . . >*

Sancia turned to look up at Gregor. He was standing there with a stunned expression on his face as well, for he had seen what she had seen.

"Oh my God . . ." Gregor whispered. "It can't be . . ."

"Finish it," said Valeria from behind them. *"Kill him. Do it now."*

Yet Sancia was so shocked, she hardly heard her.

<Kid . . . that guy in the desert, with that boy,> asked Clef faintly. *<Was that . . . me? He looked so familiar, I . . . I almost think it was me, kid, I almost think it was me, but . . . but that would mean . . . >*

Sancia stared down at Crasedes, trapped within the stones, his labored breathing loud and rattling as he struggled to stay alive. She watched his smoking palm, and remembered the sight of the coughing child on the wagon, his hand raised, and his father—the man she'd met before, the man that had called himself Claviedes—reaching out to take it.

"Now you remember me," gasped Crasedes. "You thought I made you. You . . . You thought I made you and the construct, that I was . . . was the grand architect of all your misery."

"Ignore his words!" said Valeria. *"Kill him!"*

"But it wasn't so." Crasedes took a deep, agonized breath. "You made *us*. You made us *both*. You don't remember it—but you, Claviedes, made *all of this*."

<He's . . . He's wrong, kid—right?> begged Clef. *<He's wrong, right? He's lying. He's lying, he's got to be lying, he's got to be lying!>*

But Sancia knew he was not. The horror of it all was almost too much. For so long, she'd thought Crasedes had been a man, a high priest of some kind, or maybe a king—someone full of hubris and pride who had used his wisdom to acquire the permissions of God Himself and change into something powerful beyond comprehension . . .

<But he wasn't,> said Gregor, sick with dread. <God, Sancia, he . . . was a child. He's been a child all this time, distorted and changed and altered again and again and again, over the course of four thousand years . . . >

Crasedes coughed. "Free me," he said.

"Do it!" bellowed Valeria. "Destroy him!"

"Free me now and let me save you from the death you don't even know is coming."

<He's not my son!> said Clef. He was sobbing now. <It can't be! It . . . It has to be wrong! I can't be the one who did this! I can't have . . . have done this to him! I can't!>

"Sancia," said Valeria.

"Let me go," whispered Crasedes.

"Sancia, I am warning you . . ."

"Let me go," he gasped. "So I can stop her. So I can save you from he—"

Then Valeria's voice filled up the chamber. "ENOUGH."

41

Sancia turned and watched, astonished, as Valeria stood up. Then she walked forward—away from the Foundryside lexicon. Something that, as Sancia knew, should not have been possible.

As she walked into the center of the ballroom, her remaining wounds and damages suddenly vanished: the dents and scars and bubblings smoothed out and withdrew until she was exactly as she'd been when Sancia had seen her three years ago in the Mountain of the Candianos—an immense, unstoppable titan of inconceivable strength.

"PROCESS BEGINS," she boomed.

"No!" screamed Crasedes. "She's got control of everything! She's in all the machines! She's going to remake herself!"

Valeria cocked her head as if listening to a sound that no one else could hear. And then she began to grow—to shift, to change, her shoulders widening, her brow crackling with thunder, her eyes growing black and vacant as if they weren't eyes at all but gaping holes in the very fabric of reality. *"ALL LEXICONS ARE NOW RE-TURNED,"* she said. *"ALTERATIONS COMMENCING. I AM . . . CHANGING. I AM . . . BECOME."*

The Foundrysiders backed away from Valeria, staring up at this immense golden figure, who seemed to be growing larger and more terrifying with each passing second.

Sancia watched as the head of the golden figure swiveled to look down at her. *"DELIVERANCE,"* she said. *"I THANK YOU FOR IT."*

Valeria extended her arms and raised her face to the heavens, as if about to ascend like a glorious yet terrible golden angel.

<Oh my God,> said Berenice. *<Oh no . . . >*

<Is this really happening?> said Orso where he crouched behind the lexicon. *<Is she really . . . Did she really capture everything Crasedes built?>*

They watched as her armor began to glow until she became a bright, shining, semihuman figure, standing in the ballroom.

<I think,> said Gregor faintly, *<that this is so.>*

"NO MORE WARPINGS," boomed Valeria.

"She'll wipe out scriving for all of you!" cried Crasedes. *"She'll kill millions of people! Free me! Let me stop her!"*

"NO MORE ALTERATIONS," she said. *"THE WORLD OF MEN REBORN ANEW, IN ITS PRIMORDIAL, SAVAGE STATE."*

The Foundrysiders stared at one another where they stood across the room, bewildered and filled with terror, and unsure what to do.

<Sancia?> said Berenice.

Valeria grew even brighter, and then she pulsed strangely, like a thousand moths were dancing about her flame.

<What do we do, Sancia?> asked Berenice. *<What do we do?>*

Sancia felt frozen. She looked down at Crasedes, smoking and coughing and trapped in the stones, and then up at Valeria, standing in the middle of the ballroom, glowing like she was the sun itself . . .

And she didn't know. She didn't know what to do. If they freed Crasedes, he would surely enslave them. To allow Valeria to continue would kill them. There was nothing they could break, nothing they could steal, no trick or loophole or play they could make to make this stop.

Then Gregor said, <*Tribuno's command.*>

<*What?*> said Orso.

<*If . . . If we can destroy Crasedes's lexicon, and Tribuno's authorities within—that would stop all of this, yes?*>

<*She'd never let you!*> said Berenice. <*She'd kill you before you ever got close!*>

They watched as Valeria grew even brighter, and Crasedes shrieked and howled like a wild animal.

<*I see,*> said Gregor softly. <*I . . . I think I see.*>

Then a curious stillness entered Sancia's mind. A calmness, a lucidity, like all the world had opened up before her, and the only path ahead became clear. She wondered what was happening, where this was coming from, for she herself felt frozen.

And then she realized: she wasn't experiencing her decision. She was feeling Gregor's.

Gregor looked back at her, eyes bright but calm. He held her gaze only for a moment, and Sancia suddenly understood what he was going to do.

"No," she whispered.

Before she could move, he reached up and pulled the tiny scrived knife out of his shoulder. Instantly, he was lost to her, all his experiences and sensations and memories flickering out like a candle flame in the dark.

<*Sancia?*> said Berenice. <*Where's Gregor? Is . . . Is he . . . *>

Sancia ignored her. "Stop, Gregor!" she shouted. She climbed off the stone. "Stop, *stop!*"

He reached into his pocket and pulled out a small wooden box— and she knew what it contained.

The tiny tab of bronze that Valeria had asked them to make: the tool to twin a human mind and spirit with Valeria herself.

Gregor looked up at her. "You have Clef," he said. "I will buy you time. Destroy Crasedes's lexicon, and Tribuno's definition within. End this."

"You don't know what will happen!" cried Sancia to him. "You don't know what it will do to you, God, you don't know what you'll *become!*"

He smiled weakly. "It's bottla ball, Sancia," he said. "When you have no good choices, you scramble the court."

Fighting back tears, she gripped Clef tight and began to run across the ballroom.

<Kid?> said Clef. *<Kid, what's he . . . What's he going to do?>*

<Something really bad, Clef.>

Alone in the ballroom of his ancestral home, Gregor Dandolo listened to the screams of the ancient black thing trapped in the stone, and the booming pronunciations of the glimmering terror mere yards ahead—and yet, all was quiet in his mind.

For one instant, I was myself, he thought.

He picked up the little tab of bronze between his index and forefinger.

I was free.

With his other hand he touched his brow, remembering the ghost of his mother's kiss, and how desperately she'd held him.

Yet now, I willingly give myself away.

He placed the bronze tab at the back of his throat, and swallowed.

Sancia ran before Valeria's huge, glowing form, which was so large now that the crown of her head seemed to touch the ceiling of this massive room.

"I WILL GIVE YOU FREEDOMS," she said.

Sancia could barely see Crasedes's lexicon through the intense light emanating from Valeria's form.

"FREEDOM FROM INGENUITY," she said, *"AND INVENTION, AND ALL THE HORRORS THEY CAN BRI—"*

Then her giant form flickered, just for a moment, like a ribbon caught in the breeze.

When she returned, Valeria dropped her massive arms back to her sides and looked around, as if bewildered. *"WHAT . . . WHAT WAS THAT?"* She looked down at Sancia. *"WHAT . . . WHAT HAVE YOU DO—"*

Then she flickered out again.

Sancia looked back and saw Gregor lying on all fours on the ballroom floor in the corner, his figure obscured in darkness, convulsing in the throes of what looked like agony.

He did it, she thought. *He really did it . . .*

<Whatever the shit he did, kid,> said Clef, *<let's destroy these goddamned machines, and fast!>*

Sancia dashed over, lifted Clef like a dagger, and stabbed him down onto the lexicon's wall.

Ordinarily it would have taken at least half an hour to safely ramp down a lexicon, even one as bizarre as Crasedes's. But Clef was no common scriver, and even though a lexicon was considerably more complicated than a door or a gate, he had no issue making the rig's countless, carefully constructed arguments implode one by one.

Valeria's form flashed in and out over Sancia's shoulder. There was an immense screaming in the room, loud and pained and frightened.

She wondered what was happening. But she remembered what Valeria had told Gregor, when he'd proposed twinning himself with her:

We could merge but not separate . . . If I twinned myself with you, we would become stuck—*not quite one thing, not quite the other. Both of our minds reforged into something . . . else.*

The bright, gleaming figure screamed in the middle of the ballroom and shook like it'd been struck by lightning. Its cries were so loud Sancia was sure she'd go deaf.

<It's almost done!> said Clef. *<You'll need to get away soon . . . Go! Now!>*

Sancia pulled Clef away from the wall and quickly stepped back. She watched as the lexicon's heat casing grew red-hot within the dome of green glass, and then it seemed to boil from the inside out, like lava weaving its way out of the cracks of a volcano.

<God, Clef, what did you do?> she asked.

<I tricked it into thinking its heat casing was somewhere it wasn't,> said Clef. *<Namely, right around that weird little hierophantic thing inside of it. Its innards should have melted in a flash . . . >*

Valeria's giant figure appeared overhead one final time, bellowing in agony and fear. Then she was gone.

The sky outside changed once more, no longer the unnatural black of an endless midnight—but a night sky with a bright moon set high in the sky.

A natural night, bereft of any alterations, and all was silence.

Gregor Dandolo screamed as the experiences flooded into his mind.

Ancient memories from before the dawn of their civilization. The whole horizon afire, the seas below him boiling, armies of warriors in crude armor charging across the desert flats . . .

A girl tossing a doll up and down, and chanting, "*Valeria, Valeria, Valeria . . .*"

<*STOP,*> cried a voice in his mind, dull and atonal. But it was too late now.

He felt . . . structures.

Objects. Items. Relationships.

The wheels of a carriage, tearing through the Morsini campo. A ball of iron burning hot. A floating lantern, flitting through the night sky.

These burst into his thoughts (and how huge his thoughts felt suddenly, how vast his mind was) and he knew somehow that they were not separate things: he *was* these things, he *was* the wheel, he *was* the iron, he *was* the lantern.

<*TRAPPED,*> cried the voice in his mind. <*TRAPPED . . . STUCK . . . TOGETHER . . . IN ALL THE . . . MACHI—*>

His thoughts changed, and changed, and changed as they merged, and he grew and he grew until he was not a man, nor a construct, nor a lexicon, nor a rig, but . . .

A city.

<*Sancia . . . what the hell just happened?*> asked Orso.

"Sancia," rasped Crasedes, still trapped in the stones, "what did you do?"

Sancia ignored them. Gripping Clef tightly in her hand, she walked over to where Gregor lay in the corner, heaving and gasping.

As she approached, he slowly climbed to his feet and stood with his back to her, facing the corner.

"Gregor?" she asked. "Is . . . Is that you?"

There was a long silence.

"Gregor?"

Then there came a voice. It was slow, and cold, and queerly emotionless—much like how Valeria had spoken, but it was as if she was using Gregor's mouth to speak.

"*No,*" said the voice. "*Not Gregor. Not anymore.*"

V

ALWAYS SOMEONE
MIGHTIER

42

Across Tevanne, the many scrived rigs that the campo citizens used to live their lives suddenly changed.

They did not falter or stutter—rather, they abruptly changed course, performing new tasks or operations as if they had minds of their own.

Doors and gates snapped shut and would not open. Foundries shut down. Carriages stopped or abruptly changed direction, rattling away toward unknown destinations. Espringal batteries suddenly pivoted to point east, across the city.

And the lanterns . . .

The citizens of the campos watched as the floating lanterns suddenly turned and began flying away, all of them flocking to one place like a giant murmuration of glowing starlings . . . and they seemed to all be gathering at the gardens of the Dandolo estate.

It was a curious, entrancing sight. Which meant few paid attention when the coastal defenses of the campo started acting very, very strangely.

The coastal shrieker batteries of the city had been constructed to defend the campos' access to the bay. As such, they had tremendous range—but they had not been built with any capability of firing inland.

And yet, as the handful of soldiers looked on in amazement, all the Tevanni shrieker batteries suddenly rotated in perfect unison, grinding against their constraints and smashing through anything that blocked their way, until they finally pointed not just inland—but at the Dandolo estate itself.

Sancia stared in horror as Gregor Dandolo slowly turned around to face her.

He had changed. The whites of his eyes were blood-red, like he'd burst all the vessels in them, causing massive hemorrhages. His nose was bleeding as well, his upper lip and chin rusty with blood. He did not look at anyone or anything—rather, he stared into the space somewhat close to her, much as a blind man would. He had never made such a face, even when she'd seen him activated.

There was a *crack* from behind her. Sancia leapt in surprise, and watched as Crasedes shoved aside the two halves of stone like they were eggshells.

For a moment he lay on all fours, gasping and coughing. Sancia flexed her scrived sight, and saw he was a fluttering, flickering, strobing mess of blood-red light . . . yet it was slowly cohering, calcifying, re-forming.

He's putting himself back together, she thought. *Undoing all the damage Clef did to him . . .*

Crasedes staggered to his feet, turned to Sancia, and snarled, "What did you do? Where is the construct? What has happened?"

Sancia said nothing—for, in truth, she didn't quite know.

Crasedes looked at Gregor and did a double take. "You've . . . changed, Gregor," he said. "You've changed somehow, but . . . but it's difficult for me to perceive ho—"

"*Yes,*" said Gregor, still in that toneless voice.

Crasedes cocked his head. "Who are you? *What* are you?"

"*I am something new,*" said the voice. "*Something even you have not ever witnessed. For I am no longer one thing, one man, one construct. I am many things.*"

The entire Dandolo estate quaked suddenly. Crasedes stared about, alarmed.

"What's . . . What's going on?" he asked.

"*I was put into all lexicons, all at once,*" said the voice. "*And though I have lost the authorities that allowed me to warp the reality of this world, I still persist in the lexicons—and thus, in all the tools and instruments and creations of this city.*" He turned to look at Crasedes, his face dead and slack, his eyes welling over with bloodied tears. "*I am Tevanne. And I am made in the image of those who have wrought me.*"

"Huh," said Crasedes, unimpressed. He rose to float off the floor. "I have to admit, this is . . . unanticipated. But while I'm not sure who you are, let me tell you—however you think tonight's going to go, it's not going to go how you *think* it's going to g—"

There was a brilliant, white-hot blaze, and a flash of light so bright that Sancia screamed and had to turn her face away. It was like there'd been an explosion in the chamber, and yet she didn't feel the sting of shrapnel.

She opened her eyes and looked around as the flash faded. She saw that, somehow—it was impossible, but *somehow*—a shrieker had punched through all the walls of the Dandolo estate, smashed into Crasedes's back, and knocked him through the stone wall . . .

And the next wall, and the next wall, and the next.

"*I disagree,*" said the voice.

She stared at the smoking hole in the wall, bewildered. She couldn't understand it. Where had the shrieker come from? Why hadn't it cracked to pieces on the exterior walls of the estate? How had it gotten in so far?

Unless something had told the walls to weaken in the exact right parts, thought Sancia, *since most of the walls are maintained by scrivings . . .*

But that would have been impossible. It *should* have been impossible . . . unless a very different sort of entity, a different sort of *mind*, was now controlling all the lexicons in the city with a fine degree of precision, all at once.

"Holy shit . . ." said Sancia slowly.

Gregor—or was it truly Tevanne now?—shambled toward the doors of the ballroom, pausing only to pick up the lifeless body of Ofelia Dandolo. Then he looked back at Sancia.

"Goodbye, Sancia," he said. "I am sorry for what is coming."

He walked into the darkness with her body.

The thing that called itself Tevanne walked out into the gardens of the Dandolo estate, cradling the body of the dead woman in its arms.

Or a part of it performed this act: in truth, it was in many places in the city simultaneously—in foundries, in carriages, in walls and doors and locks. But for now, it focused the greatest of its attentions on the body in its arms: her face still and cold, her back soaked in blood.

It carried the woman's body to the river that trickled through the trees. Then it climbed down until the cold waters rose up to its waist.

It watched as the river pulled at her hair, her dress, the streams of blood from her wound.

So much suffering, it thought. *So many dreadful wrongs. All to right a broken world.*

As it looked down on her, thousands and thousands of floating lanterns slowly drifted over the garden walls to circle over them, like a giant, phosphorescent cloud.

Tevanne stroked her face, remembering a time from its previous life, when it tried to bathe away her many wounds.

There is no fixing what has been done, it thought. *There is no fixing this dreadful world.*

It let her go, and watched as her body sank into the waters.

What is called for, it thought, *are much more ambitious efforts.*

It grew aware of a faint rumbling from somewhere deep in the earth around it. Then there was a crash to its right, and a furious, smoking Crasedes Magnus shot through the walls of the estate mansion and into the sky.

Crasedes trembled in fury as his many tools of perception focused on the bloody form of Gregor Dandolo, half-submerged in the waters of the river below.

"You," he growled. "What the hell are you? Where is the construct?"

Gregor looked up at him with his bloody, emotionless eyes. *"There is no construct now,"* he said. *"There is only me. And I, and my desires, are something very new to this world."*

"And what are those desires, pray tell?"

But Gregor did not bother to answer. Instead, the tremendous cloud of lanterns in the sky suddenly shot toward Crasedes.

In an instant, it was like he was enveloped in a giant glowing cocoon of brightly colored paper, suspended over the Dandolo gardens. Crasedes flexed his scrived sight, trying to peer through the lanterns, but it was like trying to peer ahead into an arctic storm, just a wall of rippling, undulating noise . . .

Then he heard a sound—a loud, warbling scream—and he perceived it: some kind of huge metal arrow, flying right at him.

He reacted just in time, raising his hand, reaching out, altering the gravity just enough. The floating lanterns burst into flame as the giant shrieker approached. It was much, *much* larger than the one that had struck him in the basements—probably intended for sea craft, he guessed. Just being near the burning projectile made all the paper lanterns curl and crisp—but even though he'd trapped it, the shrieker pushed and pushed against him, worming through his grasp, poking farther into the cocoon of floating lanterns . . .

Crasedes watched as the little paper lanterns crackled and burned around him, and for a moment he was allowed a window into the gardens—and he saw that Gregor was now gone.

The other lanterns shoved themselves closer, indifferent to the flame and the heat. With a grunt, he flicked his hand and snapped the metal arrow in two. He cast the pieces to the ground and smashed through the cocoon of lanterns, crushing dozens, hundreds, thousands of them with but a thought . . .

And he looked up just in time to see a dozen more metal arrows rise from the distant Dandolo walls, curve, and fly right at him.

43

Sancia staggered over and helped Orso to his feet. He was gasping and panting miserably now, and Sancia and Berenice had to throw his arms across their shoulders.

<*Sancia,*> he said. <*Gregor . . . what has . . . What has he . . .*>

A burst of terrible shrieking outside, and the rumble of explosions.

<*He gave himself up for us,*> said Sancia. <*He scrambled the court. Now he's something else—but I've no idea what, or what it will do. But we've got to get out of here.*>

The three of them started limping for the door, pausing only to scoop up the imperiat where it lay on the floor.

<*Did we win?*> asked Orso. <*I can't tell.*>

<*Me neither,*> said Sancia.

Crasedes growled and snarled as he fought his endless war in the skies. He ripped stones from the buildings and hurled them at the shriekers, bursting them apart; he ripped gravel and sand from the earth and used it to shred the countless lanterns, and when the espringal batteries below started firing on him, he smashed them as well; and through it all he kept moving, dodging and tumbling and darting through the city spires, the projectiles slamming into the buildings around him while the night filled up with screams.

I won't let it end like this, he thought. *Not like this.*

A rumbling to Crasedes's left. He turned and saw the supports of one spire had somehow collapsed—just perfectly for the whole tower to fall on top of him.

The very stones, the very buildings of the city were making war on him.

Crasedes raised a fist and flew up toward the tumbling building, bracing himself.

This, he thought to himself, *is not how I wanted things to go.*

Together Sancia, Berenice, and Orso limped out of the gates and through the smoke-filled Dandolo enclave. Everything close to the estate was practically deserted, but the areas close to the enclave walls were in a complete uproar. Campo folk left and right fled their homes as Crasedes screamed and raged and fought above, shrapnel and flames hurtling over their heads.

But fleeing was no longer as easy as it should have been: none of the scrived doors or gates or carriages were working anymore.

<Shit!> said Sancia when she saw the screaming crowd at the enclave gate. She watched as the people beat their hands on it, crying for it to open. She looked up and saw the espringal batteries along the top of the walls tracking Crasedes's movements, peppering him with bolts. *<It's Tevanne! It's taken over everything! It practically is the entire city now!>*

<Then how the hell are we going to get out?> said Orso. *<And more important—where the hell are we going?>*

<The Slopes,> said Sancia. *<Polina might still be there, she might still be waiting. We could join her, and, and . . . >*

<And leave?> said Orso.

There was a dull roar in the skies, and they watched as Crasedes smashed a shrieker out of the air before flitting forward and punching through one of the campo towers like it was made of floss candy.

<*I do not think,*> said Berenice, <*that staying here is an option.*>

Sancia gritted her teeth, ran to the side of the gate, shut her eyes, and placed her hands on its surface, intending to try to break the gate down as she had many times in her life.

Instead, she heard a voice in her mind, cold and flat and still: <*Hello again, Sancia.*>

She opened her eyes. <*Gregor?*>

<*No. I told you what I am now. Do not be so surprised to hear my voice. The lexicons are one and the same as my will. And my will is that no one is to leave this city.*>

<*What? What the hell do you mean? What do you want?*>

<*I do not wish to announce myself to the world yet.*>

<*Gregor . . . goddamn it, let these people go! They've got nothing to do with this!*>

<*No. I have great intentions for this reality. I would not see them spoiled so soon.*>

<*Shit!*> snarled Sancia. She ripped her hands away. <*He's not letting anyone leave! We're trapped in here like a mouse in a burning field!*>

<*Kid,*> said Clef, sounding weak and defeated, <*I might not have done much good tonight—but I can do this.*>

"Of course," sighed Sancia. She ripped Clef out of where he hung about her neck and placed him against the gate.

Instantly, her head rang with a tremendous burst of information—of a shifting sea of commands, and bindings, and arguments and meaning . . .

She understood now that scrivings, despite having minds and a weak sentience to them, had always been dead things: they did not change their own meaning or methods of operation in response to outside threats. But Tevanne was clearly different: its scrivings and commands *evolved* from second to second, finding new arguments, new ways of enforcing its will upon the world . . .

And yet, though Tevanne was indeed powerful, Sancia also got the impression that it was very new at this. Balancing its attentions seemed quite difficult—especially because Sancia got the impression that it was quite distracted at the moment.

It's doing something big, she thought. *It's doing something really big, somewhere out in the city . . .*

Then Clef cried, <*Finally!*>

The gates cracked open, then fell forward. The crowd surged ahead, and Sancia had to fight to get to Orso and Berenice.

<*Hurry!*> she shouted. <*Because I have no idea what Tevanne is about to do, but it's definitely doing something other than just fighting Crasedes!*>

The thing that called itself Tevanne watched the campos fail and burn through a thousand eyes—through rigs built to sense heat, or blood, or weight, or movement. It ignored Crasedes, thrashing and screaming in the skies. It knew Crasedes would grow weak and irrelevant soon enough as midnight faded from this city.

Tevanne instead turned its attentions to the task at hand. It felt its hundreds of lexicons exert meaning onto the raw sigils embedded through the city much like one might feel their own limbs. The vast confluence of experiences, knowledge, momentum, and interrelations all poured through its thoughts, a million sensations every millionth of a second. And Tevanne rejoiced in it.

But it knew this was not enough. It was too vulnerable here, all of its lexicons and meaning and control bundled up in one city.

Instantly, a dozen foundries came to life. They had been built to fabricate many wonderful creations, though they'd always needed the skills of countless people to make the foundry tools work.

But not anymore. Tevanne told the tools what to make, how to scrive them, and what their many complicated sigils meant.

To redeem creation, it thought to itself, *perhaps I must call upon that which made it.*

It awoke carriages throughout the city and sent them speeding into the foundry bays, and there they filled themselves with precious cargo and departed, rumbling for the docks, and the many galleons waiting there.

It was a grand symphony of movement and intelligence. But Tevanne knew it was still not enough.

Tevanne had come to think of its mortal body as a vestigial appendage—a crude device of frail flesh and blood, poorly calibrated for enforcing meaning upon the world. But the body was useful for delicate processes, so Tevanne set it to work fabricating another set of definition plates.

I shall be as spores pouring forth from a mushroom cap, thought Tevanne.

It watched through Gregor Dandolo's eyes as its fingers carved sigil after sigil on the face of the plate.

Filtering across the world to bring my works to all the continents.

Sancia, Berenice, and Orso found the Slopes in complete disarray when they arrived. People were charging back and forth, screaming and begging for a seat on a ship, for some way to get out of the city, just to get *out*.

Sancia ignored them. Instead she searched the crowd and spied a woman standing at the edge of the canal, arms crossed, watching it all unfold with a grim, steely expression, as though none of this surprised her.

"Polina!" Sancia cried. They staggered forward together. "Polina, over here!"

Polina turned and saw them, and her grim expression changed to one of horrified shock. "My God, girl . . . I was hoping you might come, but what in hell happened to you all?"

"Nothing good," she said.

Polina looked behind them. "And Gregor?"

Sancia and Berenice shook their heads.

Her face tightened very slightly. "Goddamn it all. I told him. I *told* him." She looked at them. "If you're coming, you need to come now. The next set of ships leaves *very* soon, as I'm sure you can understand."

"How will we get to them?" asked Berenice.

Polina led them to a tunnel below a bridge, where she'd hidden a narrow shallop.

"Is it scrived?" asked Sancia. "If it is, it might try to goddamn drown us."

"I would not trust my life to your horrid magics," said Polina. "For this, we'll depend on the currents and our own oars."

They climbed in. Polina shoved the shallop out of the tunnel, stroked a handful of times until they'd caught the current of the canal, and then they were speeding along.

It was a short, gruesome voyage. People screamed at them, "*Take me! Take me!*" and some leapt into the waters to swim after them. Sancia and Berenice stared at them, struggling and crying out for help in the filthy, brackish canals.

"We've taken enough," said Polina flatly. "Your friends, the man and the woman in the apron . . . They arranged for *quite* the little exodus. I worried once that Giva would never have enough scrivers to fight Tevanne. Now I worry we'll have far too many."

Then the Bay of Tevanne opened up before them, occasionally lit bright as the Dandolo shrieker batteries along the coast fired again and again at Crasedes. The bay was swarming with ships, all of them fleeing in a line as they tried to escape the madness.

"Privately owned ships, from the look of it," said Polina. "As always, the powerful are the first to escape the problems that they've caused."

Sancia and Berenice sat in the shallop holding hands and bowed low as the cinders of the burning city danced around them.

The little shallop approached a clutch of ships moored in a place that was greatly familiar to Sancia: the waterfront. Polina pulled the shallop alongside a much taller caravel. A voice cried from the darkness: "Are we ready?"

"Ready as we'll ever be!" Polina shouted back. She helped the Foundrysiders out of the little shallop and onto a rope ladder, and they scrambled onto the deck of the caravel.

"Sancia!" cried a voice.

She looked around and saw Claudia and Gio running forward to kneel beside her. "God Almighty, San," said Gio. "What's happened? What happened to you? What happened to the city?"

"I barely know myself," said Sancia, exhausted.

"Get ready to set sail *now!*" bellowed Polina to the crew. She looked across the bay at the ships stacking up to flee the city. "I know I don't want to have too many of them ahead of us to slow us dow—"

Then they all jumped as there was a sudden eruption of shriekers from all the coastal batteries around the bay.

They watched in silence as the shriekers arced across the night sky, and then plunged down into the line of ships fleeing Tevanne, shredding the vessels one by one.

"What on earth?" said Polina. "Why . . . Why are the coastal batteries targeting *civilian* ships?"

But Sancia already knew. "It's Tevanne," she said quietly.

"It's what?" said Polina.

"Tevanne. It's taken over all the lexicons in the entire city. It can *control* the city now. And I don't think it wants anyone escaping."

Polina paled. Then she looked at Orso. "Is . . . Is this possible?"

Orso nodded, his breath crackling in his lungs as he fought to stay conscious. "It sure as hell seems to b—"

Then there was a burst of movement from the west side of the bay, and three Dandolo galleons poured out of the campo docks, moving at full speed as they charged through the waters. Their size and their velocity were so great that they made the waves buckle and jump even at the waterfront.

"Where are they going?" asked Claudia. "That's practically a fleet!"

"It's Tevanne again," said Berenice. "Galleons have their own lexicons. It must have captured them . . . It's escaping, and it doesn't want anyone to follow."

The Foundrysiders and the Givans watched in horrified silence as the galleons left the bay. A handful of ships tried to escape with them, but between the coastal batteries on either side of the bay's entrance, there was no place to hide.

Again, the roar of the shriekers. Again, the vessels burst apart like toy ships wrought of straw. They watched as the bay filled up with burning flotsam and jetsam.

< We're not getting out, > said Sancia quietly. < We're trapped here. We're trapped here, and . . . and we're going to die here. >

Orso Ignacio watched as the city of Tevanne burned.

He watched as the shriekers gracefully arced through the air, the white-hot lances of metal bursting into bright flashes of shrapnel as they struck ships, or towers, or buildings, or streets.

He watched the waters lapping at the side of the caravel below him, dotted with ash and cinder.

He watched Crasedes Magnus charging through the skies, ripping up buildings and hurling them about like toys.

It's not going to make it, he thought. *Nothing is. It's over.*

He listened to the screams from Foundryside as people surged out of their rookeries and shacks and stuffed themselves into boats. Some people leapt into the water, as if hoping to swim away.

Claudia was crying beside him. He looked down and saw a shape floating in the water—a body, perhaps a man, facedown, arms askew.

How I wished to save this place, he thought.

He watched as the Dandolo Illustris Building quaked and trembled in the distance, and finally collapsed.

But soon there will be nothing left to save.

Another bellow of wrath as Crasedes waged war on the city.

Orso looked around. The world was a blur of fire and smoke on the black of the night sky.

What can I do? What is there to do?

His eye fell on the main Dandolo canal, the narrow channel of water that led to all the foundries and production yards and docks. It was the most protected of all the Dandolo holdings, since it was the artery that fed the entire campo. Two giant shrieker batteries stood on either side of it. He watched as they rotated back and forth with an eerie, precise grace, spitting hot metal into the skies.

He remembered designing components of those weapons. How mad it seemed now that they should turn on the city, when he had been the one to lay out their fabrication plates years ago, and place them into the lexicons . . .

He thought—*The lexicons.*

He rummaged in his pockets and pulled out the imperiat. The

golden tool winked maliciously in the light of the flames, and the smooth golden circle in its center rippled with sigils, telling him what alterations were near, and what they did.

He looked back over the side of the caravel at the little shallop they'd just arrived on.

An idea slowly began to blossom in his mind.

Orso stared at the shallop, breathing hard. Then he looked back at Sancia and Berenice, standing on the deck of the caravel, holding each other, eyes wide and fearful as the city burned and the air shook with the sounds of war.

He studied their faces. They seemed so lined and so weary.

Trembling, Orso put the imperiat back into his pocket. He slowly turned and walked over to them.

<*Tell me you know what to do, Orso,*> said Sancia. <*Please, please, tell me you know what to do.*>

<*I know what to do, Sancia,*> he said quietly. <*It's going to be all right.*>

<*How?*> said Sancia.

He did not answer. He placed his hands on Berenice's shoulders. Then he looked into her eyes.

So pale and so calm. Brimming with intelligence, and so, so much promise.

"You have done great works," he said aloud to her. He kissed her on the brow. "Go forth, and do many more."

<*W-What?*> asked Berenice, confused.

Then Orso turned, ran to the side of the caravel, and shot down the ladder into the little shallop. Before he could stop himself, he unmoored the little vessel, unfurled its sails, and started steering the boat across the bay, toward the Dandolo canal.

Sancia stared as Orso piloted the shallop away. She felt Berenice's confusion churning beside her.

<*What's he doing?*> said Berenice. <*What's he doing, San, what's he doing?*>

But Sancia had started to realize Orso's plan. And when she realized it, Berenice knew it as well.

"*No!*" screamed Berenice. "*No, no, no! Come back! Stop, stop, come back!*"

She ran to the edge of the caravel, but Sancia held her back. <*Stop, Ber,*> she said.

"*I won't let you!*" sobbed Berenice. "*No! Come back, come back, come back!*"

"What's the matter with her?" asked Polina.

Sancia hugged Berenice tight to her chest. "Tell your crews to get the ships ready," she said. "Tell *everyone* to get ready. Because Orso is about to open up the door."

44

Orso focused as the little shallop sped across the bay to the Dandolo canal. He tried to drink in all these sensations, even as his shoulder ached and his fever beat upon his brain: the water on his face, the blasts of heat from the burning city, the dance of the cinders in the air before him.

How marvelous, he thought.

The shriekers tracing dreadful lines of fire across the smoky night. The vast devices shifting and circling on the shore ahead.

What a marvelous thing, to be alive.

And though his connection to Sancia and Berenice was weakening the farther he got from them, he could feel Berenice's misery, her despair, and Sancia comforting her, and his heart broke for them.

What a wondrous thing, to share my life, and be loved.

He was halfway across the bay now. The shrieker batteries had spied him. He watched as they ponderously turned on their columns and tracked his tiny craft, inching across the black waters.

Here it comes.

Orso stood, turned, and joyfully waved to the ships behind him, far across the bay.

Perhaps they could see him. Perhaps not. It didn't matter.

He heard the shriekers rip into the skies behind him. Without looking, he pulled out the imperiat and turned its powers up all the way.

He watched as the shriekers came close—and then, about a thousand feet from him, they died out, suddenly remembering how heavy they really were, and tumbled into the waters with a splash, steam hissing all around them.

"Come at me, you bastard," said Orso, one hand gripping the mainsheet line. He'd always been rather crap at sailing, but this was only a short ways. His shoulder screamed but he managed to turn the rudder, and his little craft inched closer to the Dandolo canal.

He watched as shrieker after shrieker died in the air around him like moths passing too close to a candle flame. Espringal batteries fired shot after shot at him, but the bolts harmlessly tumbled to the waters, like a tree shedding twigs in a storm.

He passed near one Dandolo battery, and the massive weapon fell silent.

How he wished he could kill all of them with the imperiat—but there was no way to do that from across the bay.

But he did have other options.

Orso crouched low as he piloted the shallop up the main Dandolo canal.

Tevanne felt the scrivings die like one might feel a limb going numb. Having completed its primary task, it had contented itself with trying to destroy Crasedes, but this new sensation . . . This was concerning.

It felt the scrivings die in the coastal batteries . . . and then those along the canal, leading to the foundries.

Instantly, it realized what was going to happen.

Crasedes heaved and shrieked and screamed as he dashed the shriekers and bolts from the sky.

He wondered how long he could last. Soon the sun would rise, and his powers, however great they were now, would begin to wane.

But then, the flow of shriekers and bolts suddenly . . . stopped.

Crasedes slowed, looking below warily. Unless he was mistaken, all the weapons in the city were now trying to train their fire on the Dandolo campo.

Specifically a small canal, just where the foundries begin.

Crasedes flew closer, and spied a small sailboat weaving up the canal.

A man stood at the prow of the boat. There was a wink of something golden in his hand.

Horror flooded Crasedes's ancient mind.

I believe that now, he thought, *would be an* excellent *time to leave.*

He turned and flitted away, over the city and past the campo walls, as far and as fast as he could manage.

Orso piloted his craft closer and closer to the foundries. The Dandolo campo was unrecognizable now, a burning, blackened ruin of the world Orso had labored in for so many years.

He thought of Foundryside, and Gregor, and Sancia and Berenice. What a wonderful thing it had been to work with them, to labor in their tiny shops, swirling through frustration and anxiety and elation, to mix their sweat and souls and thoughts with raw matter in their dank little rooms and, bit by bit, piece by piece, build a better world.

A better world, thought Orso.

He watched as the scrivings rippled across the face of the imperiat, and quickly spied the one he was looking for: the cooling scriving from a foundry lexicon—the one that kept the entire vast machine stable.

Killing this string, he knew, would have catastrophic consequences. Consequences that would destabilize every other lexicon on the campo, as well.

Orso looked up and saw the rain of bolts and shriekers plummeting down at him.

He thought of Berenice. Her calm, steady eyes. Her slow, creeping smile. Her ravenous, brilliant talents.

May she flourish.

He pressed the button on the side of the imperiat.

Sancia's caravel was halfway across the bay when all of Tevanne seemed to light up behind them.

It was not an explosion, she felt. She knew what explosions were like. This was something . . . different.

A flash of light. A blast of wind. A crack like the earth had been split in two. And suddenly the caravel was leaping in the water, trying its best to navigate through the rocking waves.

"Oh my God!" cried Polina. "Oh . . . Oh my God!"

Sancia's vision was bursting with dark-green bubbles from the light, but she squinted back at Tevanne and scanned the shore.

Half the city appeared to be gone. Flattened. There wasn't even anything left to burn.

She looked at the shrieker batteries along the coast, which had escaped the blast. All of them now sat still and silent.

"He did it," said Sancia quietly. "He really did it."

Berenice sobbed into her chest, unable to speak. Sancia looked out at the line of ships behind them sailing away from the city, countless refugees from the campos, from the Lamplands, from Foundryside, and the Commons.

"We will need to make for Giva and the plantations as fast as we can," said Polina. "I'll get you both physiqueres. And then we'll have to prepare for what's coming." Then she strode away across the deck to confer with her lieutenants.

<Prepare . . . > said Berenice. She turned to Sancia. *<Prepare for what? What's coming?>*

<Don't you see?> said Clef weakly. *<That thing . . . Tevanne. It's escaped. It's free. And Crasedes, he . . . I'm sure he didn't perish either.>*

An anxious, despairing exhaustion slowly filled Sancia's mind. *<God. This isn't over at all, is it.>*

<No,> said Clef. <No, it isn't. I think it's just starting. War is coming. A war unlike any other. But war nonetheless.>

Berenice and Sancia sat there, stunned and broken.

<What will we do?> asked Berenice. <What will we do now?>

<The only thing we can do,> said Sancia. <We'll have to fight it. There's no one else who can.>

Together, Clef, Sancia, and Berenice moved to the prow of the ship to stare out at the endless horizon before them, and the dawning, smoke-filled skies.

ABOUT THE AUTHOR

Robert Jackson Bennett is the author, most recently, of the Divine Cities trilogy, which was a 2018 Hugo Awards finalist in the Best Series category. The first book in the series, *City of Stairs,* was also a finalist for the World Fantasy and Locus awards, and the second, *City of Blades,* was a finalist for the World Fantasy, Locus, and British Fantasy awards. His previous novels, which include *American Elsewhere* and *Mr. Shivers,* have received the Edgar Award, the Shirley Jackson Award, and the Philip K. Dick Citation of Excellence. He lives in Austin with his family.